A Tribal Fever

A TRIBAL FEVER

David Sweetman

ANDRE DEUTSCH

First published in Great Britain in 1996 by
André Deutsch Limited
106 Great Russell Street
London WC1B 3LJ

The places described in this novel are real, the political
events and the characters who perform them are entirely
fictional and are not intended to bear any resemblance to
persons alive or dead.

CIP data for this title is available
from the British Library.

ISBN 0 233 98997 8

Printed in Great Britain by
St Edmundsbury Press
Bury St Edmunds, Suffolk

for
KADAR DIOP
of Agence France Presse
who saved both our lives while attempting to
cross the Gambia River during the abortive
Coup d'Etat in the Gambian Republic, following
the Royal Wedding, 1981.

If I were a cassowary
On the plains of Timbuctoo,
I would eat a missionary,
Cassock, band, and hymn-book too.

Martin kicked off his boxers, stepped over the rim of the bath and hunched under the freezing shower.

'Eyeyanaa . . .'

The icy shock was vicious.

'Eye-yayayayayaa . . .'

His pecker was a tiny shrivelled thing. His nuts were gone. He could understand the theory: think of the sperm-count – no hot baths, no tight clothes. What he couldn't understand was how this arctic assault on his genitals could improve matters. He hopped round a half circle, tensing as the frosty needles lashed his back.

'Nee-ow!'

'You all right in there?' Alice's voice was barely audible from their bedroom across the landing; in any case he was too preoccupied to answer, turning to give himself a final frontal punishment. Enough. He leapt over the side and began briskly towelling his head – he would, he decided, get a haircut, a really short one to dry off faster, and look less seventies, more the new decade, the harder, spikier eighties. Goodbye flower-power, hello razor-head. He looked in the mirror – even through the silvery dampness he could see why his sixth form called him 'Ringo'.

Alice's voice strained to get through: 'Are you OK?'

'Ye-es – it's just sodding cold. My goolies have disappeared. Did you draw the downstairs curtains?'

'I always do. Stop worrying.'

She tried to empty her mind but of all her self-imposed rules this passive waiting was the hardest. It went against nature to lie, prone as a tart, while he was in the bathroom, getting himself knotted up because he was supposed to perform like a gigolo. This was the bit the people at the clinic left out, as if they operated in the land of instant erections – or so Martin reckoned when he reported back on his first session, imitating the concerned tones of the slight, agitated creature in her mid fifties who'd 'counselled' him, a thing he'd much resented. She had wanted 'to do something for Alice', adding, after an overlong pause, 'what Alice needs is hope, and that means organisation – a programme.'

This had puzzled them, but the next time Alice went in they explained it to her, four of them, the same woman with three young men who might have been medical students, they said so little. What the woman had meant by a programme sounded closer to voodoo than science. 'It is very important,' she said, 'to keep in mind the number thirteen. Every women ovulates on the thirteenth day of her menstrual cycle.' Alice had had to look away – it was too easy to laugh, to put silly questions just to break down her irritating certainties. Why not twelfth or fourteenth, and did all women mean the half billion Chinese, every Eskimo; were there no variations? Apparently not.

It came back to science in the end. They provided her with charts and a calendar and left her with the dire task of explaining to Martin that from then on he was to make love to order. Science, via its medium, the agitated lady with no sense of humour, had carefully matched her maximum fecundity to his optimum fertility, or so they thought. She had to admit he took it very well, largely because he thought it was so weird. When he went back he was told that he must not masturbate nor ride a bike from day ten and that on the thirteenth, fourteenth and fifteenth he should 'go for it like a rabbit'. It was one of the young male doctors who came out with that, the big lady having carefully absented herself from the more intimate male briefings. He had laughed himself silly all the way home and went on treating it like some new game, leaving her to bother with temperatures and all the rest of it. It was only gradually that the joke wore thin. Neither laughed when they were told she would be tested to see if her vagina was a hostile environment for his sperm. For this they were ordered to make love at 6.30 in the morning so that she could be at the hospital two hours later for a mucus test. Nothing definite was found but that cold-blooded session, in that suspended moment before the neighbours began revving up their cars, had been the point when she started to sense his aversion to the whole thing. There were no more jokes from then on. She kept track of the days, he let them turn up, as today, an increasingly unwelcome surprise. Any laughter now had a bitter edge. All those years of taking the pill when there had been no need, no need at all. Then all those years of not taking the pill, and the slow acceptance that something would have to be done. She tried to shut it out, to concentrate on the here and now, on this the thirteenth day with her temperature up the requisite half degree, ready for ovulation.

'The curtains are drawn,' she called out, lightly. 'They'll think someone died.'

That struck her as pleasingly ghoulish – the idea of her laid out, in order to conceive. In the midst of death there is life – maybe. She put her hands together and crossed her feet like a Crusader memorial but quickly uncrossed them and lay still – the bathroom light had clicked off and she could hear the pad of bare footsteps on the landing carpet.

The doctors had told Martin to do it earlier rather than later, while he still had plenty of energy, and they had advised him not to drink as this, like hot baths and jockstraps, was bad for the sperm-count. He didn't mind the boxer shorts, the cold showers were a bastard but endurable, but drink . . . That was the worst thing of all. He could take climbing into bed at six of an evening when he was still supposed to be in Olympic condition and ready to fuck for England, but God how a little drink would help him over the hump, help kick-start the old motor, help rise above the having-to rather than the wanting-to.

He advanced cautiously through the black-out. He did not want illumination, did not want to see the stuff spread out on the chest of drawers: bottles, jars and worse, the thermometer, the rolls of charts and instructions, pointed reminders of the artificiality of it all. One doctor had suggested pornography but for Martin the erotic was the thrill of the particular, the disconnected, the sensually suggestive, like the shop assistant he had watched, bending over the counter in Boots, not all of her, just the curve of her back, that was all. It was the scenario that told: the way some of his sixth-form girls always had summer blouses a size too small when the warm weather began, before their mothers could get to Anstleys for larger ones. It wasn't so much the outline of their breasts as the gathered creases in the cotton which excited him, the pull and drag on the thin material, always the desire of detail, never the loud symphonic generalities of a porno mag.

His right knee lightly grazed the edge of the mattress. He pulled away the duvet and folded himself in beside her and, as he snuggled down, he caught the scent of the cream she used for the patch of dry skin on her right shoulder, faintly medicinal, overlaid with sandalwood, like Christmas soap sets, and he thought again of that assistant forever at the moment of leaning across the counter, and he gently ran his hand down Alice's left arm, his thumb edging the

3

rim of her breast until it arrived at the underside where he could cup it in his hand. He could feel the ripple of her rib-cage and weigh the firmness. She had barely changed, she was beautiful, a Modigliani, oval face, oval eyes. Closer, he fluttered his lips across the nipple then darted downwards, making her draw in her stomach as if to escape, tonguing and teething over the hollow of her navel, just brushing it, his hand pressing into her waist.

Not so much foreplay as delayplay, giving himself time to react. He wondered how he was doing but did not want to reach down, preferring to press against her leg to feel if he was hard enough to get started. No. He needed time, time to nuzzle the contours of her right breast, fingers feathering over the last millimetres of smooth skin before her pubic hair began. His lips had reached her upper arm and he thought of those tight summer blouses with their suggestion of dried lavender from cupboards where they had been folded through the winter months and then he knew he was hard, really hard, and started to ease himself over her, and then the doorbell rang.

'Let it ring,' Alice snapped, passivity gone.

But he was already out of bed and pulling on his dressing gown.

She considered calling him back, then thought better of it. She was no more excited by these planned encounters than he was. Now at least she could get back into her old familiar T-shirt and drop the unwelcome role of *femme fatale*. She reached for the cherished garment. When she and Martin had first got together it had come from somewhere smart like Biba, a deep fashionable orange before countless laundrettes had reduced it to a thin Bhuddist saffron, sagged and frayed. Still she rarely brooded on her appearance – Martin always claimed to be satisfied so that was that. Not that she was necessarily flattered, Modigliani was his preferred benchmark – the nude on the Zurich poster was just visible by the door: a body composed of anorexic bananas, a rugby ball head with the blank eyes of a tribal mask suggesting a disturbing interior emptiness. Me, she thought. Or rather, me as my husband sees me.

She shifted a bit and hoped he wouldn't be too long. It was dangerous doing nothing, it left too much room for memories. The daylight behind the curtains echoed the long Sunday mornings in student lodgings, with no more than coffee trips to the freezing lino-floored kitchen and roll-your-owns with Old Holborn smelling of wood and tar and liquorice papers that made a twisted worm like an old vein throbbing at someone's temple. If she and Martin went out, she would slip a hand into his back pocket, so that she could feel the firmness of his backside and sense its movement as they walked along. She had wanted to touch him all the time, biting him even, quite hard sometimes. Once she drew blood but more often she left his back covered with marks like tiny stone circles, foundations for a hundred miniature Stonehenges. He used to squirm but never stopped her, except that time with the blood.

She looked at the poster again. Such skinny creatures were never meant to have babies, they were boy-women, women who did not feel that gnawing emptiness, who could never understand her uncontrollable need to hold a small living being against her own body. Not Modigliani's sort of thing, surely? And yet, why do so many of his women look washed-out and melancholy?

She pulled the T-shirt over her head. What would Martin say if she took down his scrawny tart and replaced her with a nice titty Rembrandt? She shook her head. Counterproductive probably – with a vision of rosy thighs to contend with he might never perform again, and that would hardly resolve her problem.

Martin opened the front door and looked out. There was no one on the short concrete path from the garden gate, no one in front of the garage. He stepped on to the tiny rain-sodden patch of lawn and shivered – April seemed to be holding back, the cherry tree was still a black tangle of bare branches against an already darkening sky. And then he saw him, by the bay window, a hunched figure trying to peer through a crack in the curtains.

His first thought was that this was some sort of private detective sent to spy on them, maybe even a journalist – the military raincoat and dinky Tyrolean hat would do for either role. The idea was essentially flattering, even though he could think of no reason why anyone should take the least interest in their suburban lives.

The man's head twisted this way and that, trying to see round the lip of the drapery. It struck Martin that he might just as well be a burglar who had rung the bell simply to check whether they were in or not, and being neither brave nor dressed for a physical encounter, he started to withdraw, just as the peeping tom accepted that he was never going to see much more than a sliver of interior and turned to leave.

'Ah,' he said. 'There you are. You're a hard creature to prise out of his lair.' He stopped, sensing Martin's confusion. 'Mantock, William Mantock,' he said, extending a hand. 'You wrote to us – Les Enfants du Monde – remember? You filled in our form in the Sunday Times.'

Memory returned in a rush. 'But that was months ago.'

'Ah yes.' Mantock let his unshaken hand fall back. 'Takes a while to process all the applications – we're thorough, very thorough.'

'Application? I didn't *apply* for anything, I just asked for the brochure you never sent.'

The other hand shot up, waving a brief-case. 'Got it right here.'

'I'm not sure I'm interested any more – I mean I hadn't expected a personal call.'

'But what could be better than having someone on hand to answer your questions? Anyway, we have to take a look as you might expect. Don't want any funny business if you get my drift. Not that that's a problem here. I can see you've got a very nice place.'

Martin followed his gaze along the curved line of thirties semis, each with its tree, its clipped privet, its net-curtained windows, just the sort of place, Martin reckoned, where a mass murderer or psychotic rapist would choose to live. It was another of Alice's decisions, as if some instinctive premonition had warned her that one day she would need to convince the world that she was eminently respectable and ordinary. The adoption society had thought so; all that side of things had been fine until the question of age smacked them in the face like a garden rake, springing up when least expected.

Mantock too was clearly sold on the crescent, on the sanction of half-timbered solidity, on the appropriateness of glazed porches and damp rhododendrons. But was Mantock respectable enough for *them*? He looked distinctly peculiar: mouth too wide, eyes too close and as for the hat . . . More to the point, Martin had to accept that he knew nothing about Les Enfants du Monde save for the little he had gleaned from the ad in the paper – a photograph of a black baby seated on the ground in searing sunlight, pot-bellied, nose dribbling snot, the horribly thin, the all too familiar image of African tragedy, of drought and death. Normally he would have spared himself the misery by flicking past it, only this time he had been gripped by the headline. 'YOUR CHILD,' it read, which was a clever, sleeve-grabbing ploy, on a par with the rest of the brief text which, at one level, seemed to be no more than the usual stuff about orphans of disaster, but which managed to convey the idea that the best way of dealing with the problem would be to offer help to an individual child by, in some unspecified way, taking charge of it. The word adoption was nowhere used, just this hint that the reader and the infant could in some way be brought together – through the good offices of *Les Enfants du Monde* of course. Then came the bit about the brochure and the little form to be filled out and returned.

Martin had seen it just at the point when he was beginning to accept that the adoption society was cooling towards them. There had been some talk about their willingness or otherwise to adopt a handicapped child but when that too was dropped, Martin began casting round for a way to ease Alice's distress when the final 'No' would be pronounced. He hardly expected much from the advertisement, but as it only cost a stamp he sent the form off and forgot about it. Until now, that is.

'You'd better come in,' he said. 'It's cold out here.'

They filed up to the entrance where the man carefully wiped his feet on the doormat before venturing on to the fitted carpet.

'Cosy,' he said approvingly.

Martin indicated the sitting room. 'A drink?' he said. 'Glass of wine?'

The trip to the kitchen gave him a chance to collect his thoughts. He could only suppose that this was yet another adoption society, but with a Third World connection. He wondered if he ought to get all the papers out – the report of the home visit from the Social Services, the bank statements, the medical reports. And what if they went through it all just to be told they were too old again? Better he get that out of the way while Alice was upstairs. Better not to bother her if it was all going to come to nothing.

Mantock had been busy. Propped up in the armchairs, along the sideboard and across the sofa, were large blown-up photographs of black children, mounted on stiff card, all ages, from babies to early teenagers, both sexes. A few were wretched-looking, with navels as big as fists protruding from distended bellies, hair frizzy, eyes blank. But most were rather exaggeratedly happy, beaming smiles and eager eyes peering into the camera as if searching for those who would one day come and take them to the promised land of unlimited food and unrestricted tap water. Martin guessed that there must be a couple of dozen faces spread about the room.

Mantock had lit up without asking and Martin could see the spoor of ash where he had been moving about, setting up his picture gallery.

'Your drink,' Martin said. 'And there's an ashtray on the coffee table.'

Mantock peeled the wet cigarette from his bottom lip but the ghostly cylinder of grey dust broke away before he could reach the receptacle.

'Good for the carpet,' he said, scraping it with his foot.

Martin noticed he had dropped his newspaper on the floor, notoriously the most vulgar of the tit-and-bum tabloids, though now with the inevitable photograph of the royal bride-to-be, peering out from behind her shaggy blonde fringe, still nervous of the unrelenting cameras. It was becoming impossible to avoid this Lady Di person – and they were still weeks away from the wedding.

'Well, what do you think?' Mantock asked. 'A fair selection, eh? They're mostly West African but we ought to be getting some Bangladeshis when the monsoon starts and they're flooded. This lot's drought, of course – funny old world, eh?'

Martin's gaze drifted from the shyness of lily-white Lady Diana Spencer to the gap-toothed grin of the black girl in the photograph on the nearest chair. Her hair was woven into two rigid pigtails which had been fastened together with a bow on top of her head. She was, Martin reckoned, what his mother would call 'cute'.

'Aleema,' Mantock said. 'She's eight.'

But Martin was no longer thinking of the girl – not directly anyway. He was trying to make out the background details, the things just visible behind her. He could see what he assumed must be her village, a cluster of conical huts made of dried leaves or grasses, held with hoops of plaited straw, not unlike the girl's hair. There were no other people visible and if the girl had not been there he would have thought the place was dried out and abandoned. Although photographed in black and white, his eyes could paint in the sepia colours of drought: the sandy ochre soil, the distant brown hills, the ivory bleached branches on the spiky stockade that surrounded the settlement. He had a sudden, unpleasant feeling that if he pursed his lips and blew, the entire scene would disintegrate in a puff of dust.

'Been to Africa?' Mantock enquired.

Martin shook his head. 'I was going to, once. Had a job lined up in Kenya. Teaching scheme run by the old Ministry of Overseas

Development but Alice didn't fancy it. I've always thought it was a shame really, it was only for a couple of years and it would have been a hell of an experience.'

He stopped himself. This was too confessional. The girl and the village were like those small, cheaply printed photographs he used to love in old geography textbooks, full of suggestive romance, a blurring of reality lost for ever with large-scale colour printing. He belonged to that hazy era with its tiny glimpses of an out-of-date world: porters in baggy shorts carrying suitcases on their heads, bearded missionaries teaching open-air classes, a black policeman in a fez grinning at the camera.

'There's something you ought to know,' Martin said, briskly pulling things back to the present. 'Alice is thirty-nine, I'm thirty-seven, so if that matters you'd better stop now.'

Mantock turned down his mouth in a way that indicated complete indifference to what he was being told.

'Your business,' he said. 'Doesn't bother me. You could be a hundred and ten for all I care.'

'And the reports – medical, financial?'

He shrugged.

Martin digested this for a moment before asking: 'What exactly is *Les Enfants du Monde*?'

'A service.'

'Who runs it?'

'A private group.'

'You mean a business?'

'Non-governmental, shall we say. No bureaucracy – I'm sure you know all about that if you've been at this for any length of time. Boy, do they shake you down, eh? Been going to church recently?' He chuckled. 'Bet you have. Scared to get caught drink-driving in case it gives you a record and spoils your chances. And when you think of the sort of rubbish that has kids – every sort of filth and here you are, a nice couple by the look of things, and they have the cheek to ask how often you change your Y-fronts – if you get my drift.'

Martin would have been happy to share such sentiments with a more disinterested source, but as it was he felt that this ash-stained figure rather justified the concern of those responsible for placing young lives in families.

'So what do we do? Choose one of these?'

'Oh no, no, no. This isn't a Lonely Hearts club. Would that things were so simple. You have to go in person and claim your little one, these are just . . .'

'Samples?' Martin suggested.

Mantock smiled, indulgently. 'If you like, though it's not how I would put it.'

'And where are you suggesting we claim our "little one"?'

'Next West African flight's three weeks off, if that suits.'

Martin's eyes returned to the little village scene behind the grinning girl. It was as if a door had opened a fraction, offering an unexpected glimpse into a dimly lit room.

'Don't worry,' the man was saying. 'We take care of everything. Mamatours. That's our agency. Pentern Street. Know it?'

Martin didn't but the remark brought him back to the here and now. 'And how much do you reckon all this costs?'

'Eight hundred for the holiday – pounds – each. Good flight, regular airline, best hotel, half-board, a snip really.'

'And the baby?'

'That depends when and where – there are variables, but you could reckon on ten thousand. Dollars,' he added quickly.

Martin wasn't fazed. Alice had stashed away enough to cover such a thing. They had to be the only couple among their friends who were not bouncing along on an overdraft, though he saw no reason to let this little man in on their finances.

'That's about seven thousand pounds,' he said. 'Pretty steep.'

'For a baby?'

'Suppose not – though I can't imagine its entirely legal?'

'Legal?' Mantock pronounced the word as if it were new minted and he was not entirely certain of its usage. 'That's a funny way of putting it. I'm not sure I can see what legal has to do with anything. This is a one-to-one service, a way of bringing people together and I can't imagine what could be so wrong about that. If it's legal you want then you could always go to your local adoption service. They have laws, lots of them as I expect you've already discovered, but they don't seem to have much to do with natural justice because – as you've no doubt also discovered – there's nothing very just about nature. Legal, is it?' He had started to collect up the photographs, stuffing them under his arm as he progressed round the room. 'Of course, if you're not bothered . . .'

'Oh, but we are.' It was Alice standing in the doorway, her

10

dressing gown wrapped about her like a cape. 'Bothered that is. I'd like very much to know more.'

She walked to the centre of the room and looked round the gallery of eager or indifferent black faces, turning slowly as if she were displaying herself to auction and they were the expectant bidders.

'This is Mr Mantock,' Martin said. 'He's come from an organisation called *Les Enfants du Monde* that I wrote to – oh – weeks ago. They arrange adoptions for . . .'

'Deprived children,' Mantock said. 'We bring people together.'

Alice fixed her eyes on him. 'And you just came tonight, out of the blue?'

'In a manner of speaking. We had such a backlog it's taken a while to get through the list. This is a very personal sort of business . . . I see you like that one? He's Mohammed, from Upper Volta I believe, drought's terrible there, the worst.'

Alice had picked up one of the hungry photographs, an emaciated boy with a too-large head, dazed eyes, frail shoulders picked out like the framework of a bird's wing.

'Mohammed?' she said, as if something as exact and as public as a name were an unpardonable intrusion into so private a tragedy. But Mantock was already slipping another photograph in front of her, a child in a T-shirt with a Coca-Cola logo and a smile like a keyboard.

'Jean-Baptiste,' he said. 'Lovely lad. Very bright.'

Alice felt the now familiar ache beginning to clutch at her stomach.

'And babies,' Mantock said, offering a photo of a swathed bundle, with a tiny sleeping face, just visible through a gap in the cloth.

The colour drained out of Alice's cheeks.

'Hasn't got a name yet,' Mantock was explaining to Martin. 'I suppose that's the sort of thing you'd be after – a new-born?'

Alice came back to life. 'Are you saying that it's possible?'

'You have to go there,' Martin interjected, feeling the situation slipping out of control. 'To Africa or wherever. It's incredibly expensive.'

Alice barely heard him, her eyes were scanning the tiny face.

Mantock opened his mouth to speak, but Martin silenced him. 'This isn't the moment.'

'Of course, of course. Don't need to rush things. Mind you, there is that flight and if you were thinking then . . .' He paused but the silence was total. 'Yes, well, I'll just collect these up and be on my way. Here's my card if you change your mind.'

He handed one to each of them. Martin ran his thumb across the thin paper. It was not engraved and had an amateurish letterhead with a drawing of an old-fashioned bassinet with a waving baby inside, a cartoon figure disturbingly like the old golliwog from the marmalade jars. Beneath were the words 'Les Enfants du Monde' and below that 'Mamatours' and the address in Pentern Street.

Mantock had finished and was waiting with his stack of pictures, the smiling photograph of Jean-Baptiste uppermost.

'Nice place you got here,' he said conversationally. 'Perfect family home. Well, I'll be saying goodnight, seeing as you're such early birds.'

Martin saw him out while Alice began brushing away the scatterings of ash which seemed to have landed everywhere. He had left his newspaper on the sofa, the shy-faced celebrity peeking up through the gaps in her blonde fringe. It was the sort of paper they never bought – strident, illiberal – Alice lifted it with the pleasurable anticipation of an illicit thrill but before she could turn the first page she saw that Mantock had also left one of his photographs face down beneath it.

'Thank God he's gone,' Martin said as he came back in. 'I never imagined anyone would turn up like that. I don't know why I sent for the damned brochure in the first place. Is something wrong?'

Alice had turned the card over and was looking at the swaddled baby.

Martin shook his head. 'I don't know what that little creep thinks he's playing at, but if this is his idea of a joke.'

'No,' Alice said softly. 'He's just using two really irresistible things: motherhood and pity.' She smiled without humour. 'The Devil only tempted Christ with supreme power – but then Christ was a man, you get more scope with women. Motherhood and pity, clever stuff.'

Martin put his arm around her but she continued without a pause. 'I hate the assumption of weakness, the way they know I can be manipulated. They're right, of course, I'm a maternity junky desperate for a fix, but knowing doesn't stop the craving.'

'Come on,' he said. 'We'll handle it.'

12

That produced a dry laugh. 'It's as if I told you I had cancer – you'd put your arm around me just like this and you'd tell me firmly that we'll handle it. But this is motherhood, not a fatal disease – or is there no difference?'

'Bed,' he muttered. 'I'll bring up some chocolate.'

'You don't think we should give this lot a try.' She nodded towards the baby.

This was too much for Martin. 'Now you really are off your trolley. I wouldn't trust Mantock further than I could throw that sofa. They know people like us are vulnerable and desperate enough to try anything. It's brilliant. You hand over a huge sum of money to do something basically illegal so you have no one to complain to when the whole thing turns out to be a con.'

He said all this as forcefully as possible, refusing to acknowledge the tiny grain of doubt scratching against the solid bulwark of conviction he was offering her. But when he finished speaking his mind was free to test the itch. What if? What if it were possible? What if it were a way out? The programme hadn't worked. It was possible the doctors had launched them on it merely to give Alice more time to adjust to the fact that there was nothing more that they could do for her. But she had not adjusted and so . . . what if?

'You're right,' Alice said, slipping free of his arm. 'It's a crazy idea. I'd like that chocolate if it's still on offer.'

As she walked away, the dressing gown slipped from her shoulder, revealing the washed out T-shirt beneath, a sign that bed was again for sleep, that the calendar moment had passed – not that Martin's relief was entirely without regret. He paused at the kitchen door, trying to imagine the couples who had accepted Mantock's offer, people like themselves returning from Africa with their little black bundle, arguing their way through immigration at Heathrow, adjusting to the quizzical looks of friends and neighbours.

As he filled the milk pan and lit the gas his eyes rested briefly on the row of dolls perched along the middle shelf of the Welsh dresser – a pigtailed blonde with an idiot grin, dressed in a gingham frock and pinny, with a milkmaid's ruddy complexion, sat next to a plump, almost featureless, rag-doll with heavy amateurish stitching, dressed in a hand-knitted jump suit. Alice said she'd found them by accident, at the bottom of the box where the Christmas decorations were usually dumped, but Martin had his doubts, especially after she just happened to 'find' a modern plastic doll in Woolworths, a truly nasty object, with a shiny perm and a squawk that simulated 'mama' when it was tipped on its back – it was, so Alice claimed, exactly like a childhood toy, lost some years ago, but he didn't believe her. The fourth doll was as much his fault as hers. They'd seen it at an auction on one of those days when the rotten injustice of it all had weighed especially heavy and the silences between them seemed to be getting longer. It was the description that had caught his sense of the ridiculous: 'A Victorian Triste-Doll, estimate £40.' They had felt a little foolish when they got it home – what do you do with a near life-size porcelain figure with plump cheeks, puckered mouth and down turned eyes? They were soon forced to accept that they had acquired a presence, a figure studying them in their own kitchen, a triste-doll, forever on the verge of the tears she could not shed. They had even got to calling it 'Baby', occasionally lifting 'her' down for a bit of horseplay – 'Does Baby want the nine o'clock news?' – nod, nod – 'is that yes?' Then one day Martin had come home early and saw Alice cuddling it, talking softly into the little pink ear. He had slipped away, gone for a walk, returned at his usual time, but from then on he had found it hard to keep up the pretence, though he tried for her sake, hoping to mask the depressing fact that he was growing to loathe the sad-eyed freak which seemed to watch him from its vantage point above the kitchen table.

He set out the mugs, two, perhaps there would only ever be two. They were barely middle-aged, there was a long way ahead and not much on offer save the mixture as before. The sense of being programmed, pre-ordained, worked out and completed, almost choked him. A moment ago, their peculiar visitor had wafted in with his unexpected promise of adventure – improbable and dubious, but adventure nevertheless. They had rejected it and now there was nothing but the usual routine, except that after the thrilling glimpse of beyond, it seemed even more bland than before.

With a venomous hiss, the milk erupted over the edge of the pan and spat out the gas. Martin's eyes turned instinctively towards the line of dolls. Baby seemed so sad, as if she felt truly sorry about his little accident.

'Fuck you,' he said, then laughed at his own stupidity.

It was at the third attempt, and only by kicking and tugging, that Alice was able to disentangle a trolley from the mêlée outside the supermarket. Her car was parked way away near the perimeter fence and she could see, from the mess outside and the queues within, that she had timed her visit badly. This caused only a moment's fret, she was a highly organised shopper and was little bothered by distractions as she swept down the aisles, robotically scooping up her planned purchases. Five meals had been pre-structured in her mind and her free hand darted out as if programmed to empty the shelves. There would be pasta, so up and in went a large packet of dried tagliatelle nests, a tube of purée and a large tin of peeled and chopped tomatoes – up, in – up, in – up, in.

To her surprise the rhythm was broken when the tinned tomatoes rolled out on to the floor, narrowly missing her foot. As she bent to retrieve it, Alice saw that she had taken some new sort of trolley, a higher, squarer model with a shelf at the back and two square openings at the front, through one of which the tin had escaped. It was a curiously impractical design, but she refused to waste time puzzling over it and simply settled the tin at the base and set off once more, hand flashing out along the vegetable chill counter – mini courgettes, washed and sliced carrots, four coloured capsicums in a transparent sheath, – up, in – up, in – up, in. Far from being a drag, shopping was satisfying proof of her ability to cope with a host of functions. When she was working she had handled the house without the least friction: out of school, over to Tescos, along the row, pay, out, home, cook, no problem.

There were two routes to the bakery counter: the long way via racks of cleaning things, the shorter via baby products. She usually chose to avoid the latter with its shelves of tiny guck-filled jars, the stacked boxes of Pampers, the tins of powders, all with their grinning baby faces, but this time she made herself process down the aisle, her robot arm swinging uselessly at her side. It was, she told herself, all in the mind, and the mind in question was hers and she could oblige it to behave. Satisfied with her strength, she manoeuvred to avoid a stationary trolley whose owner was studying a set of surreal plastic cutlery presumably meant for tiny hands learning to eat unaided. The woman turned, smiling as Alice passed, until she looked down with a slightly puzzled expression. It was then that Alice realised that the woman had also taken one of the new trolleys and that she had put her baby on to the shelf, so that its legs could dangle through the two square holes. It was a maternity trolley, a sort of shopping pram, it was meant for mothers with babies. As

15

soon as she saw this Alice quickly reached out and seized a couple of jars of baby food and dropped them in.

The woman smiled. 'Mine always like those,' she said. 'Beef and carrot. I always said they should do Yorkshire pudding as well.' This caused a rich, throaty chuckle.

Alice tried to join in. 'Mine'll eat anything,' she said, hoping to get the right note of maternal pride into her voice.

'Bless 'em,' the woman said.

'Yes,' Alice said, smiling rigidly. She pushed against her trolley, forcing it forward, determined to get away before the woman could ask where her baby was. She took the next corner at speed, narrowly avoiding two smirking girls in track suits who were reaching into one of the freezer compartments to jumble up the various products in a way that would take someone an hour to disentangle. Forcing her trolley into an awkward three-point turn, Alice charged to the check-out, and began feeding things on to the belt with both hands, keen to get away, but the cashier was having trouble with the cash register, tapping everything in it at least twice before the price would take.

'Sorry,' she chirped brightly, sensing the waves of impatience breaking over her.

Alice consoled herself with the thought that for once there was ample time to stuff everything into a plastic bag – after she had prised one of the damn things open.

'Twenty-six pounds, twenty-six pence,' the woman sang out, then exclaimed: 'Isn't that funny, two twenty-sixes?'

Alice didn't think it funny at all. It was appalling. All that money, for what? She handed over the notes. Perhaps the machine had been ringing everything up in dozens – but no, the bill only showed one of each. It was just living – tins, tubes, boxes, bottles, jars.

Alice scraped up her change, struggling over a recalcitrant penny on the shiny surface, stacked her bags in the trolley and made for the door. The chaos outside had worsened, the trolleys were herded like skeletal sheep milling together for safety. She forced her way through a narrow corridor, debating whether to abandon her own baby trolley and carry her bags over to the car. At least it was still light, a sign of winter's end despite the enduring cold. She would tell Martin tonight, tell him the old Alice had returned, no more calendars and dolls, they could get on with life as it was. He'd been very good, he deserved cheering up. Bottle of wine tonight and then the good news.

She stopped, her way on to the circular road blocked by a pram left on the edge of the pavement – rare enough, now that most people used collapsible push-chairs. It was a fine old-fashioned thing, all shiny black lacquer with a matt black concertinaed hood, pulled up to protect the ivory white overlay, trimmed with lace. Alice assumed that mother and child must be inside the shop and hoped that none of the local louts would junk their handsome carriage. The area around the store was notoriously rough: a treeless estate of pebble-dash crescents, with a shuttered off-licence and a pawn shop run by an ex-boxer with a rottweiller. There were notices all round the car park warning shoppers to leave nothing in their cars and to be sure to lock them carefully, so it seemed odd that anyone should think of leaving an expensive bassinet with all its bedding in so exposed a place.

Just as Alice was pondering this a plastic toy curved up from within the carriage, described an arc in the air and plummeted to the road with a bright tinkling noise. Intrigued, she left her trolley, walked over and bent to retrieve the jettisoned object – a short candy-striped stick with a transparent globe at one end, filled with tiny metal balls which rang like a bell when shaken. She leant over the pram and saw a muffled figure, a sort of papoose, more swathed woollies than flesh, except for an immense wet grin, a bump for a noise and a pair of cherry eyes. With Alice's looming appearance, the face chortled and the hands reached up, tiny stubby fingers clenching and unclenching. Alice shook the stick and produced a satisfying tinkle. The chortle turned to a hiss of delight which produced a surprisingly large spit bubble. Alice placed the stick near the right hand. The fingers enfolded it and shook it, but only for a brief tinkle before the thing was tossed in the air and out of the pram – tinkle, tinkle, and down to the ground.

Smiling, Alice walked over and picked it up, but she wasn't quite quick enough, even as she straightened up she could hear the first of the sobs, then another, than a full-scale wail. She leant over the pram, rattling the toy, making conventional coochy-coo noises. She gave the hand the stick and grasping the lacquered rim, she began to gently rock the carriage, saying: 'there', and grinning from ear to ear encouragingly.

'There now, there now. Yes, yes. Shshshshshsh. There now . . .'

The crying cut off with surprising abruptness, an imitative grin appeared and with it a satisfied mew.

'Good good,' said Alice but even as she spoke, up went the hand and out went the toy.

It was amazing how far it went. Right out on to the road. Alice went to get it still holding on to the pram, dragging it behind her. Just as she drew level with the dejected toy she heard an agitated voice calling out from some distance away but took no notice, assuming it was someone shouting at a child. She bent to retrieve the stick but as she stood up she was suddenly thrown backwards as a hand tried to grab at her face.

'My baby, my baby . . .'

Alice pulled away and saw a young woman, her face contorted with panic, yelling incomprehensible things about her baby. Alice was so busy trying to keep a safe distance between her face and the clawing hands that it was some time before she realised that her attacker must be the mother of the child in the pram. Even then, it was not until people began to gather, some of them running up from the car park to see what the commotion was all about, others from out of the store, drawn by the spectacle of two women fighting, that Alice realised that her assailant was trying to prevent what she had assumed was the theft of her child.

'She was taking my baby,' the woman screamed, frantically striking out at two men who were trying to restrain her and calm her down. Alice stood stock still, partly out of terror and partly out of some deep instinct for self-preservation which warned her not to do or say anything.

At first the sheer noise and melodrama of the woman's perform-ance held all eyes, but as she sank into wracking sobs, the crowd began to turn towards Alice. There were aggrieved mutters of 'disgraceful', 'look at her', 'someone ought to get the police'. One figure in a head scarf thrust her face near to Alice's and started making threatening noises but she was quickly edged away by one of the store personnel, a trainee manager, judging by his youth and the galaxy of spots along his chin. That, however, was the limit of his initiative. Briefly trained in the correct way to handle geriatric shoplifters, the proper procedure for an assumed baby-snatcher was beyond him.

'What's going on?' he asked without much authority, though at least this brought a moment's silence as the bystanders strained to hear what was being said. Alice decided it was time to speak.

'I was only . . .'

The mother started up at once. 'She took my baby. She took my baby . . .'

The muttered threats resumed, the woman in the head scarf advanced and just as Alice felt she was about to be engulfed, a second woman pushed through and addressed her by her maiden name.

'Miss Clevely?' she said. 'Is there anything wrong?'

The trainee manager looked relieved at this return to normality.

'D'you know this woman?'

'Of course I do. It's Miss Clevely from St Dominic's, she's my daughter's chemistry mistress.'

The words were so reassuringly old-fashioned. So redolent of all their school days, that the muttering instantly abated and even the hysterical mother was reduced to a snivelling whimper.

'I was retrieving a toy for this baby,' Alice said as loudly as possible, though afraid that her voice must be shaking in a guilty sounding way. 'It had been left alone outside the store with no one to take care of it. It threw down its toy but when I went to pick it up this woman came up and assaulted me.' She bit her lip. She had spoken instinctively, but even with forethought the words could not have been more carefully chosen to shift the blame, to play to the crowd, to turn its anger from her to her accuser.

'I was only inside a minute,' the woman protested. 'I mean, how was I to know what she was up to. You keep hearing about things like that – on the telly.' It was no use, her accent and her delivery were no match for a school teacher, for *Miss* Clevely the *Mistress* of St Dominic's. The man who had been comforting the mother had already edged away. The muttering was now all about how disgraceful it was to leave children unattended, about how it was no wonder poor little mites got snatched away and how lucky it was that the school mistress had happened along.

Half terrified over what might have happened and half appalled at the way she had saved herself, Alice offered no resistance as the woman who had come to her rescue took her under the arm and began to lead her away.

'I think you'd best have a cup of tea,' she said, marching her towards the café at the side of the store.

19

Alice half turned to look back at her trolley, piled with goods, abandoned amidst the hugger-mugger jumble outside the door. More robotic than ever, she allowed herself to be marched to a table where she sat, mindlessly toying with a paper napkin while her companion took a tray along the self-service line. Alice studied the beige camel-hair coat and turban hat and tried to match the square, rather heavy features, to a classroom face, but failed.

'There,' the woman said, putting a cup of tea in front of her and heaping it with sugar. 'For shock,' she explained.

Alice sipped it obediently, wondering how long it would be before she could decently leave.

'I'm Mrs Tancot – Maureen's mum – Maureen Tancot? – 5b?'

Alice forced her face into a smile of recognition. The woman relaxed.

'Its been some time,' Alice said. 'I don't teach at St Dom's any more.'

'Oh, I didn't realise – moved away?'

'No, left to have a baby.'

The woman's eyes ran downwards. 'When's it due?'

'It isn't. I left to have one. I haven't succeeded yet.' She stopped, seeing the disapproving look invading Mrs Tancot's face; she had forgotten the inherent prudishness of parents. 'I'm not Miss Clevely,' she explained. 'I just kept my maiden name for work. I'm Mrs Beresford.'

The woman relaxed, her daughter's morals had not been compromised by an unmarried chemistry teacher.

'It's hard,' Mrs Tancot said. 'Not having children. I started quick, year after we married, then two more in short order. But my sister had nothing but trouble, she and her . . .'

Alice let her ramble on, it was familiar stuff, the conventional attempt at sympathy by someone who had no way of knowing what it was she was supposed to be feeling sorry about. How could she, when the whole thing about childlessness was an absence, a not having, a not being? It was the invisibility of those who do not have children that had most surprised Alice when it had slowly dawned on her that she too shared the condition. It was only by gradual stages that she had woken to the fact that she could walk into a room where a group of women were gathered together in jovial conversation only to find that she could not join them. It was no use, she had no desire to listen to the women's well-meant pity. Leaning forward, Alice cut her off in midstream.

'No one has any idea how invisible you are if you don't have children. You go into a room and the women are all together talking about being mums and you don't fit, you haven't been through it, you haven't quite grown up. You may be married but you're still a spinster, excluded from a club that doesn't even recognise your existence.'

'But I thought we were supposed to envy you career women over there with the men, not shut out with us housewives chattering on about baby things? Oh well, guess I got it wrong as usual. But surely you're exaggerating, it can't be that bad, not that bad eh? I mean of course you want a baby, it's only natural, but if you can't, well you're an intelligent, educated person who's got lots of other interests in life. I'd have thought . . .'

Alice tried to shut it out. The woman was only trying to cover her embarrassment with a litany of clichés which, like all clichés, were true but ineffective when set beside that other truth, the truth that expressed itself in the hollowness she felt, in the irrepressible longing to hold another life, for it to be hers and hers alone.

Silence. The woman had stopped talking and was looking at Alice expectantly. She must have asked a question.

'I'm sorry?' Alice said.

'I was just saying that it was marvellous what they can do nowadays. My sister went through quite a lot of new things and it worked in the end. Why don't you change hospitals if you're not satisfied?'

She was right. Alice had learned how much it varied from place to place, some cared, some hardly bothered. She'd been to three now but one thing was always the same – the infertility unit was always inside the ante-natal clinic. It was like a punishment for failure, being made to walk through the waiting room with all the pregnant mothers chattering away about their soon to be realised dream, while she made her way, slim, visibly unpregnant, to the far door with its tell-tale sign and the smaller drearier room where the other sad creatures sat in silence.

She had waited over an hour and a half at the first one she visited, an eternity in which no one was called, which could only have meant that the specialist had not turned up. Eventually they had started to filter through, but no one emerged radiant with relief and when Alice was finally summoned, she found herself in a cubicle with a table behind which was a man in an unfastened white coat, reading a bundle of typed papers, flicking them over with his free hand with an impatience that told her it was not welcome news.

'So what's wrong with you?' he asked absently.

She wondered what she was supposed to say – that she'd caught a cold, been run over by a truck? In the end they had started to talk and he had arranged for tests to be done. But after a while she had accepted what she had guessed from the first, that this was a place where infertility was treated like a self-inflicted wound, and she had taken the advice of a colleague and moved elsewhere.

'I've tried everything,' she said, knowing this would not satisfy her interrogator. She had discovered early on that many women have an insatiable appetite for the gorier gynaecological details. Normally, she tried to side-step such conversations, but today she felt she owed her listener something for her help and what easier way to repay her than by trotting out all the proddings and pokings, the pills and needles, those penetrations that become as essential as coition to the would-be but cannot-be mother.

She took a deep breath and ploughed on. 'I changed from my first hospital when I realised they weren't bothered. I went to the General, they're more into getting inside you there. They do a laparoscopy – through the tummy – so that they can see if your tubes are gummed up. Feels as if you've been kicked in the guts by a goat afterwards.'

The woman winced but Alice knew she wanted more.

'And Martin – that's my husband. He was put through it, too. You know, the bottle in the lavatory routine, with everybody utterly po-faced even though you're well aware that they're sniggering like stink inside. Did you know that a wife can develop antibodies to her husband's sperm, as if it was a virus?'

'I don't like . . .'

'No more did I,' Alice smirked, brushing aside any intervention by her listener. This was her show, she was the one who had been through it and this successful mother could just sit and listen to it. It was what she wanted after all.

Alice warmed to her task: 'Grisly isn't it, and that's just for starters. You see it wasn't him in the end – the laparoscopy came up with endometriosis. Of course I should have known, I'd always had terrible periods, really bad, but I'd always believed that only wimps complained. As far as I was concerned you just got on with it. Do you know I never so much as had a half day off work – even when the pain was so bad I couldn't unclench my teeth?'

Mrs Tancot was visibly struggling to find some kind of response. 'Well we all have to . . .'

'No we don't,' Alice said dismissively. 'I've learned that now.'

'Please,' Mrs Tancot said. 'You don't understand . . . I can't bear this sort of thing, it always upsets me. I just don't like thinking about it. I had to get my sister to have a little chat with Maureen about – you know what. I hope you don't mind, but I'd really rather not know if it's all the same . . .'

It was Alice's turn to be confused – could it be true, was this the only woman on earth who didn't want to hear about how messed up her insides were? She had assumed that the little attempts to stall her narrative had been no more than a way of displaying modesty, a desire not to appear too nosy when in reality she couldn't wait to hear more. But no, this was not a genteel facade to mask a slavering desire for further anatomical porn – the woman was ashen, she was genuinely upset, her left hand, on the table beside her cup, was visibly trembling.

Alice narrowed her eyes – she felt suddenly aggrieved and vindictive. What business had this wretched creature to come over all prurient about what she had been through? What gave this woman, this mother, the right to shut out what another woman had had to suffer? No, she was not going to let the matter drop. She would go on to the end. She would make her hear out the whole sorry story.

'Periods,' she said forcefully, delighted at the facial twitch the word produced. 'And I'm not talking grin-and-bear it, I'm talking screaming agony. I put up with it because that's what I do. I don't let my body rule me and I thought I'd got it licked. The trouble was, I hadn't reckoned on just how sneaky the enemy can be. When I married I had it all worked out. Kids? Only when I was good and ready. Oh, don't worry, Martin agreed. He always does, that's his charm. Unfortunately, by the time I was ready my body had really fouled things up. Blood and pain. Do you hear me? Blood and pain. If I'd been a moaning Minnie from the start something might have been done about it; as it was, by the time they diagnosed endometriosis I was far gone. Of course that just makes you feel guilty for having braved it out, for not having been your average wilting woman with her monthly blues, for trying to control the whole motherhood thing instead of passively acquiescing in the natural process. It seems I should have let things take their course. I didn't so I'm guilty.'

That was too much for Mrs Tancot. 'I don't think, I . . . I mean, you really shouldn't blame yourself. There's always . . .'

Alice's face set even harder. 'I know the options – I followed all that stuff about Baby Louise and the test tubes and all the rest of it. What a let down. You get the idea that we'll soon be able to pop down to the Post Office and get fixed up and then they announce that it'll be years before the treatment is generally available – that is as long as our Lords and Masters allow it and nobody in a cope and mitre kicks up too much of a fuss. By the time they finally get round to it I'll need a pram to lean on, not push.'

She stopped. Why was she doing this? The woman had only tried to help, yet here she was rubbing her nose in it, when the poor thing had made it perfectly clear that she had not the least desire to be drawn into the crepuscular world of laboratory procreation. But it was no use, the more the Tancot mouth turned down in a stagey display of self-pity, the more those discreetly mascaraed eyes pleaded with her to desist, the more Alice felt driven to continue with her miserable revelations. She bent closer, making her companion look her straight in the eye. 'I read an article at the clinic about Gynaecological Potentials. Do you know they may soon be able to impregnate a brain-dead female corpse so that it could "host" the sperm of a fertile man with an infertile wife. Even the dead shall give birth. They may even be able to preserve excised wombs under laboratory conditions to cultivate test-tube babies with no living intervention. Why not? Once you refuse to accept Nature's decision there's no logical end to it. No one seems to have even considered that a fraction of all this research money might be directed towards finding a way of stopping someone like me *wanting* to have a baby?' She gulped some tea down, it was thirsty work being disagreeable. 'Did you know that when the blokes go in to wank into the bottle most of them can't get it up so the nurses slip them a dirty mag. Think of it? Even there, they're thinking of someone else as they do it. Then along comes this test-tube full of stuff to be injected into you, produced out of desire for some huge-titted tart in a porno rag. Surrogate mothers are thought to be morally OK because no joy is involved beyond a three-minute thrill with a photograph in a

24

hospital broom cupboard. As long as no one has had any pleasure out of the operation you are allowed to pacify this monstrous craving. Yet what about the surrogate? Didn't she long to hold the baby, to force it into herself the way I do, all the time, all the rotten time?'

Mrs Tancot was examining her teaspoon as if it was the only thing in the world that mattered. When she realised that Alice had stopped talking she tentatively looked up, no doubt hoping she would be allowed to leave. But Alice was ready for her.

'Anyway,' she said forcefully, 'when they found out that I was all gummed up, they put me on Danazol.'

She paused again but was disappointed to realise that the name meant nothing to the poor mournful creature staring nervously back at her.

'Danazol,' Alice repeated. 'You know – the wonder cure – only it isn't. It's a hell of a thing – you lose your desire for sex when you're on it – not that it matters – you can't conceive while you're taking the pills anyway. You even get hairy, your voice drops, you get acne. A "mild virilising effect" they call it. Anyway, we tried to handle the thing on all fronts – applying to adopt – you think that's easy? You go to church, you give up your job. Didn't you know? They insist on it – no part-time mothers if you please. The phone rings, there's no one there, whoever it was has hung up, but you know it's them checking that you're really at home, not out, not at work. You think I'm exaggerating? Oh no, I'm not. I had to throw away my career – I was Head of Science at St Dom's – and even then they turned us down – too old. I was off the Danazol by then, so the clinic said we should start trying in earnest. That's when they put us on the programme – do you know what that is?'

That was it – she had gone too far. Mrs Tancot pulled back and made as if to rise. She had heard such things alluded to but had determined never to be confronted by them.

'I must be . . .'

Alice's heart sank. Why had she done it? What on earth had driven her to such lengths? It was one thing to fight off her demons with the aid of a plastic doll, quite another to surrender to them at someone else's expense.

'It's all right,' she said, her voice subdued. 'I'll spare you the details. I really must be going. Thank you for tea. You were most kind.' She edged round the table. 'Give my good wishes to Maureen,' she said. 'I'm sure she'll do well in her A levels.'

'She's not doing A levels,' the woman said plaintively, but Alice was already through the revolving doors, heading towards her trolley.

Safely outside, she let out a long windy breath, blowing through her lips. To lose control like that was terrifying. She could not even excuse it as a shocked reaction to the incident with the mother and the pram – there really was no excuse, it was just another sickening proof of her inability to keep this thing dampened down. She had only begun to realise how powerful, how invincible it was, after the tests had really got underway and it was only when they diagnosed endometriosis that she had realised how wrong she had been to think that she could simply brush her body to one side. Throughout her year on the drugs she had radically adjusted her approach, stealth rather than confrontation, single-mindedly devoting herself to every test, every pill, every demand of the adoption society, everything down to the final mumbo-jumbo of the programme. Never again would she resist to the point of collapse, better to bend and survive. That was why she had gone for the dolls – with them she could pacify the enemy, give it what it wanted, let mothering have its way, pick up the sad-eyed porcelain creature, hold it in her arms, make all those soothing noises, keep something of her sanity intact, safe in another corner of her mind.

She found her trolley – the dented tin of tomatoes sitting dejectedly beside one of the jars of baby food and a special offer spaghetti strainer, half spoon, half fork – everything else gone. It was inevitable given the neighbourhood, yet it left her with a curious feeling of release, as if a dead weight of tins and jars and bottles had been lifted away. Though that made her think of her real burden, less easily shed. She fumbled in her bag for the car keys. How much longer could they go on with it? Even without the arrival of Mantock and his photographs they had come close to breakdown the previous night – he hated it, she felt helpless – worse – ridiculous. Perhaps it was time for another new approach, yet another dramatic shift. Her searching hand settled on something thin and malleable at the side of the bag. She knew what it was before she lifted it out and smiled at the coincidence – if it was. Seen again, its tackiness surprised her anew: *Les Enfants du Monde*. The cheapness of the printing said more about the uselessness of the

26

whole enterprise then any arguments she might think up . . .
yet . . . it was still there, in her hand: 'Mamatours, Pentern Stre
She had only to open her fingers and it would drift away, join
the crisp packets and chocolate wrappers strewn around the dank
wasteland. She stuffed it back in her bag and pulled out her keys.
The three items in the trolley were left for whoever might want
them, a donation or maybe even a payment, amends of some sort
for her appalling behaviour back there in the café.

For the umpteenth time, Martin allowed himself to be amazed that
the scuffed and dusty corridor he trudged down five or six times a
day, had once been considered worthy of the highest architectural
awards. Wallstanton Grammar, as it then was, had been photographed on the one day in the year when a Mediterranean sunlight
had caused the bold red and blue panels to glow and the wide picture
windows to sparkle. Framed prints from the magazine, hung outside
the headmaster's room, startlingly divorced from the surrounding
reality. Two generations of nervous schoolboys, awaiting punishment, had ruefully observed these images of geometric precision,
devoid of human occupants, a perfect cubist construction, arranged
along the horizon, in the ideal state its creators had envisaged.
Under slate northern skies, hacked and battered by wilful hands,
stacked about with the detritus of teenage life, this constructivist
dream was a tawdry backdrop to the everyday squalor that lowered
the spirits and defeated joy, with a thoroughness that the occasional
attempts at decoration were powerless to overcome. Various art
classes were responsible for the huge paper murals at strategic
points, attempts to lighten a rigid grid system with a touch of
human creativity. A collage of Shakespearean heroes ran along part
of the corridor that led to the library, there were papier mâché
puppet heads outside the gym and the very latest work, a tableau
depicting the life of Lady Diana Spencer, was somewhat incongruously sited inside the entrance to the prefabricated science
laboratories, a temporary structure run up in the fifties and never
replaced. The transition from Grammar School to Comprehensive
might have given a more convincing *raison d'être* to such uncom-
promising modernity, but as Martin ruefully acknowledged, this
was a building in the wrong place at the wrong time. Its purity
could not withstand the sheer messiness of human life. This
particular corridor was almost empty, yet a single abandoned, half-

perished rugby ball, like a battered fruit trailing lacy creepers, was enough to make it seem sloppy beyond redemption. The tidiest of mortals could not have coped with the place, let alone that subhuman demi-species schoolchildren.

Martin took a deep breath, pushed open the classroom door and stepped into the glum room. Junior classes in riot were better than the silent, deathlike void engineered by bored sixth formers. A group of girls were clustered round the far radiator paying court to their leader Eileen Partridge who sat, queenlike, upon her warm throne. The boys were at their desks, most of them trying to cobble together some unfinished homework, needed later in the day – yet another reason for their resenting his arrival. They were not opposed to being taught, far from it; if he had come with something to teach them, something that would help with their imminent exams, they would have welcomed his presence. But, as Martin knew, they were fully aware that the next forty minutes was going to be a complete waste of time, hence their utter lack of enthusiasm.

'Civics,' Martin announced boldly, as if the word might for once hold promises of riches to come. He unrolled his newspaper across the teacher's desk and listened to the groan from his audience. They were right, of course, this could never be anything other than an artificial discussion of something culled from the *Guardian*. Whoever had dreamed up the idea of a single civics lesson per week had not got as far as thinking of how it might really work. Oh, sure, there was a syllabus of sorts, a few pages of guff about preparing the citizens of tomorrow – about understanding the democratic process – trade union history – interpeting the media – it rolled off the brain nicely, and meaninglessly. There was no exam, so to the ambitious, nervous, insecure, arrogant individuals Martin and his colleagues were obliged to nourish, the exercise was doomed from the start. At first, lessons had been dutifully prepared, audio-visual aids marshalled, essays set and marked. But as time passed this had withered away, until, as now, it came down to a quick flick through the paper in the break before the lesson began, in the often forlorn hope of finding something – anything – with enough meat on it to stimulate the class for forty long minutes.

On this day, Martin had been so preoccupied with his analysis of the previous evening's curious encounter that he had forgotten to do even that much minimum preparation. It had taken him longer than usual to get through the normally automatic business of dressing and making coffee, largely because the remains of the night before – the alien newspaper, the sad photograph of the swaddled baby, the scalded milk pan – had each led him into drifting minutes of reverie. No matter how he reassured himself that he had been right to reject any possibility of following up Mantock's crazy scheme, and that all the things he'd said to Alice about it being illegal and a rip-off still held good, he could not help marvelling at the sheer audacity of it. It seemed to promise a total rupture from all the useless bureaucracy, all the solicitous but equally pointless medical palaver that had commandeered their lives. There was a boldness about it that lifted the heart on a grey April morning with a Civics class to get through.

He spread the *Guardian* across the desk and scanned the front page. The lead headline read 'BRIXTON BURNS – FRONT LINE YOUTHS CLASH WITH POLICE'. To one side something about the Vatican and birth control, a subject he tended to shun, while everything else seemed quite minor, save for a box along the bottom of the page which held a large article about horse racing based on Aldaniti's win in the Grand National that Saturday. There was really no choice.

'Well,' he said chirpily. 'You no doubt saw the telly this weekend and watched the riots. If you take in the coverage then it seems to break down into two camps – the black population say it's heavy-handed racist policing, while the police claim that they have excellent relations with the local community and that it's outside agitators who've been coming in and stirring up trouble.'

He scanned the room but less than half the faces were concentrated on him, most were staring out of the vast windows, the others at the grid ceiling with its recessed light fittings, half of which were now filled with protruding light bulbs instead of the flat spotlights the architect had envisaged – Mr Serrat, the school caretaker, having scant regard for Bauhaus authenticity. No one showed any sign of wanting to join in. The only faces in any way animated were those of Eileen Partridge and Andreas, a Cypriot boy who'd moved to the school last term. They were watching each other in a way that indicated there was a crush going on. Strange, Martin thought. Andreas was no Greek Adonis, being rather short with eyebrows that met above a prominent nose. He hardly seemed Partridge's sort, her preference tending so far towards conventional football heroes like Thornton over there, the most witless boy in the class.

Martin often wondered how far these crushes went – did they do it? With the pill there was nothing to stop them, unlike his own day, when the sheer terror of it kept them chaste.

'Some say,' he continued, 'that we're heading towards an American situation: inner-city deprivation, a permanent underclass . . .' He could hear himself wittering on, as if it was someone else talking. He sometimes felt that it would take only a slight effort to detach himself from his body and float free to a point above the class where he could look down on himself, blathering on autopilot. '. . . second-generation immigrants less willing to accept role as second-class citizens . . .' His eyes kept up their search, seeking out any sign of a response that he could latch on to and that would allow him to drag someone, anyone, into a discussion. Aware of this, the faces remained frozen in frigid apathy – save for Eileen Patridge who had just mouthed something – an endearment? a rendez-vous? – at Andreas.

'You wanted to say something, Eileen?'

She shook her head vigorously, flashing him a sullen, aggrieved look, as if he had failed to play by the rules. Christ, Martin thought, but she looks interesting when she's mad. He could imagine her giving any lover hell when the mood took her.

'Most of the trouble,' he went on, 'seems to come down to the concentration of particular ethnic groups in specific, deprived areas: substandard housing, poor schools and social services – that at least is one side of the argument – the *Guardian* side . . .' He laughed at his little pleasantry but no one joined in.

It really was just empty words – even while he was speaking, it had dawned on Martin that the class itself was a paradigm of what he was saying. There were no black sixth formers, he couldn't recall there ever having been any. When Wallstanton had been a Grammar School there had never been more than one or two non-white faces – the school's catchment area lay outside the sprawling run-down council estates that housed the greater part of the coloured population. Since they had become a Comprehensive, and had amalgamated with Pendlebridge Secondary Modern, there were more, but somehow they fell away, were siphoned off at O level and failed to cross into the sixth-form classes. There were Asians, not many as most were at the sixth-form college in Bishopsthorpe where Alice had taught. There was Sybil de Souza who was Goan, sitting behind Eileen, and there were the two Patels in his Upper

Sixth literature class. But such rarities aside, he had to admit that this was a remarkably white school for what was always said to be a multiracial society.

By contrast, Alice had taught classes that seemed almost entirely Asian – there had been wonderfully lively photographs of her being dressed up in a sari for a Diwali party, and the annual class photograph always had a clutch of Sikh turbans punctuating the lines of grinning faces. According to Alice it had all been very happy, but he wondered whether this trouble in London would change things, would spread north and catch fire in Manchester.

'Of course,' he went on, 'some argue that the youth are only playing up the situation for the benefit of the TV cameras . . .' He groaned inwardly. They weren't in the least bit interested. He could have been talking about cabbage farming. With less than two months to their first exams they could think of nothing but the coming ordeal. They had tests to take, universities to get into, careers to build and – judging by Eileen and Andreas – a lot of loving to do. Nothing beyond that seemed to touch them. Martin could understand, up to a point, but did they have to be so damned confined? Nothing other than that narrow scenario seemed to penetrate. They didn't mind wearing school uniforms, there were no protest haircuts, no one challenged school rules in any significant way – even though the Head was so 'liberal sixties' he would have caved in at the sight of the first punk hairstyle or pin-pierced nose, and have been secretly happy to do so. But no. They just weren't fussed to try.

Martin could hardly believe how things had changed since his own time when long hair had led to parents being summoned, to suspensions, and even expulsion. There were kids their age, rioting, burning and looting down south, and all they could do was examine the light fittings. He thought of himself and Alice: clothes chosen to break their mothers' hearts, joining CND and sitting down outside American bases. Perhaps protest was now impossible. He had to admit that if Eileen had been giving Andreas a blow job when he walked into the room, nothing would have happened to her save a mild telling off and a request that she confine such extramural activities to the prescribed breaks between lessons. He wondered if the boys got hard-ons all the time the way he and his pals had. Was Andreas, even now, poking his fingers through the well-worn hole in his pocket to give himself a J. Arthur?

31

'Andreas,' he said wickedly. 'Stand up will you? Now tell me what you think about all this?'

The boy stood up but his hands were free and there was no tell-tale bulge. He stared at Martin with a look of aggrieved amazement.

'Oh, sit down,' Martin conceded, it was impossible to coerce any of them into an unwanted dialogue. 'Let us consider another aspect of the issue: the possibility that none of these high-flown theories holds water and that the whole thing is just a bit of a frolic that's got out of hand – Eileen have you got any thoughts on that?'

She sat unmoving, silent, blank, for just long enough to show she resented the intrusion but just short of actual rudeness.

'It's a sign of Britain's post-imperial decay,' she said, perfectly aware that she had lifted the phrase from the previous week's discussion on the IRA hunger strikers.

It was a pretty cheeky response but Martin was in no position to suppress it without losing his only chance of launching any sort of debate.

'Peter – yes, you – are we paying the price for our treatment of black people, do you think?'

'Could be?'

'Is that all you have to contribute?' Martin's voice took on a slight edge that drew a scintilla of interest from his listeners.

'What I mean is,' the boy went on reluctantly, 'they've always had it bad – Africa, slavery. I mean it's everywhere, everywhere there's blacks, there's this problem. Same here ...' He waved a hand west, vaguely towards the most notorious of the depressed areas. 'It's all drugs and thieving but can you blame them? They've got no jobs, what're they supposed to do – take up brain surgery?'

There was a snigger from his peers.

'So what do you think needs to be done to address these problems?'

The boy shrugged, a genuine sign of indifference, which puzzled Martin. He had assumed that they would all be more or less pro the rioters, that they would identify with black kids of their own age, kicking over the traces. After all they listened to a lot of black music. Yet that shrug was nowhere challenged – they really didn't care. He noticed that de Souza, the Goan, was nervously flicking a finger.

'Yes?'

'The London police do seem to be very authoritarian,' she whispered, in her rather prissy, sing-song voice.

Good for her, Martin thought, she at least ought to be on the side of oppressed coloured people.

'But,' she went on hesitantly, 'they do have a most difficult job to do. When Daddy and Mommy were in Uganda it was very difficult with the Africans, they can be very violent.'

Martin could barely believe such a remark had been made. It flouted every convention, it was the sort of thing they discussed in Civics lessons, deploring it in the popular newspapers, insisting that it ought to be banned lest it poison public discourse – yet here it was out in the open in his own classroom.

'But surely,' he said, 'there were reasons. Like here – the police do harass black kids far more than whites, don't they?'

''Cause of drugs.' Thornton the footballer had spoken. Martin was even more astonished, he could not remember him ever having said anything before.

'They're into drugs,' Thornton continued. 'Most of them, certainly down Brixton. And a lot of them up here.' There was a general murmur of agreement.

'But surely,' Martin protested, 'we can't brand all blacks with the drugs thing.'

'I didn't say all,' Thornton said in a hurt tone. 'But most of them are, everyone knows that. They're very violent, like Sybil said, look at Africa, Idi Amin. I mean, whatta mess.' He finished with a satisfied ring, as if he'd just summed up brilliantly at the Old Bailey.

Martin bit his tongue, holding back so that one of them could speak up on behalf of the Third World. He would have, at their age – it had been a key issue in his undergraduate days. University had coincided with the flood of independence. Africa had been part of the faith – Oxfam lunches, long arguments in defence of one-party state democracy. Twenty years on, the names were as evocative as ever. Katanga, Sharpeville, Zanzibar. Of course things had got a bit muddled with Nkrumah and then everything had seemed to slide into chaos: the shattering image of Lumumba, in the back of the lorry, his hands tied behind him, his glasses knocked off, his forehead bleeding. Later it was Idi Amin, the Emperor Bokassa, Colonel Gaddafi, Master-Sergeant Doe, overlaid with the seemingly perpetual drought and starvation. Now he tended to avert his eyes from those parts of the *Guardian* where yet another bloody coup was being reported or where a further huge chunk of suffering humanity was being slowly erased. But that didn't mean he'd changed his basic beliefs. He could still put the case that there were clear historical reasons why the disaster had happened – he could reel them off: the colonial legacy, the unjust trading system, Cold War interference. He could see the faces in his living room, the smilers and the starvers, see the tiny background village with its brittle beehive huts and dust-bowl ground, the colours of drought: burnt sienna, bleached ochre. He had wanted to go, he still wanted to go. If he had gone to teach there, he would never have needed to ask what he was doing, never had had this ill-suppressed idea that nothing had happened, that twenty years had drifted by to absolutely no purpose whatsoever. The real reason he avoided reading about it was because there seemed to be nothing anyone could do to help reverse the decline, the very word Africa had become a synonym for the worst sort of liberal impotence.

'Are you all right, sir?' This was Mostyn, the Adenoidal Liverpool Technophile, pocket calculator at the ready, mini headphones draped around his neck.

'Mostyn,' Martin said brightly. 'Haven't you ever dreamt of going to Africa? You know: palm-fringed beaches, a blue ocean under a cloudless sky, the endless savannah with a single baobab in the middle distance and a ripple of game somewhere near the horizon where an enormous sun is rapidly disappearing?'

He could have sworn Eileen Partridge rolled her eyes, but it had been too quick for her to be accused of rudeness with any certainty. In any case, she had a point, he was conjuring up travel brochure and TV Nature Film clichés. That wasn't the Africa he wanted, either – though if they had asked him to describe his inner vision he could not have done so, there was only a vagueness, a sense of something waiting for him that he was unable to define.

'My uncle went to The Gambia on a package tour,' Mostyn said nasally. 'He got gippy tummy and spent the week crapping. Don't fancy it myself.'

This started them laughing. Martin quashed it. 'You don't think we in the West should do more to help? We did, after all, leave them somewhat in the lurch after independence and now we just sit back and watch them falling apart.'

'They get aid,' Eileen said, in a tone that implied that it was more than adequate and might well be excessively lavish.

34

'And then their leaders steal it,' said Andreas supportively.

'Waste of money,' Thornton chipped in. 'I think Mrs Thatcher's right not to let them push her around at those Commonwealth Conferences. I mean, they're ones to talk, aren't they?'

Any relief Martin might have felt at the fact that something approaching general participation was underway was tempered by his disgust at what was being said. Why did they like Thatcher so much, these young people? Why weren't they up in arms against her? She was destroying everything his generation believed in: the Welfare State, the redistribution of wealth, the need to spend and expand education – yet this lot seemed to think she was OK. She cropped up every week in some guise or other – last week it had been Thatcher the stalwart against terrorism, unbowed before the Irish menace, now it was Thatcher the upholder of Britain's honour before a bunch of importunate nignogs.

'I would have thought we were under some obligation to help,' Martin persisted. 'A moral obligation perhaps?'

They stared back as if he had started speaking Urdu. He had strayed too far from the road they recognised, the broad highway that led from school and exams to work and safety. But who was he to blame them? The days of degree equals job were gone. He had never had to think about a career. Ambition? The word had seemed slightly suspect, not his sort of thing. Alice had wanted a job but he'd put that down to her being a new woman, like wanting to drink pints and only wear make-up if you felt like it. Ambition – no. True, he had had a sort of film playing in his head, disconnected scenes: the applause as he walked into his launch party, another success, another literary triumph; his hour of glory on Face to Face, the TV audience gripped by the subtlety of his insights, logic allied to charm. But as for doing anything about it . . . He groaned, this always happened in a dismal Civics lesson – sudden unwanted introspection. Perhaps they were right these hard-nosed kids. Maybe he ought to take a leaf out of their book, take a look at himself, work out what he should be doing. Until now, he'd left all that to Alice, but she had got side-tracked. Perhaps it was up to him to help her move on. His hand went to his side pocket and the little oblong card, Mantock's seductive offer. Could that be the jolt they needed, the way out of the cul-de-sac they had turned into on the day Alice announced that it was time they had a baby?

'What did you say, Mostyn?'

The adenoidal whine had penetrated his reverie.

'The death penalty.'

Martin was about to ask, 'What about it?', but checked himself, all too well aware of the brutish responses such a question would unleash.

'Anyone see the Grand National?' he enquired disingenuously but before any hands could be raised, the bell rang, thankfully relieving him of the need to find a way out of the hole into which he had dug himself.

It did not take Martin long to find Pentern Street. He was walking quickly, almost jogging – his lunch break was only an hour and while he had a free first period, the extra forty minutes were barely enough for the two bus journeys in and out of the city centre. Once there, everything was crowds and bustle, forced off the edge of the pavement by the crush of midday shoppers, until his map led him away from the overlit department store windows, down a deserted street of scarlet brick facades with imposing carpeted entrances elaborately embellished with floral tiles and brass plates polished to near extinction. He crossed a roundabout, headed down a short sloping street, almost an alley, and found himself beneath the towering walls of nineteenth-century warehouses, their blankness relieved by regimented lines of strictly arched and barred windows. He could glimpse between them a black water canal, its towpath empty except for a solitary dog-walker.

On the next corner, two black youths leaned against a wall, while a third executed a twitching, foot-sliding dance at the centre of the pavement. Several things crossed Martin's mind in quick succession – the oddity of thinking of them as 'youths', a word he would probably not have applied to white kids; a deep suspicion of what they were doing there; the possibility that Thornton had been right about drug dealing; and finally, a hasty debate about whether it would be best to turn round and go back. He decided that it was too late, that if they were after trouble he could hardly regain the busy crowded streets before they caught up with him. Attempting insouciance, he tried to make it look natural that he should drift off the pavement into the road, passing them in a wide arc. Squinting sideways, he could see that they were not paying the least attention to him: the youth went on dancing, his friends watching, expressionless and unconcerned.

Martin hastened his walk by what he hoped were imperceptible degrees, scanning the ends of buildings for any sign of Pentern Street. Thus far the warehouses were abandoned, layers of rock posters pasted over the street-level fronts, one building entirely painted black with the words 'AFRO-CARIBBEAN CULTURAL CENTRE' falling higgledy-piggledy from roof to pavement, in a free-hand attempt at jazzy writing. He remembered something about a black dance festival, a tale of a large grant and a scandal, of a police raid and protest march. It was certainly shut for good – the main entrance had been covered with a huge door made of galvanised iron, held with massive locks which someone had tried unsuccessfully to wrench open. He could just make out what looked like an official notice pasted at the centre – probably a bailiff's order. Then he saw what he was looking for, next to the empty pub which always seemed to survive, a shop with a fascia board reading 'MAMATOURS', its window covered by a large poster which showed what, at a distance, Martin took to be a giant anthill but which gradually coalesced into a pointed mud tower that rose out of a huddle of adobe dwellings, standing amidst drifts of sand, a sea of dunes that ran to a curved horizon. It was a desert outpost, a thing out of his geography textbook, blown up to gigantic proportions. The only living things were a man on a camel, his face hidden, his head wrapped in layers of cloth. Along the bottom ran the words *'Civilisation ancienne du désert'* and Martin could guess that the scene must once have glowed richly yellow with deep red details, before the feeble northern sunlight had succeeded in bleaching it to shades of watery blue, transforming its equatorial aridity into a faded arctic wilderness. But none of this mattered, Martin had realised that he was looking at a Touareg, a warrior of the sandy wastes. Curiously elated, he pushed open the door and stepped in.

'Can I help?'

Martin heard the question before he saw the questioner. The room looked as if it had been set up by someone wanting to play at being a travel agent: two desks made a counter, behind them was a table with an old-fashioned stencil printer, the kind even his school had managed to replace, and propped against the far wall was a build-it-yourself melamine shelf unit with a few brochures – very few. It was a second before he realised that his questioner was standing nearby – she was black, very dark, and was wearing a black body-stocking which gave her the fleeting appearance of being stark naked. The simplicity of this gripping outfit was broken by a dramatic necklace of huge gilded balls and enormous crescent earrings in beaten brass. As if to give her features a chance against this form-hugging sheath, her lips were painted a glossy scarlet and her hair was teased up high, leaving her head enclosed in an Afro nimbus.

'I was hoping to see Mr Mantock,' Martin said, uncomfortably aware that his eyes had strayed to her midriff where the tight material rose over a prominent mould which was then inhaled between her legs in an embarrassingly revealing V. He was unable to disengage himself from the sight.

There was no response.

'Mr Mantock?' he said, forcing himself to look up at a face that was smiling vacantly, as if the name meant nothing to her. She walked past him, offering two sculpted buttocks, like a Rodin torso cast in wobbling aspic.

'Mantock?' Martin repeated dryly. 'Mamatours?' *Les Enfants du Monde* perhaps?'

She turned, her rigid smile unchanged. 'Our accountants are dealing with the VAT,' she said pleasantly.

'I'm sorry . . .'

She blinked, lowering a trireme of false eyelashes. 'Ah,' she said. 'You're from Quickprint? Your cheque's in the post. You'll have it tomorrow.'

Martin shook his head and was intrigued to see the mask slip a little as doubt crept in.

'You want a holiday?' she asked.

'Sort of. Is Mantock around?'

'What name shall I say?'

He told her and she disappeared, her stilettos clacking up what sounded like a wooden staircase.

Martin stared about him, relieved to be spared her alarming presence. There were two slight attempts at decoration: a pair of crossed fly whisks with beaded hafts and a tiny black and white photograph in a clip frame of a dazzling white boat, three tiers high like a modernist apartment block, berthed at a river quay with porters loading cargo. Her bows bore the name *Kankou Moussa*. A dozen dugout canoes were berthed alongside her. Across the sky, at the top of the photograph, someone had hand-printed '*la voie fluviale du Niger*'.

38

'The Niger,' Martin said out loud, savouring its familiar strange-
ness, a word forever known yet utterly mysterious. He bent towards
the little image, noting the men in shorts in the smaller boats and
an extraordinary figure on the dockside wearing a white suit and
sola topee. Like the anthill mud tower outside, it was this, not
images of game on the savannah or palm trees by an ocean, which
gripped him. This Africa was a monochrome, antique place, comic
yet imposing, like the engraved catalogues of turn-of-the century
department stores.

The stilettos click-clacked down again and the balletic figure
slipped round the door.

'You can go up,' she announced. 'First on the right, off the first
landing.'

He edged his way round her as if touching might burn, noting
the powerful scent of something lemony and expensive which she
must have doused herself with that morning. Once past he started
to climb a gloomy flight of stairs, with just sufficient light to see the
exposed tacks, still holding tufts of fibre, where a carpet had been
ripped away. There were enough steps for him to calculate the way
the encounter would go – he couldn't imagine Mantock foregoing
the pleasure of at least a little gloating over this rapid capitulation.
Martin decided to say that he had been in the neighbourhood and
thought he'd just drop in to find out more – no commitment, only
a bit of fact-finding.

He reached the landing, knocked and was bidden to enter but had
to force back the door and push his way past stacks of boxes, before
he could get into a tiny smoke-filled space.

Mantock had one of the boxes open on his amazingly cluttered
desk and was examining what Martin took to be a photograph
album, fiddling with a transparent sheet which he had pulled away
from one of the cardboard pages.

'Won't stick,' he said. 'Bloody duff, the lot of them. Made in
Korea – North Korea.'

Martin was impressed. To be standing in a room full of North
Korean photograph albums, even duff ones, was rich.

'You can go in July,' Mantock said. 'I'll need a deposit next week
and the full amount three weeks before departure.'

There was no gloating. He had clearly expected him to come.

'I thought you said there was a flight about now?'

'Cancelled. Unforeseen circumstances. It'll be July, so you'll be able to avoid all that Royal Wedding crap. Sickening, innit? Don't worry, everything will be taken care of – the hotel in Bamako is beeyootiful, believe me, a dream palace and that's gen.'

Martin did believe him, it was curiously easy to sense when he was lying.

'And the baby,' Martin said. 'How do we . . .'

'Our man'll contact you as soon as you've settled in. You'll have to take the money with you and settle up locally – they prefer it that way.'

'But what about bringing it back, there must be regulations? Documents? Has to be?'

Mantock had lifted out another album and had begun testing the pages with his fingers, which clearly did not adhere to the surface. He shook his head, though whether this was over Martin's lack of trust or the general hopelessness of the North Koreans as manufacturers of specialist stationery, was hard to say.

'We arrange for you to choose a child. We get a signed release from the family or whoever's responsible, you take it round to the government office and get the all clear. It's not very difficult when you know how.'

This was not one of the believing moments, though again Martin could not have said why. Perhaps it was the certainty that things were bound to be harder than that. Not that it seemed to matter. This was clearly a system designed to appeal to desperate people who would be willing to risk nudging the law to achieve their ends. At worst Martin could imagine turning up at Heathrow with a child, at which point there would be long, difficult and downright acrimonious discussions with the immigration people, who would, so he imagined, be forced to cave in. What else could they do? Take the baby away? Send it back? Where? To whom? They would no doubt be very angry and would make things as awkward as possible, but if he and Alice managed to get that far, who could stop them? Other than that, where was the problem? He doubted the local people would care much, given all their troubles. Why should one mouth less to feed make any difference?

It was at this point that it suddenly dawned on Martin that Mantock had actually specified a destination.

'Er, where was it you said we were going?'

'Bamako. Middle of the left-hand hump.' Mantock's hands outlined the bulge of Africa. 'It's the capital of Mali – bloody enormous place – goes all the way up to Algeria, the Sahara that is – terrible drought as you might imagine – *La Sécheresse* they call it. You won't need to pack much.'

'I haven't said I'm going.'

'Just as you please.'

That brought Martin up with a bump. It very definitely wasn't as *he* pleased – it was Alice who took care of their money, Alice who made that sort of decision. He couldn't imagine how she would react if he went back and said he'd done a complete about-face and booked a trip to Africa.

Mantock thrust the album at him: 'For your snaps, if you decide to go – you could put a dab of Gloy on the corners, or use bluetack. And take this brochure, it'll tell you all about the country.'

Martin accepted the gift but in his heart he knew it was useless, they would never go, there would be no mud huts or desert sands to fill the empty spaces.

'Do you really want a baby?' Mantock asked.

'Yes, of course. Why?'

'It isn't just the wife?'

There was no answer. Mantock eased a cigarette out of a tight packet and held the little white tube between the tips of his thumb and index finger.

'I have to smoke this – *have* to, but do I *want* to, do I *need* to? Can I divide the two? Can I give up smoking? Funny thing the mind and the body, eh?'

Martin stood up. He put the album under his arm and looked at the photograph of a giraffe on the cover of the little book.

'I'll think about it.'

'Of course you will,' Mantock said soothingly. 'Of course you will.'

From his seat at the kitchen table, Martin could see through the open door into the living room to where the television showed the face of Peter Sutcliffe, the man charged with being the Yorkshire Ripper. The sound was turned down but the story was familiar enough – the thirteen murdered women, the ultra-ordinary semi-detached house, all the improbability and horror brought together in a cheap wedding photograph the press had managed to find: the veiled bride clutching her bouquet beside Sutcliffe in his Sunday suit, outsize bow-tie and buttonhole carnation, the commonplace uniforms of suburban love.

'Scrambled eggs?' Martin said. 'I thought you were going shopping?'

'Tomorrow.' She had decided to keep the afternoon's drama to herself.

'Anything else?'

'There's cheese.'

The image of the Ripper gave way to Bobby Sands the IRA hunger striker. It would be the Brixton rioters next, Martin reckoned. There was a sort of predictable litany of mayhem, though, he reflected, seldom anything about the slow descent of Africa, except the occasional starving child, offered without context. News was left to short reports in the serious papers, bleak statistics filed by stringers and seldom backed up by lengthier thought pieces that might have explained where the places were and how they had got into such a mess. Cities and peoples drifted in and out of consciousness too quickly to stick. Tribes made war, leaders were deposed, vast numbers starved in locations Martin's teachers had failed to reveal to him, or which had changed names without his noticing, leaving a vague impression of universal terror and disease. Thanks to a paucity of foreign correspondents, somewhere below the Mediterranean, beneath the holiday lands of Morocco and Tunisia, and somewhere above the game parks and shanty towns of South Africa, the old Heart of Darkness was still beating to its usual tom-tom rhythm. Europe's fantasy of savage barbarism was intact, as if roads and frontiers had been washed away by twenty years of bloodshed, returning an entire continent to its nineteenth-century void.

Alice pushed the cheddar towards him.

'A good day?' she enquired.

'The usual, why?'

'Had any more thoughts about last night, about that man and his photographs?'

Martin's knife hovered an inch above the yellow block. His eye drifted to the side table where he had left Mantock's booklet, fortunately laid upside down, its contents hidden.

'I told you, I thought he was mad.'

'Really?'

He wondered what she was getting at. It was as if she could read in his face that he'd spent most of the day thinking about nothing else, trying to read Mantock's pathetic little brochure during his last lessons, frustrated by its lack of detail. The damned thing seemed to cover the whole of West Africa leaving the section on Mali and Bamako tantalisingly brief, and even that largely given over to official statistics on land surfaces and crop production. He had soon tired of the tables of distances, the list of consular offices, the addresses of organisations concerned with the promotion of trade and the development of health. Whatever it might really be like, the country would have to remain a romantic fiction, a place of bleached mud towns and veiled desert warriors, of the river with its glistening white boats and dug-out canoes.

'I told you,' he insisted. 'Anyway how could we leave Baby behind? Who would look after her?'

He realised it was a mistake as soon as he'd said it. The whole doll thing was beyond him, out of character but clearly necessary in some way. But he knew that any jokes about it had to come from her not him. Being coy was asking for trouble.

Her response was edgy. 'Didn't you want to go to Africa once? Wasn't there some job thing you were interested in?'

That hurt. He'd given up the only career he'd really cared about because she hadn't wanted to go, yet all she could remember of his sacrifice was some vague notion that he'd once had a passing whim about African travel.

'Yes,' he said coldly. 'You're right, I did have a job thing lined up – in Kenya if you remember.'

'There you are, then. It'll be just what you've always wanted, won't it?'

'What will?'

'Our trip to Africa.' She gave him a second or two before continuing. 'It's a funny area round Pentern Street, you wonder they don't do something with it, all those empty warehouses and the shop was hardly Thomas Cook, was it? Mantock was quite amused by our comings and goings – but not surprised. He knows the pull of the thing. It's quite neat really: I need a baby, you want to go to Africa. He even suggested it was not unlike his pathetic craving for cigarettes.'

She paused again, and waited for him to gather his thoughts.

'There was no need for that,' Martin said, struck yet again by the discrepancy between her soft look and her hard manner. 'You could have said.'

'And so could you. Anyway the joke's over, you've got what you wanted, we're off to Africa.'

'It's hardly the same thing,' he protested. 'I wanted to go to East Africa, this is West. Mali's a place about which I know absolutely nothing except that the Niger flows through it, which sounds fascinating but not quite Kenya.'

'I've booked for July.'

'Why?'

Her glance flickered towards the dolls on the dresser. 'Mostly for me – a bit for you. Mantock says we'll enjoy it because we'll miss the Royal Wedding – his idea of a joke.'

'Hilarious. And what's supposed to happen when we get there?'

Alice relaxed – he was interested. 'His man will find us – he's supposed to be quite a character. Mantock says we can't miss him, he was very emphatic about that.'

Martin massaged his temples, trying to disentangle two overlapping lines of thought. On the one hand the whole thing was crackers and very probably illegal; on the other it was a relief to see Alice in full swing again, and this could be – he cast about for the right word – a sort of therapy, a cure. That was it, they would go to Africa and get cured. To his surprise he realised that this was a plan, or at least the first steps towards one. Who knew where it might lead? Perhaps he might acquire a taste for looking ahead. It was about time he made some changes, maybe moved on, out of teaching. They'd go for their cure, come back and make a new beginning.

'Well, all right then,' he said enthusiastically.

'That was quick even for you.'

'That's unfair. I did go to Mamatours first. I even tried to find out something about the place – here . . .' He reached for the booklet and pushed it towards her.

She smiled, it was impossible not to, when he always came round without rancour or injured pride.

'Thanks,' she said.

'Don't mention it.' He watched as she flicked through the text like a polished essay marker, eyes seeking out the least sign of relevance, making hmm hmm noises as she skipped from fact to fact.

'Ah hah,' she announced triumphantly, then began to read out loud: 'In the rainy season the river rises sufficiently to permit a regular boat service between Koulikoro and Mopti, from where tours of the Dogon country can be organised. The Dogon . . .' She began to mutter to herself emitting stray phrases: '. . . 25kms via Kani Komboli along the cliffs to Douru . . .' More muttering, then: '. . . carved wooden pillars representing the eight original ancestors . . .' She went on murmuring until it was clear her eye had caught something which held her. 'Listen to this,' she commanded. 'Returning to Mopti, the Niger journey may be continued to Bamba, and . . .'

'And?' Martin said, a bit irritated by these teasing extracts. 'And?'

Alice gave a little chuckle, as if she did not quite believe what she had read.

'And what?' Martin insisted.

'And Tim – buk – tu.'

'Timbuktu? You're joking.'

'No I'm not – look . . .' She held the book close to his face so that he could see the word, printed in thick bold letters as if the author had anticipated his readers' incredulity.

Now it was Martin's turn to laugh. 'I'm not sure I believed it really existed until now. I thought it was like Eldorado or Shangri-La.'

Alice took back the book and read on: '"And Timbuktu, ancient seat of Islamic culture and fabled desert crossroads." You don't suppose that's where they send people to find children, do you?'

'I can't imagine so. But it would be quite something wouldn't it? Timbuktu – no, it's too daft.'

'There was a poem,' she said happily. 'We learned it at school – it went something like: "If I were a cassowary on the plains of Timbuktu, dumdi dum di diddy diddy, dumbi dumbi hymn-book too."'

'What's a cassowary?'

'Dunno, maybe we'll find out when we get there. You deserve a reward,' she said. 'It hasn't been easy and I'm sorry. No, don't say anything. I don't know whether I really believe in this *Enfants du Monde* thing – I don't expect it'll work and I'm not so sure it ought to. But for the moment it's all there is. We'll pull out of the adoption bit the minute it starts to look the least dodgy, OK? Let's just think of it as a holiday and we'll not get hurt.'

He leant over to kiss her but what started as a peck turned real.

'My, oh my,' she said. 'But the Dark Continent seems to have turned you on. Been consorting with dusky beauties, have we?'

He hurried her towards the door, uncomfortably aware of how close she was to the truth – his afternoon had been punctuated with flashback images of that miraculous section of black body-stocking, rising like the Mountains of the Moon, falling to the forbidden cave, a darker darkness, at once the goal and punishment of those who have presumed to cross the trackless map.

'Bed,' he said.

'And Timbuktu,' she added, switching off the light with her free hand.

TWO

'What are they frightened of?' Alice said, nodding in the direction of the young black soldier, his eyes masked by black Raybans, a hefty automatic cradled across his arms.

'Laid on by the tourist board,' Martin said. 'People expect a hint of oppression – oh, don't worry, they never touch white folk. Christ, we look a mess.' He had seen them both, reflected against the darkened window, two scruffy people with the bloated Air France jumbo lit up behind them. Manchester, Paris, Dakar, Bamako – Alice had slept on his shoulder most of the way, now her hair was flattened on one side while he had a spiky coxcomb that would never lie down without water.

Alice was concentrating on the young guard, wondering if he was watching her from behind his shades, wondering if it was easier to kill someone if you know they cannot see your eyes.

'How do you know?' she said.

'Know what?'

'That they don't touch white people?'

Martin shrugged, his eyes drifted up the breeze-block wall behind the soldier. Someone had painted it once, just as high as he could reach before abandoning the task. Above the white tidemark, high on the raw dusty wall, hung a gilt-framed photograph of a middle-aged African in a crisp beige uniform with a circlet of gold leaves around the peak of his cap. His expression was kindly, his gaze fixed on some distant point beyond the room, across the runway, into the night that had hidden any sign of Africa from these new arrivals, staring out on to some ideal vision of the future. Along the bottom of the frame rang the legend: 'Son Excellence le Président de la République'.

Martin tried to remember who he was, tried to attach a name to a news bulletin, attempted to conjure up a political stance – Communist? Fascist? Benign head of state? Kleptomaniac dictator? But nothing came. The image was contradictory – a row of medals from chest to arm suggested vainglory, while the library of leather-bound volumes where he was posed offered a world of laws and parliaments. Below was the reality, the young soldier adjusting his weapon, a bead of sweat running from under his forward tilted helmet, down over the close-shaved nape of his neck to his identity tag. His lips were very, very black and as Alice watched they parted to reveal the tip of a tongue, bright pink and disturbingly feminine. Her hand went up instinctively, in a useless attempt to rearrange her hair. The man shifted on one leg, half turning away from her so that she could see the way his ammunition belt forced the camouflaged shirt up, over the high rise of his buttocks. Stuck in the side of his belt was a bowie knife with knuckle duster finger-rings – she could imagine his palm gripping it, blood drained out of the surprisingly opal nails, the veins standing up on the back of his hand. He was very beautiful.

Her reverie was broken by a sudden shoving in the line of weary travellers. Out of the corner of her eye, she saw one of their number step out and aim a camera at the soldier. She recognised the man – he had disappeared into a toilet as the plane was about to land, re-emerging in full safari outfit: all khaki and pockets, baggy shorts, a shirt with shoulder flaps, a floppy hat with a wide rim and air holes. Back in his seat he had hung himself about with photographic equipment, strapping round a canvas belt with velcro patches on to which he had stuck a puzzling collection of accessories. Now he had unstripped one of the cameras and was focusing for a shot of the guard – that is until the helmet swivelled like a gun-turret and locked on to the intruder.

Reaction was swift. The soldier took a step forward, snatched the camera out of his hands and broke out the film in spiralling black coils.

'I say . . .' Safari-suit howled, his voice mixing terror and outrage.

But the soldier was already back in position by the wall, lost behind his Raybans.

'It was only for a picture,' Safari-suit insisted. 'You can't do that.'

He appealed for support but his fellow travellers refused to meet his eye. Only Martin seemed to be listening.

'They can't do that, can they?'

'*They* just did,' Martin said coldly.

'I thought they wanted tourists,' the man whined. 'Foreign exchange, convertible currency.'

'Look,' Martin said firmly. 'You know you're never allowed to take photographs in airports – you *must* know that. They're usually military bases. Now if you'll excuse me . . .'

The woman in front was handing back a bundle of forms. Martin took one and passed them on.

'I thought they didn't touch white folk?' Alice said. 'That was a bit harsh wasn't it? Oh, sure he's a nerd but he was only doing what tourists do.'

Martin said nothing, he was concentrating on the immigration *fiche*, trying to write with it pressed against the palm of his left hand: '*Nom de famille*: Beresford; *Adresse*: Manchester, Angleterre' – his writing was all over the place – until he stopped at the space marked '*Enfants*' and the whole rotten iniquity of it crowded in on him and he drew a thin line across the blank space like a hair-crack on fine china, then shoved the paper at the immigration officer who had been studying them from his booth with the sort of look reserved for the simple-minded.

'Any problem?' Martin said aggressively, but the man just banged his stamp in their passports – bang, bang – and waved them through with a shrug.

The baggage hall was crowded, the crush even less orderly. Porters plucked at their sleeves and pointed at their trolleys. Another soldier in dark glasses tried to hurry them on, waving the barrel of his gun to show the way.

Alice leaned towards Martin. 'Why so jumpy?'

He shook his head. 'It's just airports, they're like that. Once we get past customs over there it'll be different. We'll have arrived.'

He tried to edge towards the baggage carousel, lifting himself on tiptoe to see if anyone was waiting for them.

'Do you think they'll be here?' she asked.

'You never know, might get us started straight off – a fast car to the orphanage.'

He stopped, amazed by the spectacle before them – the carousel was not functioning and instead there was a wiry man in a loose blue shift, standing by a gap in the wall, reaching through for suitcases and holdalls and tossing them behind him with all his strength. Whether by accident or design, several had landed on top of each other and had built up into a precarious tower, a sight which had begun to attract an admiring crowd.

'Jesus,' Martin said. 'What a system.'

The crowd was growing, the tower of cases was nearly ten feet high – there was a murmur of appreciation as a large Samsonite

49

brief-case swung through the air, wavered on top of the pile but did not fall.

'Well done that man,' someone called out.

'Bet that's it,' said another.

'You're on.'

But before a book could be opened, another bag went soaring up, hovered, hit the top, shook the entire edifice, but held.

'Shee-it,' said the second voice, drowned in a spontaneous outburst of applause.

It was as if all the tensions of the flight were swept away in the pleasure of the moment. More people were coming over. The noise was rising. Martin heard a loud Australian voice, penetrating yet petulant, the sound of someone used to getting his way by persistent wheedling.

'Over here! Over here! No not there – here. Margot, you get Sharon and Lizzie on either side of you, like that and I'll christen the damn thing.'

Martin was intrigued, the man seemed to be trying to pose a family group by the tower of luggage while he focused some sort of portable film camera. Martin smiled to himself – this was bound to set off fireworks, once the baggage handler realised that one of his lives was being stolen. But no, star-struck, the man was actually preening, smoothing down his baggy outfit. Martin glanced at the soldier but even his Raybans could not hide his fascination.

'Tell you what, Margee,' the Australian said. 'Why don't you stand in with the girlies – that's it, Sharon on the left, Lizzie right – now if you get in the middle then we hang on for him to throw another of those bags so's we get a bit of movement – gotta think film.'

The girls, the eldest in her early teens, the other about nine, were overjoyed and ran up at once, giggling and urging each other on, though their mother looked anything but enthusiastic. The contrast between husband and wife was laughable. Where he was almost emaciated she was well-built, not fat, but sculptural with the dress sense of someone who knew that loose outfits were not her style. She wore a light but fitted dress with two sharp pleats and a tailored blouse – it was an appearance fully conceived by an expert, a naturally round face had been carefully moulded with darker cheek tone, the eyes made bolder with shadow, the lips brought out with a wet sheen. There was something old-fashioned, something forties about her – the way she snapped open her bag and slipped out one of those wafer-thin silver cigarette cases with a lighter built into one end, a thing Martin hadn't seen for years. This she clicked open with one hand, withdrew a cigarette with the other, giving it three neat taps on the case, before flicking up the flame and inhaling smoke, deep into her lungs delicately removing a tiny flake of tobacco from the tip of her tongue with two ruby red fingernails before slowly emitting a thin stream of smoke through each slightly flared nostril.

The husband was waving his free arm, still trying to pose the group.

'Tell you what Margee, you just stand a bit closer, eh? Go on – pleeeeze, pleeeeze, what d'you say?'

She said nothing but with a sharp sigh moved a solitary step closer. The baggage handler obligingly swung a case, the girls shrieked and laughed, it was all very good humoured.

'Not so loud,' the woman said. Her voice was low but she could as well have bellowed, given how swiftly the girls obeyed.

'Ah, lettem enjoy themselves,' her husband implored, his face a picture of misery. 'That's what we're here for. Pleeeeze Margee.'

'Are you going to get on with it or what?'

'Sure, sure. OK my friend, let her go . . .'

To Martin's amazement, the formerly sullen African grinned and complied – up went the bag, hovered, then perched on the summit, wobbled dangerously but held its place.

There was another outbreak of oohing and even heartier applause but the cameraman was far from satisfied.

'Shit,' he said bitterly. 'Hell Margs, which of these buttons is it? Christ, it must be this thing down here. Why do they make things so sodding awkward? OK, girls, one more time – here, Margot, you take the camera and I'll get in the picture. It's simple, just press here.'

The woman gave him a bleak look, dropped her cigarette and rubbed it forcefully into the concrete with a very high-heeled shoe. With critical slowness she moved forward, accepted the camera and waited while her husband posed by the tower and the ever willing African began to swing a large metal case, which even Martin could see was over ambitious now that the pile was so high. The crowd edged nearer, sensing entertainment.

Up swung the silvery case. The crowd breathed in. The heavy object peaked and began to fall. The crowd breathed out. The case

51

struck the top of the tower, the entire edifice swayed then with infinite slowness came crashing down.

It was what everyone had guessed would happen, everyone except the three smiling figures below, stoically repeating 'cheese' through toothy smiles and who were clearly in for a shock, maybe even an unpleasant bump or two. But it was the metal case that really did the damage. The girls were all right – they jumped away as soon as they heard the crowd starting to yell at them to get out of it – but their father was not so lucky. While the silver box missed his head, it managed to strike a glancing blow at his hip which made Martin wince, just from the sound alone. It was bound to leave a nasty bruise and the man might well have been cut by the hard corner, but no one was prepared for what happened next.

With an appalling clatter, his wife let fall the camera which shattered on the ground. Amidst the noise of splitting plastic and splintering glass, she staggered forward, arms reaching out to catch her husband before he too hit the concrete and was hurt even more. But it was the sight of that prim and starched figure, hurtling ungraciously before the gawping crowd, which told Martin that this was far more serious than he had at first assumed. In confirmation the man clutched his sides and started gasping and groaning as if he'd been shot. By now everyone was gathering to watch the fun but within seconds expressions had changed from hilarity to concern. It was clear the man wasn't acting, he was in real agony.

His wife had made it to his side and was attempting to hold him upright.

'Lizzie!' she barked. 'Sharon, over here.'

Obedience was immediate – which was just as well, for as they hurried up, their father's shirt began to change colour, a deep red stain spreading over his side. He yanked it up and pulled his trousers away a few inches, so that his wife could examine him. Being nearest, Martin had a clear view of a shiny, skin-coloured padded dressing held in place by wide strips of tape. The woman eased it back and peered beneath. Her expression said it all, something was seriously amiss.

'Bloody funny, eh?' It was Safari-suit. 'Christ knows what he was doing coming out here in that sort of state. Looks like he just got outta hospital. Seen it before – they cut a lump out of them and then they start running around saying how good they feel. He'll drop dead soon, they always do.'

Martin could have done without the macabre analysis, but couldn't deny that the man was right to question the wisdom of travelling in such a condition. They had been warned that the smallest cut could get badly infected, so what chance a wound on that scale?

His wife had covered him up and was trying to get him to walk away, but as they drew near she stumbled and for a moment it looked as if they might both fall. Just as Martin was about to make a move one of the soldiers came bounding over to catch them and help them in the main hall.

Martin looked down at the shattered camera, wondering if he should collect up the pieces for them.

'No use,' said Safari-suit, reading his thoughts. 'Beyond redemption that. Must weigh a ton anyway, daft thing to carry around on a journey.'

Martin suppressed a snigger, the sight of the man's weedy knees with all that dangling photographic equipment was beyond parody. He turned back towards Alice, assuming that she would have been as intrigued as he was, only to realise that she had moved on. He scanned the crowded concourse until he saw her, waiting at the customs table near the exit. He hurried over, amazed that she had managed to extricate their luggage from such chaos. A little man in an overtight khaki shirt, the buttons stretched over a prominent paunch was already riffling through the bag that Martin had packed himself. He was slowly lifting out balled-up socks and folded underpants, carefully giving each a little squeeze as if choosing fruit from a stall. Martin couldn't imagine why. He was certainly an unpleasant looking number, a straggly moustache curling wetly at the corners of his mouth, a wrist watch that looked too expensive for so minor a functionary, a row of gold pens in his breast pocket exaggeratedly advertising his literacy.

'We're gonna be last,' Martin hissed. 'If anyone's waiting for us they'll leave.'

Alice shook her head, indicating caution, the man might know some English and he was not the kind of person to irritate. She fixed a smile on her face and tried to divorce her mind from the numbingly slow way he lifted out Martin's T-shirts and jeans, then fondled the worn canvas bag with his washing things, inspecting it as if it were a jewel box.

'Is this for real?' Martin demanded.

The customs officer looked up at him without lifting his head, letting his eyes roll up to the top of their sockets.

'Shut it,' Alice commanded through her rigid grin. 'You're only making matters worse.'

Slowly, very slowly, the man returned to his task, carefully putting the spread-out clothing back in the case. He gestured – a mere flick of his hand – to show that they could lift it down, then another flick to show he wished to examine Alice's case. Martin was just lifting this up when he realised that Alice had discreetly fished into her handbag and was now holding a five pound note, just above the level of the desk.

The man looked. 'Dollar,' he grunted.

She shook her head. 'No dollar.'

The man hesitated, then carefully slid out a hand to cover the note and nodded at them to go.

Martin was frozen to the spot.

'Come on,' Alice said. 'What are you waiting for – a receipt?'

He picked up both cases and lumbered after her into the wide entrance hall.

'Where on earth did you learn that trick,' he protested, but she ignored him, intent on finding which way their group had gone.

'Over there,' she said. 'There's somebody waving at us, must be a courier or a driver. God, but there's enough people squatting around here – what is all this, a street party?' Much of the floor space was occupied by family groups squatting beside cloth bundles and old boxes tied with much knotted strings. Most of the squatters were eating, their fingers pulling slivers of food out of metal canisters held close to their mouths. They looked as if they lived there. An air of weary acceptance hung about them and even their many children were silent and still. Alice was puzzled – apart from the Air France jumbo, there were no other planes on the tarmac. She could see no Arrivals or Departures board and had heard no announcements since she entered the building. Nothing. Just this inexplicable waiting. They were clearly well-fed – one enormous woman had pulled aside her flowered cloth to reveal a full black breast the size of a football on which a round-faced child sucked heartily. As the baby fed, the mother scraped up a rice-like mixture from a tin and pushed it into the mouth of an older child squatting beside her, who chomped obediently and with obvious relish. The entire concourse was half do-it-yourself restaurant, half market.

Each group seemed to have a swollen fist of stubby bananas, a pile of yellow-green mangoes and a line of shiny lacquered fish, skewered on bamboo stakes. It was as if they had come to eat, as if that was why they were there.

Martin looked down, there was a baby at his feet – he thought a girl at first, judging by the way the surprisingly soft hair had been gathered into a clump and tied with a pink ribbon. A drool of snot ran from one nostril, the eyes were impossibly round and penetrating, both iris and pupil black. She stared back at him, clenching and unclenching tiny fists, and then he saw the raised spout and tiny wrinkled walnuts and realised it was a boy. Without consciously deciding to, Martin knelt and tickled the little face under the chin.

The surrounding group watched all this with interest, the food poised in their hands, their chewing in abeyance. Martin grinned sheepishly.

'Very nice,' he burbled, pointlessly. 'Nice baby . . . very . . .'

'Not quite what we thought,' said Alice, smiling at his confusion. 'Food, plump babies, armed goons. I wish I could see our man – Mantock said he was unmissable, which is not much help here. Oh no, here comes that idiot with the camera, still wittering about the injustice of it all. Come on, this way.'

At the exit a neon tube, vivid against the night sky, had drawn a zuzzing, whirling storm of outsize flies – black hairy ones and emerald green things like fragments of precious stone, glittering in the light. No great mountain confronted them, no huge watery cataract, no vast plain crossed by majestic elephants. They looked out on a crumbling concrete sign, the sort of thing still seen outside small villages in the remoter parts of France, only this one read 'BAMAKO 30 km', and had an arrow pointing down a narrow road, more pothole than tarmac, that disappeared with military straightness into flat reddish scrubland devoid of trees or grass.

Drawn by the noise, they turned to see the Australian being eased through the door by his wife, while one of the soldiers started barking at a taxi-driver to come up and help them.

'What on earth's all that about?' Alice asked. ·

'An accident. The man got hit by a suitcase. It fell on him. He must have had an operation and it hit him on his stitches – one of those daft things that turns out to be serious.'

'Like this,' Alice said wistfully, staring at the barren view.

'Oh God, no judgements. Not yet. We've only just got here. Come on, the bloody bus is going to go.'

The only seats left were up front, beside the driver. He smiled hugely but gave off a sweaty ripeness that made Alice blink. She pulled open the window and let in a blast of hot air bearing the unmistakable aroma of woodsmoke and something thicker, more pungent and slightly sweet and, as she looked out, she realised that there was someone staring back – a young girl in a washed-out cotton shift, carrying what Alice thought was a large black doll. Hoisting her bundle, the girl came to the window and held out her hand. It wasn't a doll, it was the baby they had seen inside, the girl must have picked it up and followed them out.

'*Cadeau*,' she said, pleading with her eyes.

Alice felt in her pockets, then remembered she had no Malian money, not even a bag of sweets.

The driver was revving up. The girl's hand reached for the open window.

'*Cadeau*,' she repeated. '*Donnez-moi quelque chose. Pour le bébé.*'

Alice looked at the tiny black face, cradled in the girl's arm. One of the emerald glittery flies had nuzzled into the corner of the left eye. Alice wanted to brush it away, but all she could do was hold up her empty palms to show there was nothing to give. The girl was unconvinced and began to tap her fingers on the glass.

It was useless. They were pulling away. Alice turned to wave goodbye and saw a shower of coins land at the girl's feet. Safari-suit had tossed out his change and, still clutching the baby, the girl fell into the dust, scrambling for the meaningless English money. There was a sudden blinding flash – Safari-suit had taken his picture.

At first there was nothing but the dusty figure-of-eight the headlights laid against the moving tarmac. A hut flashed up at the side of the road, a makeshift thing of old boards and corrugated iron, and was as quickly gone. Stunted thorn bushes came and went.

'Are we crazy or what?' Alice whispered. 'There are more soldiers over there. Look. By that lorry.'

The vehicle had been halted by the side of the road. Two uniformed men were interrogating the driver.

'I mean what's going on?' Alice said.

Martin shook his head. 'Traffic control?'

She gave a dry laugh. 'I didn't want to know about the place before we got there in case it was too dreadful – *coup d'état*, murder, mayhem. I suppose I could excuse myself by claiming that I wanted it to be as blank as possible, just a port of call, a place we were going to drop in on for a specific purpose – single-minded, clear cut. But it may not be so easy.'

A cluster of mud houses emerged into the headlights, then faded back again. There had been some figures in a low walled compound and a glimpse into a box-like room lit by a paraffin lamp.

'You're tired,' Martin said. 'It's been a long day.'

She shook her head. 'You saw those children at the airport. What did you think? Did you think one of these is the sort of kid I might end up with? This is why I came?'

'Not really . . . I was too busy worrying about the luggage. But now you mention it, I suppose you're right.'

She sighed. 'I wish the unmissable *Enfants du Monde* person had been there; if we'd made a quick start there'd have been no time to worry about things.'

She was cut off by a loud blast of electronic music as a lorry drew level, its open back filled with girls in white blouses and neat black skirts, singing and dancing as they swayed along. Schoolgirls, Martin reckoned, his interest rising. They waved and smiled but he pretended to look away, studying the line of concrete shop-houses on the opposite side of the road.

Everything was movement now – cars out of old French films, a bicycle with a refrigerator strapped to its handle bars weaving in amongst shiny oil-tankers and huge six-wheeled trucks. This had to be some kind of terminus – a line of ancient dust-streaked buses was being top-loaded with woven panniers and bulging cardboard suitcases, watched by silent lines of cloth-wrapped travellers, eyes absent and uncomplaining. Martin looked down into one of the baskets, it was filled with what appeared to be stumpy black tree branches but which he guessed must be food of some sort. Names offered themselves: manioc, cassava, plantain, yams – words from books that he had never bothered to check, African words unlikely to be encountered but now there, in front of him – Alice was right, he knew nothing.

'Look,' she said pointing to the river with its narrow bridge arching to the distant town.

Martin felt his chest tighten, it was broad and full and fast-flowing. He glanced at Alice but if the same thought had crossed her mind her face did not show it.

They bumped on to the bridge, the glow from their windows lighting up the waters below. A fisherman drifted by, balanced on the point of his pirogue, casting a net, gauzy as an insect swarm. It hovered then fell, wafting in to darkness as they passed.

Now their fellow passengers were jabbering and pointing – they had seen the tall white tower rising above the distant trees, lavishly floodlit, a brilliant illusion in the surrounding dark, their hotel.

Martin shook his head, things were getting beyond him. They had reached the far bank and he could see a gang of naked boys jumping and diving into the fast-flowing stream. As they burst to the surface they waved and yelled, free spirits, shining in the first fluid glint of the rising moon.

After the excitement of the great river the town seemed gloomy. Dimly lit streets radiated out, from a wide tree-lined square. Their hotel lay to the right but as they turned on to the drive they were forced to a crawl by a chicane of striped oilcans, manned by a posse of guards in woolly jumpers with leather shoulder patches, armed with wooden axe-handles. They looked nervous and did not smile.

'Taking no risks,' said a voice from the back seats.

'Whatta they afraid of,' said another.

'Tarzan and the apes,' yelled a third as the hydraulic doors whooshed open, drowning out the fact that nobody laughed.

'Doesn't look right,' Alice said under her breath.

Martin was inclined to agree but thought it best to swallow his words again.

They got down and walked a few sticky paces to the entrance where a flunky dressed as something out of the Arabian Nights bowed low and ushered them into the deep chill of an air-conditioned foyer. Martin whistled as he took in the wide expanse of creamy marble veined with red, dangerously polished to a reflective shine. From a high, distant ceiling an enormous crystal chandelier cascaded its countless branches, a burst of cut-glass slivers at each tip, its centre alive with livid white bulbs flashing and sparkling among the faceted glass as if it were a trapped nova, the radiant heart of this burned-out country. It was, Martin thought, the most vulgar thing he had ever seen.

Blinking, he forced himself to look away. No one had come forward to greet them. They stood, hesitant and alone, reflected in a distant mirror; his long hair, chop-cut below the ears and the hipster trousers of an earlier age said it all: out-of-date schoolteacher on holiday. He turned to look at Alice, puffy and unkempt from the journey, her denim jacket and T-shirt scruffily wrong in such a place, and he felt pity and anger meet and he reached out his hand to take hold of hers. Thus linked, they went to the reception and yet again left a record of their childlessness for which they were given a key and wished a pleasant stay.

'Someone took the cases,' Alice said, impressed despite herself. 'Do you reckon this place? Look at that light and those brass rails and all this marble. I thought . . .?'

Martin followed her gaze, taking in the line of lifts with lights flashing up the floors, the bellhops in pill-box hats and bum-freezer jackets – it was crazy and she had drawn the obvious conclusion: this was in no way the world of *Les Enfants du Monde*. He could see through to the restaurant – at its centre was one of the wooden pirogues they had seen on the river, only this one was brightly painted in zigzags of red and green and on it was arranged an ebullient display of tropical fruits: papayas like giants clubs, wizened passion fruit, guavas and whole branches of lychees strewn among heaped pineapples. Drought? Starvation?

Alice was making for the lift.

'Tired,' she said. 'Too many ups and downs.'

Martin hung back. 'I think I'll look round a bit – never know, someone might show up. You go on, I won't be long.'

Safari-suit was holding back the lift door.

'Quite a place,' he said. 'Didn't fancy that restaurant though – French.'

He got out before her. She was two floors down from the summit, though the view from the corridor windows offered little – the town was lost in the trees and too dimly lit for her to make out anything but the tallest blocks.

The key stuck in the lock, but once she had rattled it open the overpowering sense of pampered luxury returned. The room was large and deeply carpeted, thick curtains ran the length of the far wall and the outsize bed had been precisely turned down and a foil-wrapped chocolate, like a silver nipple, positioned on both plumped-up pillows.

The door swung to behind her, and Alice saw their bags, placed at the centre of the room, scruffy, battered and friendly amid this alien perfection. She took hers, stacked a few things in a drawer then shoved the case into the bottom of the capacious fitted wardrobe.

As she straightened and looked round, the sense of being anywhere and nowhere increased. The transition was crazy, from the squatting crowds at the airport to this sealed-off, padded world. She crossed the deep carpet, pulled on a cord and sent the drapes swishing apart. Now there was a view to admire – neat lawns stretched away to the wide river, lit by the glittering headlamps of vehicles passing over the bridge. Small craft crossed from bank to bank, low in the water, weighed down with people and goods. One boat, larger than the others, was being readied for a longer journey – tiny pirogues nuzzled at her sides, wiry figures scuttled up ramps bearing bundles of fruit and plastic carboys of water. She wondered where it was going and hoped it was upriver to the far reaches of the desert, out to that point where the maps showed the Niger veering away from its brush with emptiness, turning back in that curious reversal which had once been the magnet and despair of explorers.

Alice leant her forehead against the thick pane, cool from the air-conditioning. As a child she had clambered on to the chest of drawers in her room to look out on the rainy street, wishing she had brothers and sisters to help wile away the shut-in days. She had imagined other rooms, across the street, behind other windows – rooms where there was no loneliness, no solitary play, no need for the overstretched imagination to fill the long afternoon holiday hours when school would have been preferable to that slow passing of time. If she went downstairs her mother would be busy baking or ironing, the radio always on. It would be hours before her father returned and a meal set out in the dining room and some sort of life revived in the dead house, hours in which she was obliged to master time, training herself to fill out the slow seconds. How different from Martin and his brothers and his cousins and their friends, engulfed in a rollicking surfeit of happenings. She had a vivid memory of her first meal with them: someone bringing out a tablecloth, another drifting in with some cutlery, a glass or two appearing, all haphazard, inefficient and only partially complete when their mother began to carry in the food and that too in no especial order. All through the meal things were missing and brought – or not brought. It matched their conversation: continuous, overlapping, anarchic. And yes, they simply piled things up and dumped them in the kitchen and again not everything – when she and Martin went up to the room that had been vacated for them, the cloth was still on the table, along with a sauce bottle, two forks and three glasses. As she climbed the stairs, Alice thought of her mother calling her ten minutes before a meal to help set things out, of the orderly talk and the clearing away and her father drying. She stopped. This was crazy – here she was looking down on the great river, the Niger – the very name conjured up images of desert warriors and reckless explorers – and all she could think about was her bland suburban childhood. Self-defence? Protecting herself from the enormity of what they were doing, the sheer madness of coming this far with so little protection?

Until that moment she had got no further than the need to pacify her aching desire to have a child. There had been enough to do, getting organised for the trip, to keep her mind off the negative side of the deal. But as soon as she saw that child holding the little baby outside the airport, she knew that the questions could no longer be repressed. She tried to fit the tiny black face into her picture of the past, to see it in England, alone, the rain on the window, the long minutes passing. Was that what she wanted? Before, it had simply been a case of finding a child, now that she had seen the reality it was as much a question of what she planned to do with one. In the short time it had taken to get from the plane to this hotel room, self-doubt had stifled the imaginary adventure, replacing it with a troubling reality.

The glass was cool, very cool. Stick figures scuttled up the gangplank to the boat, sacks balanced on their heads. Two red lights blinked and dipped in the distance where the airport must be, no cloud fringed the sharp crescent moon. Alice sighed, here at least, it would not rain and shut her in.

Martin stood under the outrageous chandelier and wondered what he should do next. It was amazing how quickly the foyer had emptied – guests shuffling into the lifts, servants slamming through the transom doors into the secret recesses of the hotel, leaving him alone with the tinkling crystal light.

He contemplated going out, but was nervous. He peered through the tinted glass doors and watched the scruffy guards at the road block. Beyond the neat lawn that fronted the hotel he could just make out a patch of rougher wasteland and beyond that what appeared to be a roofline of rusted iron sheets. Common sense said no.

He turned back to the reception where a man was studying a telex roll and did not look up at his approach.

Martin coughed to no effect.

'I say,' he said irritably. *'S'il vous plaît'?* Where can I get a newspaper?'

The man barely moved, save to wave his hand across the hall towards the boutique.

'Madame Josette,' he said, in a tone which indicated that that was all he could manage.

'Bloody rude,' Martin huffed, moving away, but the man had slumped back into his former torpor, untouched by the white man's anger.

The boutique seemed to sell everything: international bestsellers with two-word titles in thick gold letters; an entire pharmacy of suntan creams; a seven-foot inflatable giraffe; a rack of cotton Bermudas printed with zigzag palm trees in eyeball frazzling colours. A postcard rack turned a squeaky half circle as Martin brushed passed and got his first view of a large African lady closely studying a newspaper spread on the counter before her, holding a pair of gold-rimmed spectacles at the tip of her nose as if they were lorgnettes. She was big, over six foot and broad, but her clothes had been carefully chosen to maximise her assets – a wispy grey silk jacket over a dark red blouse helped to bring out the underlying russet colour in her black skin. She was richly made-up with glossy lips and finely pencilled eyebrows and her deep black hair had been scraped back from her forehead and made shiny with oil. A tiny row of pearls ran in and out of the folds of her neck which was also hung with a thick gold chain, from which depended the heavy-rimmed spectacles – her lorgnettes. She was clearly very *grande dame*, which made it all the more peculiar that down the top of each cheek, starting near the temple, ran three livid, deep blue, tribal scars.

'Madame Josette?' Martin said.

She started, wrenched from her reading, and trained her lenses on him. After the briefest pause her face broke into a huge smile, turning up her scars and revealing two stunning rows of perfect teeth.

Martin was about to launch into his inadequate French when he saw that the paper she had been reading so avidly was the *Daily Mail*.

'You speak English?'

'A little, a little. I was in Brighton.' She said this with a happy sigh, as if the name itself signified an infinity of contentment. 'I should like very much to be there now – you see I am reading here about the Wedding.' She pointed to a half-page photograph of the Prince of Wales with his fiancée who held her hand so as to show to advantage a large engagement ring. Martin groaned – the Wedding had caught up with him. Beside her, the serried ranks of world newspapers all bore that same photograph, all announcing the 'FAIRY TALE ROMANCE' in a dozen languages.

'So beautiful the Lady Di.' Madame Josette continued. 'I was in Brighton for the Princess Anne, we had a protest.'

'A protest?'

'At the school. There was only a black and white but after the protest there was an eighteen-inch colour. It was wonderful. But you are here and will miss everything. Never mind, you would like an English newspaper. I have finished with it.'

'Thank you. But I am perfectly content to be here – well that is I was until just now, the place seems to have emptied – even the manager out there is in a bad mood.'

Madame Josette's scars stiffened. She bent near. 'Muslims,' she said contemptuously. 'It is their Ramadan that starts and they are hungry and unhappy. I of course am Christian like you. It is very foolish to fast during the *Sécheresse*. You can see they do not smile.'

'Well, you have a lovely smile,' Martin said, immediately wondering what had made him say it, though he needn't have worried, the effect was entirely satisfactory – the scars curled up and Madame Josette's amazingly long eyelashes actually fluttered.

'You will help me,' she said with sudden earnestness. 'I have a question, here with this photograph, this big woman in a pink dress with the pink hat who is . . .' she hoisted her lorgnettes and haltingly read out the caption. 'Who is . . . step-grandmother . . . of the Lady Di. Will she dare to go to the St Paul's as they ask here? They say she is not of the same sort as the real family of the Lady Di.'

'Class,' Martin said. 'Not the same class, that's what they really mean. No, I think she won't go. Definitely not.'

She was immensely pleased with this assurance and refused to accept any money for the newspaper.

'I am so *hors des choses* here,' she sighed. 'How I wish I was in Brighton for the Big Day.'

'Well I'm rather glad I'm here – I'm looking forward to seeing something of your country.'

Madame Josette carefully balanced her spectacles on the ample plateau of her bosom and looked him straight in the eye.

'I would not,' she said firmly and before he could frame a question she smiled seraphically. 'There is no need. No need at all. Here . . .' she gestured expansively, '. . . here is everything. We have a real Malian village around the swimming pool as if it were a little lake of the interior. There is the *Café de Paris* discothèque on the top floor and the *musculation* in the basement. Everything,' she concluded resonantly.

But Martin felt deprived. 'Why shouldn't I travel about a bit?'

'Perhaps the weather. The clouds come so fast in the south here.'

'The weather! It hasn't rained for seven years! Your embasssy says its difficult to travel up country because of the *Sécheresse*. Doesn't add up.'

'There is nothing in the desert, mud houses, nothing. Here is everything.'

'But I came to Mali to see something different not to sit round a swimming pool. I want to see a mud city, I wouldn't mind seeing what the *Sécheresse* has done, we saw some of it on the television – the refugees and all that. My school did a sponsored swim.'

Madame Josette looked confused by these strange doings.

'To buy powdered milk,' he explained.

'There are no refugees,' she said. 'The foreign press have exaggerated everything. The government has seen to it.'

'He could sense her indifference but he was unwilling to release her just yet, she was his first Malian and he wanted advice.

He wondered if he should ask her straight out about *Les Enfants du Monde* – had she heard of them? Were they for real? Did she know anyone connected with them? But that seemed too risky.

'I see what you mean,' he said. 'At least I think I do. Do you have children, Madame Josette?'

'Of course, seven.'

'We can't. It hurts my wife very much.'

'She should ask a sister for one of hers.'

'She has no sisters.'

'Then it is God's Will.'

'That's one way of looking at it; the trouble is we've spent a lot of time and money trying to fight it, if it is. We tried adoption but that went wrong . . . then every sort of medical treatment.' He stopped, unwilling to list their failures. 'I've seen pictures on TV of people starving here and I thought it would be good for us and good for one of them.'

'Really,' she said, opening the newspaper. 'If you say so.'

'But do you think a white couple can bring up a black child? I mean do you think it's right or not?' If he closed his eyes he could conjure up that TV appeal, the ragged line moving listlessly across a treeless void, the fleshless woman, madonna-like in a cheese-cloth shawl, holding a baby, the snot drooling from its flared nostrils as if the last of life were oozing out of it. Remembering this, his proposal was so obviously noble, what could she say?

He stopped. He had her interest but her voice had lost something of its humour.

'Was a black family ever bringing up a white child?' she asked flatly.

He said nothing.

'It would not be a first choice for you? Would it?'

He shook his head. 'But the drought, the refugees, the starvation?'

'There are *no* refugees. And if there were, taking one baby would not stop this.'

'It would for that one baby.'

'If you wish to help, there are agencies that help many. People here are trying to do these things their own way, a little money would do much. Now tell me do you think the dress will be full like so . . .' Her hands described an arc swelling out from her waist. 'Or tight like so . . .' They dropped sheer down her sides. 'I think full myself.'

Martin shook his head helplessly. It had never occurred to him to so much as think what the royal bride might wear.

'Oh, how I wish I could be in Brighton once more,' Madame Josette sighed. 'It is terrible to be so *hors des choses.*'

It was no use, Martin felt reality slipping away from him. He would have to get it out into the open or face drifting off into a world of impossible connections and chances.

'Madame Josette,' he began, a little too loud but determined to press on, despite the way her eyes continued to scan the newspaper.

'I didn't come here for a holiday. I came because of *Les Enfants du Monde*. It's an organisation that . . .'

'I know what it is.' She had not looked up but her voice conveyed her displeasure. 'That is very foolish. Very, *very* foolish. Taking children, buying children, is not right and you know it.'

'Of course I do. I'm not happy about it but in the end it comes to the same thing. We help a child.'

She shook her head, her lips pursed, the scars almost touching.

Martin continued: 'Do you know where I can find them? Do they have an office?'

She went on shaking her head, slowly, emphatically.

'So what else should I do?' He knew he sounded peevish but was beyond disguising his feelings.

She stopped shaking her head and spoke more gently.

'In the past,' she said, 'a man had many wives so there were always children – if he could not make children then his brother would . . .' – she paused delicately – 'would visit and everything was . . . done . . . and there would be children.'

Martin tried to imagine such a thing in their uptight street in suburban Manchester. Well, there was wife-swapping, or so he'd heard, but children were hardly the point, quite the opposite.

'Now for we Christians,' Madame Josette continued, 'such a thing is *mal vue* but there are always children somehow. But tell me something else – how many black people will there be at the Prince Charles' Wedding?'

'There'll be ambassadors and presidents, I suppose.'

'And that is all?'

He nodded.

'I see,' she said. 'And you wish to take a black baby back to this country where there are not really black people – not *really*. A prince will not marry your daughter – or are you wanting a son who cannot marry a princess?'

Martin had a sudden image of the children on the river-bank, those shouting, splashing boys of the fast flowing water, lost and found in the mist, re-emerging from the depths in a wild effusion of spray. Then he tried to imagine one of them, dressed in cap and blazer, walking along a pavement webbed with frost, on a grey northern morning . . .

'Well?' Madame Josette insisted. 'What is your answer?'

'All that's changing,' he said without much conviction. 'We're

66

getting black politicians, television news readers, all sort of things. Of course it takes time, but we'll get there – why, by the time any of today's children grows up it'll be completely different and we will have done something to help things along.'

He felt pleased with that, but Madame Josette said nothing – she was concentrating on flattening down her newspaper, the better to study the photographs.

'*Bonsoir*,' she said, without looking up.

It was over, his audience had been terminated. He wished her good night but as he made his way out, Martin's eye was drawn to a distant corner where, tucked away behind the stacks of beach balls and inflatable lilos, he could see a dusty display of native crafts: fly whisks with beadwork hafts, some unglazed oxblood pots, a drum. Towering over them stood a just over life-size carved figure – from where he was standing it was side view – stoop-shouldered, knees bent to support the weight of an enormously distended, heavily pregnant belly that ended in a long pointed penis-like navel. A fertility figure he presumed – two tiny children were spread-eagled on either side of the great globe, clinging on like ghekkos ascending a wall. The face was a stylised mask, its hyper-thyroid eyes offering nothing but deep slits, the gaping mouth was set in a silent scream and down both cheeks, starting at the temples, ran the same tribal incisions as Madame Josette's. But where she exuded bonhomie, this creature was full of blank expressionless menace, a hint of danger for the tourists, a frisson of the dark forces they must surely believe were waiting for them out there in the bush beyond Bamako, in the hidden recesses of a forest and savannah they would never visit. To Martin, it seemed to represent all those things he and Alice had chosen to leave out of their calculations. They had simply not thought about Africa at all – this was to be no more than a jaunt to another city where an organisation would fix up an adoption. It might not be wholly legal but it would be nothing if not neat and businesslike. But Alice had seen it first, he realised that now. At the airport when she had looked at that baby she had seen the truth. Now, Madame Josette had made it abundantly clear to him that there was another, less pleasant way of looking at what they had in mind. If he had any doubts, then this pregnant figure was there to ram home the point. They were in Africa and they had better acknowledge the fact. Martin sighed. His little scheme, his first plan had just evaporated and he was left bumbling about as usual. He wondered if Madame Josette had come from a village of crumbling mud houses, in a smoky clearing, miles from the only road. He tried to imagine the initiation ceremony when they had sliced into her face, deep enough to leave those six blue incisions, but no, the pieces did not fit, not at all and he went back into the glittering crystal world of the chandelier, still silent and deserted.

Alice turned as the door rattled before reluctantly giving way.

'The key sticks,' Martin said superfluously, stopping as he took in the luxury of the room. 'This place is a freak,' he said desperately. 'You'll see . . .' He went over to the window. 'Timbuktu's out there,' he was trying to make her smile, though the joke had little point now that it was no more than a plain statement of fact.

He tried another line. 'Shall I have room service send something up? There seems to be a menu on the table over there.'

'Do you think they'll wheel in a table, with a rose in a thin silver vase?'

'Of course. What do you want?'

'Nothing. I just wondered.'

'As you like. There's a city tour tomorrow. Should be interesting.'

'Can't.'

'Why? Don't you want to see something of Bamako?'

'It's not a question of wanting – you'll have to get out and see what's what, so one of us ought to be on hand in case there's a call. I know this is your big African trip – the old dream come true, but we're here for a reason. In any case I have to rest, tomorrow's the magic thirteen.'

There was a telling silence before his voice groaned back into action. 'I thought we wouldn't be doing that here. I mean, surely we can concentrate on one thing at a time?'

'If I was certain this trip was going to work, I might agree. But I'm not. I thought someone would have met us, either at the airport or here. As they didn't I see no reason to change anything. Not yet. Sorry.'

She got into bed and pulled up the sheets.

Martin wished he hadn't spoken – all he'd done was emphasise his own dislike of having to perform to order, which was clear enough without shouting it from the rooftops.

He started to unpack, wishing he could think of something to say that would clear the air before they slept, but nothing presented itself. He stuffed a few things in a drawer, then put his case beside hers in the wardrobe. A light clicked on as he slid back the doors but it was not until he bent to push his bag under the shelf that he saw the tiny pink arm sticking out of Alice's case, a lurid little limb, tinged yellow by the low-watt bulb. What had she done? He pulled aside the flaps and looked in and was relieved to see that the explanation was simple – she had brought one of the dolls with her – though that was pretty bizarre in itself.

He opened his mouth to ask what the hell she was thinking about, but held back – if a toy provided comfort then so be it – though it explained why she had been so quick to bribe the custom's officer, rather than live through the moment when he fished out this naked, pink object, in full view of their fellow passengers.

'You OK?' he asked.

'Mmm, why?'

'Oh nothing, just wondered.'

He climbed into bed, put out his arm and laid it over her. She settled in closer. Tomorrow they would have to make love, tonight they could sleep in peace.

THREE

Martin woke, sweating yet chilled from the air-conditioning. The room smelled odd – the way his parents' bedroom had when he ran in to wake them and found himself held at the door by something stuffy and sweet in the air. There was the sharp, slightly rancid odour of a dairy in it, and the dark fug of water in which long forgotten flowers have died. Smelling it again made him think of old people on hot days.

He swung off the bed and crossed to the window, hauling back the heavy drapes and sending light searing through the room. The river glittered in the sun, twisting to the vague point where it melted into the rippling horizon – which was only a dry truth – somewhere out in the rainless wastes, the river had been sucked into the red laterite dust, leaving its deepest curves as shallow lakes, slowly evaporating as each rainy season failed, year after burning year. *La Sécheresse*, the drought. He licked his lips. He needed coffee.

Alice watched from behind a mountain range of crumpled bed sheets. 'Happy?'

'I'm not sure. This hotel bugs me. I mean, it's hardly Africa is it?'

She propped herself on her elbows. 'You are strange – I never really took in this Africa thing until that night with Mantock. Why are you so hooked on it?'

He smiled. 'We had a street party for the Coronation. There was a fancy-dress parade and this kid called Vaughan went as a Zulu and won first prize. It was a swiz in a way – just some old stage make-up his mum had found from her amateur dramatics and a sort of nappy and a spear made out of a brush, but the thing that swung it was the dance he did – he went crazy, leaping about and making *uggabugga* noises and stabbing his spear at everyone. It was a knock-out: unforgettable. Amazing.'

'And you?'

He shrugged, slightly embarrassed. 'A cowboy.'

'And you really wanted to be an Indian?'

He nodded. 'It was the *uggabugga* bit that did it. I just longed to be out there, grunting and shaking. *Uggabugga – Uggabugga – Uggabugga.'*

Alice shook her head. 'I don't think we had a street party, most of our neighbours were retired, I was probably the only one eligible for a parade. We had a telly though, first in the crescent and everyone came in to watch the crowning – people we'd barely spoken to before.'

'Who would you have gone as if you had – Joan of Arc? Boadicea? Marie Curie?'

'No, no – nobody out of *My Christmas Book of Heroines.'*

'Who then?'

'I don't know.' She pushed back the sheets and got off the bed. 'Sounds flat beside Zulu dancing. So why don't you go see some of this Africa you've been longing for all these years?'

He turned back to the window and the view of the river. What could he say – they were suspended, obliged to wait on the pleasure of others. 'I suppose I could see if there are any messages. And you?'

'Shouldn't we do a little searching on our own. Look around. Go to an orphanage?'

Martin said nothing. He was watching a narrow pirogue being sculled from the far bank by an athletic figure wearing nothing but a breech-cloth, broad feet confidently splayed on either side of his fragile craft and he knew that the gap between the timeless Africa he could see below and the world of offices and institutions that Alice still occupied was broader than the river itself.

'I'll take a look,' he said neutrally. 'You come and join me when you're ready.'

He pulled on a clean white T-shirt and a pair of beige cotton trousers with baggy side pockets that he hoped might give him an air of one dressed for adventurous living, less Sergeant Pepperish. Moderately satisfied, he made to go, but paused at the door.

'Didn't you ever want to live somewhere else?' he asked.

'All the time when I was a kid. So many places they cancelled each other out, but never your one fixed dream. For you there was real life and then this other, imaginary world. For me there was no difference. I *lived* in fairyland most of my childhood. Then came books. That's probably why grown-up life has been quite exciting enough . . . until . . .'

He waited, unsure whether she had finished and he could leave.

71

'Someone's bound to turn up,' he said, easing the door behind him. 'Bound to . . .'

Even on so bright a morning, the great chandelier still glittered above the deserted foyer. No one manned the reception though a crudely written notice had been pinned above the key racks:

SORRY FOR NO TOURS. ALL CANCEL FOR ALL GROUP.
VERY SPECIAL BUFFET FEAST AT SWIMMING PISCINE.
SIGNED: AHMED.

Puzzled, Martin went to the glass doors and peered out. Even more men were gathered at the road block, joined by a couple of soldiers with serious guns and the obligatory sunglasses. One was reorganising the oil cans on the drive, narrowing the passage, while the other hung about the turning from the main road, ready to intercept any arrivals. Not that there was any traffic that Martin could see. He wondered who was doing what to whom – were the hotel's guests being guarded or were they prisoners? He wished he had made more effort to find out about Mali before agreeing to come. The men out there were clearly expecting trouble and the way they were sealing off the hotel made it increasingly unlikely that anyone from outside would be able to contact them.

If only there was someone he could ask.

He turned towards the boutique. Madame Josette was just visible beyond the racks of books and postcards. There was no one else and with any luck she might be feeling less moralistic than she had the night before. He went in and hovered by the swimming costumes taking in her latest outfit – a vivid scarlet headscarf, lips painted to match, tiny silver bells dangling from each ear. It was a jazzy, gypsy look, enhanced by the little appliqué roses around the collar of her blouse. He edged closer until she realised he was there, her face breaking into a scar-curling smile as she lifted up a copy of *Paris Match*, clutching it to her bosom so that he could see another artist's impression of the wedding dress.

'*Bonjour*. I am so happy,' she gushed. 'You see how it will be, narrow to the waist then full with a train so . . .' Her free hand swept out to indicate yard upon trailing yard of lace. 'Of course this is only an idea,' she said, delight transforming her scars into crescent moons. 'But they have many spies, many many spies do you not think?'

But Martin was more intrigued by her own dress, an orange frock gathered at the waist with one of those curious starched pinafores that made him think of Heidi.

'You like my ensemble?' Madame Josette asked. 'I got it in Innsbruck, we were skiing two years ago.'

The thought of Madame Josette on skis was awesome.

'It's charming,' he said. 'Very Tyrolean.'

She gave a girlish laugh and twirled round with surprising dexterity for one so large, the skirt swirling dramatically, the little bells tinkling sweetly at her ears.

'Very nice,' he said lamely, then forced himself to remember what he was doing there. 'I . . . I was wondering . . . wondering if you could help me?'

'Why?' she said cautiously. 'Is it the Moslems with their Ramadan? Are they rude in the restaurant?' She sighed gloomily. 'It was not always thus – when I was young we had a Moslem boy who was so lazy during the Ramadan my father used to beat him. Now no one is beating and the boys are very rude, very, very rude. I hope you are not upset?'

'I guess it will improve. It can't be any fun in this heat, with the *Sécheresse*, eh?'

'Here is air-conditioned,' she said huffily. 'They have no excuse.'

Martin let it drop, she was clearly warding him off, stopping him from going back to last night's disagreeable conversation.

'I was hoping to see the town,' he said. 'But they've cancelled the tour.'

'That is as well. There is a little trouble possible – the trial begins today, there may be confusion.'

'Trial? Whose trial?'

She showed little inclination to explain. 'A big trial,' she conceded. 'A man who must be punished. Unfortunately there are some who support him.'

Martin made nothing of this. 'Perhaps I might just take a short stroll near the hotel – there seems to be some sort of shanty town beyond that field in front, I thought I would have a look.'

Her scars turned down alarmingly. 'That is a *very* bad idea. The poor are not well informed, they have wrong ideas in the shanty town, they think only that rice is very expensive and do not understand about foreign debt and how much the new government is doing to put things better. Like children they believe what others tell them and today they will be disturbed. Stay in the hotel and spend money – that is the best way to help.'

Everything she said increased his interest but something told him to move cautiously. 'I'd like to buy some suntan cream.'

'Of course.'

'And some vitamin C and some tissues and . . .'

'And?'

'Do you have a telephone directory?'

'Why?'

'I need to look up a number.'

She said nothing and made no move. He was going to have to explain or there would be deadlock.

'I was wondering if there was any sort of children's home, an orphanage or something . . .' His voice trailed away, the scars were too forbidding.

Madame Josette reached for the bottles and the packet he had requested and set them in a neat row on the counter. That done she took a measured breath and spoke firmly and directly to him.

'What is your wife's name?'

'Alice.'

'Good. I would like to meet her – you will bring her here and I will speak with her – explain to her things as I said to you last night?'

'It wouldn't do any good. She's . . .' He fought, shy of the word, but it lay unspoken between them. He had a clear picture of the cupboard and the bag and the pink doll's arm and the word 'obsessed' though he had no wish to say it.

'Do *you* want children?' Madame Josette asked.

'Of course.'

'Really? As much as your wife does?'

He said nothing.

'So you are doing this for her? You have come here for her? You would like to help her, even though you know that this is not the way to do it?'

She lifted the bottles and the packet and put them back on the shelf, as if they were just more of his benign, if misguided, ideas that she was tidying away.

'But is there an orphanage?' he persisted.

74

She sighed. 'No, not as you mean.' Her eyes narrowed and again she fixed him with a look. 'Of course there are the missions. Sometimes they . . .'

'Sometimes they what . . .?'

'No,' she said, as if debating the matter with herself. 'No, this is not sensible.'

'Please?'

'Well, there is a man called Belvedere, the Reverend Belvedere of the Beulah Baptist Mission. He helps sick children – blind, some without legs . . .' She lowered her voice. 'And worse . . . much worse . . .'

Martin sagged, shaking his head.

'Very well then.' She brightened again. 'Bring your Alice to me and I will speak. Now what is it – the *Daily Mail*, the *Woman's Own*?'

He took whatever she offered and promised to accept her advice and sit by the pool. Not that it mattered, her attention had already passed to an article in one of the glossy magazines she had been lifting down. He wished her a good day and left her absorbed in bridesmaids' outfits and floral arrangements.

The foyer was still empty. Through the glass doors he could see that there was some kind of trouble at the turning on to the drive. A group of guards had stopped a car and one of the soldiers was examining the open boot. Martin groaned. It was just their rotten luck that this trial thing should be starting now. Mantock's man would never get in to see them and the only alternative was some sort of hell-hole for cripples run by the wonderfully named Reverend Belvedere. Not that it made much difference. Outside was dangerous and it was lucky he had been warned. Weighing it up, there was only one thing to do – take Alice to see Madame Josette, let them talk it over woman-to-woman and with any luck that would be the end of the whole crazy scheme – it might even be the end of the entire baby business, in which case they could fly home ready to take up life as it had been before. It was a plan of sorts and, in the meantime, there was a week's holiday to be enjoyed.

With a light step, he followed the signs to the pool – down some stairs to a passage running under the hotel and up to the gardens at the rear. He even whistled as he walked, stopping halfway along at a glass door with a painted sign offering:

75

INDEPENDENCE CLUB SPORTIF
FITNESS, MUSCULATION, MASSAGE

Beyond he could see a carpeted gym with a group of white women in jogging outfits lying face-down, trying to do press-ups, supervised by a giant African, whose awesomely muscled frame bulged from a figure-hugging singlet and skimpy running shorts. As the women strained to raise themselves a few inches from the floor, he barked orders in a resonant bass – *'Plus haut, bien, bien, bien – et maintenant plus vite – oui, comme ça – plus haut, plus haut, oui, oui...'* – moving among them, occasionally bending to scoop up an almost immobile body, lifting the requisite foot then letting it drop back. Up and down, up and down. One little old lady was doing remarkably well, raising herself high on her arms and dropping back quickly – her face a grimace of concentration, blood pulsing at her temples.

Martin stepped out, blinking in the sunlight. Madame Josette was right, this was a traditional village, of a kind. A number of thatched huts were set round a curved pool; one served as an equipment store with towels and loungers, another was a bar with high stools and converted hurricane lamps and, last of all, there was a long, narrow construction under which a party of chefs in spotless bibs and toques were setting out an excessive buffet. The lawns were dotted with sunbathers on towels and pool loungers. He could make out his own party with their subfusc English summer clothes and untended toenails. There was a couple with twins – she was wearing the sort of sun-dress unique to middle England, its tight bodice forcing a ridge of flesh at the mid-point of her bosom and a skirt which flared out in an echo of the Dior New Look. They had spread baby things over a large area and were busily at work on the twins, utterly absorbed in what they were doing. Martin looked down at the Pampers and the tissues, the bottle and nipple cleanser, the cotton buds and baby oil. Their neighbours were smiling happily at the little domestic scene. Everyone, except him, was smiling. There was nothing this young couple could ignore or leave out or decide on a whim not to do. It was all laid down and necessary. It had meaning. Without children, there was only the second bottle of wine and bugger all to talk about while you drank it. And as usual the conclusion did not ease the question. Like someone probing a sore gum with his tongue, he was unable to leave off, half enjoying the irritation, intrigued by it.

With an effort he made himself walk on, over grass strewn with gadgetry – he side-stepped an electric massager and a flashing, battery-operated board game but failed to notice one of the water sprinklers and had to make a hasty dive to one side, sprawling his length in the damp earth.

A snort of laughter made him turn angrily to see a figure in snazzy Bermuda shorts, leaning against the bar, holding a can of beer in one hand.

'Don't get upset,' the man said, still smiling. 'I wasn't laughing at you. It's the whole thing which tickles me – there's supposed to be no bloody water and yet here you are almost drowned in it. It's probably Perrier – they fly everything in from France.'

It was hard not to stare back, the man was short, barely five-foot something, Martin guessed, but a mass of black curls covering his head and falling to his shoulders, and the violent electric colours of his outfit, made him unmissable. With his dark looks and the Byronic hair he could have been an actor playing a poet, if it wasn't for the sheer vulgarity of his shirt – a mass of canary yellow pineapples struggling against a background of scarlet starbursts.

What a nightmare, Martin thought, avoiding the man's gaze and trying to pretend he was studying the Malian pool attendant, a thin, elderly man in flapping khaki shorts and navy-blue canvas shift onto which the name 'Mansa' had been crudely stitched. As he moved he spat – it was all he did – constant spitting, hawking up large frothy gobs, aiming them at the grassy intervals between the sunbathers. As he passed near Martin he gave an especially gravelly 'hurra', just missing him by inches.

'Disgusting, isn't it?' said the gaudy figure at the bar. 'He's been at it all morning – says it's Ramadan, says he's so devout he can't so much as swallow his own saliva without breaking the rules. Can you believe it?' He began to shout: 'Hey, Mansa, ya filthy bastard, stop it you hear me? It's bloody disgusting!'

The old man took no notice continuing on his rounds, morosely expectorating as before.

Martin's new companion was furious. 'There's a delegation – to see the management – care to join us?'

Martin shook his head. He didn't really care what the poor old guy did as long as he was well out of range. It had been a mean trick to dress him up like a mental patient and it could be no fun fasting. It didn't seem fair to rat on him, just because he was having a hard time.

'Suit yourself. It's no skin off my nose if you lie down in one of Mansa's filthy gobs of phlegm.' He thought for a minute. 'Will you have a drink with me? It's good for you in this heat, helps the dehydration, at least that's my excuse.' He offered his hand. 'Name's Delmonico, Barry Delmonico – they christened me Bartolomeo but it sounds too pretentious for a Scotsman – I'm ice-cream Scots, the Italian diaspora.' He fished a card from the breast pocket of his shirt; it was an unusual shade of flamingo pink with the text in embossed silver: '*Entreprises B. Delmonico, Importation et Exportation, Agence, Cabinet d'Assurances.*'

When Martin looked up the man leant over and took it back, carefully slotting it into his front pocket again. Close to, Martin could smell flowers and see the ring on his left hand, a large sapphire in a circle of tiny winking diamonds. It looked not unlike the royal engagement ring and was obviously very expensive.

But Delmonico was explaining himself in joke Italian: '. . . I binna ere twenty years, sinsa da Independence, eeza good no?'

'Where *are* you from?' Martin asked, hoping to get a straight answer.

'Leith.'

'Really? So why are you here?'

'For the beer. This *Bière du Peuple* isn't bad when it's cold, which is why I live in the hotel. The French run it, so it works – some of the time. They've got their own generator while the rest of the town's blacked out half the day. Now you are no doubt asking yourself, what line of business a man like me might be in.' He leant closer. 'Don't believe all the doom and gloom you read in the British papers, Africa's got a lot going for it, if you can find it – gold, diamonds – there's even a man from Lille who makes a mint from beans, white ones, he cans them. Not that it's the way it was under our beloved first President. No, no. Last of the big spenders he was. Built the airport, this place, the hospital, the omni-sports stadium, now that really is something, you should see it – tons and tons of cement, even I lost count – ah, deary me, what a beauty – it's this wide . . .' He made a fisherman's gesture of great dimensions, his hands at full stretch. 'There used to be a giant statue of Himself outside, we were always shit scared it would come down in a storm, and we were right to be, when we saw how easily the students toppled it. There were bits of His Excellency scattered far and wide – which was horribly appropriate when you think about it . . .'

He paused, waiting for his audience to demand an explanation, clearly longing to tell all he knew about the country's ups and downs. Martin wasn't sure how much these anecdotes could be trusted. He remembered reading press reports of a revolution and, now he'd mentioned it, there was some local politician who'd made a stir – organised some sort of union against South Africa or Israel or both? But Delmonico had already resumed his story without waiting to be prompted.

'. . . the blood was trickling down his neck making a little puddle in the hollow where his chest sank into his paunch and he was just sitting there trying to blow it out, the way you might if you were sweating by the pool and were too lazy to go and shower. Caused a lot of trouble that photo did – they should never have let that man from *Agence France Presse* get anywhere near. There was no foreign aid for a couple of years after that, so all the building stopped – I was in cement until then, lovely it was, tons and tons and tons of it.'

He sighed dreamily, no doubt seeing an inner vision of container after container, stuffed full of sacks of best Portland. But something about the horror story puzzled Martin. He was sure he had read it somewhere quite recently, but about quite another atrocity in another country, in which case Delmonico was just bullshitting.

'. . . there was nothing before Independence, just a few big colonial houses and the railway station and that was a disaster – the Frogs burned down half the trees to keep the trains running – at least the new boys put this place on the map for a while, really rattled the French when they nationalised everything – railways, electricity, the mines. Of course they all went bust when the Frogs left and the Russians weren't much good at running them and now we have French *coopérants* managing most things, so it's *plus ça change*. So what do you say to that, then?'

'Very funny. But tell me, what's going on now? The revolution, was what – five years ago? So why all the soldiers at the airport and the road block outside the hotel?'

'Nothing to worry about.'

'Is it Gaddafi?'

Delmonico rushed a finger to his lips. 'Shush. Don't even say the name. He's the bogeyman round here.' Then he laughed, a very happy laugh. 'Awfully good for business, though. You get all sorts coming through and I'm right here to help when they need me. By the way, if there's anything you want. Gold chain? Nice little stone? People find they want all sorts of things once they've settled in. All sorts of things. And with all this chaos almost anything is possible – anything.' He winked.

Martin felt uncomfortable. It was as if the man had recognised something about him which he hadn't yet seen himself. He answered primly: 'There's nothing, thank you.' Then felt priggish.

Delmonico shrugged. 'Have a wee beer at least. Hey, Mansa! Stop that hawking and fetch us a *Bière du Peuple* pronto. Another of the Great Leader's legacies – he got the East Germans to build a brewery, along with the police headquarters and the central prison. Tons of cement. The biggest thing was going to be the *Centre National de Recherche Médico-Scientifique*. I already had the cement on the way when the troubles blew up. Nobody wants it now. Don't suppose you'd care to build a skyscraper – no? Pity. Everything went kaput with the *coup* and now we're paying for it.'

Martin's attention drifted to the hotel behind them, his eyes climbing the fifteen stories of the high white tower. Yes, he did remember a revolution of some sort, or at least he remembered a shaky hand-held camera image of fleeing protestors and nervous conscripts firing ancient rifles, of an antique jeep rattling up to a white colonial palace and the news reader reeling off a list of odd-sounding names, for a government you knew would never be heard of again. It happened all the time.

Delmonico's voice drifted back.

'. . . big programme, it was. Posters and pills and student drama groups, going round the villages telling them to pull it out, before they have any more unfeedable brats. His Eminence the Black Prince didn't like that . . .'

'What are you talking about?'

'Birth control. The first President was very keen on it – mind you, he had as many wives as you could wish for, and at least thirteen children of his own, but he knew it was the one thing that mattered.'

'And the Black Prince?'

'His Eminence Cardinal Josiah Matelolo, Archbishop and big cheese of our few Catholics. There aren't many but they've got a lot of loot from overseas and on the baby issue they see eye to eye with more recent arrivals – Mormons, Jehovah's Witnesses, ten sorts of Baptists – you name it, we've got it. Anyway, the Black Prince is a man not known for his love of family planning and a keen supporter of the present dispensation, which has found it convenient to retrench on the issue. It's a disaster. Population's doubling. They're flooding into Bamako and on top of everything comes *La Sécheresse*. But that's nature's way – they breed like rabbits, nature cuts them down.'

'I hardly imagine the drought is a direct result of the government abandoning contraceptive education.'

'More people cut down more trees, try to grow more crops, use more water and bingo – *La Sécheresse*. Take old Mansa there, he's got a dozen at least, and how can he feed them on what he gets here? No, the Great Leader had his faults but he knew what would happen if people like Mansa didn't tie a knot in it. He was a very practical man before he started to believe he was the Black Messiah which is a pity, because I liked him, he always paid his bills, which is more than can be said for the present lot.' He fell silent as Mansa approached, letting loose a final gob of frothy spit, before stepping up behind the bar to reach into the icebox for a can.

It was tongue-numbingly cold and Martin's first gulp caused a sharp pain at both temples. He looked round at the sunbathers.

'What do all these people do?'

Delmonico pulled down the corners of his mouth but stopped playing the fool: 'Mostly aid, government advisors, but the Japs come on holiday even though there's nothing for them to do and they all end up round the pool same as us. They all come expecting to photograph herds of rhino or the Victoria Falls or the charge of the Zulu Impi and what they get is this clapped-out colonial railhead. After a day wandering round, they never go out again. So what're you doing here?'

'Half-term.'

'You a professor?'

'Teacher – new comprehensive. It's really rather exciting. We've been gearing up for years now, ordering the language lab – it's a great opportunity. Of course I was head of department in the old grammar school and I'm only number two now, but it's so much bigger . . .'

Delmonico was not listening. Even Alice barely listened now that

81

she'd chucked it in. It only seemed to matter when you were there – streaming, course work, permanent assessment, modular learning. He looked at the hotel again – lay it on its side and it wouldn't be too different from the new science block, until you tried to fit the rain-washed playground and the half-finished bicycle sheds into this sun-drenched scene. He shouldn't have come.

'You alone?' Delmonico said.

'My wife's with me. She's upstairs resting.'

'Play bridge by any chance?'

Martin shook his head and watched the man's momentary interest shut off.

'Hoy there Mansa! Bring us another tube and stop that fucking spitting for Chrissake.'

Martin was just about to ease himself away, when a group of three Europeans and two Japanese approached, presumably the delegation. There was a quick conference with Delmonico, before they turned and headed for the hotel.

'Sure you won't come?' Delmonico said.

Martin shook his head. 'I've got things to think about.'

The little man smiled. 'Now, I wonder what they could be, here in this trouble-free paradise? Eat, drink and be merry – you *are* on holiday after all – aren't you?'

Again Martin had the uncomfortable feeling the man knew more than he was letting on, but before he could frame a question, Delmonico was walking off to join the others.

Martin looked at Mansa, spitting near the bar. There was something furtive about him now, as if he had guessed what the departing figures were up to. Martin felt weary with the whole thing, it was too much like the petty intrigues at work, the fussy squabbles over the stationery cupboard, the tetchy insistence on matters of status. It was something the little fuzzy pictures in his geography books had failed to convey, that Africa was no different to anywhere else in having its share of human pettiness.

He drifted over to the buffet, trying to fit Madame Josette and Delmonico into some sort of pattern. He wasn't really hungry, his body-clock was elsewhere and the food looked difficult: stuff on cocktail sticks, things that had to be dealt with. He grabbed a simple sandwich and retreated to a vacant lounger under a capacious parasol and as he ate he spread open Madame Josette's newspaper. Clearly she was not alone in her obsession: prodigies of ingenuity had gone into getting photographs of the future princess, anyone vaguely connected with her had been pressed for news of her simple unspoiled nature, her kindly interest in children, her near royal lineage. It was soporific stuff which, with the heat, had him vaguely drifting away, not quite asleep but suspended in a warm haze penetrated only by the occasional whoosh of someone diving into the pool or the distant crack of ice in a glass. Perhaps this was it – a holiday by the pool? There had been no sign of any agent, no indication that anyone had been expecting him. The whole thing began to look like an elaborate con to get them to buy a holiday in Africa. And so what? It had been a crazy idea to think of picking up a child without any proper preparation. Better just to enjoy the rest and the heat and the warm red glow around his closed eyes . . .

He woke with a jolt and returned to the article. 'A Marriage made in Heaven' was the underlying theme. There was a photo-montage of royal children and a paragraph on the order of succession, leaving no doubt as to the ultimate purpose of this celestial coupling. Martin felt angry again, this incessant harping on breeding had followed him even here, to the remotest place he could think of. It was all around him, scattered across the lawn, upstairs by his bed, on every mind, in every thought, this great global coming together, this royal progress down the evolutionary line. He tossed the paper aside and looked at his watch. It was after three and the sun was no longer at its zenith. He had wasted a day. He started to force himself up but as he looked across at the pool he caught sight of a small Japanese woman carefully descending, foot over foot, the metal ladder into the shallow end. Something about the way she moved made him go on staring. Her excessive caution and the shudder when she first entered the water spoke of someone little used to swimming. She was wearing a curiously old fashioned body-hugging, one-piece bathing costume in a flesh pink that reminded Martin of photographs of his parents at seaside resorts just after the war. Her skull-tight bathing hat was the same pink, making Martin think of Alice's dolls, wigless and ambiguous, without the tiny nooks and crannies that would have made them disturbingly human. But this hairless, androgynous figure, shivering in the pool, did show signs of life – the tiny injection craters on her upper arm spoke of the vulnerable blood beneath the even skin and the flutter of her chest offered proof of her nervous heart.

She waded to her waist, cautiously lowering herself to her chin before launching into a surprisingly sharp and mechanical breast stroke that had all the brisk angularity of a style recently acquired, her head bobbing up and down like a beach ball in a storm. It was funny yet touching. She had clearly worked so hard on it before coming and Martin could imagine the terrifying moment when her instructor first lowered his arms and ordered her to begin the frog-like rhythm taught on dry land.

Martin was entranced. She was smooth, spare to the point of fleshlessness, yet so obviously supple and soft. He could have stayed and watched for hours but the delegation was bustling back, rubicund and slightly huffy, with the flush of honest men who have done an unpleasant duty. They were followed by a white man in a dark suit who signalled to Mansa to come and join him at the towel hut. Martin closed his eyes and pretended to be asleep. The whole thing was crazy – no contact, no *Enfants du Monde*, just this make-believe African village by a make-believe pond in a land dying of drought.

Alice stood before the open wardrobe, a towel wrapped round her, wondering which of her limited choices it should be. She had just decided to get back into her old T-shirt when she saw the doll's arm sticking out of her case and realised that Martin must have seen it, too. She couldn't imagine what had come over her – it was at the very last minute, she had been checking that everything was turned off in the kitchen when she suddenly reached for the doll and stuffed it on top of her clothes. Even at the time she had felt pretty stupid, but having taken the thing it seemed only reasonable that it should have something to wear, so she had pulled the clothes off some of the other dolls and stuffed them in the bag with her. When she saw it again last night it had been quite a shock. She had pushed it from her thoughts during the journey and had rather hoped Martin wouldn't discover it, though the way she had left the arm sticking out had to mean something – as if deep down she wanted him to know. So why had he said nothing? Perhaps it was pity? That was it – he was sorry for her, unwilling to make a scene.

She pulled the thing right out of the bag and held it at arm's length.

'Hello Baby,' she said in a singsong voice. 'Why so sad, little Baby? I bring you on holiday and you still look miz – now there's ingratitude.'

There was a noise outside. Alice shoved the doll behind her. No, it was all right, she could hear the breathy hum of a vacuum cleaner, it was just someone cleaning the corridor. She pulled Baby back and examined its melancholy features.

'Poor Baby. Poor me. You're my little mad secret.' She wondered if any of the other couples on the flight had been Mantock's potential adopters. But no, none of them had looked anything but ordinary – no suspicious glances, no furtive weighing up of other people. No one, in effect, who looked as she imagined herself to look. Just couples going on holiday. Sane folk, sensible people, women who wouldn't have dolls in their suitcases.

Somehow Baby had moved into her arms. She was cradling it – there it was. She rocked it gently. Part of her still able to wonder why this could happen, even if wondering didn't make her stop.

'There, there,' she crooned soothingly, though whether for Baby or herself was no longer clear. 'There, there.'

She could taste something metallic on her tongue; the acrid aftertaste of mounting anger – mainly with herself, with this surrender.

'There, there.'

She stopped – she could hear noises again, closer. Someone was rattling a key in the door. She panicked. What to do with Baby? She sat her in the armchair then hurried to the bed, lay down and pretended to read. The door swung back and a maid bustled in, dragging a trolley piled high with towels and give-away shampoos. She went into the bathroom without saying a word; Alice could see her, swilling and flushing, bent double, her slim upper half disappearing behind a mountainous rear. With a hollow bang she let the lavatory seat crash down and was back in the room, flicking a duster at the chest of drawers, advancing on the bed.

Alice shrank. The woman walked up to the chair, seized Baby by an arm, swinging her out of the way, while she plumped up the cushions. Before Alice could protest, the doll was dumped on the side table, the abused limb sticking straight out at a painful angle, one eyelid clicked shut, the other spikily open, wild-eyed and fearful. Alice felt stupid, this woman would have real babies, many to judge by her hips – why should she care?

She was already on to the next torture, this time with a vacuum cleaner, the old-fashioned kind with walking-stick handle and canvas dust bag. Alice screwed up her face as the noise mounted the scale to a high, settled whine. Perhaps the woman enjoyed it. After all the wiping and polishing it must be pleasant to stand there, rocking to and fro as the machine covered the carpet. Maybe that was why she went on so long – she must have been round already? It was intolerable the way she banged the sides of the bed, as if hitting it purposely hard.

With a last windy groan and a sagging of its belly it was over. With a heave and a rattle, the trolley was through the door and Alice looked at the tortured doll and cursed her own weakness for having brought the thing. She went to pick it up, intending to stuff it out of sight in the wardrobe for the rest of the trip, but no sooner lifted than it seemed to slip back into her arms, to snuggle down as she began to rock, pressing the rubbery frame, trying to force it into the painful emptiness that seemed to have spread right through her.

With an effort of will, she shook herself and let the thing drop to her side, dangling it by one arm, telling herself not to be so stupid. But it was no use, she would have to compromise: dress the thing, sit it on the chest of drawers as if it were at home in the kitchen in England. That would do. Just have it there in the room, looking on.

She swung it over to the wardrobe and riffled in her case for a dress, coming up with a flowered smock, a sort of milkmaid number with a collar in broderie anglaise which had been on one of the smaller, modern dolls, the one that said 'mama'. On Baby it was a tight, short, aggressive miniskirt, a curious parody of her own T-shirt. She was holding it up in front of her, admiring the somewhat surreal effect, when another noise outside reminded her that the door was not properly shut. She went to close it and saw someone in the corridor – a white woman, waiting outside the neighbouring room. It was the same woman she had seen yesterday, the one whose husband had had the stupid accident at the airport. She was everything Alice was not, her hair sprayed into place, her make-up exact – yet there was something not quite right, something slightly off-key. Alice noticed how she dragged on a cigarette held at the very tips of her fingers, her thumb keeping it firm between puffs with abrupt little taps at the end, red with her lipstick. It was the quick gulping way she inhaled the smoke which gave her away, that and the balled-up handkerchief held in her free hand, loose at her side. She was crying.

'Is everything all right?' Alice asked softly.

The woman turned, momentarily confused.

'It's Jack,' she said, as if that explained everything.

Alice started to go back but something seemed to touch the woman.

'My husband Jack,' she said. 'He's sick.'

'Don't cry,' Alice said, suddenly afraid this formidable façade might break up, right there in front of her.

'He's gone and done it now,' she said, tap-tapping her cigarette. 'The doctor's with him. A suitcase, would you believe it? A suitcase and then there's blood all over the place and doctors and what have you.'

'Shouldn't he be in hospital?'

'That's a laugh. The doctor says it's a pigsty, filthiest place in town. Better he gets seen to here. Well, I'm not playing nursey that's for sure. I mean, what was he thinking about?' She sniffed, pulling a clean tissue out of a side pocket. 'Oh God, why does it have to be like this? I mean, why can't it just be neat and easy.' She straightened herself, taking a deep breath, forbidding tears. 'Oh, don't worry, that's over. A weak moment.'

Alice tried to smile reassuringly but saw that the woman was staring at Baby. Alice had walked out with the damned thing and now her secret was revealed. She gripped the little arm even tighter, afraid of what the woman might say.

'Pretty,' she said. 'Laura Ashley, isn't it. I always used to get my two Laura Ashley when they were tiny.'

Alice smiled gratefully. 'Is there anything I can do?'

'Truth to tell there is. I don't suppose I could just have a bit of a sit in your room, could I? Never been one for illnesses.'

Alice led the way and was about to put Baby in the armchair when the woman reached out.

'Here, let me hold her, the little pretty. Got any tinies of your own – no? Never mind, they don't stay this pretty for long I can tell you. My name's Margot, Margot Zabriskie, Polish-Australian you might say, though that's from Jack, I'm as Brit as the next. My lot are from Hull originally. You on holiday too? Or is hubby working here?'

'Holiday.'

'Like us. Daft, isn't it? Jack just wanted to get as far away as possible, wanted to show the girls the world. The doctors at home said it was all right – a gall bladder 'op' should clear up easily enough, and he did seem fine at first. But when we were doing Italy

– that was before Paris then London – the trouble started. You see he was . . .' – she lowered her voice – '. . . leaking.'

'Leaking?' Alice lips curled involuntarily.

'I know. Disgusting, isn't it? I felt exactly the same. They called it a fistula; it means the scar didn't heal and the bowel juices were leaking out. Yucky, eh? Well, even then it was no big deal. We went to the Middlesex when we got to London and they patched him up, but when he saw the commercial for the Sunshine Break – yes, you know the one – with the giraffes and the desert city and the palm trees – and he thought the girls should have the experience of a lifetime, well, that's when he made his big mistake. It's the climate here. Full of bugs.' She let out a long breathy sigh. 'Not that it matters really, it's all the same in the end.'

'Why?'

'Because he's going to die. On, don't look so shocked. He's been dying since we met. Always under the weather. It's a miracle we managed Sharon and Lizzie. I suppose I should have put my foot down when he first started talking of coming here, but there didn't seem much point. It might as well be here as anywhere and it was a good chance to get away from all that Royal Wedding stuff in London. God, but they do lay it on thick. Fairy Tale Romance, I ask you. Wait'll they've been at it a few years, then ask them about romance. Poor cow, she doesn't know she's born yet.'

Margot clicked open a cigarette case and waved it briefly toward Alice as if expecting her to refuse, took one herself, lit it single-handed and drew on it with a luxuriant slowness letting the smoke come out with her words. 'Am I boring you?'

Alice shook her head. 'What will you do? Without Jack, I mean?'

'Do?' there seemed to be a dozen possibilities in the little word. 'Do? What will I do? Oh, quite a lot, believe me. You see, Jack's younger than me, a lot younger. I'd already had quite a life before we met. I'd been – well, I'll tell you all about that another time. What matters is that just when I needed to settle down, along came nice young Jack, not much experience – none, actually – but more than happy to find someone to lead him by the hand. He had a nice job, wholesale furniture, the mother was a bit of a trial but I reckoned I could handle that. What I hadn't reckoned on was the sheer boredom! You see, I'd been used to a pretty high-powered existence. Well, I'll tell you – I was in the army and I'd been used to getting out and about. Adventurous, you might say. It's what I

88

want to get back to – a New Life. A bit of fun before it's too late. Say, you haven't got a drink have you?'

Alice looked round. The duty free scotch had to be somewhere. She opened the wardrobe and saw the plastic bag. Her guest plunged into the bathroom to re-emerge with the tooth-brush glasses.

'Neat,' she said, keeping her glass in place for an extra helping. She drank as she smoked with a fixed appreciative rhythm which Alice found herself imitating, even though she seldom had more than an occasional beer.

'So I'm Margot,' the woman said, raising her glass. 'And what do I call you?'

'Alice. Alice Beresford. What about your girls?'

'Sharon and Lizzie? What about 'em?'

'Well, how do they fit into your New Life?'

'Not sure's they do. Oh, I've shocked you? They're not babies, you know. Few years and they'll be off anyway and where does that leave me? Too late for anything, I shouldn't wonder. Naw, it's not fair.'

Alice felt uncomfortable hearing her own phrase bouncing back at her. Unfair – here was she thinking it unfair to have no children and here was Margot thinking it unfair to have them.

'Anyway,' she was saying. 'It'll cheer up Jack's mother. That little Polish treasure has been wearing black since we married, so with the rehearsals over she can get the performance underway. She'll adore having the girls.'

'Did you never love him – Jack, I mean?'

'Course I did, at first, when I'd got him trained . . .'

She stopped as if coming to a conclusion. 'I'm not as much of a bitch as all this sounds – I was very fond of him. We liked the same things, bars, clubs, I'm sociable and he was terrific company till the kids put a stop to all that. Oh, we were happy all right and everyone was over the moon for us. We'd made it, hadn't we? It was what it was all about. But it doesn't stop, it's endless – and don't be fooled into thinking it's just at the start and that after six months there'll be a nanny and cleaning lady and you'll be running a factory in your spare time. Well, not for people on our income – oh no. Do you work?'

'Used to – teacher. Gave it up. It's funny really, this is the first time in my life I haven't been going to a school of some sort. Our lives have always been broken into terms, exams, school holidays, new terms – always. It's odd not hearing a bell every forty minutes. Won't you miss the girls?'

'A bit, but there's more to life . . .' She looked down at Baby. 'You trying for kiddies?'

Alice nodded. 'A marriage isn't very much without children. They give it a reason.'

'Rubbish!' Margot said, with a vehemence that startled Alice. 'Kids don't make a marriage, they end it. You're not lovers any more, you're a family. Oh, I can see what you mean in terms of making sure you have something to occupy you – the shared task, if you're lucky. But it's hardly living. Not that it lasts anyway, like sex, after a couple of years . . .'

'Well, me and Martin . . .'

But she was cut off with a majestic wave of a new cigarette.

'Bet you think of someone else when you're doing it? Sure you do. Teenage policemen, black baseball players, someone you saw on a bus the day before . . .'

Alice sniggered and had an awful feeling it was a dirty laugh. She had a clear image of the soldier at the airport, his endless legs sheathed and camouflaged. Martin had looked like that when they first met but that was ages ago, now there was the routine, the mumbo-jumbo of dates and times, set down like a Chinese horoscope.

'There was a soldier at the airport . . .'

'There always is. Here, let's have another scotch.'

Alice reached for the bottle. She was already light-headed, but why not?

'Does that list figure in your New Life?'

'You bet.'

They clinked glasses but Margot looked suddenly serious. She settled Baby on the chest of drawers and came over to sit by Alice on the bed.

'Mustn't be flippant,' she said. 'It's hell when you want kids and can't have 'em. Why didn't you adopt? You're smart, both of you, you're not on the breadline, shouldn't have been that hard, so why this?' She pointed towards Baby.

'We were going to, but they wouldn't let us in the end.'

'Why?'

'Too old.'

'Jeezus, how old's too old?'

Alice shrugged.

'What does your hubby do?'

'Schoolteacher. He's not very ambitious. I used to teach as well but I gave it up a year ago for the adoption society – then we started this new thing for having kids – I'm supposed to rest a lot. Martin's not very happy about it, he's not as bothered about kids as I am. Just wants a quiet life, I suppose.'

Margot snorted smoke. 'Sounds like you're on your own – like me. Don't think I like the sound of your hubby, you should watch him. Just the sort to get up to something if he thought it would suit him.'

Alice was about to protest but stopped when she realised that she was inclined to agree with her.

'You should join me,' Margot said. 'Forget about your miserable schoolteacher, come and have a New Life. We ought to find you someone – I'll ask Freddy.'

'Freddy?'

'He's the cocktail barman downstairs, I went on a bit of a binge last night once I'd got Jack off to sleep. Drinks, a bit of a dance, you know? You'd like Freddy, he's hung like a stallion.'

'Is he on your list?'

'Hell no, he's queer, but that's all to the good, he knows just what's what.'

There was a sharp rap on the door. Alice froze.

'Something wrong?' Margot asked.

'It's the cleaning woman, she hates me, really she does.'

There was another rap, more insistent.

'I think it's for me,' Margot said and called out. 'Come in.'

The door was opened by a tall, thin African in a dark pinstripe suit who had to be a doctor. He reminded Alice of the soldier at the airport, the same narrow, angular features, that taut racehorse look. Margot introduced them, presenting the man as what sounded like Dr Jop. 'That's D.I.O.P. pronounced Jop,' she explained. 'There are Diops everywhere here.'

The doctor smiled, bent close and whispered. Margot nodded, sighed, nodded.

'No change,' she announced. 'And the doctor here has a couple of other calls to make. Seems the tourists are dropping like flies.'

The doctor withdrew. Margot was clearly peeved but suddenly rallied.

'Come on,' she said. 'I'm going to take you in hand, it'll do me good to get out of myself. Come on. Get your war paint on.'

'But surely . . .'

'Don't say it. You want me to be the dutiful little wife, sitting by his sick-bed. Why? It's over. I'm not going to walk out on him. I'll let things take their course, but I'm not going to pretend. So into your glad rags and let's get going.'

Alice dressed in a daze, finding some old eye-shadow and lipstick at the bottom of her bag. It was weird looking in the mirror, like discovering an old holiday snap left inside a book. Modigliani she thought, oh well it's a start – she darkened her upper lids, making the sort of blue hollows that matched the paintings, not much on the lips, the hair pulled back and there it was, that narrow oval mask.

'Now that's better,' Margot said. 'Pretty as a picture.'

Alice smiled, perhaps it was better to be someone else, a portrait of a model long dead, a fiction. Ought one to offer the world a never changing image – like Baby's always sad face – be what you like but never show it?

Margot marched towards the lift as if heading a parade. They rode up to what Alice guessed must be the very top of the hotel and stepped out into a narrow corridor with a single door, upholstered in red leather, over which was an unlit sign: 'Café de Paris, Discothèque.' Inside, a small round dance floor was lit by a single spotlight and at its centre a young African was dancing, utterly absorbed in himself. He wore a tight white singlet which glowed in the light leaving most of his exposed torso a flurry of purple movement. His skimpy shorts were made of a metallic material which sparked and rippled as he gyrated to a deafening American sound. It was half dance, half aerobics – fists punching the air above him at each crash of the beat while his left foot made a half step and his right kicked high in front of him as he fell backwards on to his left hand, pushed back and jumped clear into the air, landed and danced on without a pause. It was breathtaking and painfully sexy. When he turned her way Alice could see that his eyes were tight closed in concentration while his lips mouthed a wah wah wah to the wail of the group. He had to be rehearsing a show, it was just too good to be amateur – he fell back on both hands, turned a backwards somersault but danced off again the instant his feet felt the ground. She almost applauded, then realised he might stop if she did and that, above all, was what she did not want to happen. Now he was doing rapid dizzying turns round the perimeter of the dance floor, his hands pulled tight to him, forcing up his chest and arm muscles. He was powerfully built for a dancer, more an athlete. The music crashed to an end, he stopped on the beat and threw out his arms for the imagined applause that this time Alice could not contain, clapping and clapping for all she was worth. The man's eyes opened, he saw his audience and his mouth parted in a wide white grin of pleasure as he executed a crazy pirouette and Alice laughed, a high, innocent, merry laugh.

'Merci beaucoup, merci, merci...' she muttered, smiling nervously.

'Oh, don't be such a mouse,' said Margot bluntly. 'Go for it. I've got something to see to, but you stay – enjoy yourself.'

Alice tried to say 'no' but could only watch helplessly as Margot withdrew leaving her paralysed, frozen with embarrassment. The dancer, too, had barely moved since the music stopped and was now watching her intently, as if expecting her to speak.

She unthinkingly slipped her hands behind her back and linked her thumbs. It was an unconscious reminder of times past, something she had always done when situations got beyond her as a teenager. There had been kissing sessions that could not get anywhere but were hard to end without seeming prudish – just kissing, on and on, her hands behind her back as if being sentenced. Parties where the light was turned out and there was slow dancing and more kissing. It had been an unquestioned misery, as uninteresting as washing yet believed to be just as inevitable.

The dancer gave up waiting, walked over to a control desk and quickly manipulated a row of switches. The lights changed sequence, a thudding jerking rhythm pounded out of massive speakers and he began to gyrate, his fists punching the air, his feet sliding over the floor as if it were ice.

Oh God, Alice thought, please get me out of here. The man suddenly broke into a series of falls, striking the floor with his right hand and throwing himself up again crotch-first. Alice turned and fled.

Riding down in the lift she started to laugh. The idea of her flirting with such a gorgeously sexy creature was silly. What on earth was she supposed to do? Give him sultry, come-hither glances from under lowered lashes? Hitch up her skirt and flash a tantalising length of upper thigh? Some hopes, she thought, straightening her face as the lift opened. She stepped into the foyer and cast around for some sign of where Martin might be. The whole thing was lurching out of control, charging down avenues she had never thought to travel and it would be as well for them to stick together and keep to the matter in hand. She changed some money at the reception, then saw the sign for the swimming pool and decided to give it the once over, but as she walked past the dining room she saw Margot sitting at a table with Dr Diop, and could tell from the way his hand rested on hers that they weren't there to discuss his patient.

Martin's dreams were full of longing. Asleep, he studied the Japanese woman wading through the shallow end, water lapping into the sharp V where her costume disappeared between her legs, watching closely as she crouched into her jerky mechanical breast stroke. Unable to resist, he plunged into the water and took long, laboured strides until he caught up with her. Sensing his approach, she stopped swimming and simply stood, completely immobile, waiting for him to arrive. He reached out and unzipped the back of her costume with a single fluid motion, down over the delicate ripple of her spine, down to the slight swell of her buttocks. The flesh-coloured second skin sloughed off at the merest touch, while a slight pressure on the wings of her shoulders bent her forwards, face almost touching the surface of the water, back dipped like a dancer's instep as he ran his hands over the flawless surface of her narrow, fleshless body . . . He woke with a bump, someone had flopped onto his lounger.

'Martin.'

He pushed himself up, guilt pasted across his face.

'It's very nice here,' Alice said, her glance taking in the pool and the people. 'No, really it's *very* nice. I'm not surprised you haven't felt much inclination to move.'

'That's not fair – have you see the goons out there? It's hardly my fault no one can get in. And just to put the record straight, I did try to find an alternative but that's a non-starter and in any case we are strongly advised not to go wandering off – there's trouble in town, some sort of trial, it's upsetting people.'

He mentioned the boutique, quoting 'the woman who runs it' as his source, but Alice was far from impressed. 'You sound like one of those no-hope journalists who quote taxi-drivers when they fail to get an interview with the president. Listen Martin, you said they don't touch white folk, so why this sudden fear of going outside? You could have gone, at least for a look. I thought it was you that was so keen on Africa? Surely there's someone else you could ask, someone a bit more informed than this shop assistant you've been interrogating. She isn't another slinky black beauty in a form-fitting body stocking by any chance?'

'Ye Gods, if only you knew. Look, why don't you come and have a word with her? She suggested it. She has strong views on adoption. She's heard about *Les Enfants du Monde* and doesn't much care for them.'

'Oh Martin, what do you have for brains? I *know* what she thinks. How many children has she got – a dozen? Has it never dawned on you that the least sympathetic people to childless women are other women – in particular those with children? The people who know the minimum about the longing to be a mother are those who already *are* – they've done it, they don't *need* to think about it. And not just mothers . . .'

'What's that supposed to mean?'

'I'm not really blaming you, Martin, you're in an impossible situation, but the fact is that you hardly begin to comprehend what I'm going through – no, don't argue. The fact that you're just lying here while I . . . Oh, never mind all that. It's just the idea that you imagine I might benefit from a lecture on the rights and wrongs of adoption from some woman you've just met that cheeses me off. Don't you think I've gone over it already, or do you think I'm just out of control, that I've gone temporarily barmy? No, Martin, I think I'll forgo a little chat about my mistaken intentions. Now listen carefully, I've changed some money, in fact a lot of money judging by this wad. Here, take a million or so just in case.'

He accepted a thick stack of very grubby, frayed bank notes.

'In case what?'

There was a pause, no more than a beat, but when she answered her voice was just on the soft side of angry. 'Darling, what I want you to do is get your bum off that plastic thing and hop off into town. I want you to find some poor woman with a large brood of hungry children, then I want you to give her some of this filthy money in exchange for at least one of them. That done, I would like

95

you to bring it back here so that we can all have tea. Is that clear enough OR DO I HAVE TO RAISE MY VOICE?'

'Shshshsh, for Christ's sake. Everyone's looking. All right, all right, I'll go, but why do you always have to exaggerate? There are two extremes to anything – why do you always insist on swinging about between them? Always.' He pulled on his shirt. 'First we are setting off to save a starving baby, a lost waif, an orphan of the drought, who will live because of us, while at the same time offering us the child we need and the chance to give some of the love which we feel is there for the giving. Do I encapsulate the argument to your satisfaction?'

She nodded. He pulled on his trousers and bent to buckle his sandals.

'But then,' he continued, 'we come to moral extreme number two. Herein we are a pair of grasping filthy-rich baby-snatchers, selfishly taking advantage of those whom a cruel nature hath rendered vulnerable. Have I pictured it to Madam's satisfaction? Well, balls to all that. It's like everything in life, it's neither one nor t'other, it's somewhere in the middle. It depends on circumstances. It's subtle and difficult and confusing. But it isn't black and white – sorry, unintentional pun . . .'

'Where are you going?'

He stopped. 'Dunno. See what's to be seen. Isn't that what you want? So what's it to be – a boy or a girl?'

She thought for a microsecond. 'Girl, I think. No, boy. Oh, it doesn't really matter . . . in any case you're not going to . . .?'

'Of course I'm not. I'm just going to take a look.'

'I'm sorry,' she said, meaning it. 'Must be the heat. Look it's not really dangerous out there is it?'

It was Martin's turn to milk the situation. 'I don't really know. I'll just have to be careful I suppose.'

She sniggered. 'Oh Martin, you are a wally – stop behaving like Captain Oates. Just be sensible and I'll see you back here in an hour or so. You only need to have a quick look, then at least we can say we tried.'

He nodded and tried to stroll off with as much dignity as he could muster, keeping a wary eye open for water sprinklers and hoping he would catch sight of Delmonico, his only advisor now that Madame Josette had so comprehensively ruled herself out of the role.

Mansa was lurking behind the towel hut, spitting discreetly into

96

a shaded area that he had clearly decided was his and which everyone else was now avoiding.

Along the underground passage, the gym was deserted but the chandelier still burned in the hall. He was lucky, Delmonico was just about to get into the lift.

'Can't stop,' he said pushing the call button. 'Summoned to the MPS – the Ministry of Playing Soldiers,' he winked. 'Perhaps they've decided to dig some trenches and need a lot of concrete to shore them up – some hopes but you never know.'

'So we *can* leave the hotel?'

'I can. As long as I'm on official business. Why? Thinking of doing a bit of exploring? Not the best time, not with the trial.'

'Tell me about it – you're the second to mention it.'

Delmonico said what sounded like 'General Jop'.

'Jop?'

Delmonico nodded. 'Jop spelled D.I.O.P. pronounced Jop – a well-known name round here. They're Senegalese originally – been settled here since God knows when.'

'Then who's *this* Diop?'

'Head of the army, or was, until he tried to take over last November. You must have seen it in the papers – it was quite big at the time. He might have got away with it if the French hadn't flown in the Legionnaires. Unfortunately they were too queasy. They should have shot him, but as they didn't there has to be a trial and that's a bit hairy.'

'Was he popular?'

'Not really. But as things get worse he starts to look good. As long as they keep paying the army things will be OK, if not then who can say? Not that it really matters who's in power, not since the Father of the Nation set up a one-party state. Whoever gets to the top, the place just staggers along as before.'

There was a resonant ping and the lift door swooshed open.

'You make it all sound pretty hopeless,' Martin said.

Delmonico shook his head. The door started to close but he held it back with his foot. The door gave three little shudders, in a half-hearted attempt to clear the obstacle, then settled back into waiting mode.

'I have to go,' Delmonico said. 'Business before all else . . .'

'Why go on?' Martin persisted, determined to get the conversation round to his own problem. The door tried another three shudders but Delmonico's foot held fast. 'Why bother if it's as hopeless as you make out?'

'Because I don't and it isn't. I just like an occasional moan, that's all. In fact people here are remarkably resilient. Despite the drought and the political shenanigans, they survive and that's no small feat. I feel sorry for them, they deserve better. The greatest mistake is to imagine that something can always be done – the late President thought that, and look where it got him. Maybe it's better to bend with the wind. Take birth control. It's true they've virtually abandoned it, but it's also true they have to show something for all the aid they get. What they do is print a few posters – '*ESPACEZ VOS ENFANTS – L'AVENIR DE VOTRE FAMILLE EST DANS VOS MAINS*'. He sniggered. 'Old jokes like that. They put them up in prominent places where visiting dignitaries are bound to see them, then use most of the cash to pay the army. Can't say I blame them, though it's gonna cause one helluva problem some fine day. Mind you, your average African has a marvellous capacity for coping with impossible numbers of kids – they love 'em you see, can't have enough of them and they nearly always find someone to share with – nearly always – when they're left on their own to sort things out.' He smiled to himself. 'It's the story of Africa really, as soon as outsiders start interfering they back off and the whole thing falls in. When we hit the TV screens about five years ago there was quite a flood of prospective Mums and Dads, quite a little nuisance they were.'

Martin looked away, horribly aware that the entire conversation had turned into the answer to the question he had not put. Oh well, he had nothing to lose. 'I heard there are some children who do fall through the net – that they aren't all mopped up by their families.'

'Ah,' said Delmonico, eyebrows raised in mock innocence. 'I wonder who you've been talking to? Oh never mind, keep your little secret. Yes, it's true the nuns used to collect the odd stray – now it's mainly the Baptists. People don't convert easily round here – grown-up people that is. Little kiddies are easier, especially sick ones.' He smiled broadly. 'Is that what you want? You can find them in the market sometimes if you look down – they have bits of old tyre wrapped round their knees, a flip-flop sandal on each hand so they can drag themselves along. Africa now has the wheel, it just hasn't got as far as the wheelchair.'

Martin ignored the sarcasm. 'So who are these unfortunates?'

'Anyone too crippled to work. If they're of any use someone will take them in.' He dropped his voice. 'There's still slavery you know – oh yes, especially out in the big sand pit. Nothing changes up there. But if they're so bad that they can't even be sent out to beg then I'm afraid they're down to God. The nuns used to run an orphanage but I think that's shut. There's something called the Beulah Baptist Mission but are you really thinking of taking on a black spastic or a black mongol?'

A light began to flash on the overhead panel, someone was trying to summon the lift and the door made a determined effort to force its way passed the obstacle, obliging Delmonico to step halfway in, interposing his body like a Quaker holding back the riot squad at a peace rally. The door hiccuped against him, then resumed its uneasy wait.

'There must be something else,' Martin insisted. 'Some sort of government body, there always is.'

Delmonico smiled almost coyly, as if this was the question he had been waiting for. 'You could be right,' he said teasingly, bracing himself as the door gave a half-hearted shove. 'Now you mention it, I do recall the government setting up a new agency to cope with a little flood of would-be parents after news of the drought got around. It must still exist if you're interested – now what was it called? Ah yes, it's part of the *Centre d'Aménagement du Pays, du Foyer et de la Jeunesse et du Planning Familial.* Christ, they love these titles. I blame the French. Anyway, despite the name it's just one man and his dog in a wooden shack up the hill over there – though even that's called the *Cité Administrative*, to give it its full title. They're all up there – President's palace – so called – a dozen ministries, quite a set-up.'

He smiled and fluttered his lashes and again Martin experienced the same sinking feeling that he was being crudely manipulated.

'Och laddie,' Delmonico said soothingly. 'Dinna fret yersell. Go and see – you never know, it might be the answer. A taxi'll take you but don't expect too much, the ministries here are Orwellian, most do something quite other than what they say they do – believe me.'

He swung into cod Italian. 'Delmonico alwaysa try to helpa da people no?'

'Why are you being so damn helpful?'

'It's my good deed for the day – my crown in heaven. Just tell the guys at the gate that you're going to the *Cité Administrative* – they'll think you're a diplomat.'

That said, he stepped squarely into the lift and raised his hand in farewell. Nothing happened. The lift had given up. Delmonico dabbed at the control board. The door hiccuped forward a pace then returned to its open position. He jabbed again. With agonising slowness the door edged across the opening as if expecting to be wrestled back.

'Remember,' Delmonico said. '*Centre d'Aménagement du Pays, du Foyer et de la Jeunesse et du Planning Familial,*' then laughed as the door finally closed. 'And the best of British luck.'

Out of the air-conditioning, Martin recoiled at the waves of heat radiating from a canary-yellow taxi. It must have been parked on the drive all morning. The driver, stretched out in the thin shade of one of the scrawny trees bordering the road, accepted the commission grumpily. The interior was an oven. Martin eased himself in – asking him to drive to the *Cité Administrative* while attempting to hold himself above a plastic seat, sticky and too hot to touch.

They had only moved a few metres when they were stopped at the first oilcans and Martin was made to repeat their destination. The guards looked doubtful but the regular soldier nodded and waved them through.

Martin was relieved and risked sitting back, hoping the slight, fetid breeze from the open window would start to cool them down. Hunched at the wheel, the driver charged along in a style that would have been dangerous had there been any other traffic. They had turned left and were retracing the route to the open square that Martin remembered from the night before. In daylight, he could now make out a modernist concrete bank on the far corner, rising in three sharp layers, a cubist sponge cake. It was anywhere and nowhere but only for a moment – the driver took a right into a long avenue of stained concrete shop-houses piled high with merchandise, bolts of cloth, tin trunks, aluminium pans, with men haggling over bargains and women gliding past with impossible loads on rigid heads: outsize orange calabashes, branches of stumpy green bananas, babies swung on their backs. Defeated, the driver slowed to a crawl. Martin smiled to himself, the African market had engulfed them, he had arrived. There was a tap at the window – a little boy was holding up a tray of miniature model cars made out of slivers of old tin cans, stray letters from the original brand names still visible on the tiny body-work. Trotting along, the grinning figure held them up in turn, reeling off their names – *'Deux Chevaux, Peugeot 503, Renault Dauphine'* – the history of French motoring reduced to a few ingeniously bent shards from a tin of concentrated tomato purée.

Other momentos of the colonial past drifted by: a man with a baguette under his arm, a supermarket with special offers of charcuterie and cheese pasted on its windows, the brief glimpse of a terraced café with a waiter in a long white apron, balancing a tray on his spread fingers.

The boy tapped again. *'Citroën DS,'* he said, holding up the tiny streamlined vehicle. Martin wound down his window and was hit by the pungent ammoniac pong of warm blood. They were passing a kind of open-air abattoir; a line of concrete slabs spread with ragged strands of dark red flesh, blackened with clusters of gorging flies, filling the air with the intense buzz-saw of their unhindered satisfaction. No one bothered to brush them away, and he could imagine the millions of eggs oozing on to the rich sticky carcasses, the gleeful rubbing of hind legs, the unconcerned eyes swivelling across a landscape of puffed suet and yellowing gristle.

The boy had dropped back and, as Martin turned, he heard angry shouting and caught sight of two men in long djebbas arguing furiously. It was comic at first, two grown men in night-shirts, jabbing their fingers at each other and yelling their heads off. The gathering crowd seemed to think so too, grinning and laughing, but then, with a chill, Martin realised that this was the idiot braying of a mob that has scented blood. The two were near to blows. One began to retreat backwards, stumbling into a stack of earthenware jars, scattering them. A market woman leapt to her feet and added her voice to the uproar. The man turned to run but the crowd blocked his escape. His assailant closed in, fists raised. The laughter faded. Martin stopped breathing but suddenly lurched as the driver hit the accelerator and sent them bumping away. Martin tried to look back, as eager as the others to see the blow fall, but there were too many blocking his view. Whatever happened he had missed it.

They were climbing now. The road curved sharply under brittle dying trees, up and out of the nervous city. The driver had unhunched himself, as if the worst were over – which raised uncomfortable questions about the situation they had left behind.

They took a hairpin bend and crested the summit and were on the level again. Martin had to admit that this was certainly another world – no crowds, noise, smells. It must once have been a fairly elegant park – there were still traces of squared-off lawns and he could see what appeared to be neat clapboard houses. It was a colonial retreat, a haven, safely above the heat and stench of the African city below. Somewhere, over amongst the far trees, must be the presidential palace; the other wooden buildings would be the ministries. At intervals along the road, notice boards announced their present functions.

MINISTÈRE DE LA SANTÉ PUBLIQUE
BUREAU DES POSTES ET TÉLÉCOMMUNICATIONS
RELATIONS INTERGOUVERNEMENTALES

Up close, most were weatherbeaten and crooked, some nearly illegible. The houses too were far from well maintained – here a pillared veranda starting to lean awkwardly, over there a bad case of sagging gutters and missing tiles. And that was it – decaying shacks and imposing names – no sign of any activity, no indication that this was the hub of the nation's public life.

Then he saw them – three men up ahead, armed, and looking their way. Martin caught sight of the driver, wide-eyed in the mirror. He understood the man's fear. If these men were soldiers there was cause for concern. Only one had anything resembling a uniform – a grubby tunic with a torn pocket. The other two wore rags: a faded batik shirt, a frayed woolly jumper in Barbie-doll pink. Someone had tried to spruce them up by issuing black berets, with the crossed-spear-and-star badges of the regular army, but the overall effect remained worryingly amateur, not improved by the antiquated rifles which swung at their sides, museum pieces with worn wooden stocks and scratched pewter-coloured barrels, deadlier because more used-looking than the pristine designer automatics at the airport.

'*Sauvages*,' the driver said, evidently petrified. '*Les sauvages du Nord.*'

'Drive on,' Martin said sharply. '*On y va.*'

The car eased past, drifting, as if trying not to provoke them.

'*Sauvages*,' the man said, awe-struck. '*Sauvages . . .*'

They only stared back, evidently as bemused by Martin as he by them. In any case he had seen the sign he wanted and was trying to get the driver to turn off the road and head towards one of the smaller houses where his ministry must be.

Still muttering his fear, the man rounded the corner with a squeal of brakes and bumped down an unmade track.

Relieved, Martin got out and took in the warped steps and crooked awning. So this was the place, the *Aménagement du Pays*, whatever that was, and the potentially more useful *Planning Familial*, though even that wasn't certain. At least someone was working – he could hear the clack of a manual typewriter and, bracing himself, he climbed the sloping stairs and entered an outer office, where a very large woman in a flower-print, full-length dress with capacious mutton-chop sleeves sat banging two fingers on an ancient black typewriter, which rang like a tram bell every time she took a wide swipe at the return arm. On the desk before her, lay the new edition of *Paris Match* with the full-face smiling portrait of 'La Belle Lady Di' on its cover. The typist's broad face was wrinkled with concentration and when Martin asked to see the *directeur*, she merely indicated a black plastic sofa where he would have to sit and wait. He sat, hemmed in by the exaggeratedly curved side wings which must have made it the height of fashion in the fifties. Now the cushions had deflated and a triangular rip revealed a brown spongy substance that someone had picked away.

Tack tack tack tack ping. The typewriter competed with the angry electric fault of two flies copulating on glass. He looked up and studied the large framed poster on the opposite wall. A grinning peasant couple, with a single chubby child, were surrounded by an array of consumer durables – a bicycle, a radio, a plastic bucket. Next to them stood their miserable counterparts, a glum couple with seven thin, ragged children and no goodies. The two flies zizzled ecstatically over the smallest of the children.

Tack tack tack tack ping. With a squeal of protesting ratchets the woman ripped the letter from the machine and bore it at arm's length to a door which she entered without knocking. A moment later she reappeared and beckoned him over. Martin rose too eagerly and left the seat with the noise of a wet fart. Stumbling with embarrassment he squeezed past her and found himself facing a desk, too large for the present occupant who was visible only from the shoulders up, his round, rather stern face, half hidden by pebble glasses and a full moustache. He was hardly much taller when he

rose to shake hands. A plastic strip at the front of the desk read
'FRANÇOIS-MARIE MAMADI', a souvenir of a conference, Martin
guessed.

The man's formal black suit looked forbidding despite the cuffs
covering half his hands, and Martin found himself reciting his name
and address as if he were in court.

'Please sit down, Mr Beresford.'

Martin had not expected English.

'You know my country?'

A curt nod before he went back to his papers.

Martin waited. The silence was disturbing. 'Did you like it?' he
asked, a hint of desperation in his voice.

Mamadi did not look up. 'My wife did. Will you excuse me while
I deal with an urgent matter?'

He did not wait but returned to the letter his secretary had
brought.

Martin tried to clear his mind of all that had happened, the town,
the fight, the *'Sauvages.'* He would have to make as good a case as
possible in what would probably be a very brief interview and tried
to summon up his arguments – the need to help an unfortunate
child, the love and care they could lavish on it, the advantages for
everyone – but the heat made ordered thought impossible. The
shutters must be closed to keep out the light but the gloom only
added to the sense of oppression in the leaden air, barely stirred by
an old four-blade fan that revolved dangerously about an open
ceiling hook. It was hard to see how Mamadi could be quite so alert
in this soporific cave, yet there he was, skip-reading the page in
front of him, scribbling corrections, flicking up the edges of a brown
file to double-check things on the wafery pink pages.

His desk was a triumph of organisation, the executive toys neatly
arranged: the little merry-go-round of rubber stamps, a see-saw
blotter, a space-rocket pen sticking out from a block of polished
malachite, the heavy bakelite telephone with letters as well as
numbers on the dial. Hanging behind him was a wall-size map of
the region varnished on to canvas, now yellowed and cracking as if
it too had suffered from *La Sécheresse*. It was a colonial leftover;
squared-off Art Deco letters proclaimed the territory *'LE SOUDAN
FRANÇAIS'*, a formless mass of empire without the current frontiers and with a mere half dozen roads, like red arteries, just visible
beneath its wrinkled skin. The stretched appendix scar of the single

railway line from Dakar to Bamako only emphasised the vast emptiness. It cowed Martin, especially the line of the great river which arched across it, spreading upwards from the coast of its southern neighbour to enter its borders through a thin strip of green that barely covered the narrow area around Bamako, after which the river ran through the browns of the savannah, before skirting the fringe of the vast yellow desert that yawned over most of the map like a giant cartoon speech-bubble with nothing to say. That yellow mass was disturbingly close. It seemed only a short distance to the first of the desert cities, way beyond which, across an unimaginable distance lay a tiny dot at the curve of the river, a place that must surely be the remotest human settlement on the planet, linked to the capital by a mere line of dots, not even a proper road, just a child's puzzle – join them and make a face – so fine Martin was forced to screw up his eyes to trace its thin meandering track and to squeeze out the infinitesimal printing which finally offered that mad, magical word: 'Tombouctou'.

'The desert,' said Monsieur Mamadi following his gaze. He signed the letter with a flourish, replaced the pen in its block, then clasped his hands on the desk before him to show that he was now giving his full attention to his visitor.

'Perhaps you wish to make a crossing? There are travel agencies who arrange this, though now it will be very very hot.'

Martin shook his head though it was hard to turn away from the great emptiness. He could just make out the tiny crosses at intervals down the dotted line – wells or camps? – the phrase 'just a dot on the map' sprang to mind.

'I don't think I was made for the Foreign Legion,' he said. 'With a map that size you see what it really means – it must be terrible out there, why would anyone go?'

'There are people who have to and people who want to? What else? But if you did not come to Africa for adventure, Monsieur, you came because you had to?'

But Martin was unwilling to risk the Look, unwilling to drag himself away from those desert spaces.

'The drought – La Sécheresse – it has been bad there – we saw the pictures on the television – there has been starvation?'

Mamadi shook his head. 'Foreign press reports were exaggerated. The situation is under control.'

'But the refugees?'

'It has been necessary to resettle the worst affected and that has been done. But that is not why you are here, Monsieur, and I have a meeting.'

'I was given the name of the *Centre* by a friend – my wife and I – we are on holiday but we wonder whether – you see – we can't have children and she – we – want to adopt and we thought that with the drought, after the pictures on the television . . .' He waited for the Look but it did not appear. Mamadi was staring straight at him, his expression blank. Martin blundered on: 'I have all the necessary documents – bank statements, medical report – we've had a home visit from Manchester Social Services . . .' Even as he said it he realised how ridiculous it sounded in that shuttered steaming room.

From outside there was a sudden barked order, presumably one of the soldiers. When Mamadi spoke he sounded bored.

'You are not the only one, Monsieur Beresford. The story is always the same: the pictures from the television of the drought and refugees when there are no refugees. It is all taken care of and anyway this is Africa. Families share, no child has not a family. And there is this . . .' He pulled open the drawer before him and lifted out a thin white brochure with an unmistakably British coat of arms.

'This is from your Ministry of Home Office.' He read slowly: 'Interracial adoption is not encouraged.' He put the document to one side. 'You see, even if you found a baby – and I think you will not – you could not bring it to your country. Your Ministry does not think that white people should bring up black babies, Monsieur.'

Martin looked away, how could those wretched bureaucrats be sending out such stuff? What did they think the reactions of someone like Mamadi would be on being told that white folk hadn't to bring black babies into their precious country?

'I am sorry . . .'

'Oh please no,' Mamadi said, smiling for the first time. 'Are they not right? Everybody has a home, no? And yours is so cold, I remember.'

'But if a baby is abandoned, if it is starving, surely.' He felt his anger rising. 'I don't care what that says, there are always ways round the rules. If we turn up with a baby we've saved they'd never be able to turn it away, they wouldn't dare.'

'Monsieur Beresford, for a long time they have been coming here, from America, from Sweden. There were two women from Birmingham . . .' he allowed himself a smile, evidently still amused by this. 'To all I say no babies.'

'If it's a question of money, I could always . . .'

Mamadi slowly raised a hand and Martin knew that he had made a mistake.

'It's for my wife,' he said weakly. The man's indifference was far worse than the Look. 'Surely if we went up country we might find something? The reports can't all be wrong, can they?'

'It is not possible to travel upriver just now – do not think of it. I will give you an application and I will let you know if any news of babies comes here.' Again he pulled open the drawer, this time handing over a set of pink forms interlaced with carbon paper. He rose to indicate that the interview was terminated. 'Remain by the swimming pool, Monsieur, enjoy your stay in Bamako. If there is news I will send for you. If not, go home with a nice sunburn.'

Before Martin could protest there was the sudden loud crack – a rifle shot. His head shrank into his shoulders but Mamadi looked more pained than concerned.

'Good day, Mr Beresford. I hope you have a pleasant sunshine break in my country.'

'That was a gunshot . . .'

'An accident, no one will have been hurt.'

'But who are those men, what are they doing?'

'They are doing their national service – all young men must do it. It is good for raising consciousness, for nation building. Now, if you will excuse me . . .'

They shook hands and Martin noticed he wore gold cufflinks shaped like top hats.

The receptionist had gone and when Mamadi closed the door behind him, Martin was left alone in the outer office to struggle with the form – names, addresses, first names of wife's grand-parents, occupation of paternal grandfather. After a second's hesitation he decided to make them up, Ebenezer and Hildegard sounded suitably antique. He made up more things: schools and jobs, past addresses, responses to questions about exams, taxes, social security details, all questions that could only have made sense to a French applicant. Slowly, the form evolved into a work of fiction as a strange character, half English, half French, grew across the thin pink page. But when Martin lifted a corner to check the copies, he found the carbons were so weak almost nothing had come through and he was forced to begin again, pressing his pen so hard on to the top page he created odd shadows and deep scratches as he went. Despite the pressure the last sheets were mere echoes of the original, no more than a thin purplish wispiness. By contrast, his fingers seemed to have been treated with gentian violet, so much carbon had rubbed off on his hands.

Irritably, he tossed the form on to the receptionist's desk, knowing full well he was wasting his time. The angry fly-buzzing was still going on, surely they hadn't been at it all this time – how long did flies fuck, for Christ's sake? Filthy dirty things making hundreds of germ-laden off-spring from one poke alone. He bent nearer to the glass and watched them skittering about in busy ecstasy. These were the black hairy variety, dirtier looking than the emerald glittery sort. He wondered if black hairies ever brought up emerald glittery babies and vice versa? He picked up the *Paris Match* from the desk, rolled Lady Di into a weapon and cautiously approached the glass – WHAP – the glass shuddered but the squelched mess confirmed his aim. The emaciated father with too many unwanted children had a nasty splatter of fly guk over his ragged shirt front. As he wiped the slime off the magazine, Martin felt pleased with himself. If he did nothing else for the people of Mali he had at least spared the poor beggars another litter of disease-ridden fly babies.

He went outside. The driver was already in his car, no doubt more terrified than ever.

'Les sauvages,' he said as Martin climbed in.

He fell back into the seat, beyond caring about the sticky heat. The man continued his tirade against the ragged soldiers, starting his vehicle with a noisy rasp and muttering away, his complaints suddenly rising to a loud bark as he succeeded in infuriating himself. They lurched off with a dangerous swerve. Whatever the man was saying, Martin felt sure he would agree with it – he, too, felt aggrieved at his treatment, at being so royally snubbed by Mamadi. He was also furious for being so easily rattled by that gunshot.

There was an angry yelp near Martin's window – they had almost run into a man shepherding a dozen scrawny goats down the centre of the road. Having left the hill at top speed, the driver showed little desire to slow down, despite the growing crowds closing in on his car. The goats were all round them now, panicking. Martin tried to outstare one lugubrious female, her teats sagging like a novelty condom. They were back in the people's Africa. A grim-faced man was selling what looked like gold beads, until he smiled and revealed a mouthful of his product. But who, Martin wondered, bought gold teeth like that? Did they pick one out and pop it in to try for size? Worse, were these little teeth, like so much in the market, second hand?

Ahead was another crowd though he could see that this was a performance of some kind – a man was standing at the centre of the circle, with a long, plump snake looped over his neck and coiled round his chest. The watchers were spellbound, if understandably wary, all eyes fixed on the hissing creature. The man held the tail in one hand while the other gripped the body just below the narrow scaly head, jabbing it towards the spectators, pushing the darting tongue and scimitar teeth at them, making them duck away shrieking. As he moved round, terrifying his audience, an assistant followed, holding up little folds of newspaper and calling out: 'Médicaments, médicaments. Messieurs, mesdames – si vous voulez un enfant, achetez un médicament.'

Martin was delighted – it was the old snake medicine-man, a timeless huckster, selling his potions, offering to make babies. It had a certain crude logic – the sinuous, thrusting serpent, the penetrating bite, the sharp venomous injection – and then the little packets with their helpful powder. Perhaps he should buy one for Alice – he could slip it in her tea. He smiled – his ears were filled with the engaging thump of electronic music, his eyes roamed over colour and movement. It was far from the Africa of rolling farms and game parks he had once imagined, but it was fine for all that, and as this sank in, he began to wonder if there might not be some way of holding on to it. Now that Mamadi had put an end to any hope of an official adoption, might Alice not be persuaded to find something else in this sweaty, vivid place? He looked up a side street piled with bundles of old clothing as if every charity shop in every charitable country had emptied its blessings on Bamako. The gifts were indiscriminate – woollen sweaters, thick roll-necked shirts, heavy dinner-jackets and embroidered ball gowns. Everybody gave something they didn't want to Africa, why couldn't they give him? There was always the British Council, a job for two years, maybe a sabbatical. It was the nicest plan so far.

They were speeding up again. A cyclist skidded away, yelling abuse but nothing deterred the hunched figure, groping the steering wheel, muttering his distress.

'*Sauvages*,' he mumbled. '*Sauvages*.'

Martin tried to ignore him, content to dream. In the time they had left they could look around, maybe find a school. Perhaps he could get into teacher-training or curriculum development.

He looked up. The driver had fallen silent, worryingly so. They were back in one of the market squares, only now the people were gone, the stalls overturned, fruit and vegetables spilled on to the road. A cart had shed a load of firewood – they swerved to avoid it and again Martin caught the driver's eyes in the mirror, this time glazed with terror.

'*Sauvages*,' he said, but now with low, bitter fury, gunning the car round the end of the square and heading back along the other side, trying to return the way they had come. He was not quick enough. A young boy in school uniform, white shirt, black shorts, came tearing out of a side street closely followed by an ominous figure in a crash-helmet with a black visor, wielding a long bamboo baton.

Martin's head whiplashed as the driver braked, throwing him over the front seat. Winded, he pulled himself back and saw that the boy was on the ground with the policeman straddling him, bringing down his baton with a sickening regularity – shwhap, shwhap, shwhap. The boy twisted and screamed, trying to protect his head from the blows. Blood was seeping through his fingers. More boys ran out of the side street, followed by a close group of baton-wielding toughs. The centre of the open square was marked off by a decorative line of small stone blocks. The first of the boys to reach these, bent and pulled one up, turned and threw it with all his force. Then they were all doing it – filling the air with arching bricks. A policeman stumbled. Two of his colleagues hauled him away and for a brief moment it looked as if the uniformed brigade was in full retreat. The boys jumped up and down, cheering. Then Martin heard a noise which made him think of party-poppers on New Year's Eve – thwop – thwop – thwop – then a metallic clatter as if someone was throwing saucepans into the street. Martin could see about a dozen gunmetal cannisters lying in the road. For a second that lasted an age, nothing seemed to happen. The cylinders lay where they had fallen, until with a lazy indifference, they began to ooze smoke, wispy at first, strands of grey and red, quite pretty, growing denser, then a billowing cloud everywhere at once. For a moment, Martin thought he would be safe inside the car, a mere spectator to this weird film unfolding outside. He saw one schoolboy stumble past, choking and vomiting, followed by an even more ominous figure in a gas mask, a terrible high-tech version of the carvings in the hotel boutique, a mechanical warrior appearing out of the deadly clouds swinging his unforgiving weapon.

But the car was a poor defence. It was dented and twisted from the pitted roads of the capital and what began with a vague smell of burning rubber, quickly intensified to a gagging ammoniac pong, a memory of school laboratories but a thousand times stronger. Martin began to cough and felt his eyes burning.

'Go! Go! Go!' he yelled in English, sure that terror alone would communicate his wishes.

Coughing and spluttering the driver struggled upright and had just enough control to start the car and ease it away. They could see little through the red-grey soup. They passed a masked figure hammering away at a stumbling boy whose face streamed with blood. Martin winced and doubled into his seat, choking and terrified. The cloud was thinning, they were leaving the square. Ahead a solid line of masked men, dream figures emerging out of the soft wall of gas, blocked their way. The driver was muttering again and this time Martin knew he was praying.

Please God, Martin said to himself, get me out of this and I'll do whatever you want. The line parted, and let them through.

The driver gunned down the open boulevard, took a turning at speed and bumped along a narrow dirt lane. They were not the first – a three-wheeled truck had fled this way, lost control and toppled on to its side, scattering sacks of rice which had burst over the piste like a demented wedding fête. The taxi rammed to a halt, the driver threw open his door, fell out, retching up his guts. On the opposite side, Martin followed, a vicious bile searing the back of his mouth, a thin stream of snot swinging from his nose. He retched again, then again, then once more, trying vainly to spit out the last bitter traces of the gas. He gripped his nose with his fingers and attempted to blow out his burning sinuses, covering his hands with a thick sticky phlegm so that when he reached up to wipe the acid tears from his eyes he spread vomit over his hair and cheeks.

Slowly, very slowly, he started to regain control of his breathing. Each gulp of air was painful but at least he was no longer choking.

111

He tried to straighten up – gently lest his stomach erupt again – and through his treacle-coated lashes saw that he was standing by a high metal railing and that he was the object of fascinated interest to a group of small white children who, judging by the flouncy taffeta and pretty-pretty ribbons of the girls and the scrubbed look of the boys, must have been having a party on the emerald lawn of the large white house behind them. They were all blonde and all dressed in white and they laughed and jumped up and down and tried to reach through the railing to tug at his clothes. It was no use, the bile was rising again. Martin lurched forward and felt thick vomit pour out of his mouth and nose, while he desperately tried to get air back into his lungs through his barking coughs. The children clapped their hands, what fun it was.

When the spasm passed, he saw a large black nanny, with starched apron and cuffs, trying to bustle away her charges. She flashed him a look of furious disapproval but Martin didn't give a toss. He had to drink something, had to get some water for his burning eyes, had to wash the acid out of his mouth. He staggered up to the heavy wrought-iron gates, stuck his hands through the bars, until he hit the latch and fell inwards on to the lawn. The nanny charged, urging forwards an enormous guard dressed like an American Brinks-Mat agent, though clearly unwilling to tackle a white man. Martin ignored them, peering towards the centre of the lawn where he could just make out a linen-draped table set with sandwiches and cakes and jellies and rows of bottles filled with brightly coloured liquids. He launched off, heading for this oasis, impervious to the hesitant guardian who had put a little pea-whistle between his lips and was making a noise like a berserk referee – any white man was a problem but a half-blinded, filthy, crazy white man was apocalyptic.

His hesitation was all Martin needed. With a last desperate lurch, he left the man gasping and staggered to the table. The children had got there before him, jumping up and down, laughing and chortling at the sheer wonder of it, delighted to watch Martin fall forward and steady himself by squelching his hand into something sticky – a cake or a jelly. Then he saw it – a great cut-glass punch bowl filled with a rich, ruby liquid. This was no time for niceties, he simply lowered his head straight into it and slurped. It tasted like cherryade. He splashed some into his eyes. It felt wonderful. He palmed great gulpfuls into his mouth and sniffed some up through his nose. He felt he had never tasted anything so good, so delicious. He did it again. Happier, he lifted his sticky hand and licked it, easing his burning throat with a soothing ooze of *crème pâtissière*. He sighed. Life was possible.

A little hand was tugging at his trouser leg. He looked down at the entranced face of a girl, about seven years old, her blonde hair hung in two plaits tied with pink ribbons, the ideal towards which Alice aspired with Baby, soft, simpering, pinkly girlish. He smiled at her and looked around. The house was impeccable, brilliantly white, its shutters thrown back to reveal shady rooms set with polished tables, well-padded sofas, brass lamps, flawless mirrors. The garden was tropical heaven, its borders set with dwarf palms, and orchids, overhung with the heady aroma of jasmine.

He was not to enjoy it in peace. The nanny was coming his way and even through his misty vision he could make out a look of fearsome determination on her face. She had even managed to galvanise the guard, who was hurrying after her. It was time to go. Martin lifted the heavy cut-glass bowl with both hands and lumbered off towards the gate, the red liquid slurping round his wrists.

The driver was sitting in the dust, propped against the car, vainly trying to rub the pain out of his eyes. Martin put the bowl in his lap and splashed cherryade over his face. The man cooed with relief and began to help himself but this moment of peace was quickly shattered – an enraged female voice was shouting at them from somewhere nearby. It was a shrill tirade in a language Martin could not understand but which he guessed might be Scandinavian. He screwed up his eyes and made out a middle-aged woman standing at the gates, hands on hips, giving full vent to her fury – a tall, blonde Viking in a girlish folk-weave dress with puff-ball sleeves but with an aggressive stance and tone which proclaimed loudly that she was well used to being obeyed. The coat of arms on the gatepost made it clear that hers was a diplomatic residence and it was easy to assume that she was the ambassadress and thus hostess of the children's party. Martin picked up the punch bowl, walked over and thrust it out making her hands come up automatically to save it. There was a burst of Scandawegian outrage at this rudeness but he was already back at the car and climbing in. The guard had come out, no doubt keen to show his mistress that he was doing his job, and began barking orders at the driver who reluctantly lurched back into his vehicle and started it up. The children ran to the fence to wave them off and Martin pulled the rudest face he could manage, before sinking back and letting it all drift away.

When he opened his eyes again, he saw that they were weaving through the road block at the entrance to the hotel. There seemed to be even more guards than before but no one bothered about Martin's taxi and it was with considerable relief that he found himself outside the great glass doors, a uniformed flunky waiting to ease him back into the cool, protected world. Martin pulled out a note, an ancient stained thing, held together with a piece of brittle sellotape but which clearly said '5000' in large numbers. What this meant, Martin did not know but felt it had to be reasonable. The driver took it, lifted it to his lips and kissed the face engraved on one side. At first Martin thought he was excessively grateful, even for so large a sum, then it dawned on him that the note had been in circulation for so long it must predate the revolution and that the image the man had embraced was not that of the current leader.

'*Vous aimez?*' Martin said.

'Oui, oui,' the man said, nodding vigorously, a hint of life returning to his face.

How odd, Martin thought, they rise up against him, topple his statue, hack him to bits and now they love him.

The man drove off just as a six-door Mercedes slid up and Delmonico climbed out – not the funny, garrulous Delmonico of the poolside chat, but Delmonico the man of affairs, transformed by a light grey suit, obviously Italian, unpadded and hanging loosely from the shoulders with just a slight concession to the hips. It was held by a low-slung double-breasted button. The shirt, tie and prominent pocket handkerchief were all a rich red, as was the ring he now wore, a ruby of episcopal proportions on his right index finger. Despite all this, he looked out of sorts, though he brightened somewhat when he saw Martin.

'You look awful,' Delmonico announced.

'Tear gas, filthy choking stuff. I've been puking like an old drunk.'

Delmonico looked very interested.

'Red and grey smoke, was it?'

Martin nodded. 'Why?'

'Bulgarian. Cheap and nasty. The old government got a job lot about ten years ago when the Bulgarians stopped using it – too dangerous, same stuff as Agent Orange.' He shook his head as if bemoaning the unlimited folly of mankind, though Martin found his philosophising less than convincing.

'You wouldn't be the one who found it for them, would you?'

'Never thought they'd actually use it. Even during the revolution they kept it under lock and key, someone must have forgotten the embargo when the riot started.'

'Riot?' Martin spluttered. 'What riot? It was only a bunch of schoolkids – there was no need to *napalm* them.' He started to cough again, his agitation irritating an already raw throat.

'Steady on,' said Delmonico. 'Breathe deep – there – like that – in – out – that's it.'

Martin straightened, his breath coming easier, the pain receding slightly.

'What is going on? Why are they beating up schoolboys?'

'Schoolboys can be anything up to thirty years old here – they start late, particularly in the villages. They just look young. It was the *lycéens* who started the previous revolution, so they won't take any chances this time. Who was doing the head bashing?'

'Police in riot gear by the look of them.'

'Then your schoolboys were lucky. If it had been the soldiers from up country, I doubt there'd be anyone around to tell the tale.'

'*Les Sauvages du Nord*,' Martin said, pleased to be abreast of developments.

Delmonico smiled. 'Yes, that's what the people here call them. Up country boys. Not very – how shall we put it? – sophisticated. As long as they keep them off the drink we should be OK. Otherwise . . .'

He moved towards the double doors and paused to let the uniformed flunky pull them open for him.

'So you saw our little Mister Mamadi,' Delmonico was saying. 'Smug bastard, isn't he?'

'You knew that all along.'

'Our paths have crossed. Did you try to offer him money? It's one of life's more embarrassing moments, isn't it? He's MRN – *Mouvement pour la Renaissance Nationale* – grew out of the *Jeunesse Africaine*. François-Marie Mamadi was *Secrétaire Général* until the revolution. Then they all had to lie low for a while, now they've resurfaced as the MRN – and a fucking nuisance they are!'

He said this with such vehemence a group of white women

115

studying the display in the boutique window turned to see what the trouble was.

'Mamadi is a disaster. He doesn't play according to the rules – Malian rules, that is.'

'Doesn't make sense,' Martin said. 'Why should someone so dedicated, so incorruptible, be stuck in a wooden shack running the Family Planning Bureau?'

'Ah, you've already forgotten what I told you. Nothing is what it says it is – his real job is the *Aménagement du Pays* and for that you can read getting control over the provinces again – they broke away during the troubles and haven't shown much inclination to return to the old order when everything was run from Bamako. Mamadi can't really do anything until he gets control of the army and that means getting control of the Ministry of Defence.'

Martin felt any remaining shred of patience slipping away. 'So why did you send me off to see him if you knew it was so useless?'

Delmonico fluttered his lashes again and the penny dropped.

'Good God,' Martin said. 'It's you, isn't it? You're the one – you're the representative of *Les Enfants du Monde*, Mantock said you were unmissable?'

Delmonico nodded. 'Have to be sure you know what you want,' he said. 'Had to let you see what you're up against – what we're *all* up against. There are stages – first you decide to have a holiday, then you decide you want a baby after all, but then you think you'll try and do it all legal like. Now it's the fourth stage – me!' He smiled with mock modesty. 'I spend my time here doing deals and not the sort of thing that would get me the Rotarian-of-the-Year Award but I've never made the mistake a lot of White Trash make, in thinking that the Malians are just a bunch of savages who'll do anything for money. Ergo, I know what I'm up against.'

'So what do I do now?'

Delmonico rubbed his thumb over the first two fingers of his right hand.

'Money?' Martin said. 'But I thought . . .?'

'Not here in Bamako, not with the likes of little Mamadi. Outside, over the hills and far away.'

'But we aren't allowed to travel.'

Again the thumb and finger gesture.

'How much?'

'You'll need five hundred dollars US for a start.'

116

He held out a hand, casually, as if asking for a cigarette. Martin balked.

'Five hundred dollars?'

'It's the fare – or rather, it's what's needed to get you out of town and back again, which amounts to the same thing. You don't have to give it to me now, if you haven't got it on you. Just make sure you give it to the driver tomorrow morning, early – say half five. He'll be waiting outside in a *taxi-brouse* – bush taxi to you – oh, don't look so gormless, that's just the start. There'll be a plane, it's all laid on and you might even get back tomorrow night. That will cost three thousand dollars – but you don't have to hand that over until you've landed – when you're there give it to the pilot. The rest of the deal is up to you, how much and when you pay depends on the bargain you strike. Take what you need for two nights maximum just in case – and don't ask where. I still don't trust you completely – it's for you to trust me. Just take it as it comes.'

Martin was longing to ask why he was doing all this but guessed there must be a built-in percentage.

As if in response to the unspoken question, Delmonico pulled a thick brick-shaped envelope out of his back pocket and handed it to Martin.

'I want you to give this to a man called Maktar Diop.'

Martin's eyes narrowed. 'Another Diop?'

Delmonico laughed. 'Yes, I can see it must all sound a little peculiar but this a big Diop – well biggish. He's a nephew of the General who's on trial but don't let that bother you. Just give him the package – yes, it's money. I owe him on a deal that's all. Don't worry, it'll make him all the sweeter, it could make all his dreams come true and yours too. You'll enjoy the trip. Uncomfortable it's true, but that aside, it's everything you've ever imagined and more. Mali is a beautiful place despite its problems, and anything has to be better than lying around here with these roasting pigs. Ah, Freddy . . .'

He had seen someone across the foyer. Martin turned and saw a young Malian in a loose Hawaiian shirt decorated with blue yachts in full sail, gripped at the waist by a pair of ultra-tight jeans.

'Freddy!' Delmonico called out. *'J'arrive.'* He was off, shouting back to Martin over his shoulder: 'Your driver's name is Abdel-Kadar.'

Martin's spirits sank. He had a sudden image of a wizened, sun-baked, wily old camel-drover, haggling over baksheesh, somewhere miles from anywhere. He walked over to the lift, glad there was no one around to stare at him. As it rose, he felt limp – too much had happened too quickly. He fiddled with his key in the lock but it didn't want to turn, then gave with a sudden jolt that sent him stumbling into the room. The curtains were drawn but even in the gloom he could see that someone had cleaned up and laid their things on the dressing table and cupboard with a geometric order that reminded him of Mamadi's desk. The smell was different too, a chemical spray – Austrian Pine? English Garden? Dutch Bulb Field? In the dimness he could just make out the doll, seated on the chest of drawers. He went over to look, more puzzled than ever. It was that blasted Baby with her sad face, yet all knitted out like a rustic nymphomaniac.

He turned towards Alice, stretched out under the sheets. He knew she was awake, waiting for him and he wanted to put on the lights and ask her just what she was thinking about. They didn't need to go on with this joyless business, not now that he'd got things clear with Delmonico. He could tell her, tell her there was another solution. But seeing her lying there, waiting, intent on this last fragment of hope, he knew he must not speak – not yet.

He yanked up his T-shirt and again caught the ripe smell of acrid vomit. Christ, he thought, I stink. He was dusty and sticky but he couldn't be bothered to wash – he would have to shower after-wards, so why waste time. He threw off his pants, carefully avoiding the chair where Baby modestly faced the window; there had been a row a few weeks ago when he 'smothered' her with his shirt.

Saying his usual prayer that it would all happen, he got into the bed beside Alice and lay immobile for a moment waiting for the necessary image that might carry him through.

Unsurprisingly, all he could think of was the thin, bustless figure of the Japanese woman in her tight swimsuit, standing motionless in the pool, her pale skin clear as white Chablis in sunlight, her nervous heartbeat ticking just beneath the surface. More surpris-ingly, it worked.

FOUR

Martin felt his breathing return to normal. He glanced at his watch, it was still early evening. He was glad to have got through it. Now, he was safe for the rest of their stay, a month before he need gear himself up for another bout. He felt quite chirpy.

'We ought to be languidly blowing smoke through our noses,' he said. 'Not just lying here waiting to go for a piss. It's what they do in the movies.'

'Used to.' She switched on her bedside light. 'Now they don't smoke.'

'Well, they haven't come up with anything else.'

She sniggered. 'That's 'cause they couldn't show bonking before. You just got a bit of a grope then you saw them dragging on a fag like it was the last gasper.'

She got off the bed and turned to look at him. 'Good grief, I thought there was a pong from somewhere but I had no idea it was you. How did you get that disgusting mess all over you?'

He told her at length: the weird taxi ride through the crowded town, the embarrassing encounter with Mamadi, the *sauvages* guarding the President, the riot, the tear gas, the children's party.

'A complete waste of time,' he concluded. 'Mamadi's a typical bureaucrat, he'll never get off his arse to get anything done – why should he help us? What can we ever do for him, except make his life difficult?'

It was an unjust assessment of the straight-laced little Mamadi and he knew it, but he still felt humbled by the encounter and needed to save face, if only verbally. It was all right him saying it was all exaggerated and that the government had taken care of everything, but who was going to believe him? As he told Alice: if there was any moral right, then it had to be on their side, not Mamadi's.

He looked for approval but was disappointed to see that she was barely listening – she had picked up Baby and was fiddling with the buttons on the back of the tight little dress.

'Are you listening?' he demanded tetchily.

'Sorry?'

'I said, are you listening?'

She sighed slowly, blowing out her lips, and when she finally spoke he had to strain to hear.

'It doesn't sound to me as if you're too put out. Oh, sure, you had a rough time, but I haven't heard any regrets that you didn't succeed in what you set out to do. You know, Martin, I'm beginning to think you don't really want a child.'

'Of course I do – if it makes you happy.'

'That's not what I meant. Do *you* want a child?'

'Yes,' he said, as resolutely as possible.

Alice lifted her right hand and massaged her temples, the thumb and middle finger pressing hard, as if she might somehow rearrange the ripple of convoluted thought channels she imagined her brain to be.

'You didn't let me finish,' Martin insisted, sounding genuinely aggrieved. 'When I got back I found our man – the *Enfants du Monde* rep. Turns out to be somebody I'd already met by the pool – the very man who'd suggested I go see this Mamadi character. You see he was trying to weigh me up, testing me out – almost trying to put me off, trying to get me to go round and do it myself with no help from him. He probably wanted to be sure I wasn't from Interpol or whatever. He's a weird character, name of Delmonico, though he claims to be Scottish. From what I can gather, he seems to be mixed up in everything, some of it quite dodgy. There's something going on here, something nasty and I think he's mixed up in that too.'

Alice sagged. 'So where does that leave us?'

'Oh, he says he'll fix us up now that I've proved myself. That's the good news – we're off. It means travelling out of Bamako. He wouldn't say where though. I guess it has to be somewhere where the likes of Mamadi can't interfere – what price Timbuktu? Oh, all right, no more jokes if it upsets you so much. All I know is that someone called Abdel-Kadar will collect us, early morning, half-past five outside the hotel. He'll drive us somewhere out of town.'

'And what else?'

He looked sheepish.

'You mean to tell me you don't know?' She set the doll down in the chair. 'You mean to say that we are about to launch off into the bush without so much as a clue as to where we're going? You're bonkers.'

Martin winced. 'There's a plane involved – oh, just a short hop. Delmonico thought we'd be back by nightfall. At the most two days – it really didn't sound that much of a deal to me. A tour if you like. Depends on how you choose to look at it. If we make a good start I'm sure we'll be back in this bed in twenty-four hours – I promise.'

He stopped as she began to shake her head, slowly and emphatically.

He tried wheedling. 'We'll just take a look that's all, no commitment, just a look . . .'

'That's exactly what I meant,' she said, clearly upset. 'You want to go because you want to see more of your precious Africa, I'm just the excuse. You'll be quite happy if we get out there and nothing comes of it, just as long as you've had your blasted safari. Christ, you're transparent, Martin.'

'That's not fair.'

She considered the accusation and recognised a grain of truth in it.

'The whole thing's bothering me,' she said.

'And that means . . .?'

'It means the whole thing, the whole baby thing. The failure bit, the feeling that the whole genetic history of the human race comes to a full stop here.' She jabbed at her stomach and the sharp movement nudged the chair, so that Baby seemed to nod in agreement.

This was too much for Martin. It was as though they were ganging up on him.

'I've never thought that,' he protested.

'Then why did we try to adopt a child? What are we doing here?'

'It was the tests – it was all so clinical, like some sort of experiment. That laparoscopy was the end. It hurt you and I kept thinking it was my fault, that I'd done it to you. I couldn't bear it. That's why I wanted us to go down the adoption route, it was less artificial. I mean, you don't have to have it pop out of you, do you?'

He walked to the window and looked down. Somewhere below, out of sight, where the bridge met the bank, the young boys would be laughing and yelling and jumping, chin to knees, till they exploded on the water.

'People do it all the time,' he said. 'With a drought like this it has to be a good thing. Delmonico says he can do it despite bloody Mamadi.'

'I don't believe in it,' Alice said with a clipped finality that made him turn and look at her.

'What are you on about now?'

'Adoption. I don't really think it's OK. It's always second best. Nobody wants to adopt – they have to.'

'Nonsense. Some people adopt a second child after they've had one of their own . . .'

'Precisely,' she said. 'One of their own . . .'

She could see herself in the supermarket with her little black bundle seated in a maternity trolley, dumpy black legs sticking out through the holes while busy hands tried to pick up the smaller items of shopping to throw them out to left and right. And there she would be, gathering them up, cootchy-cooing, a member of the mothers' club at last. Or would she? It would not be her baby, would it? It would be a little black baby, and thus all too obviously somebody else's baby. She would only be masquerading as a mother. Instead of taking someone else's child from a pram left outside the store, she would have gone all the way to Africa for the hijacking, but it would amount to the same thing.

'We'd better get some sleep,' she said, suddenly exhausted with thinking. 'It's eight o'clock and we'll have to be up by four.'

'So you're on for it?'

'Yes.'

'So why all the fuss?'

She shrugged. 'Why be easy? If you felt the way I do you'd spread it around a bit too.' She set the alarm for four, then picked up the room service menu. 'We'd better get something to eat, God knows when we'll next have the chance given how vague this all is.'

'Sandwiches and beer will do. And you'd better give me any details he did condescend to let you know – he must have said something about money at least?'

Martin rattled off the various sums they were expected to fork out and wished he'd had the gumption to insist on being told more.

An unsmiling figure in a white tuxedo brought them club sandwiches and *Bière du Peuple*.

'No rose,' Alice said as he left. She lay back on the bed chomping on the thick little triangles, trying not to think too much about what they were planning to do, afraid she might trigger off another wave of self-doubt. 'I was wondering,' she said evenly. 'In all these years together, have you ever slept with anyone else? Even once?'

'Yes.'

She stiffened: 'Oh, I thought you'd say no. Why did you say yes?'

'Why did you ask?'

'I don't know.'

'And I don't know why I said yes.'

'Who was it?'

'A supply teacher. She called herself Maona – can't have been her real name. We did it standing up in the store room at the back of the biology lab – you can get the picture: a foetus in a bottle, the locusts in a glass box waiting to be asphyxiated, the smell of formaldehyde . . .'

'You're making it up.'

'Of course I am.'

'Now I'll never know the truth.'

'You wouldn't have done anyway, I'm not strapped to a lie-detector, am I? Would it matter if I had?'

'Yes and no.'

'Oh brilliant, really brilliant. Very well I did – in the stationery cupboard, as it happened. Nothing very gruesome or symbolic there, unless humping against a rack of lined quarto exercise books with mathematical tables and an avoirdupois conversion chart on the covers has some deep inner meaning that has so far eluded me.'

Alice started laughing. 'Oh God, you are a nerd sometimes . . . so what did she look like?'

'Who?'

'This Maona you shagged in the stationery cupboard?'

Martin thought, just long enough to make it quite clear he was going to tell a lie: 'Dolly bird; Vidal Sassoon hair, backcombed and sprayed like a Trojan battle helmet; crushed velvet loon pants – purple with an exposed zip up the bum and a diaphanous cheese-cloth shirt that she'd tie-dyed herself in rather splotchy pink sunbursts. Oh, and no knickers.'

Alice shrieked, 'very handy in a cupboard. Oh stop it, I've got a stitch.'

It was still dark when Martin left the hotel. The car was alone on the drive. Above its dramatically curved windscreen a wooden headboard proclaimed '*Abdel Darwesh et Fils, Transports Sahariens*' in hand-painted red letters, shadowed with green.

A slight, youthful figure, little more than a boy, got out of the driver's side and half bowed.

'*M'sieur*,' he said, coming round to open the rear door.

It was breathtaking: an old Mercedes, swollen and streamlined like a fifties Cadillac, its radiator and bumpers gaudy bands of chrome, countered by a solid-looking rack, roughly screwed into the roof, strapped up with thick-ribbed jerry-cans. Roped over a boot with raised chrome fins were an extra set of wheels with very solid tank tracks. The young driver wore a short djebba of the same blue as his car; his face was thin with high cheek bones, his complexion little more than a light tan; a shiny white skull-cap, tight on the back of his head.

'Abdel-Kadar?' Martin said.

The boy smiled and held the door wider. Martin got in.

The interior was opulent, smelling of old leather and fresh-cut jasmine. He sank into well-padded seats and took in the polished rosewood trimmings with handles and nobs in early plastic which had taken on the patina of old ivory.

The one disquieting element was Abdel-Kadar himself, so young, his profile an Egyptian figurine; Nefertiti if you put a little kohl around his astonishingly clear dark eyes with their impossibly long lashes.

The boy flashed a look in the mirror.

'*Je suis Marocain. De Meknès*,' he said.

Martin let that sink in. Delmonico went up a few notches in his estimation, everything he had said was coming true. He hoped Alice wouldn't be long and that she wouldn't bring that damned doll with her.

'Where are we going?' he said. '*Où allons-nous?*'

The boy turned, grinning, and put a finger over his lips.

'You can tell me now,' Martin said, irritably. 'We're about to leave, what harm can it do?'

But there was no way of knowing if any of that had got through – the boy still said nothing, turning back and switching on the radio which gave out a lilting Arabic song. A word that sounded like *nahaam* was repeated over and over in a hypnotic chorus. The boy swayed gently, moving his shoulders to the sharp tam-tam beat. Martin could imagine him dancing rather well, hisnarrow body moving sinuously to the wailing pipe and the singer's falsetto descant with its repeated 'Nahaam, nahaam, nahaam . . .'

Martin looked at his watch. It was half-five, they ought to be getting away.

Alice was emptying her bag on to the bed. She stuffed the everyday essentials like tooth brushes into one of her side pockets and divided the money into different piles. Martin had told her five hundred dollars for the car and three thousand for the plane; she separated them into two pockets, but the real question was how much for the . . . She shook her head, even thinking about it like this seemed impossibly crude, yet what could she do? Mantock had said it might be ten thousand but she knew too well her inability to think straight with a baby in her arms. If she only took half, then they would all have to cool down and wait. That decided, she stuffed the wad of dollars into the narrow pocket of a money belt and strapped it under the waist of her jeans, then picked up Baby, opened the back of the little gown and forced the remaining five thousand dollars and the rest of the traveller's cheques and any English money into the tiny knickers, then rebuttoned the dress. Opening the top drawer of the clothes cupboard, she laid the doll inside, trying to make everything look as casual as possible, tossing around a few socks and underpants to complete the picture. That done she went to the door, stepped into the corridor and found herself facing a somewhat ragged Margot.

'Night on the tiles,' she said, her speech slightly slurred. 'Dancing with a Swede called Thor, if you please.' She giggled. 'Was that your hubby I saw crossing the foyer? He looks very busy for someone who's supposed to be on holiday. Off for a fling in the *bidonville*, is he? They always want to sow their oats when they can't have kids of their own – it reassures them.'

'I don't think he does want kids, really. That's what's worrying me. I'm beginning to suspect this whole thing is just to get me off his hands.'

'What whole thing?' Margot said, her glance taking in Alice's travel clothes and registering the fact that while it might be late to be coming back it was equally too early to be going out.

Alice paused, then a sort of devilry took hold of her – it would be quite something to tell Margot just what they were up to.

'We're off up country,' she said, struggling to keep her face straight.

Margot's brow furrowed. 'That's not allowed,' she said.

'I know, but we're going anyway – you see we're not really on holiday. We came here because we want to adopt a baby – one of those abandoned orphans you see on the telly – you know, in those programmes about the drought and the refugees. Anyway, we've found someone who says he can help, so we're off to . . .' She stopped. The look of abject horror that had suffused Margot's face was so hilarious, there was no point in even trying to go on.

For a moment Margot seemed intent on clearing her fuddled brain, as if the last traces of alcohol needed to be squeezed out before this new element could seep in.

'I get it,' she said. 'You're trying to save your marriage, you're worried he'll go off – they can of course, that's the injustice – you've got the old biological clock ticking away; he can father a kid when he's too old to lift it – as someone said about someone . . . Christ, I'm pissed.'

'It was Charlie Chaplin actually, he was seventy something, but no, that isn't the reason. Oddly enough our marriage was fine until this baby thing started up. I think if I went down and told Martin it was off, and that this was the end of the search, and that we could just settle down and live together and not bother about kids anymore, he'd actually be quite relieved. But I can't, Margot, and you can't understand.

Margot opened her mouth, then as quickly closed it. Alice walked past, grateful that the lift door was open and that there was no need for any sort of pay off. As the door swished shut Margot raised a hand and gave a tentative tipsy wave but Alice's mind was elsewhere – her mettle was up and the journey ahead was all that mattered now.

Walking under the great chandelier was like auditioning to an unseen gallery and she wondered if they ever extinguished it or whether it just glowed eternally, independent of the hotel's more mundane functions. It made the darkness outside more bleak and impenetrable, until she saw the gorgeously improbable blue Mercedes, another part of this film she seemed to be making. Where there ought to have been a liveried chauffeur, there was only a boy in a light blue shift who leapt out to hold open her door, with a smile that was wide and innocent but with eyes that examined her like a tax inspector.

Martin made the introductions. The car slid away with barely a tremor.

'He's too young,' Alice said. 'Has he let on where we're going?'

Martin shook his head. 'Doesn't make much difference, does it? Wherever it is we have to do what we're told. It's odd really, like being one of my own pupils. I'd forgotten what it's like not having full control over your life, just having people order you about – do this – do that – shut up – speak when you're spoken to – do as I say, not as I do. On the other hand, it's quite relaxing – no?'

Alice said nothing, she was looking beyond him, out of the window at her first real sight of the town. They had turned away from the river but, cleared of their market bustle, the streets were now a different world. Squalor had receded, Alice was aware of fanciful colonial buildings in a pseudo-Moorish style, square built and russet coloured to echo the great mud mosques of the north, the roofline crenellated, their shuttered windows and doors onion-arched in the Arabic manner. Under the mottled glimmer of the street lights it all had a ghostly charm. The Deco lettering and the geometric decoration, raised images of bored colonial wives in flapper dresses, of young officials on their first tour, in starched collars despite the heat, of too many sticky cocktails and sweaty infidelity under a mosquito net. Alice smiled at her rabid imagination but was glad that her humour had returned.

They bumped over a railway crossing and followed the track out of town. Elegance soon fell away, they were beyond the lit streets in a scruffier world of real mud houses, small and undecorated, alongside shacks of fractured wood and rusting corrugated iron, shanties clinging to the city's edge, still silent in the hour before dawn.

Ahead lay a brilliant pool of white light and beside it a long, low, crenellated wall – a toy castle with watch-towers at each end and solid looking steel doors exactly at the centre. Abdel-Kadar eased the car to a gentle halt, and waited.

Martin looked up – the guard in the far watch-tower had his gun trained on them.

'I think we need the money,' Martin said.

Alice delved into her pocket and came up with the five hundred dollar bills. Martin passed them over the seat to the boy. On cue, one of the heavy doors eased back and a soldier stepped out.

For a second Alice thought it was the same man from the airport – same tall thin body, same uniform, same dark Raybans. Then she saw that the mouth was smaller, the lips thinner, the potential for death more obvious: a gun, knife and hand-grenade swinging from his belt as he walked towards the car. The window went down, out went the money. The figure took it, turned, and walked back. Alice watched the retreating rear, the shirt rucked up, the sway of the hips, the endless legs, the narrow camouflaged trousers caught in heavy ankle boots. Nothing had been said, it had been as neutral as paying a toll on a motorway.

The door closed. They were alone before the secret castle again and Martin wondered how many eyes were watching them from the dark embrasures.

'Afraid?' he said.

'Yes. And you?'

'Terrified. We could always go back.'

She laughed, settling her head on his shoulder. 'If it's a boy, what shall we call him?'

'Barry,' he said.

'*Barry*! What a nerdy idea, I do wonder about you sometimes. And if she's a girl?'

'If she's a girl then it's Olivia.'

'Olivia. That's lovely. Olivia. Sort of grand but exotic, just right when you think about it. Olivia. Well, it had better be a girl.'

She closed her eyes and tried to picture little Olivia, her tiny hands, the soft dark skin, the deep black eyes.

She woke with a bump as the car rolled from side to side trying to steady itself. They had left the fractured tarmac and were bumping along a ridged track. Her watch said seven, the sky was pink. There was a faint pinpoint of light ahead and as they approached she saw it was an oil-lamp swinging from a branch overhanging the road. She was just about to ask why, when Abdel-Kadar slowed and turned into a clearing, stopping beside an ancient hand-cranked petrol pump.

They got out. The ground was black with oil and pocked with greasy puddles. Around the edges of the compound were ragged heaps of rusting metal parts and pyramids of worn tyres. Beside the petrol pump was a Jules Verne machine, a sort of die-press mounted on ornate cabriole legs. A detumescent inner tube was draped over the turntable, a new red patch cooling on its matt black skin, the acrid smell of burning rubber still hanging in the air.

'It's a vulcaniser,' Martin said with childish delight. 'This place is a museum.'

Abdel-Kadar gave a burst on the horn and a man emerged from a gap in the trees rubbing the sleep from his eyes. His frayed vest and shorts were smeared with ancient grease stains; the oil had seeped into the lines of his face and left blackened half-moons under his worn finger nails. He must have been sleeping like that, filthy and reeking of petrol, as if he had submerged himself totally into the world of the machine. Without being told he inserted the nozzle, reached for the lever and began to pump with a mechanical rhythm, raising and lowering the handle with comatose regularity, sending the fuel chortling and gurgling into the tank, spinning the merry little spiral in its yellow measuring glass.

'You see,' Martin said. 'Look at him, he's jumped from the Stone Age to the Machine Age in one leap, and they say it isn't possible.'

'What are you talking about?'

'I'm talking about us – about Barry or Olivia or whoever. This guy has managed it – he's up to his neck in the twentieth century.'

'Perhaps he needs a little modern plumbing . . .'

'That's not the point.'

Abdel-Kadar came back with three coke bottles. Martin took a mouthful and choked, it tasted of old-fashioned cough mixture. The bottle was American, the contents home-made. Whatever it was, the boy gulped it down with a relish both gluttonous and sensual. He had hitched two fingers under the collar of his djebba, raising it a few inches to air himself and Martin realised he must be naked under the flimsy shift, and quickly turned away, pulling out a note and pushing it towards the pump-attendant without checking what it was worth. The loud outburst of profuse thanks told him it had been far more than was needed but he was too muddled to care. He turned but found his way blocked by two old women, squatting on the ground at his feet, twenty or so green mangoes spread before them.

At first he was astonished at their silent arrival and confused by the sight of their naked shrivelled breasts. They stared back at him equally intrigued, one picking her nose with two dirty cracked nails, the other volubly chewing betel with large, widely spaced teeth, the colour and shape of grapefruit pips. Martin bent down and poked some of the fruit, hoping this was the correct thing to do. They seemed soft, but was that good or bad? Abdel-Kadar was quickly at his side and bargaining furiously. Martin selected four of the mangoes then settled back to watch the fun. The nose-picker shook her head and Abdel-Kadar went into a long wheedling speech before making what Martin assumed was a higher offer. It was all a bit exaggerated given what he must have paid for the tank of petrol but the boy was so obviously enjoying himself it seemed mean to spoil his fun. Offers were made and refused, gestures struck, heads shaken in parodic disbelief until the betel-chewer suddenly spat out a fizzing red gobbet that travelled an incredible distance before landing in the dust and which was undoubtedly the ultimate refusal. The boy shrugged and turned to leave, casually dropping another offer out of the side of his mouth. The nose-picker suddenly stopped and nodded, a bargain had been struck.

'Trois centimes,' the boy said proudly.

Martin felt in his pocket but there was nothing so small. Up till then he had dealt only in denominations of fifty francs. He held out a palm full of nickel but there was nothing that looked less than twenty-five. He gave a coin to the nose-picker who began to smile and nod furiously whereupon Abdel-Kadar leapt forward and raked in all the mangoes. Martin was about to protest but everyone seemed happy so he let it pass.

The garage owner produced a newspaper and the boy dumped this parcel of fruit on to the front seat. 'No need to worry about supplies,' Martin explained to Alice but she had drifted into sleep again.

'Is it much further?' he asked as they pulled away.

The boy shrugged.

'Who is Maktar Diop?'

The large dark eyes flicked up to the mirror.

'Maktar Diop,' Martin insisted. 'You must know who I mean?'

'Many Diop.'

'Not any Diop, *Maktar* Diop. What is he?'

'We come soon.'

Martin gave up. He would find out quickly enough, the trees were thinning which could only mean that they were speeding into the open savannah. He dozed a little but was shaken back to life, dry and uncomfortable. He tried to picture the map in Mamadi's office with its tiny dotted line traversing the narrow green strip before plunging into the huge yellow wasteland – at least it had seemed narrow on the map, now he saw how vast it really was. The sky was an immense palette of oranges and yellows below which the grasslands rolled away in all directions, burned-out russet and boring and after a moment's vague resistance his head fell to his chest and sleep returned.

Alice was woken by bright sunshine falling on her closed eyes, making dark red hairs curl and dance in a viscous pink fluid. She unglued her eyelids letting in the dazzling whiteness of the day. There were no trees, just the odd stunted bush, an isolated speck against the flat brown and darker reds of the dry tundra, the colours of *La Sécheresse*, dusty and dispiriting.

She leant forward and spoke to the boy. 'How much further?'

'Soon.'

'How soon?'

'Soon.'

She sank back, dismayed at the fragile link between them. It was nine o'clock, five wearying hours since the alarm had begun their day and no way of knowing how much longer this shuddering and bumping might last.

Martin was dreaming water – shifting, light-dappled water. Beneath its silvery surface the Japanese woman swam, naked and agile, turning in time to the twisting strings of sunlight. Martin dived in and sank down beside her, gyrating his body with hers, corkscrewing together just above the light-blue tiles. He let himself drift nearer so that their legs and arms gently touched, but as he reached out to enfold her she turned and dived and he began to rise to the surface, floating away from her, up, up, until he found himself staring into the sharp eyes and smooth features of the grinning Abdel-Kadar.

'Wake up, mister,' he said. 'Have drink.'

The boy was leaning over him offering another bottle of the ersatz coke.

'Drink, mister.'

Martin took the bottle and turned, blinking and confused, to Alice. She was staring out of the window at a distant dust cloud, billowing towards the horizon.

'What's that?' he asked.

'The boy said they were Peul. Cattle-herders, nomads maybe – I don't know. They were passing that's all. The boy wanted to call one over but I stopped him – didn't seen right to interfere, which is funny when you think of what we're doing.'

The car pulled away. The coke tasted even stranger than before. Martin wondered what they made it from.

'How much further?' he asked.

'Soon,' Alice said and they both laughed.

'Soon,' said Abdel-Kadar and they all laughed.

'I'd no idea it was so far,' Martin said. 'It seems only a scratch on the map but these desert cities must be days away by road – if you call this a road . . .'

The piste had dribbled away several miles back and there was little now except the vague impressions of old tyre tracks in the fine grey dust. This was not the rich, russet, laterite earth of the savannah but a grey, flat, pebble-strewn wasteland. Was it desert? Set beside images of golden dunes under clear blue skies, it was a cruel disappointment. It looked dirty, as if one were peering under a bed in a little used spare room. It was a sort of hell, and Martin knew that it stretched for ever; he could see the map in his mind, and he shot a quick glance at the mirror, watching the boy's eyes concentrating on the way ahead. He had come from Morocco and had crossed that unimaginable emptiness once – it must have taken three months, six months? He had to be very tough despite his slight frame, his girlish grace. Martin looked away but that left nothing else to think about except the shuddering discomfort.

Alice wanted to sleep again but her eyes kept opening. She looked at her watch – it was nearly ten o'clock. She looked again – half-past ten – she could remember nothing in between.

Martin looked outside. In the far distance was a long straight line of trees. He knew this was impossible. Then he saw the single wire strung between them and laughed at his own stupidity. How else had Delmonico set up the journey, how else summon Abdel-Kadar unless by telephone? And what else was the boy doing except following them directly to their destination? There was a beautiful simplicity about it all, mixed with a feeling of awe at the sight of that single fragile wire, strung across so vast and inhospitable a void.

'Is this what you wanted?' Alice said. 'Africa, I mean, the job you applied for?'

Martin weighed that up. He had never thought of anything like this grey dustbowl; Kenya after all was as green as England, very like England some people said, but the question had its point. This was Africa, a very real Africa, but was it what he wanted, then or now?

'I suppose so ... Yes, I suppose it is. I just wanted to be somewhere other.'

'Other than what?'

'Not "than what" ... just "other". Other than everything I'd ever known. Other than me in a way.' He laughed to himself, or at himself. 'Sounds mega-pretentious – Beresford's Theory of Otherness. Isn't that why you want a kid – something that is yourself but isn't, something that's another you, that can replace all the dissatisfactions of this you, just like I thought the otherness out there would replace everything I disliked about where I was and what I was? Don't even try and answer, I've lost track of the question – anyway there's something up ahead. I think we're here, wherever here is.'

As he spoke Martin was thrown forward by the car jolting over a deep ridge. He reached out to steady himself, grasped Abdel-Kadar's shouder and held on to the bare neck where the collar of his djebba hung loose.

'What's that?' Martin said, unable to stop his voice rising a note or two.

'Looks like a prison,' Alice said.

Abdel-Kadar laughed – he had understood 'prison'. 'Ce n'est pas une prison,' he laughed. 'Pas du tout.'

Alice was not reassured. The square compound, the wire mesh fence, the long rows of plain brick buildings with pressed asbestos roofs, no tree or shrub or flower bed, no bench or shelter, nothing – it all said prison, institution, camp – a thesaurus of bleak places implying internment and control.

At least it was not in use. The double mesh gates were jammed open though the car slowed, forced to wade through drifts of the grey sandy dust. Martin scanned the brick rows. They were not just abandoned, they had been pillaged – the doors and window frames were gone, each line was a shell.

'Well, this is it,' he said, and as he spoke he realised that his hand

133

was still resting on the nape of the boy's neck. The skin was pleasingly gentle, soft and dry despite the clammy heat in the car. He considered pulling away but found his grip tightening slightly and guessed that if he raised his eyes he would see the boy watching him in the mirror with his wide, knowing smile. He jumped – Abdel-Kadar had begun to hit the horn with his fist and the noise klaxoned over the silence with a report which stopped the breath in his body.

'For God's sake . . .' he yelled. 'What's the racket for? If there's anybody here they must have heard us drive up.'

'Martin,' Alice's voice was an urgent whisper. 'Look.'

A man had appeared out of one of the yawning doorways, followed by another, then a third.

'Peul,' said Abdel-Kadar beckoning them to come closer.

Martin looked round. If they were Peul then where were their cattle? The shambling figures bore no resemblance to the tall nomads in their flowing robes and wide conical hats that he knew from photographs. True they were tall, but they were also painfully thin, emaciated, their knees and hands too large for such narrow limbs. Worse, their hair was matted and they were dressed in rags – one wore a pair of torn boxer shorts, another some old greying Y-fronts, the last had simply wrapped a length of khaki rag between his legs in a grotesque nappy.

When they were about two metres away, they halted. The first two sat on the ground but the third, nappy-man, produced a curious little tripod stool, a low, squat thing with an animal's claw at the end of each leg. This he settled carefully into the dust before perching himself on it, a king holding court despite his filthy garb.

Abdel-Kadar squatted on his haunches, then waved at Alice to do the same. He spoke in a series of staccato vowels.

All three replied with a low *eeeh* noise. Then after a pause, boxer shorts said something brisk, more vowel than consonant to which the boy replied with the same low *eeeh*.

Then silence. Not an anxious silence, just a quiet pause as if each side were taking stock of the other. Alice wondered what was expected. The only worrying thing was the way the man in the nappy had slipped a hand under its khaki folds and was clearly toying with his cock – not in a sexy way, more a sort of unthinking massage, much as the old woman at the garage had picked her nose.

'*Sauvages*,' said Abdel-Kadar grinning hugely.

134

'What do they want?'

The boy jabbed his hand at his mouth as if feeding himself.

'*Ils sont affamés, pas de bouffe ici.*' He shovelled more imaginary food into his mouth.

Martin watched with growing impatience. They hadn't travelled all this way to be given a safari park show. He opened his door and got out, surprised at just how loose the dust was and how far he had to lift his feet to walk. He stomped over to one of the doorways and looked in. It must have been a dormitory of some kind, tiny sleeping quarters, burning hot and airless under the asbestos sheets. On one of the walls someone had pinned what looked like a sales brochure or an instruction manual. It showed a rather grainy sewing machine, a table model with a foot treadle and a hand wheel as big as a bicycle's. Martin wondered whether that was what they had been making here, and if so, why? Who had thought they could sell such archaic rubbish in competition with the new sleek table-top electric machines? And why here? The workers must have been housed in these roasting cells, stuck in the navel of nowhere.

Martin looked again, the brochure was headed with the name of the firm: '*Abdel Darwesh: Société Anonyme Malienne de l'Exploitation Industrielle*'. There was a box number and an address in Bamako and the names and contacts for representatives in Paris and Bucharest, and Martin felt reality finally loosen its grip on him; it was all a joke, the whole of Africa was a joke.

'Sewing machines,' he said. 'Sewing machines . . . here . . .'

At the far side of the compound, Alice was staring at the men and they were staring straight back with eyes which had a rheumy glaucomic absence as if they had peered at the sun too often, eyes that would see far while noticing little close to. Nappy-man continued to massage himself, the others sat, immobile. For the first time since those dreamy early teenage years, Alice felt herself slipping into timelessness. It was as if there was no longer anything to be done and nowhere further to go, as if they could sit there for ever and it would not matter. She sighed long and softly, and wondered if she would ever breathe in again. Perhaps she would just remain there, mesmerised, empty of everything, until the sun baked her into a brittle, woman-shaped jar.

Abdel-Kadar came sliding up. '*On y va*,' he said with an unexpected urgency in his voice. Perhaps he had sensed her mood and was afraid she might drift away.

'They're hungry,' she said, unwilling to move, longing to stay just where she was.

'*Allons-y. Il est très tard.*'

She struggled upright, went to the car and lifted the mangoes out of the paper and carried them over to the men, but when she gestured that they should help themselves, Abdel-Kadar leapt forward and spoke loud and sharply.

The men conferred.

'What did you say?' Alice demanded but the thing was clearly out of her control now. In any case nappy-man had made some sort of offer.

The boy shook his head and started to scoop up the mangoes.

'*Hia,*' the man said, lifting his stool and putting it in front of Alice. She was too terrified by his sudden advance to do anything other than gawp at him. Then it dawned on her that this was the deal worked out by the boy – the man's carved wooden stool in exchange for the mangoes. She looked at it, it was beautifully fashioned and polished, carved from a single piece of wood with no join. Such wood must be impossible to find round here, it must have been obtained by bargaining with the forest dwellers further south. What could these impoverished men have possibly exchanged for it – hides, horns? And now she was to have it in exchange for a few centimes worth of mangoes, all to satisfy their hunger.

'I don't want it,' she said, but the men had already gathered up the fruit and were following Abdel-Kadar. Alice snatched up the stool and hurried behind them, through the first line of abandoned cells, to where Martin was waiting.

'Have you seen this?' he said, nodding towards a small, white plane with a propellor on each wing. We're going to go up in that toy.'

She could see why he was worried – the lightness of their craft was easily demonstrated by the way Abdel-Kadar had set the three men to turning it, one each behind the wings, the third at the rear. It swung round with little effort, revealing a square of fresh white paint on its nose which failed to hide the original embossed letters. Alice walked closer and spelled out the name, 'MERCURIO OIL', in a semicircle under a winged foot, and as she watched, the plane turned further and she saw the tall white man who had been standing on the far side.

He gave an order and the men stopped pushing. Even without the

136

starched white shirt and the razor-crease black trousers he was obviously their pilot, and this attempt at a uniform was moderately reassuring.

He came over and offered his hand.

'Thorsten,' he said, leaving it unclear whether this was a first or last name.

'Alice,' she said. Then the word 'Thor' rose up and hit her and she wondered if it were possible ... and then she realised that if it was, he must have been up all night, drinking with Margot before driving out here ahead of them – and that made her very queasy indeed. She could see why Margot was so pleased with herself: he was what? – a young forty? Maybe a little older, blond hair going silver, but clearly fit and – well – OK. But she still didn't like the idea that he had been up all night carousing with Margot. Worse, he seemed to be on his own – no co-pilot, no crew.

A set of aluminium steps, like a decorator's ladder, was set against the side of the plane and they were bidden to climb aboard. Inside, there were two rows of two seats while the rear was filled with cases of rough boxwood with crudely stencilled letters. As she edged inside, bent almost double, Alice again had the disturbing sensation that she had drifted into a film and that at any moment she would be expected to say lines from a script she had not been given and that her silence would make them angry with her.

Martin followed, catching his brow on the bulkhead and swearing viciously.

'Watch your head,' Thorsten yelled from somewhere up front, hidden behind a curtain that sealed off the cockpit.

'Thanks a fucking million,' Martin said, slumping down beside Alice. She appeared to be nursing a piece of furniture, but before he could ask what it was all about, someone outside slammed shut the door, while Abdel-Kadar pulled down the inner locking lever with evident expertise.

'What on earth is that?' Martin demanded, preferring to distract himself with the particular, rather than scare himself with the general activity that was now taking place.

'A bargain,' Alice said. 'I bought it off one of them – in exchange for the mangoes.'

'What is it?'

'A stool.' She rubbed a hand over the polished seat then drew it back as she remembered what had so recently rested on it. 'The boy thinks they're savages but they were perfectly polite, though they do tend to play with themselves a bit.'

'What do you mean?'

'Oh, nothing. I was just being silly. I . . .'

But whatever she was going to say was lost as the plane barked into life.

Martin had always been fascinated by flight; this time he closed his eyes and gripped his seat. The run up to take-off seemed to go on for ever and when he risked a peek they were still on the ground and he was only aware that they were airbourne when the plane began to bank steeply to the right before steadying and heading into the sun. He opened his eyes and breathed out. Clearly so small a plane was not going to rise above the clouds – then he realised why – below ran the sinuous line of the Niger. Like the telegraph poles earlier, the river was now their guide.

Little clusters of shells meant villages, scratchy graffito marked out tiny enclosures, the fragile attempts at human control of the vast undisciplined terrain; the thin cross-hatchings were worked fields, few and small against the vast expanse of dull browns and burned-out reds that stretched to the horizon's hazy nimbus. For a brief moment, a pencil-line road ran near the river and a puff of dust marked a vehicle racing along below them – their predatory shadow flew over it, an eagle watching a lamb. The river meandered, dividing and leaving an island in its wake; the plane banked steeply to follow its sweep and as they straightened Martin saw a cluster of squares and lines and patches and blocks which could only mean a town.

'Mopti,' Abdel-Kadar said from behind, leaning across to point out the second river flowing into the Niger.

Martin wondered if this was their destination but just as he was preparing himself for what would surely be a trying experience, the plane banked away, following the Niger once more.

In the cockpit, Thor glanced at the altimeter, checked his track and height, locked the control column and unbuttoned the bottom of his shirt as he reached with his free hand into his bag on the neighbouring seat to take out a little leather case, the sort of thing travellers use for shaving gear. He unzipped three sides of the square and laid open the two halves, revealing a set of compart-ments, the largest holding a small metal syringe with a calibrated glass tube, looped metal finger grips and a circular thumb pull at the end of the plunger. Smaller compartments held tiny glass phials – he pulled one out, unscrewed the top, took the syringe and forced the needle through the grey rubber cover. Inverting the bottle and the syringe he shook the liquid then withdrew the plunger, filling the tube with the required gradation of liquid. He pulled the needle clear, clicked the tube with his finger to force any air bubbles to the surface, squirted a few drops clear, then gathered up a fold of flesh above his exposed stomach into which he quickly prodded the thin metal spike and began, slowly, to force down the metal loop.

He felt nothing as the insulin flowed into his bloodstream. It was over so quickly he barely thought about it any more. Of course he knew he ought not to fly alone but as the only point of all this was money and as the risks were slight and the journey short, two hours at the most, he had long since accepted it as inevitable. The only problem would be in about fifteen minutes when the river would begin to fade. In its dried-out state, it could only be followed in perfect visibility, but that he had, and would never fly without it, no matter what Darwesh or Delmonico or Diop or any of them paid him. So where was the problem? Another year of this and the money would be right and his plan fulfilled, then he would stop.

That done, he pulled back the curtain and asked if everything was all right.

Martin said it was, though he was lying – the moment the curtain parted and he saw into the cockpit, his stomach lurched. Of course he knew about autopilot, theoretically, but seeing the Swede sitting there, not holding on to anything was terrifying.

'This a regular route?' he enquired as evenly as possible.

The Swede nodded, he was reaching into his bag again, this time for what looked to Martin like a gardening magazine. The cover had a picture of a well-rolled lawn and the Swede set it down beside him and proceeded to flick through the pages.

Martin groaned inwardly. They were just zapping along with nobody in control. It was his worst nightmare. He looked down and it got even worse – the river was no longer a sure, unbroken line, it had dried up in places, leaving a series of isolated lakes. This really was *La Sécheresse*. He thought of the map in Mamadi's office with its dotted line – now the drought had made a cartographer's convention simple reality. But could they still rely on this broken line to guide them? There were almost no signs of life, just the occasional cluster of shells with no one working the earth – why should they, it was clear that nothing could possibly grow in that waterless void.

The Swede was still absorbed in his magazine. Martin leant forward, trying to make out what the great attraction was, but all he could see were more pictures of lawns – nothing else, no flower beds or herbaceous borders, no topiary or fishponds, just lawns, flat green lawns. It was not all right. It was very eccentric. He had never heard of a magazine devoted in its entirety to so limited a subject.

'Keen gardener are we?'

The Swede shook his head to indicate no.

'Just like reading about it, eh?'

Again a shake of the head. 'It's golf,' he volunteered, passing the magazine back.

Martin turned to the inside front cover. This offered yet another vista of green grass under the heading *'Golfs du Soleil'*, with the address of a company in Nice that apparently laid out golf courses. It was not after all a magazine, it was a sales brochure. Martin flipped through it. Every manner of golf course was on offer – big ones, small ones, nine-hole and eighteen-hole, golf courses with handsome clubhouses, golf courses with health spas attached.

Martin looked up. The Swede was watching him, perhaps awaiting some sign of admiration or approval. Martin did not feel inclined to give it.

'Why?' he demanded bluntly.

'Big money, real big money. It's the Japanese, they go anywhere for golf – Thailand, California, Australia. So why not here?'

Martin's eye flickered towards the window and that weary spectacle of utter devastation spread out below. They were flying over a dust-bowl, a sun-bleached wilderness.

'I'm sorry,' he said. 'Do you mean to say that you're planning on opening a golf course here in Mali?'

'Why not?'

'Oh, no especial reason.' He waited but when the Swede showed no sign of enlightening him further he handed back the brochure, now convinced that his and Alice's lives were in the hands of a complete maniac.

The Swede tucked his precious document back into his bag. It made perfect sense to him, it was Thorsen Falkner's big idea. The Japanese came to Mali anyway. They were usually bored stiff, so give them a luxury golf course and they would pay anything – the more luxurious, the more expensive, the better. Or so he had been told by one of the Australians he had worked with in the old oil company. That guy had been around Asia and had seen it at first hand. Golf courses, he had said, were a sure fire thing.

'I got a bit of land upriver from Bamako,' he volunteered.

'That's good,' Martin said, humouring him. 'Eighteen holes will it be?'

'Sure, and some practise nets, luxury clubhouse, swimming pool, health centre.'

Martin made what he hoped were appropriate sounds of interest and admiration, anything to keep the Swede on an even keel. But the man had slipped back into his own thoughts, dreaming about rolling greenswards and well-raked bunkers. It all made sense – the land was not far from the airport, close enough to the river for all the water he would need. He had found the necessary Malian partner, someone who would keep out of his way for a regular cut, but who would know who to square and who to avoid, whose cousins to employ so that they would not be pestered by greedy policemen and drunken soldiers. He had been in Bamako long enough to have it all neatly arranged – and he wanted to stay in Bamako. It suited him, the hot nights and the noisy eroticism of the bars, the easy sex, the musky aroma overlaid with cheap scent, the taste of cinnamon mixed with lager on the breath, the willingness and the lack of recrimination or remorse. Bluntly, he liked black women – the night before had been an abberation – though amusing for all that. She had been fun, that Margot, he smiled to himself. OK for once in a while and it was amusing to have someone else buying the drinks and fretting that he was all right and wondering when she would be able to get him to bed. Yes, that was definitely amusing.

He slipped away his precious brochure, ran an eye over the gauges, flicked the machine out of remote and took control once more.

'We're here,' he said, closing the curtain.

Oh hell, Martin thought, wishing he'd done like Alice and slept through the whole terrifying business. The plane banked sharply, he said a prayer.

It was only when the dust subsided and he had clambered down the ladder that Martin realised that they had simply landed on another stretch of open scrubland – a rough area cleared of the spiky stunted bushes that somehow flourished in the parched and fissured ground. No tarmac, no building, nothing.

'Welcome to the heart of darkness,' he said, offering Alice his hand as she followed him down the ladder.

Their pilot and the boy stood a little further off, staring at some distant point on the horizon.

'Where are we?' Martin demanded 'What's over there?'

'The town,' Thorsten said.

'Which town?' Though it was as if he already knew the answer, as if in some way he had known all along where they would surely end up, but had sealed it away in a hidden recess, afraid lest exposed to the light of day it would seem simultaneously comic and implausible, exciting and yet utterly unreal.

Abdel-Kadar turned and smiled: '*C'est Tombouctou. Ça vous plaît?*'

Alice was laughing quietly to herself.

'I guess it *was* inevitable,' Martin said. 'Where else?'

He looked round. There was no sign of a settlement, just this rolling greyish dust and the unlovely clumps of thorn bushes.

'Not up to expectations?' Alice said, still amused.

'Everyone complain,' the Swede said equably. 'Everybody getting disappointed, not the beautiful, mysterious desert city – just a lotta dust.'

'That's how Tennyson saw it,' Martin said ruefully. 'How it didn't match the dream of golden Africa – something about "Black specks" and "dreary sand" and "Low-built, mud'wall'd, barbarian settlements".'

Alice didn't mind, it seemed peaceful to her, neutral, placing no obligation on her to respond in the way a mighty mountain or an imposing building would have done. Even the stunted bushes had a melancholy charm. She felt for them, no one was ever going to long to get one home to cultivate lovingly in their living room. It was hard to imagine even the most dedicated botanist bothering to send one to Kew or the *Jardin des Plantes*. They were like those people who are neither noticeably attractive nor fascinatingly ugly, most people in other words, the sort who lie in equivalent places – treeless council estates, faceless blocks beside roads too wide to be crossed in safety except through a piss-smelling subway. This grey scrubland masquerading as desert was no different to those vast swathes of

Manchester which pretend to be human settlements. She almost felt at home.

'You pay now,' the boy said abruptly.

Martin thought this a bit premature, how could they be sure of getting back? He opened his mouth but said nothing, suddenly aware of how weak their position was.

Alice fished out the wad of dollars and handed it to the Swede.

'Look,' Alice said. 'Here comes the airport bus. You know, it's dead on one o'clock and, crazy as it sounds, this whole thing is probably going more like clockwork than any journey I've ever made. You couldn't get to Salford this smoothly.'

'Looks like a jeep,' Martin said. 'Like an army jeep – American, second world war, invasion of Normandy. We've passed through a time zone, we're in a place where everything is doomed to perpetual repetition. Soon we'll be joined by Napoleon and Nebuchadnezzar. We will spend the night in a pyramid and breakfast at Gettysburg on the morning of the battle. Do you know, I think I've just gone stark staring mad. Yoopeeyooooo.'

The driver was no GI, just a shape in a burnous, like a sack hunched at the wheel, the face hidden under the hood. Abdel-Kadar climbed up beside him, while Alice, still clutching her stool, sat between the two men in the rear.

Martin groaned, the tyres wobbled in the deep drifts of sandy dust, he swayed helplessly, aware that it could be miles to the town and that it was pointless to ask. He was no longer certain that there was enough time for them to get back to Bamako – it was over seven hours, nearly eight, since they left the hotel – the whole thing was a mess, out of control. He was thirsty as never before, his lips were dry and cracking but when he attempted to wet them, his tongue brushed against a tiny ulcer inside his lower lip, making him whimper pitifully. He was coming apart.

A dog barked.

'Look!' Alice said. 'Houses. Mud houses.'

Martin saw boulders, grey outcrops standing on the grey plain. He tried to get his eyes to focus but the rocks stubbornly refused to become houses. The dog barked again, which had to mean something, unless there were wild dogs roaming the wasteland. Then he saw it, a miserable hairless mutt, coloured the same dusty grey as the desert except for a livid pink sore on its neck. It lay in the thin line of shadow offered by a crumbling mud wall, and barked again as they drifted past, but made no move to get up and give chase.

'You see,' Alice said with irritating satisfaction. 'Houses. Mud houses.'

She was right, they were driving past a child's concept of a house, a near perfect cube, save where the desert winds had worn the edges and piled deep drifts at the low entrance. It looked abandoned. By the open door an enormous water jar had cracked apart like a hatched egg. In the courtyard, beyond a low crumbling wall, a chair, bleached silver in the sun, rested on its three remaining legs. Martin looked at his watch – it had all taken twice the time Delmonico had predicted. He was dazed from the journey. The world was grey. Particles of gritty dust hung in the air, the town lay behind a gauze scrim – it's size impossible to guess – a collection of cubes with the minaret of a mosque, a steep pyramid, rising from its centre. Martin knew it, knew it well – it was the scene in the poster.

'*Tombouctou*,' Abdel-Kadar said.

Martin savoured the word – *Tom-bouc-tou* – the last outpost of Islam, the first and final point on the ancient caravan route across the empty desert.

Alice was wary, nursing the stool as if it were Baby, studying the distant town looming out of the mist of fine sand, its surrounding wall an unbroken barricade with no visible entrance, a mud prison. If they turned and went straight back she knew that they could never make Bamako before nightfall. Even if the plane could get them back to that nowhere point where they had abandoned the car, once it was dark it would surely be impossible for the boy to follow the feeble tracks that led to the city. They were trapped and alone. No one had come to greet them. The arrival of white people could hardly be an everyday event, yet the only sign of life so far was the half-dead dog. She turned. It seemed to be following them, hunched and skulking in the distant hollows.

The jeep stopped and the boy jumped down. Close too, the illusion of a solid wall collapsed – the town was made up of separate compounds, close to each other like a child's building blocks, but with narrow passages between, shaded alleyways that offered access to the inner reaches of the place. Less prison-like but still forbidding.

'We go get *tampon*,' Abdel-Kadar said.

Martin had no idea what he was talking about but knew he was in no position to argue. He jumped down and followed him towards the nearest break in the wall. Alice hesitated; she wanted to ask Martin whether they were doing the right thing but he and the boy were already disappearing into the shadows. She jumped – the driver had revved up the jeep, he was taking the Swede somewhere. She was on her own, and there was nothing to do but hurry after them.

Martin had no idea what they were doing or where they were going but it didn't really matter any more. He was on a new planet with a new gravity – the grey sand pulled at his shoes, slowing him to a loping stride.

Alice looked behind. The dog had advanced a few feet, still crouched low, stalking them. She wanted to call out but was afraid to disturb the empty greyness. She walked close to the wall, scraping against the crumbling mud, stippled like a half-healed scab. Ahead of her the two men kept to the centre avoiding the deep drifts blown to either side. The walls curved slightly so that the path seemed endless. She panicked. What if she lost sight of them? She would be abandoned in the labyrinth. She tried to hurry but the soft dust swallowed her shoes. Something made her look over her shoulder. There was a shadow at the distant bend behind. The dog still followed.

Martin was elated. The walls offered sudden recessed entrances, visible when you drew level, low moulded archways with thick wooden doors. One was half open offering a glimpse of a dark room and beyond it a bright, sunlit courtyard with other doors leading to other shaded rooms.

Alice came up.

'Where is everybody?' she asked.

Martin shrugged. 'Sleeping, I guess, what with the fast and this heat.'

'So what do we do now?'

'Whatever we're told. Delmonico said it would all be taken care of and so it has.'

He walked on. She ran her eyes round the harsh, secretive space protected by its wall, the narrow opening its only link with the empty passageways. As she turned to follow, she saw Abdel-Kadar on the path behind her and wondered how he had dropped back without her noticing. Then he was gone. She screwed up her eyes, confused. It must have been the dog lurking in the shadows, yet she could have sworn it looked like the boy. She turned, and walked on, blinking as she entered a sharp triangle of light where another path crossed, leading into another sector of the labyrinth. Now the houses were two stories high with double lattice windows, Arabic arched, their shutters nudged open just wide enough for someone to peek out without being seen. She could feel curious eyes following her and imagine the flickering tongues in the dimly lit purdah behind the shaded grills.

Martin and the boy had stopped at a corner where three paths opened into a wider space. At one of the angles stood a bulbous mud construction, shaped like a beehive with a blackened hole in its swollen belly.

'It's for cooking,' Martin said peering inside. 'Here's where they slide in whatever they want to bake – it's a communal pizza oven, really.'

He walked over to a massive onion-arched door, its heavy beams studded with clove-headed bolts – it was Marrakesh, Cairo, Damascus. He reached out to touch the finely wrought metal but his hand recoiled from the heat.

Alice shook her feet to loosen the grit in her shoes. She was hungry and tried swallowing but there was no saliva to draw on. And someone *was* following them – she had seen it for sure and it wasn't the dog – a child maybe, some kid entranced by the crazy strangers stumbling about in the noon-time heat. That at least was understandable but why had no one else come forward?

'This isn't right,' she said, addressing herself to Abdel-Kadar. 'Surely there ought to be someone around? Where are you taking us?'

'*Tampon*,' the boy said firmly.

'What's he talking about. What's a *tampon*?'

'I don't know,' Martin said jauntily. 'I'm just taking it on trust, no doubt we'll find out in good time. Have you seen these . . .?'

He was pointing to a pile of newly made bricks stacked near a broken wall. He reached down and lifted a simple wooden frame, a mould for the wet mud.

'This place is immortal,' he said. 'The sun and the wind wear it away, reducing it to dust, then they rake it up and make it into bricks and build it up again. Brilliant.'

Some of the bricks had not fully dried.

'And there has to be water,' he said. 'Fine grey dust – and a little water.'

Now Alice knew it was not a child. At first she thought Abdel-Kadar had slipped behind again – the face peeping out of the shadows had definitely been his, until she realised he was not wearing a djebba – for a brief moment she could have sworn he was naked but then he was gone again. She wanted to tell Martin but he had disappeared and as she hurried to catch up, she realised that he had stepped out of the labyrinth into glaring sunshine. They had crossed the town and come out at the opposite side, emerging into an open space, sloping away to form a wide basin, beyond which the grey dunes undulated to infinity.

The sun was in Martin's eyes; he blinked and shaded them with his left hand. He could see people, little groups of them, each standing well clear of the others, a game of statues. The unmoving figures stared back at him.

It was a market of some sort, just a line of raffia mats spread under a low wooden framework covered with dried palm fronds. A half dozen shawl-wrapped women squatted in the shade, awaiting purchasers. No one moved.

Martin took a hesitant step into the full glare of the sun. He had never felt so exposed. He walked forward, heading towards the line of mats. The nearest group of men were tall and wiry, in gowns and turbans so white their deep black faces seemed almost featureless. Martin smiled and nodded as he passed, hoping the grinning gesture would count as a peaceable act.

The produce on the line of mats was pitiful: a tiny pyramid of baby onions with shrivelled papery skins, a pinch of scarlet powder which he assumed was chilli, a miniature bouquet of a dried, stick-like herb tied with a raffia bow and a small orange gourd, a mere dwarf beside the giant calabashes he had seen in Bamako. This, as much as the lost river, was *La Sécheresse*.

He looked away, embarrassed, over to where a line of Peul cattle-herders waited beside a dozen scrawny beasts, humpbacked with long upswept horns. In the middle of the open space was what appeared to be a cooking fire and near it a group of men in ragged European cast-offs, cross-legged before a pile of animal hides that looked too cracked to be of any use. It was the silent trade, the place where the desert met the savannah, and even as degraded, and dried up and dying as it so obviously was, to Martin it remained a dream out of childhood.

He was hungry. Ignoring the blank stares he walked towards the fire.

From the anonymity of the shadows Abdel-Kadar and Alice watched his progress.

'*Le marché,*' said the boy impatiently. 'Nothing buy – no good here. You need *tampon* now.'

Alice had no idea what this *tampon* might be and cared less. She longed to follow Martin. Most of the groups looked harmless enough, though she was less sure of the cluster of men, swathed in dark-blue cloths, who were crouched beside an irritable group of tethered camels, snapping at their minders with trap-like teeth. One of the men was trying to pacify the angriest, rattling a chain of cast-iron bells near its ear. Alice saw a woman, a bent creature, scrabbling about gathering pellets of camel dung and rolling them in the dust before tossing them into a sack she dragged behind her. These were real desert people, Bedouin or Touareg, she could not tell which, but either might be dangerous. She stayed where she was.

Martin had reached the smoking brazier. A pot, set amongst the glowing charcoal embers, glittered with a stew of molten silver. A swarthy man with wispy curls escaping from the sides of his filthy turban, pumped the flames with a small leather bellows. Seeing Martin he set these aside and reached for a roll of grubby cloth which he laid in the sand and unfolded to reveal a superbly wrought sword.

'*Hattini* . . .' the man said, opening his palm and tapping the blade with the back of his hand. '*Hattini . . . shoof, shoof . . .*'

Martin took it. The haft was inset with enamelled calligraphy, tiny slivers of red and green set within thin silver cloisons. It was superb, a memory of some distant Andalusian past, yet his tools were no more than a tiny hammer and a stubby metal punch. Martin set it carefully on its dirty rag.

'*Hattini,*' the man insisted. '*Hattini . . .*'

Martin shook his head. It was beautiful but they would need an entire day to haggle a price.

The man shrugged and reached for another bundle, extracting a beaten silver brooch in the form of a flattened hand with five equal fingers. It was crudely made, a cheap back-up when the sword failed to please. Again, Martin refused and again the man reached for another, smaller bundle, unwrapped it and held up a dull brass picture frame. Inside was a newspaper photograph. It was the soon-to-be royal couple. The man gave a satisfied, black-toothed grin.

'Shoof, shoof . . .'

Martin looked at the Prince and Lady Di and the dream evaporated. The momentary vision of himself as the adventurer way out beyond the tourist line died with that tacky frame and its cut-out image. These things were made for the others who came here, and why not? Timbuktu was not that far away from Bamako if you had a plane at your disposal, and no doubt Delmonico had a good line helping foreigners who wanted to dream of being explorers for a day.

'Shoof, shoof,' the man insisted, but Martin had no desire to see whatever rubbish he had now pulled out of his sack. He moved towards the edge of the open ground, heading to where the dunes began, away from the people, from the pathetic group in their ludicrous western rags, the torn pullovers and fraying pin-stripe trousers.

To his left he could see desert men standing by their camels. One held two tablets of salt, a Moses down from the mountain, and Martin felt the sun-hardened eyes inside the dark slit of his indigo bandages studying him, assessing his worth. A she-camel snapped vicious teeth as one of her offspring tried to nuzzle up to her teats. Martin could feel the anger in the air and wondered what held it in check. Where was power in Timbuktu? What was it that controlled these watchful groups?

He crested the rim and slithered down the sandy dust until the town was lost behind him and he was quite alone and could look out over the uninterrupted desert, relieved to have escaped for a moment the silent watchers.

Alice saw Martin disappear and wondered what she should do next. She felt betrayed – he had started this whole thing and now he was gone, wandering off as if this were just any old day trip and not the most dangerous journey of their lives.

There was some movement among the distant nomads, one of their camels was being urged upright on its ungainly legs while two of the men struggled to force its head into a halter. Alice was so entranced that it was some time before she acknowledged the undeniable sensation that there was someone standing right behind her. She turned her head, centimetre by centimetre, hoping to be confounded, relieved that it was only Abdel-Kadar staring at her.

But then she took in the explosion of matted hair, the wild intense eyes, the painfully emaciated body, the distended swell of the belly, the dark hanging penis. She screamed lifting the stool like a weapon. The creature started towards her, hands outstretched. The real Abdel-Kadar wheeled round and let out a ferocious burst of Arabic. The naked boy stumbled past them and out into the sunlight and Alice saw that his ankles were shackled to a metal bar which forced him to hobble along. And she saw the cruel-looking red weals where the rod chaffed his skin. He was remarkably agile for all that, one foot thrown in front of the other with manic energy. As soon as the first group of men saw his approach there was uproar, people shouting and waving their fists. One of the tall men in white reached down for a stone and threw it with full force. The mad boy dropped to all fours and scampered off like a hunted beast. Suddenly everyone scrambled for pebbles, hurling them after the racing figure, weaving and dodging until he crested the rim of the dunes and disappeared from view.

'Oh God,' Alice shrieked. 'Martin.'

As if sensing the mounting tension one of the camels started to honk and wheeze and tug savagely at its restraint. Abdel-Kadar pushed past Alice and ran off down the slope.

Lost to himself, Martin sat with his back to the town, feet half-buried, trying to put his thoughts in order.

The desert was not flat, it rose and fell in deep hollows and steep clefts, making it hard to see much beyond the next rise. Nor was it empty, countless large black scarab beetles scuttled about, their double pinprick trails perforating the dust.

The sun was already falling from its zenith and through the glare Martin could just make out a series of larger black specks that might be tents, even a camp of some sort, perhaps the refugees everyone denied existed.

He stood up, turned and smiled with pleasure at what he took to be Abdel-Kadar coming to find him but in a fleeting second he realised his mistake, seeing the gangling arms, the shuffling gate, the first sight of the rigid metal bar, its thick anklets rattling and crashing as the boy struggled to stay upright as the slithering sand drifts cascaded behind him.

Mouthing gibberish, he stumbled forward, eyes fixed on Martin who dodged to one side and made a run for the market. As he

150

crested the rise he saw that the formerly silent watchers were now a baying mob.

Alice had been running to warn him when the first sounds of anger broke out. She was quickly hemmed in by turbaned men in striped djebbas, carried along by a press of sweating limbs. She saw Martin appear over the edge of the dune and run for the safety of this advancing crowd. Hard behind him came the shackled creature, throwing himself along at an alarming rate, his face a mask of demented intensity. The front rank of the crowd went wild with fury, cursing and fist shaking and throwing whatever rocks could be wrenched from the sandy dust. And still the boy came on, laughing at his tormentors, imitating their wilder excesses – waving his arms about, slobbering and shrieking. Then suddenly he fell silent, turned and dived to the ground as if into water, swimming through the dust, his whole body undulating towards Martin.

Martin stood alone, mesmerised by the sight of the boy, wriggling and slithering through the dust towards him.

At first Alice thought there was some sort of desert wind blowing up, the low breathy groan seemed to rise from the ground itself.

'Wooaa, Wooaa, Wooaaaaa . . .'

Then she realised it was the crowd, unleashing its collective anger in a deep bass moan.

'Wooaaa, Wooaaa, Wooaaaa . . .'

Alice called out but her voice was lost with the din.

'Wooaaa, Wooaaaa. Wooaaaaaaaaa . . .'

More stones, more little explosions of dust. One struck the demented boy on the shoulder. He looked up, threw back his head, and let out a terrible howl from deep inside some hidden well of agony.

'Wooaaa, Wooaaaa. Wooaaaaaaaaa . . .'

The crowd moved forward, drawing Alice with it.

'Wooaaaa, Wooaaaa, Wooaaaa . . .'

The blood was thudding in her temples. When she looked up she could see they had formed a semicircle at the centre of which lay the naked boy, now quite still. Three metres away Martin stood alone, staring down at him. He was a parody of Abdel-Kadar, a joke imitation. In the silence he heard, from far away, Alice calling his name. Where was she? Where was Abdel-Kadar? He turned.

The spell broken, the boy leapt to his feet again, yelling nonsense,

151

jabbing an accusing finger, screaming ever louder. Martin drew back, stumbled, steadied himself and cast round for help.

'Wooaaa, Wooaa, Wooaa . . .'

The boy was almost on him. The front rank of silent watchers parted. A tall, elderly man, another Moroccan, in a long grey djebba stepped into the arena holding a solid-looking walking-stick high above his head. To Martin's immense relief, the mad boy stopped and cringed.

The man snarled something that sounded to Martin like a curse, one strong enough to send the creature scrambling back a few feet. The crowd purred approval. The grey figure advanced on the boy, stick menacingly poised, ready to crash down on the naked frame.

Martin wanted to call out 'No!', it seemed wrong to punish him. But the stick merely whistled through the air in a warning circle – down it came, the boy leaped away, hands propelling him along the ground, fettered legs pushing behind him.

Within seconds he was back over the edge of the dunes and lost to view.

Alice breathed gain. The resonant moaning echoed away and was gone.

The man lowered his stick, bowed from the neck, his free hand rising from chest to lips to forehead in the classic Arabic greeting.

Martin was too confused to acknowledge the gesture. He looked from the man to Abdel-Kadar, astonished at the similarity, but before he could frame a question his saviour had reached into a pocket sewn on the front of his djebba and with a theatrical flourish, produced a business card.

The lettering was heavily embossed: *Abdel Darwesh et Fils. Transports Sahariens – Tanger, Taroudannt, Bua, Tombouctou, Bamako. Livraisons Commerciales, Voyages en Groupes, Safaris Touristiques.*

Martin looked up.

'Mon oncle', said Abdel-Kadar and both Moroccans bowed.

'Who was that boy?' Martin demanded.

'This my uncle,' Abdel-Kadar insisted. They both bowed again.

'Thank you,' Martin said. 'Thank you for your help . . .' Abdel-Kadar translated, Darwesh listened then responded at surprising length, his voice rising and falling in mellifluous Arabic, a speech rather than a reply. Martin was mesmerised, what on earth could the man be saying?

152

With a final wispy wave of his hand he finished and waited for his nephew to translate.

'Welcome here,' said Abdel-Kadar.

'That's all?' Martin said.

'He invite you the house. Tonight after fasting, you come.'

'That's impossible. We have to get back to Bamako, you know that. Tell him I thank him for his splendid generosity but unfortunately I am otherwise engaged.'

The boy said nothing, though whether this was because the sentiments displeased him or more simply because he had not understood, it was impossible to know.

'We – go – Bamako,' Martin said talking with deliberate slowness. 'Go Bamako – tonight – no?'

The boy smiled and said something to his uncle but Martin was sure that he had not heard the word Bamako. He looked at his watch but the inside of the glass was coated with drops of water, the sweaty heat had condensed like dew on a leaf. He unfastened the strap and saw the greenish smear on his wrist where the cheap metal had left its cuprous traces. He reckoned it must be about two but it was impossible to be sure now that time was melting away. Without a watch there was no way of knowing if they could get back or not – yet where could they possibly stay in such a dump? What could they find to eat? Martin let all that sink in as he refastened the useless object to his tainted wrist. Better to be cautious.

'Tell your uncle, that if I stay, I shall be delighted to dine with him tonight.'

The boy grinned his huge white grin – so he did understand – and said a single word which had to be yes.

Watching all this from a distance, Alice was as confused as Martin had been by the speed of the incident and the abruptness of its finish. She had stayed where she was as the crowd splintered back into its component elements and now found herself alone and exposed at the centre of the market. She too tried to see where the crazed boy had gone but had lost sight of him when he crested the ridge. If he was as dangerous as they seemed to think, why had they not locked him up, why leave him half free like that? He looked so much like Abdel-Kadar it had to mean that he too had come across the great desert. Perhaps that explained it.

She heard someone clicking his tongue, trying to attract her attention. It was the blacksmith grinning through stained teeth and pointing at the carved stool. She hugged the hard, wooden object to her. It was hers – it was a sign that she had survived, out there in the endless bush. The man grinned and jabbed with his finger and she felt foolish – it was only a piece of wood after all. With a decisive thrust she handed it to him and watched as he turned it this way and that running his fingers down the stumpy legs, all the while nodding his approval. Satisfied, he reached inside his djebba and fished out a pouch dangling from a thong round his neck. He groped for a second, then pulled out a double strand of tiny black beads punctuated with larger coral-coloured balls from which hung a curious flat metal shape. He laid it on his palm and offered it to her. She accepted, letting the strange object dangle, flashing in the sunlight. It was made of beaten silver – a lozenge with a hollow circle at its top-most point and smaller diamond shapes at the side and bottom points, making a sort of stylised human figure or a vaguely Celtic crucifix. The whole thing was finely decorated with incised cross-hatching and a bold pattern of punched holes.

'Touareg,' the man said. 'Prenez, prenez.' He held the stool close to him and gestured with his free hand that she should keep the pendant. At first she was so surprised by his wanting to exchange silver for wood, that she could only stare, puzzled and unsure. It was extraordinary, a few cents worth of mangoes had finally bought precious metal, but when she turned to tell Martin she saw the tall man with the stick, bowing and gesturing with his hand and beginning to move away.

For a moment, Martin was mesmerised by Darwesh's manner. He was walking away with the stateliness of a pasha, a self-conscious fantasy amongst these pitiful clusters of hungry, ragged people.

'Excuse me,' he called out. 'But could you tell me where I can find Maktar Diop?'

Darwesh flashed a look at his nephew – play-acting was over.

The boy turned to Martin. 'We go for tampon,' he said. 'Must have tampon, come come . . .'

He had mentioned this tampon thing before but it was a word missing from Martin's limited French.

'Tampon,' said the boy, tugging at his arm. 'We go.'

'Where is Maktar Diop?' said Martin stubbornly.

Abdel Darwesh snapped something curt in Arabic, his face had clouded over, leaving Martin with the uneasy feeling he had gone too far.

A sudden braying from one of the camels broke the silence. One of the drovers rattled his length of bells in a futile attempt to stop a quarrel. So much anger, Martin thought.

Darwesh was questioning his nephew in staccato Arabic, occasionally looking towards Martin as if to confirm what he was told.

People were beginning to move away. The white-robed figures strolled towards the gap in the mud wall, the blacksmith left his fire, over the roofs and out into the desert came the sound of a muezzin high on the summit of the great mud ziggurat:

'Allāhu Akbar – Allāhu Akbar – Allāhu Akbar – Allāhu Akbar.'

Darwesh wagged a warning finger at his nephew and turned to give Martin the Look. He must now know the real reason for their journey, Abdel-Kadar must have told him that they were a pathetic childless couple in search of another man's child.

'Ashhadu an lā ilāha illā – Llāh.'

Darwesh's hand gestured his goodbye – chest to mouth to forehead – though this time with an indifferent air, then he too turned away and joined the others obeying the call to prayer.

'We go to Maktar Diop,' the boy said. 'But first *tampon*.'

'Who was that boy?' Martin said. 'And why was he fastened like that?'

'He crazy, he run into desert, that stop him.'

'Is he your brother?'

'We go for *tampon*.'

'He is, isn't he? He looks like you under all that hair and filth.'

'*Tampon*.' Abdel-Kadar said, walking away.

Martin shook his head. The whole thing was adrift.

Alice watched the last white-robed figure pass through the gap in the mud wall. The call from the minaret had ended and she was unsure what to do next. Looking down at her squat shadow, she felt again that peaceful timelessness she had experienced, a lifetime ago, when she had sat with the three men. She scanned the endless rippling dust, awed by the illimitable distance, amazed at what they had done. In the safety of the hotel it had seemed no more than an outing with the possibility of finding the child she craved; here amongst these silent, sullen people she knew just how foolish that had been. Then she saw the mad boy again, crouched on the edge of the dune watching them. How did he eat? Where did he find water?

155

'Come, please,' Abdel-Kadar called out. *'Tampon.'*

She drew level with Martin.

'I don't understand?' she said, but the remark was so open there was no possible answer.

'I'm hungry,' she said, trying to get matters back to a practical level. 'And thirsty, really thirsty.'

But still he said nothing.

'D'you hear me?' she insisted. 'I said I'm hungry and thirsty, and I want to go to the loo.'

He laughed.

'It's not funny.'

They were so preoccupied they barely noticed that Abdel-Kadar was leading them out of the tangle of narrow passages, into broader streets of newer houses, some of which seemed to be made of a kind of stone. A donkey looked up from feeding in a pile of scattered refuse and watched them pass. Up ahead the road seemed to open out – Martin could see a broad circle of the same neo-Moorish buildings they had passed in Bamako and guessed this must be the old colonial administrative quarter.

'*Français,*' said Abdel-Kadar in confirmation. '*Les colons.*'

Rough, hand-painted signs indicated newer functions: provincial agencies, inspectorates of this and that, the same run-down unkempt government bureaucracy. It was odd, Martin reflected, how the last vestiges of French rule were crumbling away while the old Timbuktu lived on, eternally renewed.

Then he realised that one of the square concrete blocks did not fit the usual pattern. It was the first building he had seen in Mali that was freshly painted. It could have been done that morning it was so painfully white in the glaring sun. Even the little border stones lining the path had been whitewashed and the surrounding area swept clean. To Martin, there was something unnerving about this unexpected evidence of good order.

'*Tampon,*' said Abdel-Kadar sensing his hesitation. 'Here is police, *tampon.*'

Martin ignored him and turned to Alice. 'Do you see this? I don't like it. What if we've been set up – I wouldn't put it past Delmonico, he's already proved a barefaced liar over the time it would take us. It'll be the end of the day soon and we're clearly stuck here and at the mercy of whoever's in charge – and we've brought a lot of money . . .'

'*Tampon,*' Abdel-Kadar said yet again, this time making a frantic stamping motion with his bunched fist. '*Tampon. Passeports.*'

'Rubber stamp,' Martin said realising now what the word meant. 'But we haven't left the country. We don't need a bloody *tampon.*'

'*Tampon,*' the boy said sternly, motioning to them to follow him up the stairs.

They advanced warily but when they stepped over the threshold into another gloomy, run-down room there was instant relief – it was the same old hopelessness they had been getting used to, a far cry from the spick and span exterior.

'*Banjou,*' said a voice from somewhere in the shuttered half-light. Martin could just make out an African in a crumpled khaki uniform, open at the neck and sweat-stained under the arms, seated at a desk so small it might have come from a school. There was a litre bottle of beer perched precariously on the edge. Martin turned to Abdel-Kadar but the boy's expression had frozen into a wary neutrality. He was on his own now.

'*Banjou,*' the policeman said again. '*Banvenou à Tombouctou.*'

There was a sudden snort of laughter to Martin's right. Another equally scruffy policeman was stretched out on a bench clutching another litre bottle of beer to his chest.

'*Soyez la banvenou,*' said the second.

'*Passeports,*' Abdel-Kadar said.

The policeman at the desk took them and studied them with the slow concentration of the illiterate. Eventually, he came to an empty page and held it down flat while he breathed on the face of a rubber stamp which he crashed down so violently the little desk shook. He did this with two other stamps covering the entire page. Martin took his passport back and looked at the man's handiwork. One stamp, probably official, had a worn coat of arms and the vague outline of the word '*République*' followed by an illegible motto but the second was nothing but a crude cut-out flower and could have come from a child's printing set, while the third was definitely home-made and simply read '*TOMBOUCTOU*' in crudely incised letters with the '*B*' reversed.

'*Dollar?*' the man said with a happy grin on his face.

'*Pour le visa,*' Abdel-Kadar explained, then seeing the potential for argument on Martin's face quickly added: 'Pay, is better.'

Martin put the passports on the desk and debated whether to refuse.

'Pay,' said Abdel-Kadar guessing his thoughts.

'Do as he says,' Alice chipped in. 'We've no choice any more – you may not like it but we're as good as prisoners here.'

Martin looked from Alice to Abdel-Kadar to the policeman. For the first time in his life he had no appeal to any authority that could return his rights to him. Here was the power in Timbuktu and he was at its mercy just as much as those hungry shuffling figures in the market place. Something deep inside him revolted against accepting it. He was free, no one could push him around like this, no one ever had, he was after all – white – which was what it all came down to.

'Pay,' said Alice softly.

His shoulders sagged. He fumbled in his back pocket and drew out a crumpled five pound note.

'Dollar?' the man said, smiling less.

'No dollar,' Martin replied, petulantly.

The man hesitated, then snatched at the note and stuffed it into the drawer in front of him.

To Martin's dismay Alice suddenly spoke:

'I'd like to see one of your commanding officers, the man in charge if you don't mind.'

'No speak,' the man said. 'Frangsez? No Eengleesh.'

This produced another guffaw from the recumbent figure on the bench.

'This is hardly the moment,' Martin said. 'Just leave it, will you?'

Alice was about to argue when a door to her right swung open and a tall, very tall, African in a neatly pressed uniform with braided flashes on the shoulders stepped through. The two policemen leapt to their feet, the one on the bench spilling a quantity of beer down his front. The officer ignored this as if it were beneath contempt and proceeded to scrutinise the new arrivals.

Alice stared back. It was the soldier at the airport, the guard at the barracks. He was darker than the two drunks but with a clearer, more even colour, his face narrow and angular, his eyes hidden behind impenetrable black lenses in thick horn-rimmed frames. 'You are English?' the officer said, though clearly aware of the answer. 'There is a problem? You have your stamps, no?'

'We already had a visa.' Martin said.

The officer gave him a pacifying smile. 'Of course you did but we have learned that tourists like a souvenir of their visit – it is what they come for – to be able to show they were here. There is nothing else, as you will discover. You *are* tourists, aren't you?'

Martin turned sharply to Alice willing her to keep quiet. 'Yes,' he said as firmly as possible. 'We *are* tourists.'

'Good, then Abdel-Kadar will take care of you – there is the folk-music display and the souvenirs.'

'I think we had better be getting back,' Alice said.

The officer shook his head.

'Why not?'

'There is trouble.'

'We didn't see any.' Martin protested. 'Nothing at all. There's just time for us to get back if we leave now.'

'There are many things you did not see, how could you have seen everything that happens out there? If I say there is trouble that is all you need to know and I say it again – there is trouble, you cannot leave today.'

Something about the way the man spoke puzzled Martin, his English was perfect, too perfect, but it was the curious accent which intrigued him. It had that odd nasal cockney twang that Hollywood actors use when they play Brits.

'You studied in America?' Martin blurted out, then instantly regretted saying it – if he wanted to show off a British accent then Martin had clearly pointed out his failure.

The man reached for their passports, stared for a moment at the gilded coat of arms, then tossed them across to Martin as if to say: keep your Englishness.

'Your English is terrific,' Martin said 'Really good.'

Alice wished he would shut up – everything he said sounded patronising and it was obvious, to her at least, that this was not the sort of person you talked down to.

'I was wondering,' Martin went on, oblivious to her warning frown, 'about a boy we saw out there. He was clearly mad and shackled to a metal bar – though I can't think why as he can move at a helluva pace and if it's supposed to stop him from heading towards the sunset it can't be much of a success, can it?'

'It is for slaves,' the officer said, his voice flat. 'They put them on captured prisoners for the march to the coast.'

'That's terrible,' Martin said. 'I thought that sort of thing was well and truly over.'

'You do not like the idea of slavery?'

'Of course we don't,' Alice interjected, goaded by the suggestion of insincerity. 'His ankles were bleeding. It was unnecessary.'

'You are right of course, though it was the boy's family who shackled him like that – and they are descendants of the Arab slavers who used to take the people round here. They have to keep him in that thing to show the people they are punishing him, otherwise he would be killed. Everything is blamed on him: anything missing he has stolen; every wall that falls he has pulled it down with his bare hands; he is our scapegoat.'

'Can't you do something?' Alice asked.

'What? Put him in jail here? Would that be better?'

Martin looked round. Abdel-Kadar had slipped out at some point.

'Is the mad boy related to our driver,' he asked, 'and to that man Darwesh?'

The commandant nodded. 'They all crossed the desert together, which is what caused the problem – something happened out there.' He stopped speaking English and gave a command in Arabic which sent the nearest drunk scuttling out of the room while his companion tidied up the rubber stamps, lifting the desk lid and laying them neatly inside.

Martin could not resist a vengeful smirk at the man's discomfiture.

'Glad to see you run a tight ship here,' he said. 'Makes a welcome change from the general shambles we've seen thus far.'

Alice groaned but the officer seemed to weigh his words before responding to Martin's praise. 'You find this little scene depressing,' he said slowly. 'The rubber-stamp nonsense with these drunken fools? But surely it was no more than you expected from the natives? But no, you are embarrassed. You did not come to insult us, you came to help us, to help those starving children you saw on the television, to offer one of them so many good things – food, clothes, education, all the things this insane country has so appallingly failed to provide. Is that not so? You have so much to offer, yet here is this disagreeable man with his irritating ability to speak your language, making crude remarks which imply that your true feelings are not as pure as you think they are.'

Martin's heart sank. It was as if the years were slipping away, as if he had wandered into one of those sixties protest meetings at university, the ones where all those grindingly boring Nigerians and West Indians were banging on about their injustices to a white audience delirious with self-punishment. On top of everything the accent was now pure Boston grandee which might or might not be his base speech, just as Delmonico's Edinburgh might or might not be his. He could imagine him on some East Coast campus – a star of the Movement, laying any girl with half-way liberal opinions – a guilt-fucker. Well, he, Martin Beresford had grown out of all that crap – after Idi Amin, after the 'Emperor' Bokassa and all the others, after the economic catastrophe, the violence and now the famine, it didn't hold up the way it once had when the world was young and if he wanted to trot out the old arguments then Martin was quite willing to tell him so.

'Now look here,' he began, but Alice cut him off. 'What did yo mean?' she interjected. 'About us coming here to help a child?'

There was silence from Martin as he, too, saw what she was getting at.

'You're Maktar Diop,' she said.

'*Commandant* Maktar Diop.'

But Alice was not to be deflected now. 'What I want is . . .'

Now he cut her off with a wave of his hand.

'Here you cannot always have what you want exactly when you want it.'

He seemed pleased with the remark and Martin had the impression he had been practising it for some time. It was a relief to realise that someone with his education must be driven to holding imaginary conversations with himself in so dismal a place. As police commandant he could hardly have many friends and as for his colleagues . . .

Indeed, having said his piece, Diop seemed suddenly satisfied, turning to Alice with the air of a concerned host.

'You must be thirsty? Or you need the rest-room perhaps? It is through here – oh, do not worry it is very clean – between this drunken world and mine there is a *cordon sanitaire*.'

Martin stood at the door, transfixed – the room *was* spotless, the desk polished, the papers as neatly arranged as Mamadi's had been. Then he remembered the white facade, the only freshly painted surface he had seen since his arrival in Mali. So this was the power in Timbuktu, this was the man with whom little Mr Mamadi, far away in his distant impotent capital, wrestled for control of a deteriorating dust heap. Commandant Maktar Diop, so smart, so elegant, so cynical.

The commandant ushered Alice through a far door, then poured

161

out two glasses of water from a silver thermos jug silvered with icy condensation – a little miracle on its own. He handed one to Martin who had to force himself not to gulp it down in one go.

'So how are things in our capital?' Diop asked.

'Hard to say really, no one's encouraged to go out much. Delmonico says it's the trial – they've brought in conscript soldiers from up country so it's all a bit frightening – oh, I'm sorry, I forgot it's your uncle who's on trial.'

'Sorry? We are used to it – my father was executed when I was a boy. He was Minister of *Ponts et Chaussées* – Public Works, you would call it. As you can imagine, there was a lot of money in the contracts and our first President expected some of it. My father was less than cooperative.' He shot Martin a piercing look. 'You find this a little unbelievable and for once I sympathise with your suppressed thoughts – there are not many who would refuse to take a bribe here, but my family is different. We are Senegalese, my grandfather had a doctorate from the Sorbonne, he was one of the first of our people to become a practising *avocat* in France. He wrote poetry – he is our national poet.'

He stood up straight and began to recite as he must have been taught to do when a schoolboy.

> *Fille noire au bord des larmes,*
> *Ton guerrier a pris les armes,*
> *La lutte a commencé.*
> *Ô baisse ta voix triste:*
> *Ta liberté en vue . . .*

His voice trailed away, whether because he had forgotten the rest or had simply lost interest, Martin could not have said.

'What went wrong?' he asked.

'The President. Or rather, his friends – La Banque de L'Afrique et de L'Orient, Schneider et Cie, Texas Construction – they all owned a little bit of him . . .'

'According to Delmonico they could all have had their share after the rioters had finished their work.'

'Do not believe everything Delmonico says – in fact do not believe anything he says. He makes up horror stories to scare the tourists – I suppose he was made to eat one of his toes?'

'He did say he was hacked to pieces.'

'Nonsense. He was tried for corruption and misappropriation of public funds *in absentia* – he was on his farm in Normandy at the time and there he died – last year actually. Probably of drink – *le trou Normand*. No, the present government does everything legally. They think that by doing exactly as the World Bank says, we will solve all our problems and like good children we will be allowed to grow up and join the adults at table – one day. They are as stupid as my men out there who think that drinking beer makes them something special – they confuse a temporary sensation with reality. I do not. And now please, the money from Delmonico.'

Martin had to admire his restraint. He handed over the envelope and even then Diop forbore to open it in front of him.

'Where were you in the States?' Martin asked.

'Harvard, after school in Washington, my uncle was first ambassador. Now you want to know how I can stand this place? The answer is I can't but I have no choice, I am in effect a prisoner.'

Alice had been standing at the bathroom door listening to all this. She felt so much better for the splash of water over her face that everything seemed possible again – and then, when this tall, smart figure suddenly broke into poetry she had felt positively light-hearted. Of course she had not understood all the words but they sounded proud and uplifting.

'What did your poem mean?' she asked.

'It was a call to arms, not tears – to stop weeping and take action. It was written by my grandfather, but his sentiments are mine entirely. He was a great friend of Senghor, my family were originally from Senegal, they both created *négritude* in their Paris years, though few credit N'Daiye Diop with that now.'

He said this with such a bitter edge that it was a relief when he broke off and stared straight into the distance, lost in thought.

Now for it, Martin thought. Enough pleasantries, time to get down to business. He wondered what the set-up might be – was there some sort of centre, an orphanage, or what?

'Don't want to rush you or anything but it's getting on and if it's all right by you we'd like to – er – get on . . .'

'You are right,' Diop said. 'It is late. Abdel-Kadar will take you to the *campement* and get you a room for the night. You will be able to eat there.'

'But I thought . . .'

Diop made a brusque chopping motion with his right hand.

'Do not think so much. Learn African patience.'

163

'But Delmonico said that you . . .'

'Tomorrow.' He paused dramatically, then added 'Perhaps . . .'

'Now really. You can't treat us like this. We came here to make a reasonable . . .' Martin's protest trailed on but Alice was no longer listening. Things were not to be as simple as he thought but why should they be? They were trying to find a child and why should that be easy? Why should Martin object if they had to wait another day?

'. . . we can't just wait around like this.' His voice was rising by the second. 'We've got things to do. We were told we'd be back tonight. If we go missing there'll be a hell of a fuss.'

Diop shook his head slowly.

'I think not,' he said quietly. 'You had no idea where you were going and I hardly imagine that you told anyone about a trip that you knew you were not supposed to make?'

Martin sagged.

'Let's go,' Alice said, tugging at his arm.

Martin looked at her angrily. 'Whose side are you on? Why just give into him? We were told . . .'

But she was turning away and he knew he had lost and, pushing past her, he stormed out of the room.

'Abdel-Kadar will see to you,' Diop said, not unkindly.

Alice paused in the doorway.

'It's too easy,' she said. 'We were beaten before we began, so there can't be much satisfaction in kicking us now we're trapped here.'

'Tomorrow,' he said, 'I promise.'

'I believe you,' she said, her eyes fixed on his left hand, gripping the edge of the closing door, his knuckles finely wrinkled, the deep black lines contrasted against the light opalescent finger nails. He wore a thick gold wedding ring.

'Do you have children?'

'Three. They are under house arrest with my wife in Bamako – that means they are hostages. We are all trapped. You in your head, me in this room.'

He closed the door.

The two policemen were drinking again as she passed through the room. The touch of discipline had lasted but a moment. She wondered how Diop kept them under control. No one in Bamako would object if they knifed him one night. She shuddered, the idea distressed her, he was beautiful.

Martin was standing at the foot of the steps down from the veranda, facing a group of children each with a hand held out and a pathetic begging look plastered on their expectant faces.

A high thin voice said, 'Floos. D'jebel floos . . .'

'I do wish someone was on our side,' Alice said, looking to where Abdel-Kadar was standing, waiting for them to join him. 'That boy is just out for himself, like all of them.'

Martin thought of Darwesh and wondered whether he was powerful enough to control Diop but rather doubted it. Alice was right, they were on their own.

'We have no choice,' he said. 'The boy isn't going to take us back until he's told to, so that's that. What were you and Diop talking about in there?'

But her attention had been caught by a distant noise – Martin heard it too – a windy lilt of flutes, the sharp *braa-bap* of a hand-beaten drum.

A line of figures was snaking out from behind the nearest of the shuttered concrete houses.

One of them had a thin trumpet with a swollen ball near the end which wailed like a snake-charmer's pipe. There was the hollow crash of tambours, and a woman appeared, dressed in a tight *bustier* and diaphanous pantaloons which left her midriff exposed. She wriggled her hips enthusiastically, her hands flapping above her head, her feet stamping the ground, sending up little explosions of dust like the stones thrown at the demented boy.

It was an amateurish belly-dance, but worse than her inept rhythm was her tacky costume. Rows of golden coins should have been sewn into her headscarf, massive ivory bangles stained red from her henna'd hands should have clacked and clashed as her wrists flicked into the air, tinkling silver chains should have shimmered at her ankles. Instead there was only a desperate woman in a few gaudy rags, weaving about, trying to hold their interest for a moment.

Alice could take no more and hurried over to Abdel-Kadar.

'*Spectacle folklorique*,' he observed, indifferently.

'Rubbish,' she said angrily. 'Did you set this up – oh never mind, just get me out of here.'

Seeing her move away the performance fell apart. The musicians

165

raced after her, holding their hands out and shouting: '*Floos, floos, D'jebel floos.*'

Abdel-Kadar pushed the front-runners back, trying to keep a way clear for Alice to get through.

'*Floos, D'jebel floos . . .*'

Martin tried to catch up but found himself surrounded by pawing hands. The dancer was in front of him, her fingers almost touching his face. He remembered the incident on the airport bus and delved into his pocket, shouting: 'Here's some *floos* . . .', tossing the coins as high in the air as he could.

For a brief moment they hovered in the sunlight, glittering like the emerald-green flies, then, with the slowness of expectation, they began to fall.

A pained roar came from the musicians as they threw themselves to the ground, scrabbling in the dust, kicking and punching to get at their share.

Serves the bastards right, Martin thought as he hurried after Alice and the boy. He approached the narrow entrance of the labyrinth but the drifts of sand slowed him down and he paused for breath. He damned everything: the heat, the grey dust, the greedy natives, but when he turned and looked back, he saw the woman who had tried to dance for him – standing alone, empty-handed, crying.

FIVE

The shadows were longer than the buildings were high. Alice imagined the women in the shuttered houses, quietly preparing the dreamed-of meal in this last hard hour of the fast. For herself, she was beyond hunger, light-headed to the point of happiness.

Everything was a little crazy – the building ahead of them was a fantasy out of Beau Geste, standing on its own in the desert, a short distance from the grey city wall. Two storeys high, each floor a line of Moorish arches, it was a Foreign Legion fort out of a *Boy's Own* adventure.

'*Le campement*,' Abdel-Kadar said.

'French,' Martin added. 'Some sort of colonial rest-house – thank God . . .'

They went inside.

Two floors of arched colonnades enclosed an inner oblong court-yard open to the sky. Arched doorways led to single rooms on both levels. '. . . Or an Egyptian prison,' he added gloomily.

Alice did not agree. It had charm – the glimpse of desert through the arches, the descending sun flashing through the geometric tracery along the edge of the flat roof.

'Look here,' Martin said. He had crossed the courtyard and passed through one of the arched doors and stepped into an old French film, a bistro from an imaginary pre-war Paris. A long zinc *comptoir* ran the length of the room; hanging on the wall behind was a photograph of the President in what looked like a collarless Mao suit, and a yellowing notice outlining the law relating to the *Suppression de l'Ivresse Publique et Protection des Mineurs*. At the end of the room yet another arch led through to an outside terrace set with round bistro tables covered in checkered cloths, on which stood empty wine bottles with drippy candles waiting to be lit. Beyond, lay the rolling vista of dusty desert.

Martin picked up a menu. It was a single sheet divided into boxed columns, the way menus had been when he first went to France with his school. Even the food was the classic *prix fixe* fare of another age – *carrottes râpées*, *harengs à l'huile*, stewed main dishes: *gigot* with *flageolets*, the inevitable *steak frites*.

He looked up and saw a bald-headed African behind the bar watching them closely. He wore a striped Breton sailor shirt like a costume; all he needed was a black beret at a rakish angle and a wet Gitane stuck to his lower lip.

Abdel-Kadar spoke in rapid staccato bursts – clearly the man did not merit the long, unctuous phrases he had shared with his uncle. The African nodded to everything, pointing out a printed sheet in a frame by the door. Martin went to look but all the prices were in old French francs, thousands of them, and quite meaningless.

'You take any room,' Abdel-Kadar said. 'Take sheets here.' He lifted some pressed white squares from a pile by the door and topped them with a towel and a tiny bar of soap.

'You wife eat here,' he said. 'You come my uncle?'

Martin took the linen in his arms and looked at Alice, silhouetted in the doorway. He could hardly leave her in this empty place, even though she did seem unusually contented.

'I'm not sure,' he said.

'You come,' said the boy, leaning close to him and looking hard into his eyes. 'You enjoy.'

'There must be a way on to the roof,' Alice said. 'I'm going for a look.'

Martin followed with his pile of sheets, the boy turned away and headed for the entrance. Martin watched him disappear through the dark archway and knew he would have to see him again.

Alice found a stairway to the upper floor, then a narrower flight that took her up to the roof. She could see down into the courtyard where Martin was trying one of the arched doors. The wooden board gave with a rusty squeal and he found himself inside a cool barrel-vaulted cell. Motes of dust danced in the shaft of light from the entrance. He could make out a metal-framed bed, draped with a gauze mosquito net, one side torn and thickly stitched like a bad wound. A lumpy mattress was covered in striped ticking with a raised piecrust edge, its surface an archipelago of ancient yellow stains. The gritty dust had seeped under the door covering everything. He dumped the sheet and went over to a second door with a round switch to one side. He turned it, but nothing happened. There was just enough light to see that it was a bathroom. He went in, stood on the tiled platform of the squatting lavatory, lowered his clothes and relieved himself noisily. A solitary bulb dangled from a frayed plaited flex; there was something clinging to it, a long-dead insect, its empty carapace soldered to the opal globe, forever embracing the thing that had scorched the life out of it. So there had been electricity once – he wondered about water. There was a deep square washbasin, the sort of thing found in old sculleries, with a tap at the end of a free-standing copper pipe. He forced it with both hands, afraid the whole thing might rip away from the floor. It resisted, then gave with an asthmatic cough and a splatter of red brown water. He caught some on his handkerchief and drew it over his face, as if smearing away greasepaint. The trickle had stopped but he turned off the tap, more out of habit than necessity.

Back in the bedroom, he flopped down on to the filthy mattress, so heavily the mosquito net snapped from the ceiling, sending lengths of parched gauze crackling down around him – he lay, enveloped in a lacy shroud, a Victorian corpse laid out in a wedding gown.

There was a musty smell but it was too nice to be lying down for him to think of doing anything about it. Unexpected parts of him ached. He was no longer sure what time it was. What had been hunger was now a permanent gripe somewhere inside a great void. He hugged the net closer and thought of Abdel-Kadar's neck and the soft cornelian skin, miraculously free of the dust which smeared everyone else. Then he thought of the Japanese woman in the pool, the tension between her ungainly battle with the water and the grace of her body. He closed his eyes and she swam towards him, jerkily, her spine arching and unbending, her tight buttocks clenched and released, clenched and released – then he saw the face of the mad boy, its rigid, manic concentration, the legs held by the stiff metal bar, swimming towards him through the dust.

Martin opened his eyes – there was a mosquito somewhere. Its distant petulant motorbike whine went into ominous cut-out. He instinctively waved a hand but knew it was only a gesture – he had no way of knowing the direction of the attack. He tried to forget it, to concentrate on the mess they were in, but it was like the rest of his life – an unwilled drift into dead-end situations. Thus had he married Alice, thus had he become a schoolteacher, thus was he now rolled up in crinkly white netting in a filthy caravanserai in the middle of nowhere. He stiffened as the whine revved up, circled, then went silent again – it was like a war film, the shrieking bomber, the terrible nothingness before impact. The net was useless, wrapped so tightly about him the insect had only to prod its little needle through any of a thousand holes to suck at his blood. He had already rolled over, trying to free himself, but had only succeeded in getting still further enmeshed. Bugger, he said and fell to the floor with a crash – at least that ought to confuse the little bastard!

Lying there he remembered Darwesh's invitation and was very tempted. The prospect of a grim meal out on that open veranda, with Alice saying nothing all evening, was very unappealing – how could she object if he went? If she had stuck by him at the police station he might have forced Diop to do something. She had hardly made it easy for him.

Struggling upright, he wrenched at the stiff gauze until his right arm was free. A line of angry red bumps ran from elbow to wrist, but rubbing at them only made them angrier. Bugger, he thought again, then realised he was hungry, very hungry indeed. He went out into the courtyard, dark except for the dim glow from the door of the café, then went up the steep stairs where Alice must have gone, rehearsing the little speech he planned to make.

In her first moments on the roof Alice had felt the world revolving round her. To one side the desert ended in a hard crimson line, the sun a bright orange hemisphere half lost behind it, too bright to be stared at for long. When she turned towards the town, it was so intense and clear in the horizontal light, it seemed to her that she was facing an object both natural and magical – a crystal formation of cubes and angled slivers, a city of ice in the desert.

Immediately below, in the space between the *campement* and the first line of mud houses, was a wide circular excavation, with steep paths leading down into its hidden depths. She wondered what it was for but was too exhausted to do anything but look. It was all beyond her, anyway. The beautiful Diop would do what was needed in his own time. There was little point in fussing and she rather wished she could be spared Martin and his belly-aching when it all seemed so perfectly clear.

She reached into her right pocket and pulled out the silver pendant. It was the colour of iron in the dying light. She hung it around her neck, tucking it out of sight inside her shirt, and saw how dry and chalky the sun-baked skin was along her lower arms. She was turning to dust like the town. A quick rub with her fingers gathered up the dead layer into a thin black worm, like the varicose fags they had smoked as students, hopeless things that you could barely keep alight for two puffs. She pulled it away, leaving a lighter patch of fresh pink flesh. She was being remade anew – even the world had changed. She looked behind and saw that the sun had all but disappeared leaving only a final explosion of light along the earth's rim, causing all colours to slide into red. The greys of the town were scarlet and crimson; the sky, salmon; the earth, blood. She had read about it but never thought to see it – the drunken dusk of desert places. No wonder they forbade wine. It would have been a wild excess in this vast wash of luminous burgundy.

As she stood, she saw that she too was a russet monochrome: her darker shadows edging to deep plummy purples, her arms and hands a livid lobster. She felt even lighter-headed and only slowly became aware that Martin had joined her.

'There you are,' he was saying. 'I wondered where you'd got to. God, the light goes quick here, the sun just plummeted. Feel more relaxed now?'

She said nothing. He was almost invisible, a dark silhouette against the faint carmine tinge at the end of the earth.

'I've had a sort of invitation,' he began cautiously. 'Abdel-Kadar's uncle, the one with the walking-stick in the market, has asked me to his house. I think I ought to look in, out of courtesy, seemed an important sort of man . . .'

Again, no reaction.

'I don't suppose I'll be long, just going to look in . . .'

Alice felt reality creeping back. There was a deep ache in her shoulder, she revolved it slightly. What was he saying? Something about going to a party? She closed her eyes and tried to shut out his bleating.

'. . . be back soon, I dare say. Never know, might find out more about the set-up here. The café thing here looks all right if you want a bite to eat. Looks French.'

'I'll be OK,' she said neutrally. 'Don't rush.'

His dark outline blended into the black wall.

Alone again, she tried to hold the first star at the centre of her concentration, but it seemed to blink and twitch and she found herself moving around the awakening constellations in a restless arc.

Martin hurried across the courtyard and out into the dusty space between the *campement* and the town. Everything was red, the earth crimson – the mud houses a deep maroon. He had been so

171

sure that he would find Abdel-Kadar waiting for him that he was momentarily confused at the sight of an old man crouching some way from the entrance, who immediately got to his feet and began walking towards the town without exchanging a word.

When the man disappeared into one of the dark passageways leading into the warren of earthen houses, Martin realised he would have to follow. He scuttled to catch up, but as he penetrated the narrow gap between the crumbling walls he saw the man disappear down another path, his bare feet leaving only the slightest trace in the fine dust. Martin quickened his pace until he saw the man ahead of him again, his long djebba floating trance-like against the dark-red walls. He turned again, left now, seemingly unconcerned as to whether Martin saw him or not. This alley was long and straight with latticed windows on to the street. Music rose from hidden courtyards on either side. The path forked, and at the angle the arched mouth of a beehive oven glowed red, the smell of baking bread still hanging in the air. Martin was hungry and tired – it was hard wading through the cloying dust in heavy European shoes, hurrying lest he lose sight of his supposed guide, terrified he might end up lost in the impossible labyrinth. The man drifted right. Martin followed but found it hard to keep up – the narrow gap between the houses was closing in and his shoulders were now brushing the walls on either side. His guide too was forced to slow down, lessening the gap between them until Martin was almost behind him. He was very old, grey hairs curled from below his turban, his shoulders stooped and his feet splayed form a lifetime walking barefoot. Where, Martin wondered, was Abdel-Kadar with his fresh, sweet-smelling body.

They emerged into a small square with a blasted, leafless tree. Ahead was a high crenellated wall with a massive carved door inset with a bold pattern of star-headed bolts. The man rapped twice. It swung open on to a wide courtyard hung with coloured lanterns. Martin stepped in and paused as his eyes adjusted to the flicker of light after the darkening town.

'Al'hamdulillahi . . .'

It was Darwesh, wringing his hands and chortling with delight, as if Martin's appearance had fulfilled his every desire. He grasped his elbow and steered him into the square, an open space spread with woven mats and coloured carpets on which squatted men of a similar age and girth. Martin could make out a couple of women through the far arches, working at large metal pots balanced on charcoal braziers. Perhaps others were peeping out from behind the lattice blinds of the seraglio windows projecting from the upper storey.

He allowed himself to be tugged inwards to a place on one of the mats, where he was nudged down with his host beside him. A group of musicians opposite were playing pipes and tambours. A boy in a fez stepped on bare tiptoe between the guests, offering a tray of sweetmeats. Those nearest to Martin reached over to shake his hand and touch their foreheads. The man to his right said, 'Welcomes, Welcomes', to which Martin replied, 'Thank you. Thank you', after which conversation lapsed and he was grateful when another boy approached with small fine-china cups of sweet mint tea, so hot it was painful to grip the rim between thumb and finger and almost pointless to try to blow the liquid cool.

More women were working in the cooking area beneath the arches, watched by a large, dark-skinned matriarch. At her prompting, a figure appeared in a long bloody apron carrying the carcass of a lamb which he hung from a hook on the wall between the arches, blood streaming from its slit throat, and proceeded to strip away the creature's fluffy coat, unveiling an obscene pinkish nakedness. Martin knew the man, it was the blacksmith from the market. It all looked very promising, two browning carcasses were already turning on spits above glowing charcoal braziers the first rich aromas of roasting meat were wafting his way. He swallowed his saliva and was glad when a boy came over with a tray of plump dates filled with swollen knobs of bright green almond paste. He took two. They were delicious. He could see other good things being set out on large round platters. There were, Martin reflected, worse things to be doing – like being with his wife.

The lambs turned. A weird figure, his djebba tucked into his belt like baggy pantaloons and a sheet coiled around his head in a careless turban, brought a hookah with a bright coal in its upper chamber which he set before Darwesh. Martin hadn't smoked for years, and tobacco on a very empty stomach might be disastrous. His English-speaking neighbour tugged at his sleeve and shook his head. 'No good, no good,' he said, pulling a long thin pipe from a leather pouch, followed by a cube of what Martin guessed must be hashish. The man went through the process of crumbling the dust into the pipe and lighting it from the ember above the hookah. Having inhaled deeply he offered it to Martin, who took the pipe to his lips and drew on it, long and deep, holding the smoke in his belly before releasing it with a windy sigh. The man giggled encouragingly and refused to take it back. Martin inhaled again and felt the years slip away – it was university again – the smoke, the hunger, the tiredness, set him adrift. The music was insistent and loud. Conversation was unnecessary. It was all very easy; perhaps too easy – the one lingering doubt, which even the frequent to and fro of the pipe could not completely suppress, was why exactly had he been invited? Arab hospitality? The famous courtesy to visitors? An act of simple politeness? It was possible, yet something – some inner voice which even the aromatic smoke could not quite suppress – said that there had to be more to it than that. The spits revolved, the lambs turned, the music pounded, the pipe passed and repassed. Now there was another bustle of activity near the arches. Laden dishes and trays appeared, carried by young men and boys. Martin strained to see if Abdel-Kadar was among them, but could not make him out if he was.

Darwesh got up and went to inspect one of the lambs. He was handed a dangerous-looking scimitar with an engraved blade and a multicoloured handle from which two gold tassels dangled. He raised the weapon and carefully sliced a chunk from the carcass which was deftly caught by a boy holding a brass salver. Their host lifted this charred flesh in his fingers, bit into it and nodded theatrically to indicate his approval, an act which provoked an expectant murmur of pleasure from around the courtyard. Dipping his hands in a proffered bowl and wiping them on a towel, Darwesh left his servants to carve the meat and stepped back through his guests to his place beside Martin. Bowls of water and towels appeared and as soon as Martin had washed Darwesh clapped his hands imperiously summoning two men who staggered forward with a large wooden platter loaded with lemony saffron rice, dotted with sultanas, raisins and nuts and overlaid with huge chunks of the lamb. Around the edges of the tray were small mahogany bowls of a vivid red liquid, which had to be chilli, while a larger bowl was piled with little pyramids of dark meat which Martin guessed must be chicken livers.

'Eating, eating,' said his English-speaking neighbour, leaning towards the food to show him how to scoop up the rice and meat in his right hand and nudge it into a ball before tweaking at the tender, greasy flesh. Martin obeyed. It was delicious and the people around him laughed pleasantly at his noisy relish. With the next mouthful he risked a quick dip into the sauce – it was hot but not too hot and the reaction that this produced among the watchers was gratifying – clearly they had not expected him to touch the stuff.

'Hot, hot,' said his echoing neighbour. 'Eat, eat. Enjoy, enjoy.'

Martin gorged. The others likewise, quickly and noisily.

'Eat, eat,' said the neighbour. 'Eat, eat. Enjoy, enjoy.' Darwesh clapped his hands summoning a young man in a short shift-like garment and high traditional fez who hurried over with a silver dish covered with a domed lid. He knelt, lifting it with a flourish, exposing what looked like five strips of greyish leather.

Again he was invited to 'eat, eat', but this time he hesitated, acutely aware that everyone was watching him. Whatever the greyish strips might be, they were clearly considered a delicacy. Happily there was nothing immediately repellent about them, no eyes or other soft organs, just this rather tough leathery looking hide. He lifted one and tried to bite into it but the tasteless strip resisted his teeth. He clamped his jaws repeatedly, but seemed hardly to dent the stuff.

'Good?' the man asked.

Martin smiled weakly, still chomping, wondering what it was he was struggling with – stomach-lining, a heel (if lambs had such things), the earlobe maybe. Was it an elaborate hoax? Would they suddenly fall about laughing? He reached for the silver bowl and offered his host a strip – if it was a joke then it was about to be exposed. Darwesh bowed and delicately lifted a long thin strip and, sighing with pleasure, popped it into his open mouth and began to chew. After a moment he swallowed and it was gone. It was no use, Martin decided, he would never get it down like that, his only hope was to try and bite the thing in half. He ground his teeth and the thing snapped. He tried to tease up some saliva, then tried swallowing again. Both pieces sank heavily. He needed a drink, the hash and the rice had dried his mouth to a personal desert. Swallowing the two strips had parched him even further. He pointed towards his glass and more mint tea appeared, so sweet it left his lips sticky. The silver bowl with the strips was offered again but this time he made a gracious gesture towards his fellow guests who accepted his offer with alacrity. Martin returned to the main tray and continued to stuff himself with rice and lamb, happy to have passed the test.

As huge earthenware bowls of fruit were being brought out, it was Darwesh's turn to attempt a conversation. He said something in Arabic.

'You businessman?' the neighbour translated.

Martin shook his head.

'You professor?'

Martin nodded; the title was exaggerated but would suffice. If this was leading up to something, it was still too early to say what.

Water and towels passed round again and a little boy ran up with a silver sprinkler to drip orange-flower water on to their hands. One man caught him in his arms but the lad wriggled free amid a burst of raucous laughter. The pipe passed again. Martin rather wished his host would leave him in peace, he felt woozy and wanted to forget everything in the pleasing sensuousness seeping through him.

But Darwesh spoke again.

'You go soon?' the neighbour asked spreading his arms like an aeroplane.

'Next plane,' Martin said. 'Back to Bamako, then home.'

'France?' the man asked.

'England.'

The two men conferred with much use of the word *Angleterre*. Then the man explained: 'His son Paris. Study to be *médecin*. Very hard for money. No *devises*.'

That was just about clear – Darwesh's son was a student in France and his father couldn't get foreign exchange for him. Given the drift of the conversation the next remark was not unexpected.

'You take for him no?'

Martin didn't need to think about this: 'No!' he said firmly.

Before the man could protest the orchestra started up with a loud crash on the drums and a sudden clattering rhythm on the tambours which had all eyes turning towards the space at the centre of the courtyard. The music quickened and a dancer rushed on tiptoe, out of the arched shadows into the light. She was veiled from the crown of her head to her waist with a headband weighed with a circlet of gold coins. Her wrists jangled with silver bracelets, her ankles clashed with the heavy rings of henna-stained ivory. A tight red bustier propped up her discreetly covered breasts, more silky veils in blues and yellows sprouted from a single diamond embedded in her exposed navel. Martin felt overwhelmed by the unreality of it all: the stars and the moon, the scent of orange-flower water, the tambours and pipes, and the dance of the seven veils.

The svelte creature began to revolve, billowing her veils, jerking each buttock up and down in turn as her delicate feet patter-patted against the hardened earth and her fingers plucked at the diaphanous scarves, sending first one then another drifting away. Martin thought of the Japanese woman, her fleshless frame, her slim boyish body, of . . . He stopped, some instinct told him Darwesh was observing his every reaction. So what – if this was the 'thing' the lecherous bastard thought he wanted, then he was right. By God he wanted it. Were there seven veils or six or eight? The little diamond winked as the belly rotated. A veil drifted before his face leaving a vague hint of musk. The dancer stamped her little feet, as near to the front row of squatting men as possible. She wriggled her midriff, causing the slight peak of her belly to rise and fall and her navel to expand and dilate. Why did the tiny jewel not pop out? It was the sexiest thing Martin had ever seen. She turned, trembling her buttocks in the face of the nearest spectator who suddenly lost control and made a grasp for them only to find himself clutching air as she side-stepped and danced to the opposite side of the yard. Another man held up a rolled banknote until she saw it and wiggled her way towards him, offering first her front then her back until it was clear he preferred the latter, carefully folding the note and teasingly inserting it into the rear cleavage, leaving the stem exposed as she danced away. The place was suddenly alive with waving banknotes. She picked her way through the squatting crowd letting them stuff the stiff paper rolls fore and aft – into the cleft in her bustier, down the front of her waistband, but mainly, so Martin observed, into the valley at the back until it sprouted a dozen stiff tubes. More veils fell, the music grew louder and faster, the dancer turned more wildly, forgetting their money, more concerned with her own dervish spin. It was mad and frightening, she was possessed and Martin was suddenly convinced that she was moving towards him. Surely she would veer away, dance off into the crowd, return to the centre – but no, she was still advancing, her arms rising and falling as she made one last dangerous whirl, as the music ended with a final crash of drum and tambour, and she fell, as if struck by a hammer blow, right there into Martin's lap. The audience went berserk, shouting, cheering, applauding, banging whatever was to hand. There was a loud female lu-luing from the upper rooms, which proved Martin right about the silent watchers. He looked round to see what would happen next and realised that Darwesh and the echoing neighbour had slipped away during the dance and that there was no one left to help him. Nervously, he looked down at the exhausted dancer who opened her heavily darkened lids and stared back at him through the fine veil that still covered her face. Martin screwed up his eyes and peered into the flimsy gauze and saw the lips turn into a grin. There was no mistaking who it was. Despite the heavily roughed mouth, the powdered face, the kohl-fringed eyes, the henna'd hands, the glittering, shimmering veils. But before Martin could speak, Abdel-Kadar was on his feet and nimbly skipping through the cheering crowd, back to the safety of the darkened inner rooms.

Alice watched the bloodshot sky fade through purple to raven black, spattered with cold white stars under a sharp Islamic moon which picked out the arches round the courtyard. In this silvery disguise it was suddenly hard to bear. The failure and the scruffiness and the poverty she had so far witnessed had been tolerable because they were squalid and unlovely – to let them be beautiful for an instant was to admit a deep hurt.

There were lights in the desert, pinpricks, shifting stars, a prancing firefly-flash out among the dunes. Now she saw order, they advanced two by two, in a snaking line. Cars? Lorries? Buses? There were a dozen pairs, dipping out of sight behind a ridge, resurfacing with a burst of fiery spray.

It was no business of hers. She got up, went down the two flights of stairs, through the archway, past the bar, out on to the terrace where she chose one from all the empty bistro tables. The headlights were passing to her right; she deliberately ignored them and picked up a menu. There was a printed sheet clipped on to the regular fare – the choice was impressive: *boeuf en daube, petit salé, escalope de veau à la crème*, with wines to match, château-bottled, premier cru. Aware of someone behind her, she turned and saw the fat barman in his funny *apache* outfit, waiting for her to choose.

'S'il vous plaît ...' she began, but the man simply turned and walked away.

There was nothing to do but wait for whatever might come. She must be facing north, out into the desert, with home an unimaginable distance across the empty wastes. No matter how far, no matter how exotic the destination, there was always the return, yet in a sense – the only sense that really mattered – they had come too far to go back.

She heard a sudden braying laugh –

'*Aaarf, aaarf, aaarf . . .*'

– and looked up sharply. Who would dare to be so rude?

'*Aaarf, aaarf, aaarf . . .*

There was nothing. Just the braying laughter.

'*Aaarf, aaarf, aaarf . . .*'

The fat man came back with a tray. He slapped down a plate with half a fried chicken, an unmarked bottle of dark red wine, with a small thick glass which could hold little more than a good mouthful, then he retreated. Alice looked at the fowl, yellow with oil and surrounded by hefty chips, soggy and unappealing. So what. He had left no cutlery, she ate with her fingers, reaching for the litre bottle, struggling to hold it in her greasy hand. The wine was coarse but again, so what.

'*Aaarf, aaarf, aaarf . . .*'

She looked up, a frog, a huge, scabrous, greenish brown monster of a frog had hopped into the circle of light cast by the oil-lamp.

There were others, dozens of them in a half circle behind, but this lead frog was so much bigger it had to be a she, bloated with spawn.

'*Aaarf, aaarf, aaarf,*' she went, then the others joined her: '*Aaarf, aaarf, aaarf, aaarf . . .*'

Alice was thoroughly mystified. Frogs lived by water, not here in this dry desert. Where was the river or the pond where that fat creature could release her slimy bubbles ready for old man bullfrog to do his fertilization bit?

She tore another mouthful of the slimy chicken and washed it back with a harsh gulp of red wine, while out of the corner of her eye she watched the mother frog hop forward a fraction. The others moved up, in unison behind her. So that was what she wanted – food. But did frogs eat chicken – ought they to? It seemed somehow obscene for anything not human to feast on such greasy flesh.

The frog seemed to follow her reasoning – '*aaarf, aaarf, aaarf*' – she insisted. Alice tore off a strip and threw it far into the shadows where she would not be able to see what would happen. The frog turned with a series of clumsy belly heaves and disappeared after the titbit, '*aaarfing*' as she went.

Alice wiped her mouth with the back of her hand and swigged

down more wine. Distant drumming wafted in from the town. Why should Martin be the only one to have fun? She could hear more of the wailing snake-charmer music and the sharp slap of a tambour. It was unfair, a party, music and dancing – Diop might be there. He would be a wonderful dancer, sinewy and self-absorbed, unmindful of her jerky seventies bop. She pushed her plate away and got up. The fat man had gone, she was free to do whatever she wished. The courtyard was a deep tank, the night and stars were lights playing on its surface. She swam through dark waters towards the darker entrance, then froze as she realised there was someone coming towards her, two figures outlined against the arched doorway. They couldn't see her and turned aside before getting near. Alice heard the rattle of a door and the harsh grating of a match and was blinded by a sudden burst of light, followed by the shaky glow of a candle. It was Thorsten, the pilot, and a small figure entirely veiled. The door was pushed shut, leaving Alice wondering why there was all that draped modesty when the woman was willing to come to the *campement* with the Swede?

Walking softly on the balls of her feet, Alice made for the doorway. Outside, beyond the open ground, over the roofline, shafts of light rose from the hidden courtyards as if lifted by the music. She walked towards the dark outer wall unsure what to do, worried in case she ought not to be doing it but unable to stop herself. A darker shadow marked an alleyway and she headed into it, hoping it would lead quickly into an open square, somewhere better lit and less terrifying. If one of the two doorways ahead was open she could look – maybe go – inside. But everything was shuttered and bolted. Just past the second door there was a narrow opening between two walled courtyards that must lead into the heart of the labyrinth. Telling herself she was crazy, she hurried down it, quickening her pace lest she lost her nerve, turn back and run for the safety of the *campement*.

The passage narrowed slightly. Her arms brushed against the mud walls. There was something at the end, something lighter. Stepping out of the tunnel she saw two entrances, both firmly closed, but a bright light shone up from one courtyard and there was the sound of frenzied drumming, the hum of conversation and the pleasant scent of roasting almonds. She wanted to knock but did not dare. There were two paths ahead – she chose the right for no particular reason, following walls so high she could barely see the stars and was surprised to step out into a wide space with a stone cairn at its centre, a monument of some sort. There was something unusual about the big house behind it – the moonlight fell on a bronze plaque high on the wall with an inscription which Alice realised to her surprise was in English. She strained to make out the words – a Major Laing – killed in the desert – 1826 – she tried to imagine it, without planes and jeeps and smiling guides, Major Laing on his own, in that mud house, then out in the desert, the knives drawn from under the long robes. She swallowed, her eyes drifting to a nearby window. It had lattice shutters. One was pushed back but beyond was total darkness. She could no longer hear the distant music and the utter silence disturbed her more than anything so far.

She took a path, curving to the left, so sharply she could not tell what lay ahead. This too began to narrow, forcing her to hold her arms out before her. It was impossible to turn but the thought of retreating backwards, blindly, drove her on. There was something malign at work, something teasing her, playing on her fears, and when she squeezed herself into the next open space she knew it had won – she was confused and lost, no longer sure how many times she had turned. The walls were now so high she could not see the minaret and had nothing to which she could align herself. Two passageways offered themselves but neither seemed better than the other. Had there been an open door she would have conquered her fear and gone in, trusting that her status as a scatty tourist would protect her, but there was nothing, only the neutral sides of the perfect maze. She told herself to snap out of it – rats were put through similar tests and doing anything had to be better than limply waiting there. 'Come on,' she said out loud then plunged down the middle path and hurried on as fast as she could, hampered by the sand in her shoes, but unwilling to stop to empty them for fear she might lose heart again. And then it happened.

A figure stepped out of the darkness. She saw him before he saw her, his uniform, unbuttoned at the neck, his cap at a skewed angle, a bottle dangling from his right hand. He stumbled as he came towards her. It was one of the policemen from the station, clearly drunk. She had no sooner registered his condition than he saw her – or rather, he saw something. Leaning forward at an unsteady angle he advanced, eyes squinting, attempting to focus. His expression was menacing. He snarled something. She stuck up her chin as if to say: 'I am untouchable.' It worked. He stopped, a cracked grin of recognition blossoming across his bleary face. But to her dismay he raised his free hand as if to strike her. She flinched but the hand only stopped and turned palm upwards.

'Floos,' the man said. 'D'jebel floos. Donne-moi de l'argent.'

He wanted money, which she would certainly have given had she possessed any but all the cash was in her bag or with Martin.

The man advanced, still holding out his palm. 'Un petit cadeau,' he said. 'Deutsch marks, haben zie . . .'

Without thinking, she turned and hurried back the way she had come, not running, she guessed that might provoke him, more a firm lolloping stride.

Behind her she could hear his polyglot pleading: 'Hey lady, give dollar.'

She hurried on. Surely he was too drunk to do anything more than call after her: 'D'jebel floos.'

She heard him still. He seemed no further away.

'Donne-moi un cadeau. De l'argent.'

He was closing on her. There was another narrow passage just ahead but she dared not squeeze into it for fear it would slow her down too much. A little way on was a wider alley – she took it, the voice still pleading but more distant. She ran into another square and stopped, feeling safe enough to pause and weigh up what she was doing. Before her was the broken wall she and Martin had passed earlier with its stack of new mud bricks beside it. She walked towards them but froze as she heard the voice close behind.

'Hey lady, give me dollar . . .'

Terrified she dashed to the wall, seized one of the heavy mud bricks, turned and hurled it in the direction of her tormentor. There was a satisfying clunk and a yelp of pain – but satisfaction immediately gave way to terror – it was bound to enrage him. She plunged down the nearest passage, no longer pretending to walk, running wildly, but as she rushed into the next open space she instinctively turned to see if he was after her and with a sickening jolt ran smack into a waiting figure. Hands took hold of her as she sank to her knees and looking up she saw the trim uniform, the slim figure, then the narrow features of the commandant.

'Help me,' she said, letting herself go limp so that he would catch her and raise her up.

'What do you want?' he said.

182

She shook her head, feeling the gun holster pressing into her side and smelling something appealingly clean but unsweet after the cloying dusty heat of the town. She was sorry when he set her on her feet, relaxing his grip and stepping back.

'What do you want?' he said again.

But she could only shake her head, her mind fixed on the drunken policeman, wondering if she had hurt him, afraid it meant serious trouble.

'Come,' Diop said, irritated by her silence. She hurried after him, terrified he might disappear, but it was only a short walk before they emerged from the labyrinth and were out in the open desert.

His jeep looked shiny and science fiction in the blue moonlight but he swung himself into the driver's seat as if mounting a camel. She scrambled up beside him, feeling silly, convinced he was going to return her to the *campement* – a naughty runaway, brought home by the local copper.

He revved up with a shattering noise and lurched off along the line of the outer wall. Alice clung to the seat afraid she would be thrown off, squealing as he took a sharp angle that set them heading into the void. Her relief that he was not taking her back quickly gave way to a fear of where they might be going. He was looking straight ahead, peering into the illuminated figure-of-eight the headlights threw before them. Alice forgot her fears and studied his profile – his eyelashes were the longest she had ever seen, curved like a hasty signature.

She looked away, afraid he would sense she was staring at him. To her left she could just make out the last of the stray mud houses dropping away behind them, almost lost in the dust cloud they were churning up. The ground was covered with flecks of snow, little eddies, caught in the wake of the jeep. Next there were boxes. Cardboard boxes. Dozens of them, first in small heaps, then in large dumps, all surrounded by flurries of white snow. Snow in the desert, snow everywhere. She laughed out loud.

Then she saw the tents, sage green army tents in long lines radiating from a central circle with a flagpole and a lifeless flag. There were people, immobile, lying in the shadows of the tent flaps or clustered in groups beside a line of military trucks stacked with more cardboard boxes. Boxes everywhere – the snow was packing material, scattered chips of white polystyrene. When Alice looked behind she could see people struggling to their feet and shuffling along in their wake. She was about to ask who they were when Diop stopped in front of a large tent marked with a roughly daubed red crescent whose edges had blurred into the canvas. A line of women squatted near the entrance, babies laid across their arms. A group of men sat slightly apart, their heads covered by the cowls of their djebbas. One woman was trying to feed her baby, squeezing a length of pap, as black and as wrinkled as a dried date, into the passive mouth. The child looked less as if it were being fed than as if its mother were dragging the tongue out of its unprotesting throat.

'Refugees?' Alice asked.

Diop shrugged. 'They have been "resettled".'

'What will happen to them?'

'Nothing. There has been a government report, a delegation from Brussels, a commission from UNRA, a paper from the World Bank, so nothing. Fortunately the European Community sends food – they have been growing too much maize flour recently and so it comes here – they make porridge with it. But what do you care – is it not what you hoped to find? No disaster, no baby?'

'Please take me back,' Alice said.

He ignored this, pushing aside a tarpaulin, hung across the entrance, bending to go in.

Alice looked at the men, sensing their hatred. One of them stood up – he was probably only stretching his legs but the sudden movement terrified her and she quickly ducked under the cloth, hurrying after Diop.

The interior was long and narrow. A row of mats ran down either side with a middle corridor that led to a closed curtain. Diop must have gone behind it. The women on the mats nearest the entrance were heavily pregnant, waiting their time. Beyond them women nursed newborn babies. There was little noise, the occasional snuffle from one of the children, a hiccup which might have signalled the beginnings of a cry but didn't.

A single oil-lamp hung on the central pole, drawing the eye, sending all light concentrically out, ending in far corners of darkness where shadowy bodies lay stretched in sleep or hidden suffering. It was over-consciously dramatic – Rembrandt, Joseph Wright, van Gogh. Lit from above, the women looked posed, a dagguerotype for a nineteenth-century *carte de visite*.

Near her feet, a naked girl – about two years old, Alice guessed – sat alone, sucking her wrist. Alice took a step toward her, glancing about to see if anyone disapproved before she knelt and smoothed the loose curls. The child studied her. Alice smiled and ran gentle fingers above her waist, slightly tickling. The girl released her wrist, gurgling with pleasure.

'Pretty,' Alice said, stroking the little back – the child was soft and warm. Alice wanted to lift her but was afraid this might be going too far. She wished she had thought to bring something – sweets, biscuits, something she could have passed round.

The canvas partition was yanked aside. She felt Diop's anger before he spoke.

'This is Dr El-Assawy,' he announced. 'She is in charge here.'

The woman behind him was wiping her hands on what looked to Alice like a traditional blue bordered tea-cloth. The brusqueness of her movements showed as much anger as Diop's voice.

'Dr El-Assawy is Egyptian,' Diop was saying. 'She has come to help our refugees. She is a very helpful person. Perhaps she will help you.'

He hates her, Alice thought, they have been arguing and he has not won. It was obvious that the doctor would not be easy to manipulate. She wore no make-up and her skin had the lemony pallor of a naturally dark person who avoids the sun. Her medical status was confirmed by a tightly-waisted, white dress with a red crescent sewn over the breast pocket. Her hair was held in a white headscarf. She handed the tea-cloth to one of the women without taking her eyes off Diop.

'Les camions,' she said. 'Vous m'avez promis.'

'La situation n'est plus ce qu'elle était, elle est très mouvante. Ce n'est pas le moment.'

'Il me semble que ce n'est jamais le moment qui vous convient. Et pouvez-vous me consacrer le jour qu'il faut?'

Diop turned to Alice.

'I'll wait for you outside,' he said.

El-Assawy tried to call him back: 'Vous m'avez promis . . .'

But he was gone.

The two women faced each other, separated only by the little girl on the floor between them.

Alice mumbled something apologetic but the woman seemed too upset to do more than dismiss her words with a brief shake of her head.

'He promised me,' she said in English.

She bent, picked up the child and carried her across to a woman sitting in the shadows. Then set about rearranging a line of pans which looked perfectly well placed to Alice.

'Why do you need the lorries?' she asked.

'To leave – not next week, now.' She hit the last word with a bang on one of the pans. 'You should not have come here. It is very dangerous and travel is forbidden – you knew that, didn't you?'

Alice said nothing.

The doctor continued: 'I cannot prevent the commandant giving you one of the children, he is the legal authority here, but I see no reason to help.'

Alice turned away sharply.

'I realise it must be very hard,' the woman continued. 'These women here have baby after baby and now death after death, and nothing will stop them. It must seem unjust.'

She put the last of the pans to one side, lifted an enamel jug and poured water into the bowl, lifted it with both hands and carried it to the partition curtain. Alice went to hold it aside and was surprised to see a naked woman laid on the floor under an oil-lamp, both hands resting on the steep slope of her pregnant belly. Her hair had been cropped *en brosse*, her feet were fissured and caked with dirt. She eyed Alice warily.

Three other women squatted near her, one so ancient she seemed to have shrivelled inside her skin. The other two were young. One massaged the pregnant woman's legs with a kneading motion, half baker, half potter. The other held two babies in her arms with two more sleeping on a mat at her feet. As if on cue, the pregnant woman's face contorted with pain and the wizened figure began to intone in a low singsong voice.

El-Assawy let the drapery fall back.

Out of sight the woman released a teeth-clenched howl that made Alice shudder. She looked across at the doctor but her expression revealed nothing. Alice braced heself, expecting a further outcry but was still jolted when it came.

Behind the curtain, woken by the noise, one of the babies set up a low breathy sobbing. Alice could hear one of the women shushing it.

She felt suddenly aggrieved at being lectured to in this indirect way. She turned on the doctor: 'Do you have children – of your own?'

'I have my work?'

'Didn't you want children?'

The doctor went back to rearranging the pans but Alice was not to be deflected. 'Didn't you want to have a baby?'

'Wanting something too much can make you unfit to have it.'

'Oh no,' Alice said sharply. 'It's too easy to play judge but I won't be blamed – I was told there were abandoned babies here, babies in need, perhaps a baby for me.'

The doctor gave up on the pans and turned to face her tormentor. 'I was in the Sudan before this and once in Bangladesh after the floods – you people get there almost as quickly as we do, quicker sometimes. Oh sure, you have a kind of moral case but is it so true? Do you really want to give love or do you just want to get it, to get the one thing missing from your oh so fortunate lives?'

The following silence was almost tangible, even the hidden baby had stopped snivelling, as if stunned by the hardness of her tone, as much as the words she had chosen.

El-Assawy pressed her fingers to her forehead, massaging the ridge above her eyebrows. 'I'm sorry – it is the worry here. I get angry but you see, I don't think anyone should have children to get love. Love is passed on, they will give it to their children and so on. You must find something else for your own life, not someone else.'

Alice turned and strode towards the entrance. 'I can't help it,' she said over her shoulder. 'There was a time when I was like you – I never thought about it, but then it just crept up on me.' She lifted the tent flap. 'I know all the arguments, all of them – it's just that they don't help.'

Outside, clear explosions of stars drifted downwards as if drawn to the distant lights of the town. It was cool and ghostly and beautiful; each isolated pile of boxes a grisaille still-life in the silvery shadowless waste. For a moment, Alice savoured the impossible oddity of being there.

She looked back. There was no light from any tent except the one she had been in. Even the poor people of the town had their music and their lights, while this place was totally silent.

As if her thoughts had been read she was suddenly blinded by a powerful yellow beam, forcing her to screw up her eyes and shield her face with her hands. It had to be the jeep. Diop must have been sitting there in the darkness watching her. How stupid the whole thing had become, how childish and petty. She turned away from the glare and began to walk back to the town. She did not look back, even when she heard El-Assawy's voice behind her.

'What are you doing?'

Alice said nothing.

'Where are you going?' the doctor insisted. 'You can not just walk off in the night. This is not your Piccadilly Circus.'

'Don't worry,' Alice said. 'I'm sure you've got enough to think about.'

'Yes I have,' she said, drawing level. 'Quite enough. But that does not mean I do not care.'

She took hold of Alice's arm and refused to be shaken off. Without anything being said she steered her in a half circle, away from the town, and only when she was sure Alice would walk unaided did she release her grip. They had walked a cautious hundred yards before the older woman spoke again.

'Diop told me you are a nurse.'

'Why should he say that?'

El-Assawy laughed quietly. 'To make me help you. He also threatened not to give the lorries unless I gave one of the children. He can be ruthless.'

'You don't seem to mind?'

'Mind? No, I suppose I rather admire him. What stops this country is not poverty but the poverty of what the people want. They do not want enough, they are happy with so little – only a few like Diop get angry enough to want to do something about it. Very angry in his case – angry at being himself, I'm afraid.'

'You like him?'

'In a way. But I'm not going to help him unless it will help the children.'

'You'd give in – for a lorry?'

'Of course. Are you upset that your idea of happiness is part of someone else's bargain? Why not? You come with money, Diop needs it, I need a lorry . . .'

She left it there. Alice thought of the mangoes, the wooden stool, the strange silver emblem hanging round her neck.

Somewhere behind them the jeep started up. Its headlights swung round, showing the way ahead in its two narrow beams.

To Alice they had hit on what looked like a group of upturned boats. As the jeep approached, the light increased and she could see they were half-oval shapes, some sort of large tent made out of curved spars of bound branches covered with woven mats. El-Assawy was heading towards one which stood slightly apart from the main camp. Its entrance was guarded by three veiled men, squatting before a charcoal brazier, a little metal kettle steaming on its glowing embers. A dozen or so camels were herded nearby. Clumps of stunted thorn bushes had been uprooted and formed into circles, each holding a tethered goat. The surroundings were swept and orderly, no empty boxes, no 'snow drifts' to be seen. These were real desert people but they clearly knew and accepted the doctor. One of them reached for a little cup and filled it with a stream of brown liquid from the kettle and offered it to Alice with elaborate chivalry.

'Try,' El-Assawy said. 'It is very refreshing.'

The china was unexpectedly fine and very hot. She held it gingerly between thumb and first finger and blew discreetly across the surface of the liquid before trying a cautious sip. It was delicious – strong and sweet, thick with mint, very refreshing, the scent clearing her head wonderfully.

The jeep glided up and stopped ten metres from them. The lights went out but she could see the dark outline of Diop, sitting on his high seat watching them.

Again El-Assawy took her arm, this time guiding her through the opening. When she straightened, Alice found herself bathed in a dappled, honey-coloured glow from the moonlight filtering through the raffia mesh of the curved roof. Her eyes ran along the ribbed supports; she was Jonah in the belly of the whale. The feet-flattened earth was brushed clean. An enormous bed, almost a platform, stood high on carved posts that ended in splayed, inverted columns. The thick coverlet of brown and white pelts cast over it, the hide shield swung from one of the ribs by leather thongs, its cured skins painted with a bold geometric pattern and a squat sword in a darkened leather scabbard lying across the end of the bed, all created the illusion that she had stumbled into the tent of some Homeric hero. Everything was finely made – the intricately woven baskets, and the inlaid chest strapped with cast metal bands held with a complex wrought-iron lock. She ran her hands over the intricate floral frieze carved along its rim and peered at the swirling Arabic script engraved on the metal straps. Until that moment Africa had meant recycled oilcans, plastic buckets, ragged unsuitable European clothing; here at last was skill and beauty.

It was when she tried to get a better view of the strange high bed that she realised they were not alone. A woman lay on the floor propped against one of the columns, a baby clamped to her breast. Her eyes were shut, their swollen rims caked with dried matter, her long hair clotted with sweat and dust. The child was so emaciated its buttocks were two flat pools of wrinkled skin. The sharp little shoulder blades seemed about to burst through like new teeth.

'Her husband is dead,' El-Assawy said. 'There was fighting in the camp three nights ago, over food. This happens often now. The tribe is broken by the drought and they have nothing except this.' She indicated the bed and the hangings. 'The men outside were friends of the husband. They have been protecting his tent since the fighting, but they too will go back into the desert soon and then . . .'

'She is ill?'

'Dying. It will not be long now.'

Alice cringed. The woman could not understand but it still seemed wrong to dismiss her so lightly to her face.

'Can't you do anything?' Alice said, knowing it was a silly question but feeling the need to ask.

'The child will live,' was all the doctor said.

It took a moment before Alice understood what she was saying.

'But I want my lorry,' El-Assawy went on. 'And you will have to give Diop whatever he wants and even then you may have trouble at the airport when you leave. You really must think very carefully before you agree. I am only doing it because I know that no one will take care of the child. The mother is not Touareg, those men outside think she is a savage and that the child is cursed, and when she dies they will gather up the husband's belongings and take them back to the tribe – but the baby . . .' She ran a finger across her throat, then looked Alice straight in the eyes, waiting for her answer.

'Please,' said Alice.

'You want the child? You are sure?'

'Yes.'

'I do not know how long it will be before the mother dies – a day, two days. I will talk with Diop, he is the one to arrange things. Please wait here.'

Alice had a passing urge to insist on being part of the discussion – there was something unnerving about being caught between two such strong-willed people, both with agendas of their own. Then she remembered the dying woman – a totally helpless pawn, let alone the child. She leant nearer. Was it a boy or a girl? There was no way of telling. She wished El-Assawy had not shown her this; it was of the same order as being forced to listen to the sufferings of childbirth, obliging her to go through some sort of shared agony, a surrogate birthing. She studied the woman's stretched face and prayed that her suffering would soon be over – then realised the inherent selfishness of her prayer, but could think of no way of purifying her wish.

She was so intent on these meandering thoughts, it was some time before she realised that Diop had entered and was standing just behind her.

'You are lucky,' he said, nodding towards the woman. 'You came at the right time. Oh, do not look so shocked, she has less to fear from dying than she had from living – look.' He pulled up the hem of her long skirt revealing a heavy iron band welded round her left ankle.

'They still take them when they can and the child would have been brought up a slave if they let it live, which I doubt. Only the drought could have made them risk coming so close to the town, they usually keep them hidden, far out there at the water-holes.

He bent and prised the child from the breast. The mother murmured something, but was too weak to resist and sank back into her silent torpor.

'A boy,' Diop said, holding him out towards her. 'Lucky, eh?'

Alice was surprised how easily he slotted into the crook of her arm, the tired face blinking up towards her, a bubble of spit playing on his tiny lips. Alice could feel the firmness of the body against hers, not the rigid feel of a doll, but something yielding and alive. The fine frizzy hair had been cut to leave a central Mohican ridge, the skin was light honey, a Mediterranean skin. It was more than she could have hoped for. In her mind she could lift it out of this Homeric scene and into the bright light-washed spaces of the supermarket, seat the child in the appropriate trolley, glide down the aisles, his eyes wide with delight at the passing array of colours and shapes, at the faces bending near to coo and smile. No darker than a suntanned Italian. The mouth blew another spit bubble. Alice was afraid the mother would suddenly rally, find a hidden reserve of strength, cry out against their scheming. But when the baby gave a deep sob and Alice held out a finger for him to suck on, everything seemed to be for the best.

'I want money,' Diop said briskly.

'I've got five thousand dollars.' She started to reach under the top of her jeans trying to get at the money belt while holding the baby in position. Then she realised he was laughing again.

'Real money,' he said. 'A hundred thousand dollars. With that I could save this country from all the crooks and idiots who are wrecking it. Once we had an honest thief who took what he could and spread some of it around. Now we have a Minister of Health who spends money that could build a hospital attending an international conference on medical management. Next year we are going to host a world symposium on water resources. We will have to build a new airport for all the heads of government who will attend. I do not wonder that you laugh at us. We are ridiculous.'

'I don't laugh. Not at all. But what would you do with the money?'

'There is a man called Darwesh here. For the right amount he will get me what I need. Give me what you can and I will give you this baby, when its mother dies.'

The little figure in her arms slobbered on her finger. Was it smiling? Yes, it had to be. It was happy. She gave it a little bump and sang a few notes down the scale.

'I only brought eight thousand and I had to give the pilot three.'

'Not enough.'

The baby began to whimper, sensing the tension in her body. Diop leaned over as if to take it.

'You can get more,' he said coldly.

She nodded.

Diop lifted the baby away and laid it back at the mother's side. There was no reaction.

'Give me the five thousand now,' he said.

She pulled out the wad of notes. He crumpled it in his fist as if it were a stone he was about to throw.

'I will send the baby to Bamako – afterwards. You, meanwhile, will get more money, another ten, and give it to the messenger. I want you to find Delmonico and tell him that the twenty-ninth of July is still the day. Your money will help – you may even have a place in Malian history. But please do not forget – the twenty-ninth of July is still the day.'

Alice reached inside her shirt and pulled the necklace up and over her head. She looked at it, then gently laid it against the woman's left hand. There was a slight rustle as if she had touched it – enough for Alice, enough for her to believe it meant acceptance, a final bargain struck, on that day of exchanges.

Outside, they found El-Assawy sitting with the three men, sipping tea and smoking a long black cheroot. She raised a questioning eyebrow and Diop nodded. The two of them were soon in conversation about *les camions*. Alice left them to it, climbing on to the jeep and waiting for Diop to drive her back.

Martin was confused. Just when things ought to have been hotting up, everyone seemed to be drifting away. There was nothing formal about this slow haemorrhage, he heard none of the ebullience of the welcome as guests eased themselves to their feet and made for the door. Darwesh was not in evidence and even the echoing, English-speaking neighbour had gone.

Martin had hung on, hoping Abdel-Kadar would come back, but now he was beginning to feel exposed, sitting alone but for two other guests, deep in conversation, at the other side of the courtyard. Joints cracking, he stood and went to the arches where the boy had disappeared. A heavy iron-clad door barred his way. He pushed but it was solidly locked. He looked up at a latticed window and was sure he saw a face hastily pull back into the shadows. Through the dregs of the hashish he knew what they were up to – they had locked him out.

Martin called out the boy's name but there was no answer. He pressed his ear against the door, yelled 'Abdel-Kadar!' and listened. Was that laughter? Were they sniggering at him, somewhere in the shadows? They must all be in on it – the women who had slaved away, cooking the meal, Darwesh, the boy, the rest of the household. He looked at his watch – it was midnight, he had been away far too long. Even the last two talkers were now gone. Muttering to himself, he crossed the empty courtyard, stepped over the door frame and found himself alone in the street. No one was waiting to lead him home. Was it part of his punishment? Had they planned to tease him, arouse him, abandon him? With a hefty clunk the double doors closed behind him. Bastards, he thought. Perhaps they no longer cared; he had had his chance and had blown it.

Steady, he told himself, think what you're doing. It would be all too easy to plunge into the labyrinth and get hopelessly lost. The one sure thing was the minaret, moonlit and clear over the irregular roofline, there at the very heart of the maze. Keep it to his back, walk only away from it and he would reach the edge of the town, where he could circle the perimeter and arrive back at the caravanserai.

For several metres the way was straight. His confidence grew, but when the path began a leisurely curve, drifting under a series of arches that linked opposing roofs then curved more strenuously, he knew it was not working. Within minutes he was facing the minaret once more. Stoically he turned round and retraced his steps but found that the path divided and was unsure which of the branches he had come down. He chose the right, for no especial reason, but having walked only a short distance he realised it was a cul-de-sac, with a massive door at the end, richly carved with Arabic calligraphy and with a huge central knocker in the shape of a ringed lion's head. He resisted the temptation to rouse the occupants and retraced his steps, but by the time he reached the main alley he could no longer remember the way he had come. It had taken only minutes for him to be thoroughly enmeshed in the tangled grotto.

In a way, it was relaxing – when any path was as good as another, it hardly mattered where he went. Whether the minaret was before or behind him was irrelevant. He took a left, because he had just taken a right. He took another left, then a right and found himself standing in the desert. Having accepted defeat, the labyrinth had graciously expelled him. He looked back at the irregular roofline like a grinning line of bad teeth and felt suddenly weary. He had been awake for God knew how long and the final effects of the hashish were drawing down the shutters, sapping whatever remnant of energy he had. The *campement* was a short walk to his right. There was a flicker of light somewhere inside its arched doorway, but even the brief distance to the entrance seemed interminable, his legs dragged down by the cloying sand. Then he saw the jeep, parked outside, and a sharp prick of fear jabbed through the fug of his exhaustion and summoned up a last burst of strength. His mind raced – it had to be Diop, but why? Alice? Trouble? He made his legs go faster, scuttling through the arch, scanning the courtyard, expecting anything.

Steady, he told himself, don't get in a state. The bar was lit up; he went through and stood in the doorway looking out at the veranda where they sat, Alice hunched in her chair, Diop rocking back, his legs stretched out in sharp V, a hand resting on an old-fashioned revolver with a worn, wooden handle sticking out of a time-polished leather holster. Martin knew what role Diop was playing – he was the sheriff in a Western, propped in his chair on the broadwalk on Main street waiting for the rustlers to mosey into town. Arrogant bastard, Martin thought, then felt suddenly and deeply insecure. Guns were no part of his world. He had never touched one in his entire life. Even as a kid he had only played with fantasy weapons – the Dan Dare space rifle that fired sparks and made a noise like a bird scare. Beside a man with a real gun he felt childish. That Diop should be sitting there with Alice was bad enough, but that he should be so completely in control of the situation was intolerable. Martin was on the point of overcoming his fears, enough to ask what the hell was going on, when he heard a disgusting noise, something between a laugh and belch.

'Aaarf, aaarf, aaarf . . .'

But when he looked round there was no one. Only the three of them. No one else.

Diop rocked back even further, as if falling was not a possibility. Martin loathed him.

'Aaarf, aaarf, aaarf . . .'

This time Martin looked beyond Alice and saw the fat bloated creature resting on its front paws, like a sumo wrestler assessing an opponent.

'Aaarf, aaarf, aaarf . . .'

As if interpreting his thoughts Alice posed the question: 'How come there are frogs in the desert when there's no water?'

'Ah, but there is,' Diop said, 'if you know where to find it, and they do. These frogs have proved very useful to me, very useful indeed.'

He looked at Alice as he spoke. 'That one is pregnant,' he said.

She looked away. She had had enough of the subject.

'Why do you hate everybody?' she said quickly. 'The people here – you really despise them.' She stopped. That was going too far but he didn't seem to mind.

'The people here were slavers once. Even quite recently they raided the Peul and carried off children. Now *they* are slaves, bought and sold for a bucket of water. *La Sécheresse* has changed everything. It is like a prison where a mere nothing – a packet of cigarettes, a few pills – can make a man king. Mali is a prison. Here the currency is water.'

'Why are you here?'

'You mean, why am I not in Bamako? Why is someone of my education stuck out here listening to frogs and arranging for stray white people to steal babies?' He laughed to himself. 'Because I am dangerous. Or might be.'

'But surely the country needs . . .'

He waved away the platitude.

'This is not a country – not yet. It used to be called a *territoire* which is nearer the truth. It's a massive piece of a massive continent. It is the space between a lot of smaller pieces which make more sense – *they* have harbours or a single united tribe or an entire river with access to the sea. Mali is the rest, the hole in the middle, the bit nobody knew what to do with. It is hard to feel patriotic about a void.' He saluted and sang: 'God bless my native void. God bless my native void. God bless my void.'

'*Aaarf, aaarf, aaarf* . . .' echoed the frog.

Alice giggled.

'Do you know Mamadi?' Diop asked.

Alice shook her head. 'Martin met him. He sounds very . . . straight?'

'Yes, that is a fair word. Mamadi and his friends are what every liberal-minded, concerned person wants for my country. No more left-wing radicals, no more socialism, no more cooperative villages. We are now into the middle classes, democratic capitalism, market-based pluralism . . . Mamadi is all of that.'

'Not such a bad thing, is it?'

'Tell that to your desert friends. One shower of rain and they'll start slaving again. There are tribes in this country that are still fighting pitched battles with hand-forged spears. Every time one of their chiefs dies they bury a girl child at the four corners of his hut – alive.'

Alice looked him straight in the eyes. 'You made that up.'

'But you believed it when I said it, because in your heart you know this country is not at all like your home, and that you cannot turn it into England overnight. In any case you don't really care – or at least you didn't until you got here and found yourself obliged to think about it. Go home and it will cease to bother you. Or perhaps you think that with a Malian baby in your arms you will have to take some continuing interest in the nation's affairs. You could start an Anglo-Malian society. No doubt our ambassador in

Brussels – Mamadi's cousin at the moment – will come over and give you an annual cocktail party which will cost just about what it takes to feed the refugees for a year. Or maybe you could have coffee mornings for other adoptive mothers of Malian babies so that you can all be supportive.'

'Stop!'

'It doesn't matter,' he said quietly and not unkindly. 'Soon you will take a baby and forget where it came from. Then it will be an English baby. Mali will work out its own salvation.'

'Any fool can get pregnant,' Martin said, suddenly stepping into the light.

Alice whirled round but Diop made no move.

'This place is bulging with unwanted kids,' Martin went on. 'And a hell of a lot of them seem to be dying.'

'And so you propose to help by taking one away,' Diop said, his voice disturbingly quiet.

Alice was alarmed. Why had Martin come? He was sure to mess things up. Having reached a sort of understanding with Diop, the last thing she needed was for Martin to blunder in and wreck it.

'Leave it . . .' she began, but he was already pulling up a chair between them and had that grumpy 'I-know-my-rights' look on his face which could only spell disaster.

'Commander Diop has been offering to help me,' she said primly but firmly.

'Oh sure, and how much will that set me back. I suppose this is a business arrangement?'

Diop shrugged: 'From a people who did nothing but take when they were in a dominant position I find any suggestion of our greed somewhat laughable.'

'*Aaarf, aaarf, aaarf* . . .' went the frog.

'*Aaarf, aaarf, aaarf* . . .' echoed the semicircle of frog followers.

'Even the frogs are amused by what you say,' Diop said, colder than ever. 'I think you should leave this matter to your wife.'

But Martin was not to be easily cowed. 'All I've seen here are a lot of things left by the French which have been allowed to run down. This place is sinking back to what it was before they came, all in the name of *négritude*, anti-colonialism, whatever you're on about now. All I see is a junk heap and don't tell me its the fault of the French or those they left in control, because it's nearly thirty years since they went and you're still killing each other.'

'Martin!' Alice said sharply, though she knew there was no halting him now.

'Why *do* we always have to take it lying down?' he said to her in his pleading voice. 'We used to believe all that anti-imperialist stuff at university, how we raped the world and gave nothing back. But now we're here and we can see the track across the wilderness, the railway over the mountains, that single telephone wire going on and on and on . . .'

'You are a fool,' Alice shrieked. 'A bloody stupid fool!'

'But I . . .'

Diop scraped back his chair and sat upright. When he spoke it was in staccato bursts. 'Seven years of drought – no resources – corrupt leaders stealing what little there is – promised help which never comes.' He paused then began to speak in a low, bitter, monotone. 'Who are you to say these things – did *you* build the road, the railway, the telephone line? Who are *you*? A *lycéen* on holiday with his wife who cannot have a baby, who thinks it will make them feel good to take back a living souvenir.'

'*Aaarf, aaarf, aaarf* . . .' intoned the blubbery frog as if she agreed with every word.

It was so like the 'rhubarb, rhubarb' of the old comedy shows, even Alice forgot everything and giggled.

'I amuse you?' Diop said, his voice glacial now. Alice hung her head, it had all gone too far, but she was unable to think of any way of stopping it.

'*Aaarf, aaarf, aaarf* . . .' went the big frog as if unhappy that they were not paying her enough attention. She hopped a few feet further into the light '*Aaarf, aaarf, aaarf* . . .'

The other frogs joined in: '*Aaarf, aaarf, aaarf* . . .'

Martin stared fascinated by his first clear sight of the fat thing. She really was a monster, mottled and nobbily as if suffering from some wild skin eruption, some terrible punishment for a lifetime of disgusting debauchery. Her entire body was a drinker's nose, inflated, throbbing.

'You bore me,' Diop said. 'What right have you to tell us what we should do? If you were black for a day you would kill yourselves.'

'*Aaarf, aaarf, aaarf* . . .'

To Martin's dismay Diop was reaching round to unclip the gun holster. There was nothing to stop him venting his fury in any way he chose. No one knew they were there. They had money on them. He was insanely angry. The gun was in his hand. He was lifting it.

'No!' Martin said, stiffening with terror. 'Please . . .'

But Alice had guessed what he was going to do.

'*Aaarf, aaarf, aaarf . . .*'

Diop lifted the weapon to eye-level, peered down the barrel and, as she screamed, squeezed the trigger. The deafening report echoed into the desert, followed by a reverberating silence.

Martin forced his eyes open. Where the mother frog had been there was now a nauseous mess, green slime, an ooze of spawn with froggy-eyes, vomit.

SIX

Martin's night was a film, half-remembered from student days, an unresolved thing of shadows and suggestions, of wandering, lost in a dusty labyrinth, searching for a door but finding only unbroken walls of crusting earth, each turn deepening his loss. His feet dragged in the loosening drifts until he saw a figure, cloaked and hooded, turning the corner ahead of him, but when he reached the bend, the way ahead was empty. He hurried on. At the next corner he saw the black robe slip into a narrow cut, halfway along a high wall, sloping backwards like a pyramid. Martin called out, the figure turned. He thought he saw the face of the Japanese woman staring from under the hood. He struggled through the sand, the hood fell back, it was Abdel-Kadar grinning impishly. He stepped through a doorway and Martin ran up. Nothing. No trace in the dust. Martin retraced his steps. He saw another door, carved, studded, open. He stepped through. The hooded figure was waiting. He raised his head. It was Diop, the revolver in his hand. He fired.

Martin woke with a jolt, slapping his arm where the mosquito had bitten. He was covered in vicious red marks. Alice was breathing with the uneasy snuffling of one who has cried herself to sleep. She had lost weight, her face had recaptured something of that waif-like quality he liked so much. Too bad, the whole thing was such a mess.

Easing himself clear of the tangled bedding, Martin got up and dressed himself from the heap of clothes on the floor, ignoring the musty odour of yesterday's sweat. He slipped through the door and crossed the silent courtyard, blinking at the hot daylight through the arched doorway before stepping out into the dusty space between the *campement* and the town. There was no one waiting. No Abdel-Kadar, no old man. He knew he ought to go back inside but somehow he just walked on, half-expecting to see the hooded figure of his dream, beckoning him into the labyrinth. But no, the dust was unmarked and looking up at the narrow passage between the crumbling walls he told himself that he would never find the house unaided. He wasn't even sure why he wanted to. When the time came to go back, Abdel-Kadar would come for them, so why this urge to look for him now?

Even so early, it was too hot to stand in the sun. He edged into the shade of the wall, just inside the labyrinth. The threshold crossed, he relaxed and took stock. There was no point in going back; only exhaustion had fended off a blazing row last night. Despite his frantic questions she had refused to say what if anything she had arranged with Diop, leaving him in agonies of doubt. Had he interrupted them before they had come to some arrangement? Had his intervention prevented her from doing a deal? He rather imagined it had, but it was impossible to be absolutely sure. No, the commandant had been so maddened, the whole thing had to be over. They were going to go back empty handed and all they could hope for now was that that arrogant bastard would let them leave in peace – just let them fly away as baby-less as when they arrived, and no bad thing either. He kicked up a little flurry of sandy dust. What a fool he'd been to fall for the baby trip second time round. Now they'd paid real money – thousands of bloody dollars for a plane trip to this mud heap. There was no baby, that much was obvious.

He looked ahead to see if he recognised any of the buildings but it was useless. He let himself drift forward, slowly, just for the exercise. There was a left turn, he took it, then a right. High on the walls, peeping out just below the roofline, he could see split palm trunks to carry away rain-water. Like a fridge in an igloo, he thought. Yet there was water somewhere, there was the frog – he shuddered. What a bastard.

It was better go back before he got hopelessly lost. He started to retrace his steps, then stopped again. It was as if his desires had entered an uncharted labyrinth of their own, a place of half-glimpsed things – he thought of the Japanese woman in the pool, arched in the water, then kohl-rimmed eyes, the narrow fleshless body, Modigliani, spare, as much boy as girl, no motherly hips or lactating breasts, just sinewy limbs and firm, unblemished skin.

He had somehow turned again, or had he? He was lost but then he had expected to be. Funny, the nearest wall seemed to have fallen in. He could see over, into a shabby courtyard piled with drifts of sand. It was a vision of what the town would be like if the inhabitants dropped their guard. He wondered how long it would take the desert to complete its work – a month?, a year? There was a wooden signboard still fixed to the lintel of the broken doorway. Amazingly, it was in English – the first line was lost but below he could just make out: 'World Beulah Convention, Alabama, USA'.

The rest had been violently scratched with knife-strokes that had left deep furrows in the dry wood but he could still decipher the times of church services and the name of the pastor, the lettering scored from left to right with a deep sawing motion, but just readable as 'The Reverend Austen Belvedere'. Martin blew through his parched lips – a dry, silent whistle. It was the name Madame Josette had offered when he had enquired about orphanages. Funny she had said nothing about Timbuktu? He wondered what had happened to the mission, let alone its minister – the place looked worse than the usual abandoned dwelling, more as if it had been deliberately wrecked. He stepped into the courtyard but there was nothing, a dusty square without a single trace of whatever the Reverend Belvedere had once presided over. Martin shuddered – it said too much about his and Alice's own presence in this alien place. Even the scarab beetles left a greater impression on the desert than they would. They had no place here and certainly no cause to take anything away with them. Theirs was a world which did not touch on this place at any point, two planets orbiting apart. He stepped back into the street and carried on, still without knowing why.

Turning out of a narrow cutting between high walls, he realised that he had reached the minaret. Close to, it was a high narrowing pyramid bristling with exposed branches, presumably used to climb the outer walls when they were resurfaced with mud. The mosque itself was long, straight and plain, the entrance a dark hole, a pair of worn leather sandals carefully placed to one side. Kicking off his own shoes, Martin stepped over the raised lip and entered what he took to be a high corridor running left and right. It was only when he moved a little further inside that he realised he could see down another open passage running front and back. Move forward and the next two columns shut off the cross passage – it was a unique sensation, the forest of thick square columns holding up the high flat ceiling were so staggered that at no point was it possible to see other than along two passageways. It was infinity without space; wherever you stood, you were always at a crossroads, never out in the open. It was the creation of a desert people longing for the enclosing safety of shadowy places. If there was a Moslem Puritanism then this was it, no gilded mihrab, no intricate calligraphy, no encrusted stucco ceiling, just this arid holiness, a place for mystics and hermits, tangled-haired madmen blinded by searing sunlight, seeking the dark solitude of caves for their rambling prayers.

Martin walked left and right, up and down, it was all the same. The only light came from the door through which he had come and another some way ahead and a third to his right which opened into a small, enclosed courtyard with two steep mud staircases leading up to the roof. He chose the left-hand flight, pausing at the top step, surprised at the size of the dusty expanse of the roof, ridged by crossbeams laid over the columns. It was an odd sensation to be walking over this vast sheet of sun-dried mud, impossible to believe that it would not simply break under his feet. At the base of the minaret he found the narrow hole that led inside and began to climb, his hands pressed against the walls to stop his stockinged feet from slipping on the crumbling steps. The winding space was barely wide enough for him to squeeze round, but after a complete circle he came to a narrow arched slit that offered a limited view over the town, a thing of cubes and flat squares with no human activity to disfigure the abstract purity of paths, courtyards and flat roofs.

He went on, the stairwell growing narrower and steeper. It was impossible to decide whether he was more afraid of getting stuck or of slipping backwards. His relief, as he bent double to push out through a low aperture, was short lived when he realised that he was standing outside, near the tip of the tower on a narrow sloping ledge with no protecting wall. The distant town seemed even more toy-like and geometric but now he could see why he had always lost his way – far across the roofline was another minaret, smaller but similar enough to have confused him when he tried to use it as a marker.

He wanted to turn but saw the sheer drop to the path below. Clinging to the fissured wall, he strained to see behind him without having to move too far. This was the edge of the town, beyond was the desert, the same rolling hollows and stunted thorns, though now there were lorries, twenty at least, and men, a lot of them. He risked turning a bit further, desperate to know what was going on. It took a while for him to make sense of it. There seemed to be men in army fatigues loading the vehicles, some of which had what he took to be military markings – stencilled badges and numbers. The canvas awnings were camouflaged in swirls of browns and ochres and there could be little doubting that the boxes were ammunition cases. There was even an open truck with a large field-gun mounted on its back, held in place by a thick mesh net. Then he saw Diop jump down from one of the vehicles, followed by Darwesh. Martin pressed himself against the wall, afraid he could be seen from down there. What if it was prayer-time and the muezzin was on his way up? One of the lorries was revved noisily. He risked another look and saw Abdel-Kadar standing beside his uncle, listening to Diop who was ticking off points on his fingers. With a final broad gesture, he finished, walked over to his jeep, swung himself up and drove off. Martin breathed easier. Then he saw that Abdel-Kadar was taking his leave and realised that it must be time for them to return to Bamako and that he had better get down and back to the *campement* before he was missed.

He twisted himself round and lowered his foot onto the first step, slipped an inch, and grasped desperately at the dry wall until he was sure he had a safer foothold. The descent was painful, step by unsteady step, his knuckles bloodless from pressing against the crumbling walls. Down in the cool corridors, he paused for a moment to catch his breath. It was hard to know which had scared him most – the terrifying vertiginous stairwell or the sight of all that military hardware.

Breathing a little steadier, he stepped out of the cool half-light into the white glare of mid-morning. His stockings were sandy and grated in his shoes but his thoughts were elsewhere. Something was going on, something with a smell of danger about it, real danger, far beyond a few scowling guards in sun-glasses.

He had been turning right and left without thinking and as before this abandon seemed to placate the spirit of the labyrinth, which promptly expelled him into the desert. The ground was covered with footprints. He backed away, cowering in the shade of the last building, afraid that he had come out near the lorries.

He risked looking up and saw the minaret, behind to his left, where the vehicles would be, which meant that if he headed right he would be walking away from them. Praying he wasn't mistaken, he set off through the thick drifts piled against the outer walls; there was no shade and the sun was rising to its zenith; it was crazy but what else was he to do?

He tried not to keep looking behind him – it did no good and slowed him down. The only light in his gloom was the thought that he must look like something out of one of those desert jokes, the crazy figure stumbling towards a mirage of a bar with ice-cold lagers served by blonde bimbos in bikinis. Only it wasn't that funny. Nothing was any more. He felt profoundly sorry for himself, he had only got into it for Alice's sake. It was her need he had tried to satisfy and now here he was, frazzling to death with a band of armed thugs just behind him. Why, he demanded, of no one in particular. Why?

He was so preoccupied with life's injustices, that it was some time before he realised he was no longer heading straight forward but had begun to head down a slope. He stopped, still trying to focus his rage. In the end it all came down to Alice, remove her from the equation and so many other things fell into place – a different sort of life, living abroad, even a different sort of desire. She was the barrier to it all. Without her . . . Someone was coming towards him, a woman striding up a steeply sloping path. She had a bucket on her head and as she crested the rise it spilled a little water. Martin stepped aside to let her past and saw that the track led down into what was clearly a deep man-made crater, a hole in the desert at least a hundred metres across and probably the same down. The path sloped abruptly away from him, then began to spiral round out of sight to some far point where the water must surface. He was entranced – it was the power in Timbuktu, control it and the place was yours. And then he understood what Diop had meant the night before when he said that he was grateful to the frogs, for it must have been they who had shown him that beneath the dusty surface of the desert lay the river of life.

He started down. It was easy at first, no more than a gentle slope but soon the path became a crumbling slide, worse than the minaret. It was like slipping down a sand-dune and when he tried to slow himself by grasping the sides his hands set off a mini-avalanche of dust. He could imagine a twisted ankle, sitting alone in pain, unable to climb back. Slithering down was one thing, but grappling back up the disintegrating sides would be twice as hard. He stopped himself and turned to retrace his steps. Suddenly, someone grabbed his hand, holding it in a grip that was strong, very strong, and he heard a clash of metal and a high childish voice going 'Echta-echta', like a wet throaty cough. 'Echta-echta'. Martin tried to pull away but was held fast. He forced himself round and came face to face with the mad, shackled creature. 'Echta-echta-echta.' It tugged at his arm, grinning wildly. Martin reeled. How on earth . . .? But then why not, it was a logical place for the boy to have his lair, a place to hide from sun and people. But why was he trying to pull him further down? Martin dug his heels into the soft dust and tried to yank his arm free, but the boy was incredibly strong and dragged him on regardless. Martin tried reasoning, then shouting, then pleading. The boy pulled harder, another section of path crumbling under them. They both stumbled and for a second the boy had to save himself, releasing his grip and falling forwards. Martin threw himself back and started scrabbling up the track. 'Echta-echta-echta', the crazed creature was after him. 'Echta-echta'. He tried to grab Martin's leg but released it when Martin kicked out wildly, landing a foot in his face. 'Echta-echta'. He came again, faster than Martin, manacled legs no hindrance in such thick dust, his feet moving as one, as if swimming through the thick drifts. 'Echta-echta', he pounced on top of Martin, knocking the breath out of him, pinning him down. It was pointless to struggle any more. Martin lay still waiting to see what he wanted. 'Echta-echta-echta'. The boy emitted another stream of guttural, spit-flecked noises. He was playing with himself, jerking his long circumcised erection, jacking himself off with a demented fury. 'Echta-echta'. Martin looked at the grinning idiot pumping his flesh and thought of Abdel-Kadar and tried to pull back as far as possible. Sand dribbled down the sides of the slope and ran under his collar but nothing mattered. His every yearning – the narrow waist, the wide, dark eyes, the sensuous mouth, the androgynous body, half girl, half boy – had become this slobbering creature.

'Martin!'

It was Alice. The boy froze. Martin pulled his arm free. The boy fell away, hunched as if waiting for a beating. Martin felt a horrible empathy with the mad creature as he squeezed against the side of the slope, trying to be invisible.

'Is anyone down there'?

The spell was broken. Martin clambered over him and started for the surface.

'Are you mad or what?' Alice demanded. 'What were you thinking about? If Abdel-Kadar hadn't put two and two together we would never have found you. We've looked everywhere else.'

'He's down there,' Martin said hoarsely. 'The mad boy, he's down there – I thought he was going to kill me.'

They hurried over to the jeep and clambered into the rear seats. Abdel-Kadar was watching him in the mirror, the displeasure evident on his unsmiling face.

'This is power,' Martin said, clutching Alice's hand. 'It controls everything – life and death, and there's something else going on here, something we ought to keep well away from. I didn't realise they would start as soon as we brought them the money.'

'What on earth are you babbling on about?' Alice said. 'You keep us waiting all morning and now you . . .' But she never finished the sentence, her anger cut short by a sudden blow against the side of the vehicle.

The naked boy was hobbling along, banging against the jeep with all his force.

'Drive!' Martin yelled, but the drifts were too thick and they could only lumber away at a steady crawl.

'What does he want?' Alice demanded, as the boy leapt to grab at Martin, his genitals swaying free as he mounted the running board.

'Drive!' Martin yelled. Abdel-Kadar stamped the accelerator, bucking them forward and lurching into the desert. Still the mad boy hung on.

'Get him off,' Martin cried. Abdel-Kadar swung left then right, skidding in the dust, clashing the gears. With a look of angry disbelief, the naked figure lost his grip and fell, his twisted face blurring to nothing in the rising dust cloud.

Martin sank back, exhausted. In the shocked silence, Alice succumbed to a flat melancholy. It was over. Behind them, the labyrinth would be deserted in the afternoon heat, later there would be the blood-red sunset, the call to prayer, the music rising from the secret courtyards and despite everything she felt a pang of deprivation at the realisation that she would never see any of it again. The telephone wires stretched ahead of them.

'We're in over our heads,' Martin said, still breathing too fast and talking in a rush. 'That money Delmonico sent – Diop is starting a revolution with it. I thought it was a bloody bribe not an arms deal. I mean that makes us accessories . . .'

'I know,' Alice said calmly. 'I gave him another five thousand.' She ignored the garrotted sound from his throat. 'I couldn't tell you last night, not with the way you were laying into Diop, you'd just have spoiled everything. Anyway, we have to get him another ten in Bamako for when Abdel-Kadar comes back with the baby.'

Martin looked so pole-axed Alice laughed.

'I'm sorry,' she said. 'But that is what we came for, isn't it? Cheer up, it's a boy. He's sweet – eyes like Abdel-Kadar's. Light-skinned – almost an Arab.'

Martin instinctively turned to the profile concentrating on the road ahead, wondering again how much he understood and if he did what he made of it.

'How?' Martin said.

'How what? How did I find it? How are we going to get it?'

'All of that. Start at the beginning.'

She told him about the camp, about El-Assawy and the desert people, glossed over the bit about the dying mother – why should he have to share the feeling of guilt that still clung to her memory of the darkened tent? At least one of them could think it was just a good deed, taking away some poor orphaned kid.

'I don't see why we couldn't have taken it with us,' Martin said suspiciously. 'Even if we didn't have the money, Abdel-Kadar could have hung about Bamako till we got to a bank. No?'

Alice side-stepped: 'We're supposed to tell Delmonico that the twenty-ninth is still the day.'

'What are you talking about?'

'It's a message from Diop to Delmonico – the twenty-ninth is still the day.'

'I don't think we should get any deeper into this – it's grown-up stuff, real guns, real bombs, way out of our league. Why don't we just go home and forget about the whole thing?'

Abdel-Kadar's eyes had been moving between them, gauging reactions, now Martin saw they were fixed on him, as if willing him to keep silent.

What neither he nor Martin could guess was the confusion in Alice's thoughts. She had no doubts about Diop and their agreement; despite last night's madness she trusted him implicitly. The baby would be sent, of that she was sure. She ought to be happy, she knew that too. What she had wanted most was about to be granted but her mind could not resist turning back to that canvas tent, to the woman giving birth, to the angry voice of the doctor lecturing her on the morality of love. She had rejected it then, she was less sure now.

The Swede was already revving up the plane as they approached. He turned to greet them as they clambered on board and Alice was amazed how spruce he looked, as bright-eyed as before, freshly pressed shirt, sharply creased trousers. She could see the crumpled mess Martin was in, and was sure she looked no better. She was exhausted, drained; even as the plane lifted away her eyes began to close as the dust sealed them in, her chin slumped to her chest and she slept.

Martin was still shaken and nervously alert. He waited till they were up and the dust cleared, eager to see the town disappearing below them, a Lilliput of building blocks, neat cubes and square spaces, a labyrinth with what monster at its centre? He shuddered and turned to see the boy, then realised that Abdel-Kadar had not come with them, he had stayed behind, and just as Martin grappled with the consequences of that surprise, he saw the line of trucks, travelling along in its own dust storm, heading south as they were. He eased himself forward in his seat and spoke to the Swede.

'What's that all about?'

'Ask no questions . . .'

'How long would it take to drive to Bamako?'

'Two days and two nights non-stop – but what makes you think that that is where they are going?' He smiled as he said this.

'I just guessed,' Martin said. 'You know, don't you? You know something's going on, something our friend Diop back there has dreamed up?'

'None of our business. It's Mali business, not white business. White business is business.' He laughed at his own wit.

Prat, Martin thought, but went on trying to get to the heart of the issue.

'Would you do anything for money?'

'Could be,' he said. 'Yes, why not. They is going to do what they do anyways, so what's wrong to make a dollar?' He thought again, then waxed philosophical: 'You know I like it here and I don't want them to get a bad way, but it's their business, like I say, it's not our business.'

'What are those lorries going to Bamako for?'

'Maybes the soldiers want to drink and dance a bit. Good clubs in Bamako – want to come some time?'

Martin slumped back in his seat, telling himself the Swede was right, it was none of their business, why should he care if they wanted to kick the shit out of each other. He tried to calculate, two days and two nights, would he and Alice be gone before anything happened – whatever anything might be?

The same three ragged men helped Thorsten with the plane. He produced the keys to the Mercedes and drove them back to town, resolving Martin's major worry, though clearly the Swede was in it up to his neck with Darwesh, Diop and their cronies. He wished the boy had come with them, he helped pass the time.

It was late afternoon before the first baobab stood clear against the horizon, an upside-down tree with its roots in the air. It made the void seem emptier. They passed close enough for Martin to see long pods, dry and brittle, hanging from the barren branches. The seed-balls inside were like the cellophane covered pills that Alice used to pop out every morning when they thought there was a medical answer to their problem. Now it had been resolved quite simply and, like most things, it had come down to money in the end. Martin tried to picture himself in this new role, fitting the face of the child at the airport on to the portrait, surrounding it with people they knew, but it did not get rid of the Look – Alice had said the boy was light-skinned but everyone would know he could not be theirs. Now there would be other looks to add to those of mere pity, nastier looks. He closed his eyes and tried to dream up the Japanese lady in the pool but his thoughts kept drifting back to the path into the cistern and the figure waiting in the shadows.

He woke in a darkness deepened by the enclosing forest and he realised that they were passing the garage and that its light had not been lit. There were no sudden pinpoints of light through the foliage, no signs that someone was cooking or sitting under the leaves, listening to the radio. He turned down the window and heard nothing and smelled nothing, no music, no woodsmoke.

As they bumped on to the first stretch of pitted tarmac Alice struggled painfully out of sleep.

'Nearly there,' he said.

The glow lighting the sky ahead had to be the barracks. Alice had not thought much about the return, now she realised they might have to replay the scene acted out when they left the day before. She made a quick total of the loose ends of money tucked here and there but knew it could not be as much as the original bribe.

Thorsten slowed to a crawl under the crenellated walls. The heavy metal gates were open and there was a soldier outside, standing over a man who was squatting on his haunches with his hands on his head, eyes fixed to the narrow space in front of his interrogator's heavy boots. The Swede pulled off the road and waited.

The soldier's left hand was clutching a can of *Bière du Peuple*. He lifted it to his lips and took a long swig, then half turned to see who it was that awaited him. Yet again Alice thought it might be the soldier from the airport, thin and lanky, but the face was different, the lips thinner, the eyebrows higher above his impenetrable Raybans.

When he realised the soldier was watching him, Thorsten leapt out of the car and stood obediently to attention.

'Stay where you are.' Alice hissed at Martin, which was superfluous as he was incapable of movement.

The soldier lifted the beer to his lips and finished it without taking his eyes off the Swede. He crushed the can to an egg-timer, then let it drop, quite casually, half turned and gave them their first sight of the heavy automatic dangling at the end of his right arm. This wasn't one of the old rifles with worn wooden stocks that they were almost used to. This was a high-tech black metal assault rifle with a long curved magazine like an erection clipped on to its underbelly and a shiny telescopic viewfinder. Two extendable legs made an inverted V at the end of the barrel. This was a serious object, a light machine-gun, a weapon of war. It seemed to rise a little in the man's hand, rise and point its curved erection towards them. Martin had a sudden flash replay of Diop and the frog – but before he could say anything a truck appeared in the gateway, nosed on to the road, turned close to the Mercedes and headed off, out of town. It was an enormous lumbering thing on high double wheels whose hubs were lost above the top of Martin's window. He flinched back from the noise and the nearness of the metal giant but it was no sooner gone than another and then another swung out and past them. The ground vibrated, the air roared with engine noise and blackened with burning fumes. Thorsten was trapped against the door, centimetres from the wooden side panels, almost lashed by the flapping tarpaulin covers. Martin had a blurred glimpse of military insignia: crossed sabres, jagged lightning bolts, a victor's wreath, a clenched fist. How many were there – fifteen?, twenty? It was only when the last veered away that he saw through the open rear flaps the two rows of men in green fatigues and combat helmets, using their automatics to steady themselves as the massive zigzag tyres crunched over the crumbling potholes.

'Oh God,' said Alice. Now that the road had cleared, she could see the prisoner, spread out along the ground, a trickle of blood running from crown to chin, his eyes rolling upwards, a plaster saint, dropped and cracked. The soldier had raised his gun to hit him again, then thought better of it. He turned and walked over to Thorsten and without saying anything used his free hand to reach inside the man's shirt and pulled out a thin gold chain with a medallion dangling from it. With a snap it came off his neck. Satisfied, he lowered himself just enough to see into the car. Martin pressed back against his seat, wishing himself invisible, and smiling as if in a photo-booth. The soldier said something to Thorsten in guttural French – he sounded almost bored – a few clipped sentences which Thorsten answered briskly, eager to please.

The guard weighed this up then said: '*Floos.*' As if he had thought of something brilliant.

'He wants money,' Alice said. 'That's what *floos* means.'

Thorsten said something back, bargaining despite the weakness of his position.

The man said something which had to be a figure and the Swede essayed a counter-offer which provoked a roar of rage. The man's free hand leaped up and took hold of Thorsten's throat, the huge fist engulfing the narrow tube as if to crush it like the beer can.

Martin closed his eyes. Alice groped inside her shirt and eased some notes out of a final hiding place.

'Here,' she yelled holding them out of her window.

Seeing this waving wad of currency the man loosened his grip and hurried round to grab it, only to explode with perplexed rage when he saw they were not dollars – Alice had brought along some lira, left over from their last trip to Tuscany three years before.

Thorsten tried hastily to reassure the man that the notes had real value and that, in any case, it was all they had. For a terrible moment he seemed unwilling to swallow this, turning the top note over and over, examining the strange words and pictures as if they might suddenly yield some meaning. Slowly, very slowly, Thorsten got back into the car and started the engine. He waited a moment. The man did nothing. The Swede eased away, no one breathing, too conscious of the gun to even think of looking relieved. At the next corner they turned alongside the railway line again, past the Moorish villas, unlit, ghoulish. Suddenly they were back into the square with the white hotel tower ahead of them.

A posse of soldiers sat or lay about beside the striped oilcans along the drive. The lawn nearest them was covered with crushed beer cans, though they looked to have drunk themselves sober, and waved them through without stopping. Alice went straight inside but Martin hesitated.

'You handled that very well,' he said.

The Swede shrugged. 'Used to it, just go humble and don't ever give them reasons to get mad. Anyway they never kill whites, too much trouble. Just as long as we do as we're told we OK.'

'What now?' Martin said.

'Go sleep. Or come to dance, over there in the *bidonville*?'

Martin smiled, impressed by the man's stamina if nothing else. He thanked him but refused, but then, as he was getting out of the car, he saw the newspaper the mangoes had been wrapped in, lying on the floor at his feet. 'ONLY A WEEK TO GO' sang the headline over an artist's impression of the wedding dress, spread across four columns. Martin wondered if Madame Josette might like it. He reached for the crumpled page and stood on the kerb, skip-reading, then suddenly his eyes glanced across a date – it was the day of the Royal Wedding – the twenty-ninth of July. It was too late to form the question, the Mercedes was disappearing into the night.

He joined Alice under the comforting glitter of the chandelier, no longer the vulgar thing it had seemed when he first arrived. After the deep darkness of the outside world it was a miracle of exquisitely fashioned glass, the ultimate triumph of electric power coursing in from somewhere unknown, to explode vividly into light. It looked wonderful.

'I want to sleep,' Alice said. 'There's so much to do now.'

'Alice,' he began. 'Are you sure . . .' But she was at the lift, her arms folded across her breast as if she was already carrying her baby.

The restaurant was closed. He walked towards the coffee shop, its tables set with little candles in red jars, reminding him of those hilltop cemeteries you see in Italy as you flash past on the remorseless autostrada. The waiter's face was a rosy mahogany, his gums blood red, his teeth pinkly opalescent. Martin strolled down the cold buffet with a plate too small for the heapings of soggy salads and the thin wafers of baked meats. Back at his table he realised he wanted wine, something red, thick and drunk-making. The list had heart-stopping prices, but he found an Algerian plonk with the reassuringly simple label, 'Sidi Ben Abbas, Société Algérienne des Vins' and a hearty sounding 12° prominent in the bottom right-hand corner. Bearing his order, the waiter walked round a glass partition, swirled with frosted glass flowers, to a long counter where Freddy, Delmonico's friend, dressed in a hip-hugging bolero jacket and a large red bow-tie, was serving drinks. Martin was intrigued – perched on one of the high stools was the wife of the Australian who had had the accident at the airport. Her cocktail dress had a generous cleavage, her very high heeled shoes had straps above the ankles, and she was sipping a green drink from a frosted glass, holding a cigarette in the same hand and exhaling smoke in two thin streams. There was something about the way the barman lowered his eyes that convinced Martin they were discussing something *risqué*. He was unsure which shocked him most: her desertion of her sick husband or her easy familiarity with this dubious Malian servant.

'Monsieur?'

The waiter wanted him to taste the wine. It was no *grand cru*, but at least the nutty flavour helped mask the chemical taste of the bottled salad dressings. When he finished the food, there was still a comfortable half bottle left and he sat, staring into the rosy glow, rigidly working his way through it. In the pink he thought, literally in the pink – an upside down hell in which everything glowed very nicely thank you. He lifted high the last glass, a defrocked priest mocking his office, and studied the ceiling through the rich ruby lees, as if the external world had subsumed the warm burgundy tinge he felt inside. His plan had worked well – not perfectly but well enough. They would have a child, a son. It called for a celebration. He lifted his glass, intending a silent toast to Africa, and realised that there was a dark shadow behind the red liquid. He lowered the glass and found the Australian woman glowering down at him, arms akimbo.

'I was worried,' she said, 'about Alice. When you didn't appear yesterday I thought something must be wrong.'

Martin was in no mood to be put on the spot and tried to deflect her.

'I hope your husband's getting better?'

'He isn't. He's dying. Peritonitis the doctor says. But never mind that – did you find what you were looking for?'

He wondered how she knew but did not feel inclined to elaborate.

'Aw, shit. That's what I was afraid of,' she said. 'I'd better go up and help the poor cow take care of it.'

'No, it's not here yet, it's coming, I mean we didn't have enough cash so they wouldn't hand it over. I'll sort it out tomorrow.'

Margot exhaled through her nostrils. The thinness of the smoke streams was a comment in itself.

'Why? For Alice, for yourself? Can't you see she doesn't need a baby? It's a big con. It's foisted on us when we're little girls. We do it to ourselves. For Christ's sake, there are all sorts of urges, but most of the time we try to get them under control. What's different about this one is that everyone keeps stirring it up like crazy.'

'Now look here . . .'

'No. You look here. I'm going to do everything I can to stop this before it's too late. I don't trust you – you're up to something and I don't know what it is, but when I do I'll dump you in it. Alice is a nice kid, she deserves something better than a washed-out marriage and a substitute child.'

She turned on the spot and her heels clacked away.

'Bitch,' Martin said loudly, but too late.

He signed the bill and stood up, the chair tipping over behind him. Stupid thing, he thought, bending to straighten it before walking away with the stiff poise of someone over-conscious of doing something quite ordinary.

The Japanese woman was getting into the lift with a man who, to Martin's irritation, had to be her husband. There was something about the way they dressed that suggested togetherness – she, in a flounced gingham skirt, ankle socks and pink tennis shoes, he in sports shirt and long white trousers. Martin hurried over and joined them. They rose to the top floor where the doors opened on to a small corridor with a single door over which a neon sign flashed 'Café de Paris Discothèque'. Martin followed them in and waited while they took a table on the edge of the dance floor, then chose a seat opposite, so that he could peer through the gloom at her.

So early the place was deserted. A solitary waiter brought her a flamboyant cocktail, frondy with leaves and topped with a tiny paper parasol. Martin ordered Scotch, forgetting to ask for a *bébé* and getting almost an eighth of a bottle poured over loudly cracking ice. The place was weird. From so high they ought to have been looking out on the noble panorama of the moonlit river and the vast savannah, instead the windows had all been blocked off and the boards painted with expressionist scenes of Parisian life: the Arc de Triomphe, the Eiffel Tower, Sacré Coeur, the Place du Tertre. The music matched them, an endless loop of plink-plonk French pop-songs, dated cover versions of Anglo-American rock numbers reduced to a music-hall singalong. Martin didn't care – *she* seemed to like it, swaying in time to the music, taking occasionally sips through the barber's pole straw in her glass. Martin took a hefty swig of his drink and coughed, it was rough and not from Scotland. Still, with all the heat and wine he was thirsty and a second swig saw it off. Without being asked the waiter brought another.

The couple rose, walked on to the dance floor and began jiggling about to one of the bumpier melodies. They were like puppet skeletons, grinning and picked clean by the ultra-violet lights, their limbs flying apart, then jerkily reassembled in a comic *dance macabre*. Martin was entranced and not at all pleased when he realised that someone was pulling a chair up to his table.

'Well, well,' said Delmonico. 'Back so soon and didn't even come to see his old chum. Are we a daddy then?'

'No *we* bloody well aren't. It took a day there and a day back – what was all that shit about a quick trip?'

'Tut tut, laddie, it all depends on conditions out there, even you must see that. So what went wrong? The telephone lines are down, a bad sign. Some of our wilder friends used to make neck-rings out of the copper but that was years ago. Now it has to be a wee bit more serious – no?'

'What would I know, given how naive I am?'

'There there, just tell me what it was caused all the trouble?'

Martin told him about the lorries and the ammunition cases and his encounter with Darwesh. 'He's some sort of gun-runner, but the bit I don't understand is the message Diop asked Alice to give you – "It's still the twenty-ninth of July" – which just happens to be the Royal Wedding day. What on earth is going on?'

Delmonico gave a little laugh. 'Great day, laddie. His Excellency the President of the Republic will be there – in St Paul's Cathedral, an honoured guest of Her Majesty the Queen, along with one of his wives – which exactly is still to be decided upon, or so I understand.'

Martin shrugged. It was hard to see why anyone would care.

'You fail to see the connection?' Delmonico said slyly. 'But then why should you? You live in a land of general elections and ballot boxes, a land whose head of state can take a trip abroad without risk of mayhem breaking out.'

'I see,' Martin said. 'Or at least I think I do. Is that why friend Maktar is getting ready to march?'

Delmonico smiled coyly.

'Why are you paying for this?' Martin insisted.

'Sound investment. The first President was too much of a crook – messed up the whole thing in the end – but this lot are just stagnating like a bunch of country bankers. No risks, no profits. Young Diop has dreams, visions.'

'Why tell me all this? Aren't you afraid I'll rat on you?'

Delmonico shook his head. 'And let on what you've been up to? I doubt you'd risk that. Anyway you're up to your neck in it now.'

This was too much for Martin. Why was he always so damned sure of himself. 'I don't reckon your country bankers are as dopey as you imagine. We saw a military convoy heading out of town as we came back. I guess they know something's going on.'

Glad to have upset him, Martin took a good swig of the whisky. His whole body twitched involuntarily.

'I wouldn't,' Delmonico said. 'It's gut rot.' Then he grew serious. 'If they are going to try and jump him, then it all depends on how much he's been able to get out of Darwesh. Could go either way. No bets on this one.'

'We put our little mite into the pot. At least Alice did.'

'What did you and he cook up?'

'I didn't cook up anything, he and Alice made all the culinary arrangements. We didn't have enough money so he wouldn't hand over some kid he'd found for her and now we have to get all the loot we can lay our hands on and he'll send down the goods . . .' He stopped, suddenly putting two and two together. 'At least that was the plan, but if what you say is true I doubt I'll be hearing from your Mr Diop again.'

'You don't seem too fussed?'

'Frankly I'm not. I got carried away with this crazy notion and now I'll be glad to see the back of it. I ought to have known she'd get in up to her neck. She's not all right, you know – unstable, took it bad not being able to have kids.'

'You should pray they do get through. It could solve all your problems – give her what she wants, then you can have what you want.'

Again Martin experienced the horrible sensation that this creepy little man knew more about his desires than he did himself.

'I don't know what you're talking about.'

'Don't you just? And how was Abdel-Kadar? Helpful? Oh, all right, get on your high horse if you must, it's no skin off my nose. In any case what are you doing up here – little woman not well or are we looking for something else? Take my advice: if you want a black tart its best to go down to the *Café de la Place* near the market, this place is the pits. Any minute now it'll fill up with white kids from the embassies, and young Malians from ministerial families. They go to the *lycée* together and they love this place, it's a little bit of Paris for them.'

Martin took another gulp of the hooch, draining the glass. Through the thick rings at the base he saw a black face smiling at him.

'This is Freddy,' said Delmonico.

It was the barman, changed from his uniform into a sparkling disco outfit, almost a suit-of-lights, a T-shirt encrusted with circles of mirror and chunks of coloured glass. He shimmered unsteadily before Martin's wonky gaze, and seemed altogether unreal, his skin too smooth, his eyes too dark, a painted model. He was wearing the shortest, briefest hotpants, in a livid day-glow green, from which his legs seemed to extend for ever, thin and hairless. Delmonico's hand gripped one of these brown stems just above the knee.

Martin turned away and tried to focus on the Japanese still randomly jigging about. The happy thought struck, that there was nothing to stop him joining them. People often danced on their own in discos, he'd seen them.

'Scuse me,' he said, getting up, and stumbled headlong on to the dance floor. He hadn't seen the step and just managed to right himself before crashing into the dancers.

There was an irritating cry of 'Whoa there!' from behind him but he tried to look as if nothing had happened and started to bounce about, dancing for all he was worth, completely carried away, in a world of his own.

He tried to watch the woman but there was no sign that she was aware of his presence. He edged a little nearer as the music speeded up and the flashing lights turned them into a flickering zoetrope of jerking, arm-flapping marionettes. Martin went at it like a fledgling trying to take flight, throwing back his head and letting the banks of lights in the ceiling strobe through his brain. Round and round, round and round and round and WHAM there was the floor.

'You all right?' It was Delmonico with Freddy bending over him. The Japanese were on the other side, hands stretched out to help him up.

'It's all right. Nothing to worry about – slipped, that's all.'

Delmonico grabbed him under the elbow and hauled him to his feet.

'I said I'm all right, for God's sake.'

He tried to hurry to the door but the four of them kept up with him.

'Do you want me to come with you?' Delmonico asked. 'Don't want you passing out in the lift.'

Martin just shook his head and got in. He stabbed at the board but nothing happened. He pressed again, all too conscious of four pairs of eyes examining him.

'It's all right really,' he kept repeating. 'Nothing to worry about, nothing absolutely nothing.'

With teasing slowness the doors hushed together, leaving him with one last image of Delmonico shaking his head, Freddy grinning from ear to ear, and the Japanese couple executing a deep bow. The lift sank to his floor and opened. Just along the corridor was what looked like a hospital trolley, equipped with a drip-feed. He jiggled his key in the door until it gave with a violent rattle, banging against its buffer. He switched on the bathroom light, stepped into its livid glow and tried to clean his teeth. A deep-red sludge came off his tongue and clung to the curve of the basin. Even the full force of both taps failed to shift it and he had to nudge it loose with his fingers.

Back in the room there was just enough light to make out the mound of Alice on the bed. He went over, sat on the narrow space on her side and stroked her hair.

'What are you doing?' she said, sitting up so fast he fell off the edge and hit the floor with a hard thud.

'I just thought . . .'

'Well, think again.'

She yanked at the sheets, pulling them over her. He got up, limped round to his side and got in, carefully leaving a space between them. He wondered if she would agree to separate beds when they got back. He wondered where Baby was. Then he slept.

SEVEN

Martin got to the lavatory just as the pain became unbearable and a crippling contraction released a violent stream of hot liquid. There was a pause. He attempted a diagnosis: amoebic dysentery, bilharzia, hepatitis, jaundice, kwashiorkor. The pain returned – another terrible contraction and then the amazing release, the splattering flow. He was so doubled-up, his chin felt cool against the lavatory bowl. It began again – pain, contraction, release. He extended his diagnosis: blackwater fever, beriberi. There was no more pain. It was over. He must have totally voided himself.

He jabbed the flush and watched it whirlpool away, the satisfied gurgling reminding him that he ought to drink more in case he dehydrated. There was a bottle of water by the bed, but as he made to leave, the pain winded him again and he was forced to sink back on to the pan as another hot stream burst loose.

'Puer, whatta stench . . .'

It was Alice at the door, her face wrinkled with disgust. 'Smells as if something died here. What on earth were you doing last night?'

'Had a drink or two that's all. I think that's what did it – uff . . .'

He had slouched forward again, gripping his midriff.

Alice fled.

He tried to breath it into submission – in – out – in – out, out, out – better. He straightened a little. Dare he risk getting up? He was clammy and a bath might revive him. He cautiously walked over to run the water. So far so good. He eased himself in, kneeling and waiting for the level to rise enough for him to dunk his head. With his nose just hovering above the surface he reached behind and sluiced his backside. That was a lot better. He looked up. Ahead of him, the familiar accusing El Greco stared back from the tap, rebuking him for the past two days, a hotchpodge of sun-baked images that suddenly narrowed to the Japanese on the dance floor, his burbling drunken nonsense.

'Oh shit-Christ!' he cried, trying to stuff the ghoul of retribution back into the upholstery of memory.

'What did you say?' Alice called out.

'Nothing. Just singing in the bath.'

He turned up the cold tap, letting silvery condensation hide the face of aggrieved conscience. He wallowed for a moment more, then eased himself out feeling marginally better, though his guts seemed suspiciously elsewhere. Towel-wrapped in the bedroom, the dull light through the drapes picked out the squalor in grisaille – the dried scrofula of croissant beside the bed, a sucked peach-stone with its sticky Van Dyck beard, a wounded slice of cantaloupe with the imprint of Alice's teeth. He twitched.

At least she was dressing Baby, which might hopefully indicate that all the nonsense of the past two days was over and that life could get back to abnormal. She looked even thinner, their exertions had taken a toll, though he had to admit the loss was no bad thing.

'You all right, love?'

'You'd better hurry,' she said. 'The traveller's cheques are over there.'

He wanted to protest, to ask why she was playing around with the bloody doll if she still meant to go ahead with this thing, to tell her that in any case it was all over, that there was a civil war in the offing and that the smart young Diop would have more on his mind than sending her a baby. But all he could manage was a personal whinge.

'I've got terrible runs. Daren't go out just yet.'

'Abdel-Kadar will be here soon.'

'Of course he won't. How could he, with all the trouble out there? It's a revolution, we'll probably have to be evacuated.'

'He'll come,' she said, yanking Baby's bib over her head, less gently than before. He went back to the lavatory to give it one more go but there was nothing.

'What's he like?' he said at the door. 'The boy, what's he like?'

'He's sweet. Big brown eyes . . .'

Martin fought back the desire to say that all African children had big brown eyes. It was clear she had no vision of the child other than as a baby. It was a baby, like Baby was a baby. It didn't matter what it was like because it was like a baby.

'And the mother?'

Her brow furrowed, 'Maktar . . .'

Ah yes, Martin reflected, Maktar Diop the midwife. Whoever the mother may have been, she was now as disposable as placenta. Maktar would take care of all that.

221

'One day he'll want to know . . .'

Alice turned, noticed Baby's unfastened button and reached over to deal with it.

'*He'll* want to know,' Martin insisted.

When she spoke the voice was so thin and sharp, he could have sworn it was Baby giving the order.

'The traveller's cheques are over there. I've signed them so take my passport with you and you'd better hurry.'

The boutique was transformed. The racks of bikinis and suntan oils and postcards had been pushed aside to make a path to the back of the shop where the folk-art was displayed. The pregnant fertility figure had been put to service as a tailor's dummy and was now pinned up with paper shapes, the mask-like visage protruding above a flounced and ruched collar of cut-out paper. It was a mock wedding dress of lavish proportions and excessive frills. Bent double, before it, Madame Josette offered the world a truly tremendous *derrière* englobed in yellow organdie, as she busily tacked up the front hem, absently singing a half-remembered song; one no doubt learned at that distant language school on the Sussex coast.

> *The farmer has a wife,*
> *The farmer has a wife,*
> *Ee-eye-addio,*
> *The farmer has a wife . . .*

Martin coughed. She unbent in one smooth, upward sweep, turned and beamed; her upper half demur in saffron silk clasped at the throat by an outsize cameo brooch with what looked like a head of Caesar.

'Good day,' she said, raising her lorgnettes. 'But you are pale?'

'My stomach,' he groaned, clutching at his middle for dramatic effect.

'*Crise de foie*,' she said, all brow-furrowed concern. 'Is it here?' she rubbed a hand over the broad expanse of her midriff. 'Or perhaps like so . . .?' She jabbed a finger in and out of her navel. 'Or perhaps it is this.' Her fingers kneaded her gut while a look of intense agony passed over her features.

'Like that,' Martin said, poking his own belly sharply. 'Pain like that.'

'Ah hah,' she exclaimed triumphantly, turning to swing open the high doors of the cupboard behind her, revealing shelf upon shelf of little boxes and bottles.

'For the *crise de foie*,' she explained as she ran her lorgnettes along a line of labels weighing up the possibilities. She settled on a dark-brown bottle sealed with a government stamp, inside which were a dozen or so pink ovals, with a ridge down one side, like tiny effeminate rugby balls.

'These,' she said firmly, 'will do you good.'

He thanked her, popped one out and swallowed it with difficulty.

'You are perhaps surprised at my endeavour?' she said, eyes twinkling. 'I am following the *Mirror*.' She indicated an artist's sketch of Lady Di in an imagined gown, which she had pinned on to an example of local art, a crudely painted scene of some huts by moonlight. 'It is the only way to be *dans le bain*. The drawings are so, so . . . *faible* . . . I have not a good impression, but see here how one has the effect . . .' She flounced the paper train which rustled crisply, like greaseproof paper baked on to a cake.

'Terrific work,' Martin said, genuinely impressed. 'You have real talent.'

'The nuns.'

'Of course. Tell me, isn't it a little unusual here in Mali, to be so interested in something like this, I mean something so, so . . . well foreign?'

She cocked her head on one side and considered the question carefully.

'Ummm, yes and no. There is the football, many are following Everton.'

'Everton?'

'Yes – foolish *n'est-ce pas*?'

'Well, yes.'

'They should support Arsenal, no?'

Martin felt reality slip away. The blunt visage of the 'mannequin' with its absent eye-slits seemed to outface him. Madame Josette smiled hugely, her scars grinning upwards in unison.

'You are thinking that the natives should worry about native things, that it is silly for this black lady to be bothering with the Lady Di, that perhaps it is a sign of neo-colonial mentality and that where I should be concerned with the *indigène* I am too involved with the *métropole*? Or perhaps you have not fully thought these things through?'

She stuck a pin into the short sleeve of the dress and moved towards the counter.

'I was a student in Paris during the struggle for independence. The French put our leaders in prison in Madagascar. We protested.' She smiled without moving the scars. 'I came back with my *doctorat* for the celebrations – a new flag – *Un peuple – Un But – Une Foi.* And now what do you think I think? About my country, I mean. About independent Mali?'

'You must be very sad.'

'Yes. But do I wish to return to the way it was before?' The scars curled up, the eyes twinkled. 'No, I do not. That is the answer to your question which you had not thought. This . . .' She indicated the wedding dress, the newspaper clippings, the stacks of magazines. 'This *c'est l'anthropologie.* You have a 'obby?'

'I used to collect stamps.'

'Good,' she said, pulling open a drawer. 'Here is a gift for your 'obby.'

Martin took the little perforated oblong. It was beautifully engraved in two shades of red, the fine lines picking out a camel above which was a short Roman sword wreathed in flames, the whole thing overprinted with a crudely stamped Cross of Lorraine.

'It is a *Timbre de la Libération.* It was a Vichy colonial stamp – the camel is for *Le Territoire,* the burning sword for *Les Forces de l'Ordre.* After the Liberation they printed the cross of de Gaulle, so it is very rare. It is a present.'

'He studied it again; there was a tiny border of interwoven lightening flashes, clearly fascist in inspiration.

'I really didn't think of the war stretching this far. Silly, really. I suppose I thought somewhere so remote would have just ticked over until it ended.'

He took the proffered stamp.

'You're very kind, but . . .'

'But?'

'But I'm not sure I'll have time to start my collection again. I've got rather a lot on my plate at the moment, which is why I came to see you. Is it safe to go into the town today? I thought there might be trouble?'

Only a slight downturn of the scars showed that the question irritated her.

'Why do you think this?'

224

He was studying her shiny lips so intently he noticed the ridge of lipstick where she had omitted to make the final smoothing motion. He thought she was going to fire a question back at him but, as he watched, her expression settled into one of bland self-possession and she contented herself with offering him another list of the many activities the hotel was planning for that day.

'. . . a *spectacle folklorique* by the pool, so interesting, and the buffet will specialise in seafood. Tonight there will be cabaret in the Café de Paris Discothèque which you must not fail to assist.'

Her English was breaking up and with it her desire to distract him.

'So you see,' she ended abruptly. 'There is no need to go walking in the town.' The smile left her face as if something unpleasant had just occurred to her.

'But where are you yesterday and before yesterday?' she asked. 'You are not coming for a paper.'

He shifted uneasily, this was difficult but telling the truth seemed the only way of getting her to answer his question.

'I went up country.'

'Because of babies?'

He nodded glumly. 'To Timbuktu,' he volunteered and was not displeased to see the amazed look on her face. At least the journey merited some respect even if his reasons for making it were laughable.

'And you saw Maktar Diop?'

He had not expected that and his silence was her answer. 'I see,' she said. 'And this is because of Monsieur Delmonico, I think? They are so good friends, always to help people with what they want. What is it you want? No, do not say, it is better not to know. But I will be your good friend, not Delmonico, and I will tell you that sometimes it is better not to have what you think you want. Sometimes you put our hands together and say "Please God give me". But God knows best and does not give. So you go and take it, but perhaps you were not meant to have it.'

Her right hand reached for the cameo, her stubby middle finger tracing the laurel wreath about the imperial forehead. She laughed to herself.

'The French thought they could find here what they had not been given, they did what you are trying to do, they adopted us. Oh yes, and *they* had *your* reasons: to help us, to save us from hunger and thirst, to give education and make work, as good parents should. And should we have loved them as you want a child to do? Ah, but you are seeing what I mean now . . .'

A week earlier and he would have made the point for her, now his mind was cluttered with confusing images of decay and decline that muddied the argument. It was, he told himself, as if nothing had been cleaned or repaired since the French left. It wasn't the inability to carry out complex technological feats – that he understood – Christ knew, he couldn't do them himself. It was more the elementary things that remained undone that so wearied him: sweeping the streets, mending a broken shutter or even, despite Maktar Diop's solitary exception to the universal rule, arranging for your own premises to be properly painted. Why the squalor, why the filth, why the stench? If the poor did not know, why had their educated leaders not told them what to do – or *made* them do it if need be – and if *they* did not know, then why not have someone from outside show them a better way even if the word was colonialism, even if it was now so utterly unacceptable it could not even be said? He looked up, suddenly afraid that she might guess what he was thinking. Her scars had gone down and she was leaning forward as she always did when there was something unpleasant to relate.

'You must be very careful,' she insisted. 'You ask me if there is trouble in the town to which the answer is not yet but maybe soon. I suggest you to do as you are told from now on. If you do, all will be very well. This is a small thing, the end of a problem, leave it and enjoy.'

He had no quarrel with that – the thought of Abdel-Kadar handing over a little black baby, even one as light-skinned and cute as Alice had described, filled him with stomach-turning dread.

Madame Josette had returned to her dress-making, pulling the paper gown tighter across the huge pregnant belly, for all the world as if the royal nuptials had already attained their ultimate goal.

She glanced up at him. 'You do not like my statue? It is not your English cup of tea? It is Dogon, old, you can see where the little insects have eaten the knees . . .' She lifted the ruched paper hem to show the bent joints punctured with tiny holes. 'It is not a woman – that surprises you? It is the Dogon religion – they believe the first creature was a . . . I do not know the word . . . it was a man/woman. Anyway, the man/woman gave birth to the first twins . . . you see

226

them here . . .' She lifted the paper folds higher, revealing the two tiny figures clasping the sides of the distended globe. 'They are the Adam and Eve of the Dogon and they gave birth to all the people.' She let the gown fall with a sniff. 'Primitive no? They also believe that a Dogon is not a man until he has made a man.'

Martin felt a sudden all-encompassing loathing for this fat, swollen termite-ridden thing, this pregnant hermaphrodite with its pendulous milk-heavy tits, its wobbly knee-bending weight, its utter grossness. He longed for the spare and narrow, the smooth and the hard to the touch, anything but this wooden facsimile of fleshy excess.

When she next spoke, Madame Josette's voice was kinder, as if the worst of her lesson was over and he could now relax a little.

'We do not believe like that,' she said. 'It is not necessary to have a baby is it? Not for you at least. Did you find one . . .?'

The question was so abrupt, only instinct saved him.

'No,' he said, hoping that the literal truth would add conviction to the word. 'I didn't find a baby after all. I came back empty-handed. Turned out a complete waste of time.'

She narrowed her eyes but seemed to accept this. 'Good. Now tell me, who is the Lord Lichfield?'

Martin breathed easier. 'He's a photographer – a cousin of the Queen – why?'

'It is here in the *Cosmopolitan* – "Lichfield Lens on Lady Di".'

She held up the spread, showing a wispy soft-focus portrait – more a hairstyle than a person.

'How lovely she is – ah me, I am so *hors des choses.*'

Martin asked for the *Guardian* and received a *Telegraph*. He paid and thanked her.

'*Bonne journée,*' she said with a frown that ordered him to remember what she had told him.

'Have a nice day,' he replied, thinking it better to use the Americanism than leave on an empty note.

Out in the foyer, workmen were arranging swags of blue, white and red material over doors and windows. Mali might be in chaos but the hotel went about its business as if nothing else mattered.

He opened the newspaper expecting something on the crisis, then remembered that Mali was of no interest to anyone in Britain. If it went up in flames there might be a paragraph, filed by one of the agencies a few days later, though even that was far from certain.

There was a photograph of Lady Di's father, a bumbly sort of cove with a teddy-bear grin. No doubt the British nation would take him to their hearts. The lead article was an account of a television interview given the evening before by the Prince and his fiancée which, from the portions transcribed, appeared to have been of a mind-curdling banality. They hoped, so it was reported, to have children. Which was, as Martin realised, the point of the whole thing. It was a royal breeding ceremony. He thought of the King and Queen of the Belgians, the sad little tragedy of their childlessness, their entire lives shadowed by it, as if nothing else mattered.

He was moving towards the lift when the pain returned, stabbing into his guts and making him clutch at his midriff again. Bemoaning his rotten luck, he rushed to the nearest toilet, dropped his pants and let out a thin wet spurt of gas. He waited, raising himself slightly to peer through his legs – nothing. He tore a clutch of tissues and wiped himself and there it was, a blob of jelly, shot through with a thin red vein – it could have been one of Baby's eyes, half melted in the churning cauldron of his tortured guts.

He flushed and washed his hands, strangling his wrists, the way doctors do.

Still unsure of his bowels, he went to Delmonico's room and found the Scotsman draped along a sofa near the window, playing Noel Coward in a cherry-red silk dressing gown with a black foulard at his throat, talking into the telephone, in what Martin supposed was Bambara. The contrast between Delmonico's urbane, fluting tone and the hard consonantal bumps and prolonged solitary vowels was intriguing, though less so than the naked figure of Freddy lying face-down on the bed, his face covered by his encircling arms, the run of his spine like a reverse question mark losing itself in the perfect, polished mahogany, *coco-de-mer* buttocks. Martin tried not to stare, but after Delmonico had languidly waved him to a chair, there was no other distraction save the disturbing perfection of Freddy's trim, muscular torso. Martin tried looking out of the window, but this room was not as high as his own and offered only the tops of trees and the rising slope of the distant hill. The interior, however, was no different from any other in the hotel; Delmonico had not stamped his personality on it. Most of the floor space was stacked high with boxes, Martin lost count at fifty, all plastered with air-freight codes and bright red symbols indicating how fragile the contents were and which way up they should be stored. One had been ripped open to reveal a brass and onyx carriage clock. There had to be enough to staisfy every household in Bamako capable of paying for one. Even someone with a total lack of entrepreneurial acumen like Martin could see that this was overstocking on a flagrantly capricious scale.

"Orrible, aren't they?' Delmonico said, Cockney-like, as he gently set the phone back on its receiver. 'Mantock sent them, I ask for photograph albums and what do I get? Clocks! Christmas presents for the top brass, they like something – shall we say "colourful", – though who can say who will get one this year. Something is going on but just what it may be is anybody's guess and, as is the way here, everyone down to the poorest beggar knows that trouble is brewing, a prediction which inevitably tends to fulfil itself. But all of this is academic – *n'est-ce-pas?* What you want to know is, should you go on? You are no doubt thinking of all the future heartache you may be bringing into your life – the messy, noisy babyhood, the hell of school days, the agonising adolescence, the grim moment when that cuddly brown bundle wakes up to what has happened. Rejection, it's called, the realisation that your real mummy got shot of you . . .'

He said this with such vehemence Freddy stirred and drew his left leg up to his chest before drifting back into sleep again. Delmonico looked fondly at the doubled-up figure, then turned back to Martin.

'I don't know why you people want to have kids, anyway – where's the fun in it?'

'Didn't you ever want to have a son?'

'Wouldn't have been much point in wanting would there?'

'But didn't you?'

'Of course.'

'Well?'

'I grew up. So why don't you – but no, I forgot, it's not you, it's your wife – it's always the wife – it was with my mother. Oh yes, I'm adopted so I know how it is. The father is always out of it, just along for the ride, never really able to *be* a father because he doesn't feel in his heart that he is. Mine could never punish me, no matter what I did. I only saw him get worked up once, when I nearly died of pneumonia. I was seven and when I came to at some point he was sitting on the edge of the bed crying his eyes out, probably afraid he'd be accused of failing to look after this thing he'd been lent, as if he'd broken next door's lawn mower.'

'How did you know you were adopted?'

'A little shit at school told me. He'd overheard his mother saying that my mother wasn't my mother. I smashed his face, then ran home and blurted it all out. Of course she explained that she'd meant to tell me one day – and then I got the usual spiel about how, even if they weren't my real Mum and Dad, it didn't make any difference. In fact it was better, because they had *chosen* me. It's the word they all love – *chosen* – it's supposed to make you feel special.'

'And doesn't it?'

'Hell, no – makes you feel like a puppy in a pet-shop window.'

He stopped and looked sharply at the ceiling. There was a mosquito whine, distant but menacing.

'They even get through the air conditioning,' he said. 'Amazing. Anyway, as I was saying – some things are meant to be, like coming to the end of the line – letting the candle go out, as the French, so poetically, put it.'

'You're not suggesting you're homosexual because you were adopted?'

'I'm saying that the people who adopted me weren't meant to have children and aren't going to have grandchildren – there's a grand design somewhere in it all.'

'That's ridiculous.'

Delmonico looked away again. Freddy swung himself off the bed and started to pull on his clothes.

Martin heard the mosquito – it was as if he was still in that hot dark room in Timbuktu – then he saw Delmonico staring fixedly out of the window and when he followed his gaze he saw that the mosquito was really a distant helicopter rising above the tree-line. It dipped, then passed out of view, blades first – thwop, thwop, thwop . . .

'What *is* going on?' Martin demanded.

'It's still not clear.'

'But no one is going to be able to get from Timbuktu just now, are they?'

'How much you paying?'

'Another ten thousand dollars.'

'They'll come,' Delmonico said. 'For that they'll come. Take a clock. Go on. Don't be so stuck up, it might be useful.'

Martin picked up one of the boxes.

'We all adopt something – or someone,' Delmonico said kindly. 'With me it's Freddy. Oh yes, it's a sort of adoption – sons and lovers. I'm going to send him to university.' He dropped into stage Jewish: 'My son the doctor.'

Freddy had sat up and was buttoning a shirt decorated with outsize pink elephants.

Martin wanted to laugh but stopped himself. 'Thanks for the clock,' he muttered.

'You're welcome.'

With the door closed behind him, Martin stood in the corridor weighing his options. He fumbled in his pocket and pulled out a coin. It was old and dirty and worn but he could make out the profile of the first President on one side and the crossed spears and motto on the other.

'President I go to the bank,' he said out loud. 'Spears I don't.'

He flipped the coin, caught it on the palm of his right hand, then slapped it onto the back of his left and looked – the President. He decided to cheat and do it again. Flip and catch and slap. The President once more. Now he would have to find the bank.

Alice had made a cot by pulling out the top drawer of the cupboard and emptying the clothes in a heap on the floor. Next she took her faded Biba T-shirt and ripped it along one side seam and laid it inside, the way she'd seen in a film, a lifetime ago. She was so busy, she ignored the knock on the door and the fact that someone had come into the room. If the maid wanted to clean, so much the better. She plumped up the saffron cloth and wondered what she might use for a pillow.

It was the silence which stopped her; whoever it was, was staring. She turned.

'Well,' said Margot. 'I've been looking all over for you.'

'We ended up in Timbuktu. It took longer than we thought and there was trouble.'

'Same here. There was a riot somewhere in town the day you left. We could hear shooting. Quite a lot of people left yesterday, just went to the airport and took the first flight. Thank God the Frazers decided to stick it out – they've been looking after the girls. You know, the couple with the twins, so it's perfect.'

'I'm sorry, I should have asked. How's Jack?'

231

'Sleeping. Best thing really. So where's yours?'

'Gone to the bank.'

'He'll be lucky. Everything's shut as far as I can see.'

Alice panicked. 'Don't say that. They've got to be open, we have to get the money . . .'

'Whoa, steady on. What's all this, then?'

She walked over and looked into the drawer, then turned to see Baby propped on the dressing table.

'You're hardly making a bed for *her*, are you? Oh it's all right, I saw that husband of yours last night and I know he's likely to walk in here at any moment with a little black baby in his arms. This, I take it, is its bed.'

Alice nodded, then told her the story. Told her about the journey and the mud city and the camp. She skipped anything about Maktar, subtly reworking the whole thing so that it sounded as if there was some sort of agency in Timbuktu and that all they had done was to go and register with it. It was the story she intended to use from then on – she was even coming to believe it herself.

'Shee-it,' Margot said, pulling her cigarette case out of a side pocket and fumbling to get it open, her usual dexterity gone. 'Are you sure you know what you're getting into? No, of course you don't – how could you? Let's just hope they don't turn up – no, don't look at me like that, I'm only thinking what's best for you. My God, what a chance you're passing up. You could get out of your marriage with no hang-ups about kids; start again, have a life; and here you are trying to chain yourself to it.'

She tossed the cigarette away unlit.

'That husband of yours is a shit, that's why he's doing this. He's stitching you up and I'm going to see that he doesn't get away with it. Come on – I think we both need a drink.'

Alice looked up from the make-shift crèche and glanced at her image in the wardrobe mirror. She really had lost weight these last few days. She half turned and admired the dip of her side-view.

'That's my girl,' Margot said, reaching out to pick up Baby and carry her over to the chest of drawers. She laid her, none too gently, in the ruched up T-shirt, then nudged the drawer closed with her hip.

'Bye, Baby Bunting, Mummy's gone a'hunting. Come on . . .'

The foyer was now completely swathed in blue, white and red ribbons. Alice sauntered towards the boutique and saw the large, smartly dressed black woman glueing the cut-out head of Lady Diana Spencer on to what seemed to be a larger-than-life carving, incongruously dressed in a paper wedding dress. It was easily the most bizarre and inexplicable thing she had ever seen in her entire life, but as she began to frame a question, Margot hustled her into the restaurant, ordering champagne even before they had reached a table.

'*Banjou Mesdames*,' the waiter looked moody, no doubt hungry and thirsty.

'Buck up,' said Margot, dismissing the menu. 'It may never happen.'

The poor man retreated, confused.

'Now listen to me,' Margot said. 'This crap has got to stop. It's that rat of a husband of yours who's dropped you into this, I bet. He wants you tied up with a kid so's he can start chasing firm young flesh – I've seen him eyeing the potential, and I bet you have too? Yes, I thought so. I can't let this happen, you're so like I was before I woke up. Why don't you come with me when we get out of this? We could travel a bit, make a fresh start – the New Life, remember? Whaddaya say?'

The champagne arrived. Margot stuck a finger in each glass to calm the rising foam. 'Cheers,' she said.

Alice took a good swig and sneezed as the bubbles ran up her nose.

Her glass was refilled – the gloomy waiter advanced with the menus and was repulsed again.

'It's no use,' Alice said. 'We don't want the same things, not really. You're lucky, you've got it down to a few simple goals. I still don't know what I want – besides a baby – and I'm not absolutely sure about that any more. I watched a woman in labour the day before yesterday. It brought home a very elementary truth about motherhood.'

'No pain, no gain?'

'Sort of.'

'Well, at least that's a start. I'll drink to that.'

They clinked glasses.

'There's nothing I can do,' Alice said. 'He's out there getting the money right now – they may even be here with the baby. If he comes back with it, then that's that – isn't it?'

She stopped, something had occurred to her, something so obvious she was amazed that it had not crossed her mind before.

'You haven't seen your friend Thorsten lately, have you?'

'Thor? Yes, he came into the bar last night after your hubby staggered off – why?'

'He didn't happen to say what he might be doing – what his next job might be?'

'What're you driving at?'

'Please,' Alice said. 'It's important. Did he say anything about going to Timbuktu?'

'No. Well, not exactly. He didn't mention where he was going, but he did say he'd just had a call and that he would be off again tomorrow – today now. Does that answer your question?'

Alice nodded. It probably did. She could see the tent, see the woman. If she had died just after they had left, then Thorsten would have been summoned to fly back and pick up Abdel-Kadar and the baby. She tried to work it out – the flight there and back and the drive into town. If Abdel-Kadar was waiting at the air strip and Thorsten flew straight back, then they could be in Bamako that afternoon. Would they come to the hotel? Perhaps not. A bit tricky to hand over a baby under that huge chandelier. They'd probably try to find them somewhere, try to arrange a more discreet rendezvous.

'Penny for them?' Margot said.

'Oh don't mind me, my thoughts are all over the place, I don't know what I want any more. I suppose I still owe something to Martin but in a way this is his last chance – oh I know what you think about that but it's how I feel that matters. He has a right to be a father despite everything and if he comes back with the child I'll go on with it. But if he doesn't, then . . . then I just don't know.'

'Attagirl. Look, I've got to be going – someone to see. You get yourself some food and I'll call by later and see where we are. I just hope he comes back empty-handed, I really do.'

She gave Alice a peck on the forehead and beckoned to the waiter. '*Madame?*'

He was wearing a sort of white mess-suit with a velvet bow-tie in deep maroon with matching cummerbund. Alice wanted to apologise for keeping him hanging about while she drank champagne, for rejecting food when he must be hungry, for lounging about in this amazing luxury when she could now imagine the barren compound in which his family must be housed. And yet what did her champagne-pity mean to him? They were an arm's length from each other, yet centuries and continents apart. She shook her head and told him she would take the buffet. He nodded glumly and withdrew. He had lost a tip and there was even less to smile about now.

Margot walked with her to the counter, then slipped away. Alice was hungry. She overloaded a plate and found herself a quiet table on the edge of the room where she could study her fellow lunchers. At a glance they seemed to divide into a few stray pool-siders in jazzy shirts, who had decided to forgo the *al fresco* buffet, and clutches of sober trousered businessmen – jackets were draped over chair backs – earnestly doing deals.

The tourists were split into ethnically separate tables, European or Japanese; the only black faces were at the business tables, presumably local functionaries being wined and dined for contacts and contracts. Given what was about to enter her life, Alice might have found such visible apartheid worrying but somehow she felt that she and Martin would handle it – she smiled at the vista of earnest multiracial dinner-parties with similar parents that stretched before her. Once word got round of where they had acquired their child, the irresistible glamour of Timbuktu would no doubt ensure them a certain measure of notoriety.

No, it wasn't the racial thing that bothered her so much as her growing doubts about the whole enterprise, the vague feeling that there had been something in Timbuktu that was now deflecting her from her avowed purpose. She felt it even more forcibly when she thought about the couple with the twins. In a sense they had everything she had long believed she wanted: little mouths to feed, the fawning attention of everyone around them, the undisputed status afforded by parenthood. Yet now, with the prospect of joining them so close to hand, what she saw was less a freedom from longing and more a journey into a long, narrow tunnel with no end in sight and no turning back.

The sharp ping of a bicycle bell made her look up. A classic bellhop in tight trousers and waisted bolero, pill-box cap at a jaunty angle, was weaving through the tables, holding aloft a notice board with the name Zabriskie chalked on it.

Ping, ping, ping, ping.

The boy crossed the room. There was a manager in a dark suit by the entrance, scanning the room for any sign of a response. With infinite slowness Alice raised her right arm.

The boy was looking in the opposite direction but someone pointed her out, drawing every eye in the room her way.

The boy hurried over.

'*Voulez-vous m'accompagner?*' he said, half bowing.

She tried to smooth her skirt as she walked and felt a nugget of mascara, like a huge wart, caught in the corner of her left eye. Somehow she got to the door and was ushered into the empty foyer by the waiting manager, his face a picture of unctuous concern.

'Madame Zabriskie?' he began. 'I am afraid I have bad news – your husband – I'm afraid . . .'

'He's not my husband,' Alice said.

The man coughed behind his hand and smiled indulgently.

'Nevertheless,' he said, 'Monsieur Zabriskie is dead.'

Martin looked down the drive and worried. There were no taxis and no guards at the road block. Clutching his boxed clock he walked purposefully along the road and turned towards the square. No one tried to stop him, there was no traffic at all, the silence was intrusive. He turned towards the market hoping for bustle and colour, but the shop-houses were shuttered, the wooden stalls empty, as if he were being punished by having the pleasures of Africa peremptorily withdrawn. Opposite rose the tiered concrete cube of the *Banque Populaire du Mali*, gaunt and forbidding, heavy concrete walls patterned with the grain and knot-holes of the wooden moulds, the ghostly memory of dead trees. It had the empty air of a looted pyramid, offering little incentive to ascend the steep flight of stairs to the overhead walkway that led to the entrance. In any case, Martin could see little reason to change all their solid traveller's cheques for a barrow-load of grubby Malian francs, now that there was little likelihood of anyone getting through from Timbuktu. He drifted past the squat columns on which the structure was raised, continuing down a tree-lined street of substantial residences, most with a flagpole and a Mercedes on the drive.

He could smell smoke, not the satisfying aroma of burning wood but something throat-catching and acrid. It was coming from behind a line of ornamental railings surrounding a well-tended garden, which made the crude bonfire crackling at the centre of the lawn all the more incongruous. Martin watched, intrigued, as two white men in suits hurried out of what was clearly an embassy, arms full of papers and files which they dumped into the flames, pulling back as the blaze roared up. This was, Martin realised, not the place to be caught spying but as he began to hurry back towards the bank a lorry turned off the square and advanced towards him, its drab olive paintwork and stencilled markings making its military functions all too clear. Without hesitating, Martin took a sharp turn up the pitted track between two shuttered buildings, breaking into a run as soon as he felt he was safely out of sight.

He had to be heading towards the open-air abattoir he'd past on his first day – there was the now familiar stench of rotting vegetation and usual incessant dentist's drill of impatient flies. He heard voices and slowed down. There was a market of sorts, woven mats spread on the road, with a few rush paniers around which a crowd of shoppers were scrabbling frantically for what Martin could see was very little. Some were trying to rake up anything they could find, shouting their offers at the market women and as soon as one had gathered up all he could carry, he quickly hurried away. Martin saw Mansa, the spitter from the swimming pool, hanging on to the leaves of a bunch of blackened carrots in a helpless tug-of-war with a respectable looking figure in a dark blazer. The man faked defeat, then suddenly yanked back, sending Mansa flying, clutching a useless bunch of leaves, wide-eyed with surprise and dismay.

It was clear to Martin that he had strayed too far from that invisible line behind which white folk were immune. This was a grey area, he was exposed and vulnerable and he retraced his steps feeling as trapped and helpless as he had in the labyrinth in Timbuktu.

Back at the embassy he could see one of the diplomats poking at the dying embers, slivers of charred paper dancing in the hazy air, and through the heat ripple he could see that there were people being ushered into the chancery, adults weighed down with luggage, children hanging on to toys and games. Martin groaned, it didn't take genius to work out that these people would hardly be seeking sanctuary if it was only a question of a few trucks doing battle, miles away in the African bush. Something nasty was clearly about to hit Bamako and him too if he wasn't careful, a realisation that produced surprisingly mixed reactions – oh yes, he was scared, very much so, but he was also elated, light-headed at the possibility that at last something big was going to happen, something that would knock all his grumbling doubts and ill-formed longings out of play.

These conflicting emotions wrestled for control of his legs. More people were being bustled up the drive, it was beginning to look as if everyone bar him was preparing for a siege. He weighed up the few options open to him. If he were to be imprisoned in the hotel for an indefinite period, then it made sense to have local money – which also neatly resolved his problem with Alice. Cautiously scanning the way back he advanced on the bank, though even at that distance the broad line of darkened windows running beneath the concrete layers showed that no lights were burning within. Even as he climbed the stairs he knew that the automatic doors would not open and as he sat down on the top step, and looked back across the square to the hotel, he was appalled to realise just how easily an entire capital city had been brought to a halt. He was not entirely alone – on the ground below a ghekko was doing primordial push-ups in the sunlight, scaly sides inflating and deflatinig, high protruding eyes studying an improvident insect that had strayed too close. Zap. There was a brief, tail-lashing, wing-whirring struggle – the insect broke free but landed only a short distance away, dazed, one gossamer wing left in its enemy's grinning serrated mouth. The ghekko cocked its ancient head to one side, contemplating the puzzled gift, – zap – a final frantic whirring, a deep sag-throated swallow. It was all over.

Martin stood up to go but doubled as the sharp pain hit his guts again. He would have to relieve himself, but where? He hurried down the stairs, sending the tiny dinosaur scuttling for cover. A little further down the street was an entrance to the area behind the bank, a scruffy garden with unkempt stunted bushes that might provide some cover. Forcing a way in, he scythed apart fronds and branches to reach a small clearing where he dropped his trousers, squatting down as low as possible, letting out another hot stream of evil-smelling fluid. It was over in seconds but how to clean himself? There was a large, vividly green leaf on the nearest plant but there was no way of telling if it might be some sort of stinging nettle. He touched it gingerly. It seemed harmless. He plucked it and rubbed it on his arm – no rash, no pain. Eyes closed, teeth clamped, he ran it under his scrotum and over his sphincter – fine. With a sigh of relief he fastened his zip and readied himself to rise and it was then that

238

he saw the lit-up window on the far side of the building and an inner voice, previously unheard, warned him to take great care.

Still bent low, he edged forward, just far enough to get a better view of the room. There was a long polished table around which a group of Malians, some in suits, some in military uniforms, sat, listening intently to someone just out of sight. Martin duck-waddled sideways a fraction until the entire room was visible. The speaker was short and had his back to Martin. He was pointing out positions on a large map hung on the far wall. It looked oddly familiar. Then Martin realised where he had seen it before. The speaker turned, it was Monsieur Mamadi.

Martin dropped as low as he could, his new-found instinct firing off warnings like signal rockets. Whatever was going on in that room, he needed no telling that he was not supposed to know about it. He started to back away, an inch at a time, afraid to snap a branch or crunch a stone. It seemed to take for ever, but at last the window slid from view. Still backwards and doubled up, he emerged from the undergrowth, and waddled out on to the street, clutching the clock like a protective fetish. He was just straightening when a hand clamped tightly onto his right shoulder. He froze. He was dead. They would never believe he had gone in there for a shit. He was a spy. They would shoot him. He was so stunned, it took some time to realise that the hand had relaxed its grip and was slowly kneading his tense neck muscles. Even when the change registered, he could hardly believe the obvious, that whoever was standing behind him was giving him a gentle massage. Confused, afraid, fascinated, he turned and looked straight into the grinning face of Abdel-Kadar. He was wearing Western clothes, tight faded jeans, a cotton shirt in a darker blue. Then Martin saw the Mercedes parked at the foot of the steps, its impeccable body-work hideously scratched and dented, one side window an icy pattern of force-lines. Standing by this disaster was a man in uniform with a filthy bandage over one temple and dark-black bruising around the neighbouring eye. Martin recognised him as one of the drunken policemen from Timbuktu, though judging by his scowling face he was no longer the happy boozer of two days ago. Martin wondered how he had got that way, then he saw the bundle in his arms, swathed in rags and his heart sank.

Abdel-Kadar followed his eyes.

'Baby,' he said bluntly.

'I couldn't get the money. The bank's closed. Everything's shut.'

The boy cast a glance over the concrete cube, absorbing the evidence, then motioned to Martin to follow him.

The policeman stiffened as they approached. Martin had a sudden, terrified feeling anything might happen. The man had a revolver. There was no one around. He was entirely dependent on the boy for protection.

Abdel-Kadar said something to the man who, with obvious unwillingness, allowed the bundle to be lifted from him and placed in the crook of Martin's left arm, balancing the box held in the other.

Martin looked into the gap in the bindings. A little black face, all eyes, stared back at him.

'I've no money,' he said desperately.

The policeman seemed to get his drift.

'Floos?' he demanded of the boy, who tried to pacify him. The man looked very unconvinced.

Abdel-Kadar reached into the car and lifted out a padded parcel, a little larger than his hand.

Martin looked at it with instant suspicion. It was very well wrapped, like something from a fancy shop, sharp folds overlaid with sellotape, a neat cross of frizzy yellow string, the knots coated with blobs of cardinal red sealing wax. It was a parcel playing at being a parcel.

Abdel-Kadar nudged it against Martin's right hand forcing his fingers to touch it. It was soft, soft as the baby. He gave a little squeeze – it yielded but with a hint of something within, like the baby's arm. He pulled his fingers away.

'I give you baby,' the boy said. 'You take this to your home for Monsieur Darwesh. His brother will collect it.'

Martin shook his head rapidly.

The boy came closer, his body touching Martin's, his eyes locked on to him, soft and dark, his lips barely parted.

'Take it,' he whispered.

The parcel was rubbing against his crotch. Martin squirmed, his mind churning with the hideous memory of the water-cistern and the slobbering creature forcing himself upon him.

'No!' he yelled, surprising himself.

'D'jebel floos,' the policeman said, his voice confused and impatient.

240

He reached out to grab the baby back. Abdel-Kadar tried to deflect him but he was too strong and was not going to be stopped. Without thinking Martin held out the box and shoved into the man's grasping arms. This confused him. Was it money?

'You must take,' said the boy, nudging the parcel at Martin. 'Take or bad trouble.'

The policeman ripped open the box and yanked out the carriage clock. For a brief second he was held by the gaudy amazement of the shiny brass fittings, the little revolving balls swinging first this way then that, this way then that. His brows knotted – incredulity began to give way to fury. Whatever it was, it was not what he had been promised. Enraged he shook the thing with all his force, there was a quiet but audible click followed by the unexpectedly loud chimes of Big Ben – Ding Dong Ding Dong – Ding Dong Ding Dong – Dong . . . Dong . . . Dong . . .

The midnight strokes echoed across the still silent space like a car alarm in the night. The policeman threw the offending thing to the ground, shattering its face and scattering its mechanism everywhere. But as he lurched forward to retrieve the baby, the glass doors of the bank parted and a cluster of heavily armed soldiers dashed out, looking round to see what all the noise was about.

Martin turned and began to walk away, the baby clamped in his arm. He was eerily calm telling himself not to rush, ordering himself to walk as nonchalantly as possible. He remembered the Swede outside the barracks, remembered he had said they don't kill white men. He kept walking. At each step he expected someone to call out that he should stop, but no one did. It was a miracle. They were letting him go. He risked a look over his shoulder, and saw Abdel-Kadar and the policeman bent over the car while the soldiers searched them. Ahead was a turning. Martin made it. He was safe. He could see the tower of the hotel. He walked on, his thoughts in turmoil. Which plan did this fit into? What particular scheme was he acting out now? Someone was walking beside him, a kid in ragged cut-off shorts staring at the bundle in his arm.

'Oh Christ,' Martin said to himself. 'He thinks I've stolen it.'

Then he realised that he had.

The manager pulled back the sheet like a conjurer revealing a disappearance, only to find this grim cadaver still there. Jack Zabriskie looked ghastly – grey, sunken, bird-like. The manager paused to let the bereaved absorb the sight, then dropped back the cover. It settled airily on to the point where the nose stuck up above the rest.

'The maid found him,' the manager explained.

'She would,' said Alice bitterly. 'She goes into the rooms without knocking. She's no business bursting in on people when they want to be left alone.'

'Please, Madame Zabriskie, you are upset.'

'Where are Sharon and Lizzie?'

'Your daughters are with Mr and Mrs Frazer in 324. Perhaps you would like to speak with them alone?'

Alice felt the urge to laugh – she had just acquired a complete family, and why not when Margot didn't seem to want them anymore.

The manager was still talking, she made herself pay attention.

'. . . the burial or perhaps a cremation?'

'I'm sorry I don't know.'

'Of course . . . it's all been so sudden. Perhaps you would like to sit with him for a while. I can come back and go through the details later. Please understand that if there's anything – anything – we here can do . . .?'

Alice looked down at the vaguely human shape, as if Margot's husband had been made of wax, now melted by the African sun. Everyone always wanted to help, in the manager's place she would have said the same thing, and meant it, just as he probably did. But there was never anything that anyone could do. She looked away, trying to settle on some neutral point on the white wall. It was sentiment without feeling. We think we grieve for strangers when we are really grieving for our own mortality, which is why funerals are such satisfying celebrations of survival – you get to leave. She wondered if she ought to cry. Did she have a handkerchief? Probably not.

She let the thoughts roll on – were all emotions as selfish as that, or at least partially so? She had already accepted that her desire to have a child had had little to do with love as there could be nothing for her to love until the desire was fulfilled. Merely wanting to love could never be selfless, it was hunger of a kind – which was what Dr El-Assawy had tried to tell her. Strange how everything led back to the camp and the tent. If she closed her eyes she could see the doctor with her pale face and exhausted look. Yet for all that there was something impressive about her that Alice could not erase, something that seemed eminently preferable to the grinning guzzlers in the restaurant or this sense of helplessness beside the dead body of a stranger. El-Assawy's was a proper exhaustion, a tiredness from work that had to be done. Even her anger came from a just cause and not the petty expression of frustrated selfishness.

'If there's anything – anything – we can do . . .'

'I'm *not* Madame Zabriskie,' Alice said. 'She's somewhere else. She went for a walk.'

The man's expression passed from confusion to irritation. He straightened himself and when he spoke his voice had lost its caring, slightly unctious tone.

'I really don't think that this is . . .'

'I'm sorry,' Alice said. 'I was having lunch with her before the bell-hop came round and I thought . . . Oh, never mind. I'll go and find her, she must be somewhere round here.'

The man looked far from happy but before he could protest again, Alice was backing towards the door.

'I'll go and find her,' she said. 'Someone will have to tell her her New Life has begun.'

Inside the lift she hesitated over the buttons. The place was so big and Margot could be anywhere. She pressed for the top floor but the disco was empty, the dancer gone; she walked to the centre of the dance floor lit only by a shaft of light from the open door behind her. Its tiered seats and the disc jockey's raised podium, made it more like a court than a place of entertainment. She began to revolve – one, two, three – one, two, three – humming a sad little tune whose unremembered words had been all about the loss of love. One, two, three – one, two three. How furtive marriages are, she thought, her mind on Jack and Margot. Once they must have had something. They had had two girls, yet look at them now, the sunken corpse, the vivacious Margot. People make love in the dark because they are in the dark. One, two, three – one, two three . . . She saw the sheet draped over Jack – how quickly he would cease to be real to his daughters. Soon their grandmother would be everything. She stopped turning, irritated with Margot and her New Life – what right had she to abandon her daughters?

There was a door behind the music console, with the word '*Privé*' on a red card. For want of anything better to do, she pushed it open and stepped into a grey service area. A bare bulb hung by taped wires from a length of flex. There was a mop and bucket against the far wall and a second door which led into an unpainted stairwell which descended in giddy stages down the entire depth of the tower. It was a place no guest was ever intended to see, a looking-glass world of stained concrete and bulkhead lamps. She started down, gripping the rail to counter the spinning vertigo. On the first landing, a stack of broken trestle tables was topped with an old tea-chest overflowing with crumpled foil decorations, dumped after Christmas and forgotten. She tramped down six flights, pausing beside an old armchair with escaping stuffing, a missing leg, balanced on a stack of menu cards. On the ground beside it, were old tin-lids heaped with cigarette butts, and a dozen filthy coffee mugs, one frondy with green mould. It was a staff hideaway, a quiet corner for off-duty moments, relaxing in squalor, released from the oppressive glitter of the public world. She went on to the bottom, pushed open another door and found herself in a large studio, at the far end of which, two men were painting an enormous hanging canvas, covering it with an idyllic country scene that could only be France – striped vineyards, a distant château with a round *pigeonnier*, a gentle range of sun-dappled hills, topped with cotton-wool clouds.

The artists were engrossed in their work and she slipped past unnoticed, pushing against a far door and stepping on to a thick pile carpet. She had slipped back through the looking-glass into a room with exercise machines and weights and training equipment, some sort of gym or health club. The place was deserted, or so she thought until she stepped further into the room and her eye was caught by something moving, reflected in a wall-size mirror running the length of the far wall. In it she saw Margot, naked and stretched out on a high treatment table, lying on her front while her back was massaged by a giant of a man in a tight singlet, his arm muscles rippling as his huge hands kneaded into her flesh. His body moved to a peculiar rhythm, oddly unrelated to the flow of the massage. Then Alice saw what Margot was doing – lying slightly on her side so that her face was directly in front of the man's crotch so that . . . Alice stopped even thinking. The reality of what Margot was doing was so . . . so . . . She turned and fled, across the studio, back through the looking-glass into the stairwell, up the first flight and out of the first door she came to.

She stood in the foyer, blinking under the chandelier, bewildered. There was even more striped bunting. She hurried to the lift and went back to her floor, but as she stepped out she walked straight into the manager. She had completely forgotten about Jack, lying there, dead.

'Madame Zabriskie is coming,' she lied. 'She'll come, as soon as she can.'

And muttering apologies, she hurried past, fiddled with the lock and threw herself into the safety of her own room, where she stood, shaking and trying to catch her breath.

She had had quite enough of the outside world, now she wanted her familiar life. She pulled open the drawer. Baby lay, eyes clicked shut, as if dead and buried in this crude sepulchre. Alice reached into the drawer and gently undid the string on her tiny track suit and peeled it off. Naked she looked cruelly artificial – the slight gaps where the arms, legs and head were joined to her torso, the unmarked curve of her shiny belly, the absence of a navel dropping into the nothingness between her thighs where a vagina ought to be. It was better. Unreal and unchanging. Alice set her on the chest of drawers and stroked her brittle hair.

'Sorry,' she said. 'Mummy's sorry.'

The door opened. She was about to scream at the maid for daring to come in without knocking when she saw that it was Martin. He must have bought something in the town, something crudely wrapped in filthy rags. She was about to ask what it was when there was a pained hiccough and the bundle started to cry.

'It's hungry,' Marting said, laying it gently on the bed, unpeeling the bindings like a nervous Egyptologist.

The sight was pitiful, a tiny emaciated frame under an outsize head, knees like skulls, chest all fingers-and-thumbs, the belly extended with a protruding navel, the shrivelled genitalia.

'Boy,' Martin said.

'But it isn't him,' Alice said. 'Mine was lighter, like a Touareg, this one's too dark.'

'You see, you see,' Martin said, 'Bloody Diop, the cheating bastard!'

'Did you see him?'

'Of course I didn't, he's in the middle of a civil war. Don't you take any notice of anything. Abdel-Kadar came with one of those drunken policemen from Timbuktu. God knows how they did it. The town's in turmoil, it looks like the diplomatic corps is about to cut and run, everything's closed and yet they got through all right.'

'If everything's closed, how did you get the money?'

'I didn't. I was waiting outside the bank when they rolled up.'

'So how did you pay them – you must have paid them – didn't you?'

He shook his head sheepishly.

'They didn't want money, they wanted me to take a parcel back to England for them – well, I wasn't going to fall for that old trick.'

'So what did you do? How did you get the baby if you had no money and you wouldn't take the parcel?'

'There was a bit of a to-do with some soldiers and I just walked off with it. Simple as that. Anyway what does it matter – they were trying to cheat us, bringing a different kid. So we didn't pay.' He paused, then seemed to come to a decision. 'Look on the bright side – what does it matter which kid it is, as long as we've got one – eh?'

There was another distressed wail.

Martin pulled clear the largest rag which had been used as a diaper. It was smeared with yellowish liquid. He sniffed experimentally. There was a vague scent of damp lino in old houses which he suspected was more the filthy cloth than the baby's excrement. There was nothing solid at all, just a thin yellowish consommé. A brute like that policeman wouldn't have bothered to feed or change him.

'What are we going to do?' Martin said.

'I don't know.'

'Don't know, what do you mean you DON'T KNOW? For Christ's sake, you wanted this. You must have known we'd have to feed it – it's not made of plastic.'

He hoisted the little body off the bed, producing a puzzled sniffle. Hanging free, the stretched frame seemed even more emaciated, a skeleton wrapped in cheese-cloth. Martin slowly turned it round, carefully appraising it like a collector in an antique market. He looked closer – there was some sort of bruising under the arms, blotchiness like the bubbly surface of a blackberry.

'Oh God, he's got a rash – look – there's an eruption, like hives. It's an infection or an allergy. Did you bring anything? Germoline? TCP?'

There was still no response from Alice. Martin held the child closer, forcing her to see the angry swellings. She tried to look away but he insisted, forcing the child into her arms. For a moment she seemed unaware of what he had done and he wondered if she was going to let it slip down, the way she sometimes did with her dolls when things got too much for her. Another hiccoughing cough seemed to alert her to the tiny presence and to Martin's relief she hoisted it further into her embrace, using her free hand to loosen the remaining rags around the face. She stroked the smooth hairless head – there was no sign of that Mohican tuft she had noticed on the child in Timbuktu. Indeed there was no resemblance at all – the features were broader and heavier, more like the dark-skinned townspeople here in Bamako than the lighter more aquiline features of the desert dwellers. Not that it made much difference – if Martin had brought the real infant, she still would not have known how to deal with it.

Martin made himself calm down. There was no point in getting angry with her – it was too much to expect that she would have an instinctive knowledge of what to do with a child and even if she had, there was no way she could have brought all the stuff babies need – nappies, feeding bottles, cotton buds – let alone the special medicines that a sick infant should have.

'It's no use,' he said. 'I'll have to get help. Can you just hang on to it till I get back?'

Her lower lip started to tremble.

'NO!' he yelled. 'No tears. Not now. Hold on till I get back – got it?'

Alone, she sank into the armchair, the little body pressed against her. In the fading light only its wide, unblinking eyes were clearly visible, and in the gloom, the figure of Baby seemed to watch over her treachery from its vantage point on the chest of drawers.

Alice had no idea how long she had been sitting there before she heard the familiar struggle with the lock, and Martin came back, leading the maid, her hips a-bustle as she walked over and lifted the baby out of Alice's arms. Nothing was said, she undid the shoulder of her dress and bared her breast, holding out the deep-black nipple to the child. The child did not react. The woman nudged the little head towards the proferred teat, but only when his mouth made contact did he begin to feed.

Alice had opened the cupboard and was lifting out tiny clothes: a pair of knickers, a pinafore dress. She reached for Baby and began to dress her, smoothing down the little garments, fluffing up her bedraggled curls.

When the little boy had finished, the woman shouldered him for wind, gently tapping the sharp little back. Martin found some antiseptic cream in their emergency kit and carefully smeared some on to the tender blotchiness under the arms, making the child whimper in distress. The woman lifted away the tiny hands, offering a clearer view of the infected area. The child snivelled. Throughout all this Alice continued to nurse Baby in her arms. Ignoring her, Martin went to the cupboard and pulled out a doll's nightdress. As he held the bottom open, the woman slipped in the child, then fastened up the neck. There were no nappies but one of his shirts would do. They laid the baby on the bed and wrapped him up as best they could, then lifted him to the open drawer where he could sleep. Martin slipped the woman a banknote. She nodded, refastening her dress. When she had gone Martin lay on the bed, staring at the ceiling while Alice sat in the armchair, rocking Baby, backwards and forwards, backwards and forwards . . .

EIGHT

It was as if he had not slept. He could remember running down and down the endless spiral ramp into the depths of the cistern, getting no nearer to the distant water. He felt clammy, the air was laced with the confusing odours of unwashed bodies and bruised fruit. The air-conditioning was ferocious, but they were only recycling their own filth. He eased himself upright. Where was Alice? She was not in the bed. A thousand terrible possibilities cascaded into his fugged brain, then vanished when he realised that she was still sitting on the floor, back to the wardrobe, legs straight in front, holding the thin black baby to her exposed left nipple.

'It keeps him quiet,' she said. 'That's all.'

It seemed to be true. The little mouth was puckered about the dry teat, obeying the obligations of nourishment with none of the rewards.

Martin went to the bathroom fearing the worst but he too seemed to have dried out. It gave him the courage to face the day, though he had no energy to wash and simply put on the same clothes he had been wearing for two days now. Fastening his jeans he decided he would have to get some baby things, feeding bottles, sterilisers – maybe the boutique would have some.

'You must see that man again,' Alice said, as he came back into the room and made for the door. 'The one in the office, the government man. We need papers – for Simon.'

Martin looked down at the emaciated figure, obediently mouthing her purplish nipple, cosy in Baby's nightie.

'Simon?'

'Yes, it suits him, don't you think? You'd better hurry, the office might close early for Ramadan and it'll make less trouble at Heathrow tomorrow. They can't send him back, can they? We could get that man on the *Argus* to help. What was his name, Ferguson – Terry Ferguson.'

'You've no idea – everything's shut, the entire population has stocked up for a siege. There's no point in going out – this is a ghost town.'

She stormed over to the window and yanked back the curtains. 'Well,' she said. 'What's so different?'

She was right, a line of vehicles crawled across the bridge, not as many as before but enough to show that life went on. Down below, by the pool, Mansa was setting out his deck loungers.

'I don't understand . . .' he began but she cut him off.

'Joke's over. Simon is what matters now. First go to the boutique and get whatever baby stuff they have: bottles, steriliser, powdered milk, whatever . . .'

He was about to protest that that was precisely what he'd planned to do, then thought better of it. She was on an efficiency jag and it might be unwise to provoke her.

'. . . and after you've brought the stuff here, go and get the papers sorted out while I feed him – and don't take no for an answer. Do try and stand up for yourself, don't let him push you around. This is for Simon and you're his father.'

The word hit him like a blow between the eyes.

'Well?' she said. 'What are you waiting for?'

He mumbled something about being on his way, and left.

The lift took for ever to arrive. The glass-fronted panel where the daily menus were posted had been draped with the now ubiquitous blue, white and red ribbons and the *carte du jour* was decorated with a crowing cock and the announcement that *Monsieur Prévost, chef de cuisine, vous propose un soirée de toutes nos régions* in the main restaurant, followed by a list of six courses running through *foie gras de canard* with Sauternes, on to *aumonière de saumon* and ending with a *vacherin glacé*, all for a truly colossal amount of francs. In the foyer the workmen were still high on ladders draping bunting and swagging rosettes. In the restaurant, the waiters were gathered round a gas cylinder, inflating countless blue, white and red balloons, floating them into a waiting net, ready to be hauled to the ceiling.

Martin was totally confused. It was as if yesterday had not happened; the men had returned to their post by the road block and, while there seemed to be no regular soldiers controlling them, at least someone was back on guard. The boutique, too, was functioning normally – save that Madame Josette was in a towering rage.

'Look,' she fumed, slapping the cover of the *Daily Mirror*. '*She* will not go.'

The 'she' was withering.

'Who is *she* to refuse? Well . . .?'

Martin looked. The 'she' covered half the page, flamboyant in flamingo pink with what looked like a dead chihuahua on her head, and another in her arms. She stood four-square beneath a banner headline: 'CARTLAND NOT FOR ABBEY'.

'She uses boot polish for her lashes,' said Madame Josette in a horrified whisper, then wailed: '"Boot polish" . . . what is this then?'

'But isn't it better she doesn't go, I mean I thought that was what you wanted? After all she has no dress sense – not like you.'

He waved a hand in a painterly gesture over her Liberty lawn blouse and pearl-grey pleated skirt, as crisp as a Venetian blind. Her scars turned up.

'But *you* have taste. *She* should not have made this refusal, it is not for her. Oh, to think she can choose while I have no chance at all – *c'est le désespoir.*'

Martin's attention wandered, his eyes roaming the racks of suntan creams and diarrhoea pills, settling on the little jars of baby mush. He edged a little further along the counter to see if there was any equipment on the other side of the rack.

'You need something?'

'No – er well yes.'

'Perhaps there,' she said, pointing to a distant display case draped with a patterned cloth. He moved towards it as nonchalantly as he could and lifted the cover. Beneath were ranged row upon row of condom packets, laid down by country of origin, the rubbers of all the nations, a tribute to Madame Josette's customary sense of order and pattern.

He let the cloth fall back. 'Oh – ah – no,' he stammered.

'Then what is it you wish?' she asked soothingly.

'A feeding bottle, teats, a steriliser, powdered baby milk.'

'But I thought . . .'

'It's a gift. For that couple with the twins. They're so nice, I'd like to give them something.'

'The Frazers. But they have everything, except the little meals which they buy here.' She raised her lorgnettes and studied the rack. 'The beef and carrot, the banana and pear, the chicken and pea – especially the chicken and pea. The twins are beyond formula.'

'I still want to buy it.'

She trained her lenses on him, then slowly lowered them to her bosom where they lay like portholes on the side of a commodious liner.

Her silence was humiliating – whatever she had guessed, she was keeping it to herself. She bent below the counter and brought up all the things he had requested, the equipment in one box, the powder in a large tin, both decorated with an ecstatically grinning white child, plump to the point of obesity.

'The Cartland woman believes in the Royal Jelly,' she said, tactfully deflecting matters back into neutral regions. 'But this I do not have.'

'That's quite all right,' Martin said, holding out a large note.

'There are no newspapers at all,' she said. 'The airport is closed temporarily. A little problem that you should not worry about. Life, as you see here, is going on.'

'Well, it didn't look that way yesterday – diplomats burning files, people snatching at any food they could find, the banks closed – I don't call that "going on" do you?'

'That was yesterday,' she said, leaving the phrase hanging.

'Nevertheless,' Martin insisted. 'A mere twenty-four hours ago, everyone thought the balloon was going up.'

Dated airforce slang was not part of her repertoire. 'No balloons, not yesterday. There will be balloons tonight, but not before.'

'Never mind. What I'm trying to say is that everyone was preparing for the worst, now they're almost back to normal – why? What's going on?'

She sighed deeply, as if pained by the world's incessant folly.

'People hear rumours, they believe them, when they see it is not the truth, they forget. It is so easy to make a mistake – especially for you where everything is so strange. In Brighton I was very confused at first – how cold everyone was, no one talking, no one smiling – then I understood, it is manners, good manners to leave people alone, yes? Everywhere is different. Be *very* careful.'

He thanked her, raked in his purchases and bolted.

Back in the room he found Simon laid on the bed, with Alice trying to distract him by dangling one of Martin's socks over his face. He took absolutely no notice, his eyes glazed with a sad indifference which almost outdid the mock grief on Baby's porcelain features.

Martin switched on the little bedroom kettle and began to unpack his purchases. He lifted off the plastic over-lid and tugged at the ring-pull to unveil the powder beneath.

'Looks like cocaine,' Alice said.

Martin shuddered, remembering Abdel-Kadar and the packet. He'd almost erased yesterday's drama. Now he was about to return to the dangerous streets of Bamako.

'Why don't we just take Simon home? As you said, no one would dare stop us once we got to Heathrow.'

She shook her head. 'We have to get out of here and how do we do that with an African baby unless we have something to prove it's ours?'

'But that's the problem, it isn't. Who gave it to us? What organisation fixed it up? Where are the adoption papers? Alice – listen to me, Alice, please – when push comes to shove, I stole that baby . . .'

'NO!' Her voice hit top C without a run up. He thought she must have raised the entire hotel.

'Don't scream,' he said. 'For God's sake, calm down. I'm on my way. Look I'm going . . . look . . .'

'MARTIN!'

He froze.

'Martin, I am not putting up with any more of your twisting and turning. Get that piece of paper, whatever it is, but GET IT!'

He ran down the corridor and into the open lift, his mind on nothing but escape, and found himself squeezed against two men in white coats, beside a trolley covered in a sheet. They stared impassively ahead as Martin studied the odd way the white cloth jutted up – it was a peculiar shape for a dinner trolley and it was only as he left them at the ground floor that it dawned on him that he had shared his ride with the mortal remains of Jack Zabriskie.

Along the restaurant ceiling the balloons sagged in their loose netting. A gaggle of chefs pattered about with cartwheel platters of charcuterie and bowls of salads. On a central table an enormous shark-like fish, whorled with mayonnaise, stared blankly at a whole suckling-pig skewered with kebabs. Martin shook his head and walked out.

There was a solitary taxi on the drive, fortunately with a different driver – the previous one might well have refused to cooperate. Even so, the new man looked wary and far from pleased to learn their destination. With good cause – the guards were unwilling to let them pass and with no regular soldier to sort things out, Martin was reduced to repeating *Cité Administrative'*, over and over, in a hopeless attempt to wear them down. In the end, he found himself fumbling in his pocket and passing over a five hundred franc note to the nearest pair of hands. The effect was immediate, bodies removed themselves, the car edged forward and Martin felt childishly proud at having achieved such a dubious feat.

It was a short-lived pleasure – they were no sooner out of the drive than they could see that their way into the square was blocked by a red and white striped barrier, manned by an armed policeman, waving his hands in circles to indicate that they should turn back.

This was too much for Martin's driver. *'C'est la fête des Blancs'* he hissed, clashing gears and gunning his vehicle into a noisy spin. *'La fête des Blancs,'* he repeated as they screeched away, and then kept on saying it over and over again, as if the irritation somehow pleased him.

Their road led through a patch of rough open ground, pitted with glossy black puddles of sump oil, their surfaces sheened by the overhead sun. The place was dotted with greasy machinery – pistons and engine casings, radiators and fan-wheels – ready for the men, oily too in their blackened dungarees, cannibalising lorries, working under the skeletons of smashed cars held up on pillars of brick. It was Mali's quotidian miracle of recycling – from mud mosques to these Frankenstein vehicles, crudely stitched together from anything to hand, then adopted and customised with bright paint and orgies of chrome.

Another road block lay ahead. The driver took a corner with a squeal of burning rubber, a cheering round of *'fête des Blancs'* and somehow got them back on the road, climbing out of town to the ministries above.

Now, Martin thought, for the tricky bit. He braced himself for trouble but saw at once that something had changed: the scruffy *sauvages* had been replaced by a platoon of alert, if anxious-looking, soldiers in snappy black uniforms and silver helmets, who held their guns ready in white-gloved hands. It was this, and the gold-braided sleeves and red epaulets, that convinced Martin that they were something special – most likely an honour guard for the President in his palace beyond the trees.

Happily they were too preoccupied to waste any time on a passing white man, waving them through with a look of complete indifference. Martin sat back, attempting to rehearse what he intended to say as they approached the familiar dilapidated house. There, at least, nothing had changed. The same woman sat banging at the same ancient typewriter, barely looking up as he explained that he wished to see Monsieur Mamadi again, merely waving him to his place on the sticky sofa. He picked up a week old copy of *La Voix du Peuple Malien*, entirely given over to the reprint of a speech to the *Assemblé Nationale* by the President, whose blurred retouched features stared out from the cover. He wore a white cap and slightly tinted spectacles and, despite the fuzzy reproduction, appeared to be a strong-featured man with a pursed, oddly feline mouth which suggested a potential for ill-temper. His discourse did not inspire, though Martin presumed that much of it would be in local code, understood by those to whom it was directed. Words like 'co-operation', 'unity', 'regional development', must have a reso- nance beyond the apparently dreary officialese. As he read, Martin realised that he still had no idea what the man stood for, outside the confines of his own country. Did he lean to the East or the West? Was his aid American or Chinese, were his advisors French or Cuban, did his farmers fertilise their crops with gifts from West Germany or did Bulgarians staff his hospitals? To all this the ex- colonel, now Commander-in-Chief, gave no clue, his thoughts preoccupied with *les accords euro-maliens* and *les nouvelles struc- tures de l'enseignement public*. From outside, it had been possible to see the continent purely in terms of drought and famine, yet within the thin off-white sheets of this official gazette, such things were not even hinted at. Here were five-year plans and new administrative committees, overlaid with references to the 'struggle for indepen- dence', or the 'new Third World order'. And all this from a man destined to stand in St Paul's Cathedral in a few days time, watching an hereditary white prince turn his fiancée into a princess amidst all the ceremonial trappings of ancient wealth and privilege, at a cost which must be a significant proportion of the Malian national budget. Martin could see the sneer on the lips of Maktar Diop.

He put down the newspaper and saw that the door to the inner office had opened. Beyond it, little Monsieur Mamadi was struggling into a smart black jacket, his cuffs sparkling with huge emerald links, a double row of pearl buttons twinkling down his front, high- heeled patent leather boots wetly glistening as if he had been wading through the sump puddles by the car repair shops. He was clearly about to leave for something important. Martin tore himself off the plastic seat and threw himself towards the door.

'You must help me,' Martin said. 'I need an adoption certificate – for Simon.'

With a heave and a grunt Mamadi got his arm through the sleeve of his jacket allowing him to wave his liberated hand up and down his front as if to say: 'Look, you see I am all dressed up!'

'Please,' Martin insisted.

'Who is Simon?'

'My son.'

'You said . . .'

'I found one.'

'You do not find sons, this is not a fairy tale. In Mali there is no stork to leave babies under bushes. Now if you will excuse me, it is the *Quatorze Juillet*.'

'I found this baby the day before yesterday – maybe I shouldn't have but I did, and now I need the right papers to take him home. Believe me, it's the best thing for him, he's been starving and we will look after him, you must see that.'

In his own breathless silence, Martin suddenly took in the wall where the map had been. Now that it had gone he could see that its crinkled canvas had covered an old tongue-and-groove partition, faded to tobacco yellow, in the centre of which still hung a recruiting poster from the first world war, a cartoon portrait of a grinning African Spahi holding a rifle in one hand and a bundle of banknotes in the other, racing towards a group of quaking Huns, who were obviously waiting to be hacked to bits by this grinning savage.

Mamadi flicked an eye in the direction of his gaze.

'Thousands died,' he said. '*La Somme, Verdun*. There is no monument, but the French authorities paid the same war-widows' pensions as those in France, a fortune here, so no one has ever complained. Who needs a monument?'

'I'm not responsible for the past,' Martin said, abandoning diplomacy. 'I didn't create the British Empire, let alone the French – I've been an anti-colonialist since university, ask anyone. I don't care what you do, it's your business. You lead your lives, I'll lead mine. But what can this baby mean to you? It's going to starve to death along with hundreds of others, my wife saw them in Timbuktu. All dying. What difference can one make?'

Mamadi stopped trying to edge past him. Martin's heart sank as he realised what he had said.

'*Tombouctou*,' Mamadi said quietly. 'No, don't tell me, I can guess, Delmonico. It's really about time we taught him not to interfere. Very well, Mr Beresford, I will strike a bargain with you – tell me exactly what you know about Maktar Diop and you shall have your adoption certificate.'

'Suits me. Didn't care for the little rat, anyway. Too goddamn superior for his own good. What I know is that he's got money, lorries and guns. The money from Delmonico; the vehicles and bullets from a very suspicious character called Darwesh. More to the point, he's got a lot more trucks and guns than were sent out yesterday to deal with him. If you ask me, he's probably won round one already and is on his way here for the final show-down.'

'I could have you shot.'

'Me – why?'

'For taking the money from Delmonico to Diop. Oh, stop – I am not going to – you have been useful in your stupid way.'

He went to the drawer, took out what looked like a scroll, signed it with a flourish and pushed it toward Martin as he stormed through the doorway.

Before Martin could say anything, a riot of noise broke out: voices barking orders, vehicles revving up, motorbikes savagely kicked into life, all suddenly drowned by the piercing blare of police sirens.

Martin rushed on to the veranda. The presidential Citroën, flag-flapping, headlights flaring, was coming down the road from the palace surrounded by chaos striving for order – outriders struggling to form two lines on either side of their leader, a cluster of black Peugeots jostling for position in the following procession. One of these halted momentarily for Mamadi to climb in, then hurried to regain its place in the line. The dust was blinding, the strobing roof-lights of the police escort flashed through a red cloud, while the heavily armed soldiers in the troop-carriers covered their faces with their hands, like bystanders in a quattrocento frieze averting their rude gaze from the brilliant miracle.

As the last wails of the sirens drifted away and the swirling grit began to settle, the returning silence was eerily complete, even the birds had stopped singing. Martin's driver launched a hearty gobbet of spit into the road.

257

'*Fête des Blancs*' he said, even more vehemently than before, but so quietly only Martin could hear him.

Margot leant against the open door, head cocked to one side, a cigarette glued to her lipstick, her right eye blinking in the curling smoke, evidently tipsy.

'Christ, you've done it now.'

Alice clutched the baby closer. 'I'm sorry about Jack,' she said defensively. 'They came to tell me but I couldn't find you. How are the girls?'

'Upset. S'only natural. They'll get over it by the time they get home. He's being flown back for mother tomorrow, so I'll put 'em all on a plane in London and kiss them fond farewell.'

She came nearer and peered down at the child with obvious distaste.

'Looks like we've all got something to take back. What'you going to do with it?'

Do with it? She was going to do everything with it. She opened her mouth but found nothing to say.

'Seems to be all there,' Margot said. 'Though you never can tell. Scrawny thing, though, are you sure it's going to make it?'

Alice shook her head. There was something not right but she did not know what.

Margot suddenly leant forward and jabbed a finger directly at the wide, staring eyes. Simon did not blink. Margot bent even closer and pulled a massively comic face, twisting her mouth and wrinkling her nose. There was no reaction.

She stood back and brought her hands together with a loud crash. Simon did not move an inch.

'What's the matter?' Alice demanded.

'Let me see – give it here.'

Alice held tight, shaking her head.

'What are you afraid of?' Margot said sharply. 'Come on. Let me have a look.'

Reluctantly, Alice edged the tiny bundle towards her.

'That's better,' Margot said, pulling up the doll's dress and easing it over the baby's head. 'Thin isn't the word, God it's leaking diarrhoea, you can count the ribs – and what's this – it's not just baby rash – what'd you put on it? Well, whatever it was it hasn't

258

worked. God in heaven, this kid's sick.' She pushed him back into Alice's arms. 'I'm going for Dr Diop.'

'Why?'

'You know why – you've been sold a pup, that's why.'

Martin hung on to the back of the driver's seat as they swung into another squealing three-point turn. Their earlier road was now closed to them and Martin's attempt to reason with the police at a newly thrown-up barrier had got them nowhere. He had tried taking a note out of his pocket but the man was clearly under stricter orders than usual and turned away before the gesture matured into a full-scale attempt at bribery. Now they were heading out of town, away from the route they most wanted to follow.

Martin sank deeper into the lumpy, springless seat – after Timbuktu he knew better than to try to impose his own order on the flow of events. In any case, they were already curving left, which ought to mean that they would pitch up at some point far down the Niger, after which they only had to follow the river-bank back upstream to arrive at the bridge and the hotel.

Clever, Martin thought, but before he could congratulate his driver, it dawned on him that this would bring them out on the wrong side of the police barrier. Oh what the hell, he thought – there was no alternative and worrying about it would get him nowhere. He was beginning to understand the languid patience of the waiting passengers at the airport, to comprehend how it was that the guards and taxi-drivers could hang around outside the hotel all day long doing absolutely nothing. It was the spirit of the place – he could see its effect in the first shop-houses by the road, each one selling the same identical piece of machinery as its neighbours, same red and green fly-wheels, same glistening dollops of opal grease. Why did they cluster together? How often did the owners make a sale? He could see one, stretched out on the concrete floor of his tiny emporium, an arm cradling his head, the other twitching away the flies, waiting for that one customer who for some never-to-be-explained reason would decide to buy his machine rather than the identical ones on either side. Then what? Go out and get another, then lie down and wait.

Martin gave up. He might understand but he would never completely feel at ease with the enervating mix of fatalism and indolence that seeped into everything. He ordered the driver forward but it was useless. The way was blocked by a crowd of schoolgirls in dark blue skirts and white blouses, and all the driver's angry curses could do nothing to make them move.

Martin was less upset – he could make out the tower of the hotel over the roofline and at a guess the way ahead must lead into the square beside the bridge. Anyway, the girls were cute. He got out, handed the driver a note, wiggling his fingers to show he intended to walk, then eased his way in amongst the warm young bodies, picking up the pleasant hint of soap and coconut oil. For some reason they seemed to be standing at attention, staring ahead, silently waiting for something – then he noticed that each had a tiny blue, white and red flag dangling at her side, like the draperies and ribbons in the hotel and the parti-coloured lettering on the menu in the lift. It all began to fit together – the driver's *'fête des Blancs'*, Monsieur Mamadi's *'Quatorze Juillet'*, and he wondered why it had taken so long for the penny to drop.

He pushed forward, easing through the rigid bodies, knowing now what he would find. The bridge and the river lay to his right but straight ahead, across the square, was a compound of concrete offices, a small village in itself, with a tall pole on which flapped that same tricolore flag. It was, as Martin had already guessed, the French embassy and the cause of all the fuss and bother. Today was the Fourteenth of July, Bastille Day and sure enough, parked near the heavy security gates, were all those official cars he had last seen on the hill, prominent amongst them the presidential Citroën. Through the railings he could see the guests gathered on the lawns, clutching drinks and making small talk. Anybody who was anybody in Bamako must be there. Behind him, the people went dozily about their business, waiting for the daylight to pass and with it the end of their fast, while before them was spread this elegant reception, with its champagne and canapés, its smiles and handshakes.

There was a sudden burst of applause and an immediate flurry of activity outside as the drivers hurried from the shade of the trees and scuttled back to their cars. It was over. A tall figure, immaculate in a long grey robe gathered at the shoulder, with a tall embroidered cap on his head appeared at the entrance.

At once, the schoolgirls sprang into action, waving their flags and screaming in high-pitched unison.

The police and soldiers snapped to attention, saluting. An elderly grey-haired white man in a dark suit, clearly the French ambassador, followed to the gate, and shook hands with his parting guest who had to be the President.

The schoolgirls shrieked ecstatically. His Excellency waved and smiled in their direction, then bent to get into his official car. Once again there was the infernal din of the outriders and the police sirens but this time the schoolgirls almost drowned it with a piercing lu-lu-lu-lu-luuing sound. The car swept away and the noise stopped at once – as if the current had been switched off. Like unplugged robots, the girls lapsed back into their supine boredom. Martin was astonished. He looked round expecting at least one to be still shouting, still enthused by the excitement of a moment ago. But no, it was over, they were already being trooped away, taken back to whichever *lycée* had leant them for the occasion.

Across the road, other guests were taking their leave. Martin could see the diminutive figure of Monsieur Mamadi shaking hands with his host and when he stepped into the street Martin could also make out his companion, a large woman, a third taller than him, draped in a voluminous golden tent which began its airy descent just above her copious bosom, leaving her smooth brown shoulders bare. Atop all this, her head was encased in a mighty swirl of gold cloth, an enormous golden wheel was clamped to each ear, golden bangles fettered her wrists. She was magnificent, she was Madame Josette. Martin blinked. Yes it was, it was Madame Josette – or rather Madame Mamadi. He jumped up and down like the school-girls, trying to catch her attention. But she looked neither to left nor right, sailing through, sublimely indifferent to the gawping crowds, smoothly gliding by, as if beneath her glistening tent she moved on hidden wheels.

As they progressed, Mamadi smiled and shook hands with his fellow guests but his wife merely nodded a fraction or raised an eyebrow, regal through and through. Martin felt tremendously proud of her, and wondered if everyone else was equally impressed. He turned to look at the crowd, trying to gauge its reactions, and as he did so his eyes fell on Abdel-Kadar, no more than a dozen yards away. Nearby, the bandaged policeman, wearing a striped djebba, was staring straight at Martin with a look of pure venom. The boy held up the parcel. Martin shook his head. The two figures moved towards him, forcing their way through the densely packed crowd. Martin tried to escape, but the line of schoolgirls was solid and unyielding.

'Please,' he said desperately, pushing with all his weight.

Some of the girls half turned to see what the fuss was about, yielding enough space for him to squeeze through until he was stopped by the police barrier. A quick glance told him Abdel-Kadar would soon catch up. The way his companion held his arms crossed could only mean that he was hiding a weapon of some sort. There was no alternative – Martin dipped under the barrier and walked into the road as boldly as he could manage. Only the colour of his skin could have saved him. The policeman hesitated, the soldiers raised their weapons but waited. After a walk that seemed to take most of his life, Martin went straight up to the majestic golden figure, waiting for her car, utterly indifferent to the surrounding fuss.

'Why, Madame Josette,' he exclaimed, as nonchalantly as possible. 'Fancy our meeting here.'

She revolved a smooth 180°, a diplomatic smile pasted on her face. Monsieur Mamadi's eyes rolled into their sockets, leaving nothing but slightly bloodshot whites.

Martin glanced back across the street. For the moment Abdel-Kadar and the policeman were held at the barrier but it would not be long before all the guests drove off and there would be nothing to stop them crossing the road.

'I wouldn't normally have interrupted the party,' Martin said desperately. 'But I felt I just had to come up and congratulate you on your truly magnificent robe, it's . . . it's . . . very . . . imperial.'

Mamadi let out a snort of laughter which caught him completely unawares. He had thought the little man bereft of humour.

'Heh, heh, heh – she is an imperialist . . .' This amused him so much he doubled up with mirth and even his wife could not control her scars which turned up in a mixture of pleasure and amazement.

'Oh, Monsieur,' she said, 'how droll you are. But now we must go – our car has come.'

A large shiny black Peugeot had slid up beside them. Mamadi reached for the door.

Martin cast about wildly. Further down the avenue the police were already dismantling the barriers, it was only a matter of time.

'Perhaps you could give me a lift – just to the hotel, it's my wife, she's not been well, she needs me.'

The scars indicated irritation.

'This is an official reception, my husband has much to do just now . . .'

'Please. You must take me! It's a matter of life and death.'

'Come, come. You must not dramatise things so.' She bent and deflated into the back seat with no loss of poise. Mamadi scuttled to the far side and hopped in, barely visible beneath the gathered waves of gold.

Martin looked across the road. The police had already taken down the crash barrier a short way from Abdel-Kadar and his chum. It would not be long before they were free to cross.

Martin bent to the window.

'Please,' he said, pulling his face to enunciate the word, unsure whether they could hear above the motor and the air-conditioning.

The window slid down.

'Very well,' said Mamadi.

Martin got in beside the chauffeur, faint with fear. As they eased away he saw Abdel-Kadar, his face stony, the index finger of his right hand laid along the side of his nose in a gesture which promised evil.

'This gentleman came to see me this morning,' Mamadi said, addressing Martin as much as his wife. 'He has asked me to arrange an adoption for him, he has *found* a child.' He said 'found' witheringly. 'He found it in *Tombouctou*. Did you know this?'

Madame Josette was impassive.

'What a wonderful country we have,' he went on, 'that those who need to can find a baby. Not even in the advanced United States is there so clever a thing. There they need doctors and tablets. Here, nothing.'

They had driven round the square and had been allowed through the barrier on to the road to the hotel.

'How do you like it here?' Mamadi enquired dryly. 'The Russians built it, and the bridge, for one of the Pan-African Congresses – heads of state with large retinues flying in to pass resolutions threatening this and that. So the Americans built something else, then the French gave us I forget what. Our first President was going to have everything – a modern airport, hospitals full of machines, factories with smoke, an army with advanced weapons, huge monuments – our first President thought monuments were important. He even talked about an atom bomb, how no one would ever treat us as they had in the past if we owned just one missile with one warhead.'

'Was he mad?'

'No more than most. There was a time when I thought he was God, he made me feel so proud. That was before we found out how much he had been used by his smart European advisors. One of these "experts" talked him into building a hundred kilometres of three-lane motorway when what we needed was thousands of kilometres of single-lane all-weather piste for the same price. But oh how good it felt when you saw him on the newsreels opening the superhighway, the *Autoroute d'Afrique* with all those Europeans standing in the sun waiting for his car to arrive, lining up to shake his hand. Then there was the Hopital Marie-Christine – named after his official wife – it had every high-tech gadget you ever heard of. Of course what we really needed was a corps of barefoot medical assistants to trek around the villages, but they don't make you feel good the way an iron lung does. He wanted a radio telescope for the university but he fell before he could sign for it. It would have cost four times the annual national budget but we would have been glowing with pride at each swing of its massive perabula.'

As they drew up under the high concrete awning, a flunky ran out to open the door. Martin cringed at the sheer weight of all that megalomania hovering over him. It seemed to provoke Mamadi.

'Do you love your country, Mr Beresford?'

'I'm not one for all that patriotism thing.'

'Do you hate it?'

'Well, no – I suppose I rather take it for granted.'

'You are very lucky. We will leave you here at your hotel – built with a loan which we cannot repay. Please go straight in, there is some danger.'

'What are you going to do?' Martin asked, reminded of Diop and his trucks.

'That is hardly your business. All you need to know is that this poor country is now being ruled by men with their eyes open, not by children who think their day-dreams are real. Goodbye.'

Watching the Peugeot disappear, Martin seethed. He bent his head as far back as he could and stared up the soaring sweep of the high white tower. The Malians might have overthrown their great leader but they were still proud of his zany schemes. For all his protestations, Mamadi too liked monuments. Gazing up, Martin had a horrible vision of what the world would be like if the Malians ever had power – the Great Leader had been right – one missile, one warhead was all they needed. 'God help us', Martin thought, and hurried inside.

The African in a pin-stripe suit, who entered the lift as Martin got out, was so obviously a doctor that Martin assumed he must have been treating Jack Zabriskie, so that it was only when he saw Margot at the door of her room that he remembered she was a widow and quickly adjusted his face to an expression of understanding sadness.

'I'm very sorry . . .' he began, but she waved this away with her cigarette as if performing a conjuring trick.

'My God, you've done it now,' she said savagely. 'You must be three sorts of idiot to have let them dump that poor little wreck on you, but I suppose it doesn't matter to you, does it? It was always a case of tying up the troublesome little woman. The more the difficulties, the more she'll be off your back. I wouldn't be surprised if you hadn't asked for damaged goods. It would explain everything. Well, I'm not letting you get away with it – Alice deserves better than to end up slaving for two, she needs to break free – God knows we all do – and I mean to see she has her chance.'

She was so instantly venomous, Martin's only thought was to get away. He took a step forward, meaning to get past her as quickly as he could.

'Don't you threaten me,' she said, her voice rising dangerously. 'I may be a woman, but I know how to handle myself.'

She had brought up her fists like a boxer, the cigarette end smouldering on her bottom lip, the classic image of cinematic pugilism.

'I haven't the least intention . . .' Martin began, but it was no use, she stepped forward and jabbed with her right hand, an inept but lucky blow which connected smartly with his nose.

Martin let out a yelp and covered his face with his hands.

'Oh Martin . . .' It was Alice standing at the door, her hair dishevelled, her eyes red with weeping.

'Don't worry,' Margot said. 'I can handle the brute.'

She did a little dance from right foot to left, clearly limbering up for another round when Martin lowered his head and charged past into his room and locked himself in the bathroom, where he tried to staunch the flow of blood from his nose with a non-too-clean handkerchief. He could overhear the two women talking in the corridor before the door closed and there was silence.

'Are you alone?' he called out.

'Yes.'

'She's mad,' he said, giving the room a cautious scan. The baby was lying on his back on the bed, wrapped in another shirt, while Baby, pink and naked, had been sat, legs out, on the chest of drawers from where she could view her new rival with unblinking interest.

'She's only trying to help,' Alice said.

'Help who?'

'Me.'

'That goes without saying. She was ranting on about Simon. What the hell's the matter?'

'Everything. Dr Diop says he's blind and deaf. It's a disease – they don't know what it is, it's something horrible. He's wasting away. Look . . .'

She pointed to a pile of Martin's shirts, each stained with a damp colourless patch.

'He passes that stuff all the time, front and back. He's dying, Martin.'

'The bastards, they pulled a fast one on me. Thank God I didn't pay them. D'you know they tried to grab me today? I was scared stiff – thought they were going to knife me. Mind you, I wish I knew where they were hiding out so's I could let them have this back. Now what are we going to do?'

'Do?'

'Yes. You don't think we are going to take it home, do you? At least the Australian cow's right about that. It's out of the question.'

'But it's *our* baby now, we have to take care of him – get doctors, find a cure.'

'It's *not* ours, it's somebody else's and whoever *they* were didn't want it either. It'll never be allowed into Britain sick like that – it might be contagious.'

'But we've got a certificate, haven't we? You said they wouldn't dare turn us away, the newspapers would take it up. You said, didn't you . . .?'

Martin hesitated, just long enough to convince Alice that whatever he said must be a lie.

266

'There's no certificate. Mamadi wouldn't give me one, the bastard.'

Alice's face split in two – her eyes narrowed in anger, her mouth turned down in fear. She stumbled towards the baby and lifted him into her arms.

'Now, let's be reasonable,' Martin said, hoping to wheedle things into calmer waters. 'It's all been a big mistake, but we can just about put it right. It'll be best for Simon, we'll get him fixed up in a place that'll take care of him, then when we're back home we can sort something out. I'm sure we can put our names down for an agency again – you could even have more treatment if you wanted, honest. What do you say, eh? It's for the best. Believe me.'

She was shaking her head so furiously he thought she might hurt herself.

'Don't, Alice. You're getting worked up. It doesn't help things. Let's just be rational about it.'

Her head seemed almost to revolve. Martin panicked and knew he would have to do something quick lest she start screaming – she'd got hysterical before and it had been really frightening.

'Stop it!' he yelled. 'If you want this fucking baby then have it – but I'll tell you this, it won't have me for a father . . .'

The head stopped rotating, her face sagged – all of her sagged as if the Great Puppeteer had loosened his grip and let all the strings hang loose. Her misery was childish – puffy and quaking. A big sob gathered momentum and broke in a series of monkey chortles. Her grip loosened and Simon slipped down the crook of her arm. It was Baby all over again. Martin knew he had won.

He waited a moment, but now there was only silence.

'We'd better dress him up,' he said quietly. 'We'll have to find somewhere to put him – a hospital, an orphanage, somewhere.'

He went to the chest of drawers and pulled out the last of his shirts, carried it to the baby and began to wrap it round the thin loins.

'We've got to,' he said to the little face blindly directed at him. 'We don't want to, but it's for the best.'

He lifted the bundle into his arms and walked towards the door. For a moment he thought Alice was going to let him go on his own, but as he waited by the lift she came slowly down the corridor, holding the still naked doll by its right arm, letting it dangle loose by her side. They rode down in silence, stepped out into the foyer and froze – the vast space was crowded with Malians in voluminous coloured robes – both sexes. There was a sprinkling of whites in dinner-jackets, their wives elegant in French couture, with the waiters back in their Arabian Nights costumes – turbans and pantaloons – passing among them, offering trays of fizzing champagne flutes. Martin tried to follow one, hoping to get past discreetly in his wake – an impossible hope, for as soon as he began to cross the polished marble floor, a corridor of shocked silence opened up before and behind them. Halfway across, the waiter turned aside leaving them fully exposed, shuffling forward, baby first, through the cluster of new arrivals crowding in from the line of limousines circling the drive. An astonished doorman held the glass door open to let them through. Out on the pavement, Delmonico in a white dinner-jacket, bright red Bermudas and long black knee-socks, appeared to be welcoming the guests as if the party were his. He was so preoccupied with a large African in a white military mess-coat, a broad gold stripe down his tight trousers, that he was initially unaware of the extraordinary spectacle which had formed up behind him. It was only when he realised that the person he was addressing was staring, wide-eyed and incredulous at something over his shoulder, that he turned and got the full force of the bizarre family group.

'Shit,' he said, with a degree of awe in his voice which rather pleased Martin.

'Look here – er – Barry, I'm in a spot of trouble and was wondering if you could help out.'

'Are you mad, Jimmie? Do you know what's going on here? It's just about the biggest thing in the social calendar in these parts and you turn up like a remake of the Inn of the Sixth Happiness. Piss off, for God's sake.'

'No,' said Martin petulantly.

'What do you mean?'

'I mean exactly that. I'm not moving till you help me. I need somewhere for this child. It's sick, it's dying. I need an orphanage, a hospital.'

Delmonico's eyes appeared to swivel.

'Damaged goods, is it? Damaged goods? Oh, very nicely nicely. The customer isn't satisfied and the customer is always right. I thought you wanted a child not a Christmas puppy? It's a human being. If it really was yours and it was sick, you couldn't just send it back, could you?'

'That's different.'

'Precisely.'

More guests were arriving, some obviously important. Delmonico made an unctuous bow in the direction of a tall thin black man in a long red robe. On his chest hung an enormous folk-art cross onto which a negro-Christ had been hammered with the same outsize nails used on the Timbuktu doors.

'The Black Prince?' Martin asked.

'Yes. Now bugger off.'

'Not until you tell me where to take it.'

'You'd better give it to God. I understand he never says no.'

'I don't understand.'

'In the shanty town – go straight in from here, keep on looking left, you'll see what looks like a wooden church-steeple over the rooftops. It's the Redemption Chapel of the First Beulah Baptist Mission, proprietor the Reverend Austen Belvedere.'

'Belvedere,' Martin echoed, his voice subdued by the bizarre inevitability of the name. It was as if an encounter between himself and the ubiquitous minister had been ordained since that moment when Madame Josette first mentioned him. He had a sudden clear memory of that battered weather-beaten board in Timbuktu – now it seemed that nothing could finally erase that name.

'Belvedere,' he repeated, just to be sure. 'Over there you say?'

'Yes, yes. What's the matter with you, can't you understand simple English? Now for Christ's sake sod off.'

Martin edged past him, crossing the drive in front of an enormous Lincoln with an American flag on one wing and a satellite receiver on the roof. As the ambassador got out he greeted Delmonico with open arms.

'Thanks,' Martin yelled back, stepping on to the wet lawn and heading towards the distant ragged paling.

Across the roofline, neon strip lights were stuttering on and a distant amplified muezzin summoned the faithful to prayer. The smell of wood smoke filled the air as the enfolding night ended the fast. They left the lawn, crossed the road, and stepped on to the stretch of rocky ground. It was hard, very hard. Moving from the springy lawns to a cracked lunarscape was a lesson in itself, so dry, so rocky and deeply ridged they both stumbled as they walked.

269

Ahead lay a long, crudely built palisade of broken planks and rusted iron sheets. In front of this was a deep storm drain like a moat. Dry now, it was choked with old cans and broken bottles and heaped with yellowing vegetable stalks. The air was busy with flies, persistent noisy things, little troubled by his waving hand. Again, Martin smelt woodsmoke, light and pleasant, but now overpowered by a sweet odour, rising from the ditch – the sweet costive stench of rot, the repulsive sugariness of putrefaction. He gagged and pulled back. An unsteady looking plank lay across this deep gully and he took it at a run, wobbling dangerously before staggering on to the opposite bank. He turned to help Alice. She hesitated, sniffing the air, scenting the earthy aromas of soil and vegetation, fresh and real after the unhealthy, recycled air of the sealed hotel. She hoisted Baby into her arms and jumped. Martin tried to catch her but she shook herself free and walked off on her own, keeping a clear distance between them.

Martin hesitated, looking back. The hotel was no longer visible over the jagged roofline. He could still smell decay and hear the persistent rise and fall of flies, as if someone was tuning a distant radio, never quite finding a station.

As if attempting to welcome them to this unappealing jumble of blank mud walls and unpaved streets, a distant electric guitar executed a twangy riff, a drum rolled and a lilting falsetto sang: *Oh A-fri-caaa, les nuits d'amour de l'A-fri-caaa.'* Martin could just see the spire away to their left and turned at the next junction, glancing at Alice to make sure she was following. Her face was orange-yellow under the pallid neon light, shiny and plastic, as if the doll really was her child. He looked down at the boy in his arms, but he too had an unreal tinge, greyish like India rubber.

'You OK?' he asked, but she looked through him, her expression a mask of misery. He prayed she would hold on and not break down in this Godforsaken dump.

He looked around, frantically searching for the right way. They were following a low wooden railing along the edge of an open space which was lit by fairy lights, swung from the branches of a leafless tree. Tables and chairs were arranged around a central dance area and on a podium five Africans in identical red shirts thumped out the insistent samba-ish beat while the singer begged for love – '*Les nuits d'amour, de l'A-fri-caaa'*. It was too early for much business; a knot of beer drinkers stood at a long thatched bar but the only dancer was a solitary woman in a tight black miniskirt which forced out her bottom like a shelf and a bust-gripping white top which ground her breasts to a millstone cleavage. Ribbons, blue, white and red, were fastened into the knotted furrows of her hair, matching the bunting swung between the tree and the thatched roof like isobars predicting inclement weather. The woman's eyes were closed, she was in ecstasy.

Even with the blare of the music, Martin could hear the breathy sound of sobbing – he turned and saw Alice, staring intently at the dancer, a solitary tear coursing from her left eye carried along in a thin wash of mascara. He stared fascinated, as the little glistening drop ran over her upper lip, fell through the valley of her lips and on over her chin to the void below. Martin was suddenly afraid that everything had gone too far. She really was a Modigliani, the sad-eyed oval repeated in the face of the doll, and with that realisation he sensed something of the aching chasm that divided them, his calculating need to end the whole thing so distant from her deep, excruciating misery.

Again he reached out and tried to hold her and again she twisted away and stalked off. He hurried after, walking too fast, his shirt pasted to his back, his breath coming in painful rasps. There was a woman ahead with three children following her. Alice moved to one side to let them pass. She was tall and big-hipped, swaying along in a tightly wrapped cloth that must have been printed with a face given the one large eye stretched over her thrusting backside. She balanced a slopping bucket of water on her head, carried from God knew how far away, with a baby strapped to her back, another swarm of flies circling its lolling head and again Martin smelled the sweet stench of rotting vegetation and marvelled that any child could survive in such filth. He thought of the couple at the hotel with their fluffy white towels, their bottle and nipple cleanser, their packages of disposable nappies, and all the rest of the hyper-sterilised feeding and wiping gear without which they could not manage, and he looked again at the three little girls in their ragged cotton shifts, traipsing barefoot after their mother, wide-eyed at the sight of a white couple with a black child and a naked doll, walking in their *bidonville*.

It was then that Martin realised his arm was wet – Simon must have done something. He held the little bundle away from him but it was too late. He was soaked.

271

Alice turned to see why he had stopped and for a passing second it looked as if she might smile, but no, as grim-faced as ever, she came over and lifted the child away, hoisting him into the crook of her arm alongside the doll. With her free hand, she deftly unknotted the shirt from between the legs and wiped him down with one of the dry sleeves. He was perfectly peaceful, as motionless and uncomplaining as Baby.

Martin reached to take him back but the fierce, bitter look that flashed across Alice's face made him pull away.

'Go on,' she snapped. 'Let's get it over with.'

'It's for the best,' he protested. 'He's sick. He needs help.'

'Spare me your reasons, Martin. I don't need them. It's all over . . .'

Trying not to think what she meant, he hurried them through a narrow alley on to a street of more substantial houses. The spire rose above number 46, a concrete building with two doors side by side, and a painted notice-board which showed an open Bible across which a bird descended, wings outstretched in a nimbus of golden rays. Under it were the words: 'Redemption Chapel, Hall of Worship of the Beulah Baptist Mission of the World Beulah Convention, Alabama, USA; pastor the Reverend Austen Belvedere DD (Miss.); Divine Services: Sunday, Prayer Meeting 10.00 am, Sunday School 3.00 pm, Family Worship 6.00 pm; Adult Baptism by arrangement'. The smaller door had a knocker. Martin rapped sharply, the noise echoing somewhere far inside. He waited. After a moment, distant footsteps approached, growing louder like a comedy sound-effect, flip-flopping towards them until the door was opened by a slight man with thin silver hair over a hollow face with stretched white skin that had been too long under the African sun and was now weathered rather than tanned. He wore a grey short-sleeved shirt with a white dog-collar, grey trousers which ended, to Martin's amusement, in cosy tartan carpet slippers. He looked for all the world like an elderly, rather absent-minded academic summoned from his library. Grey eyes settled on the naked form in Alice's arms and the shiny doll hanging beneath. For a moment nothing was said. The rheumy gaze drifted wearily from baby to Baby and back again, then withdrew into some inner place of sanctuary, safe from the foolishness of this world.

'Reverend Belvedere?'

The man nodded and stood aside to let them in.

272

'We heard that you helped orphans, that . . .'

A gesture made it clear that there was no need to explain. He closed the door and led them down a narrow, empty corridor into a low-ceilinged kitchen dominated by an ancient black-metal stove. He waved them towards a pair of severe-looking ladder-backed chairs at a long scrubbed table. When he spoke, his long nasal vowels and descending cadences belied his church and his degree; this was no hellfire hillbilly evangelist but a sort of weary Southern gentleman. Brittle-looking fingers, stretched with parchment skin, vaguely emphasised his words.

'Yes,' he said, picking up Martin's question as if he had just finished asking it. 'Yes, we do. Though we are dreadfully over full just now. Perhaps more to the point is how you came by the child – you are, I take it, visitors here?'

Martin stumbled into the story of Timbuktu, nothing of which produced the least reaction in his listener – Delmonico, Maktar Diop, the delivery of the baby, the discovery of its sickness.

'When was he last fed?' Belvedere asked in the embarrassed silence which followed the tale. It hit Martin like a punitive rod – here was someone whose first concern was the child. The only one so far.

'This morning.'

The grizzled eyebrows went up. He sighed.

'I doubt it matters. It may even be a mercy, though one shouldn't even think it.'

'We would make a donation,' Martin said, then had the bitter feeling he was reliving his encounter with Mamadi, offering money to an honest man. 'Thank you,' Belvedere said, which made it worse.

He stood and asked them to follow, leading them through the kitchen into a cosy living room enclosed with books. More volumes lay on the floor near a heavy sofa. Others lay open on chair arms and side-tables. They negotiated these, to emerge through a latched door into a small inner courtyard, scrubbed and empty, with a withered drought-stricken tree at its centre. Barren as it was, something about the place spoke of past pleasures – the stucco scrolls over the arched doorways, the broken shutters at the windows, the yellow and red flower patterns on the cracked tiles, still visible under the inevitable layer of red dust.

At the opposite side of the yard, Belvedere held open a door and let them walk past him into a high, barn-like space whose crude undressed brickwork marked it down as a factory or storehouse. To Alice it was the field hospital again, though this time there were beds, all sorts of beds: iron-framed army bunks, utility wood-framed single beds, there was even a very large and thickly padded affair which must once have been part of an expensive imported boudoir suite. They were ranged down either side of the room, some just frames, a few with striped ticking mattresses, lumpy and stained, all without sheets. There were two or three babies to a mattress, some curled up on one side, some laid flat, their heads at an odd, broken angle. Three shawl-veiled women sauntered about in no discernible pattern, wafting large leaf-shaped fans to disturb the flies which rose in irritation only to return when the draught moved on.

Martin looked round for someone to take the baby and saw a woman in a travel-stained dress which must once have been white. He took in the red crescent over her breast pocket. She looked tired beyond exhaustion, but her face brightened when she saw Alice.

'Diop gave us the trucks,' she said, her eyes indicating the far corner of the room where a group of women were seated at a long table, feeding their children. 'We got through this morning, it wasn't easy. There was some fighting – soldiers from the government, Diop killed them. He let us go ahead, fortunately the Reverend Belvedere had a place for us.'

'Round one to young Maktar,' Martin said. 'You two know each other?'

'Doctor El-Assawy runs the emergency hospital in the camp at Timbuktu,' Alice explained, but stopped when she realised the doctor was staring at her bundle. Alice opened her mouth to speak then fell silent as the other woman's eyes drifted down to the dangling doll. Alice tried to push it behind her but it was too late. She waited for the look of pity to cross that unsmiling face but there was nothing, no judgement, just an air of mild weariness that yet another problem had been landed at her door.

'I'm so sorry,' Alice began. 'I'm so sorry, I . . .'

'We were cheated,' Martin interjected, hoping to stave off another crying jag. 'Diop sent this kid instead of some boy he'd promised in Timbuktu, a Touareg boy or something like.'

El-Assawy shook her head. 'Impossible. He was with his men, always ahead of us. He had no time . . . in any case this child is not from Timbuktu.' She held out her arms for the baby but Alice did not respond.

'Go on,' Martin said. 'He's sick, it's for the best.'

El-Assawy flashed him a look that ordered him to keep quiet. She offered her arms again. 'He's right,' she said. 'It's for the best.'

Alice looked down at the sightless eyes, the tiny fists clenching and unclenching, the little opal nails.

Unfazed, Martin was trying to explain about Abdel-Kadar and the policeman. 'They probably got the kid here in Bamako, just trying to get the cash for themselves.'

The two women ignored him.

'It isn't just because he's sick,' Alice said. 'I couldn't have gone on anyway – even if they'd brought the boy you showed me. I knew, even before Martin came back with this one.'

El-Assawy's eyes dropped back to the dangling doll. 'But I thought you had to have a child?'

'No. After Timbuktu something began to change. Put it down to shock if you like – or aversion therapy if that's still on the menu.'

She held out her arms, offering the baby. 'What happened to the mother?'

'Still alive when we left.'

'The child?'

'I do not think we will ever know. Perhaps . . .'

'There is no need to spare me – the commandant said it would be killed.'

'Yes.'

'How do you handle that?'

She was momentarily confused by the unusual word but soon worked it out. 'Handle? How do I hold it? I suppose by trying to save another one.'

Alice looked down at Simon as if to say, 'And this one?'

El-Assawy took the point, laying the little form on the nearest bed and beginning gently to feel the stomach, barely touching but enough to cause the tiny arms and legs to twitch with the discomfort.

She shook her head, a gesture of uncertainty rather than despair.

'It could be one of a dozen diseases, there are tropical illnesses we know hardly anything about, though most have the same symptoms – the terrible diarrhoea like this, though here it is very bad. The poor child is wasting away and when it gets this far it does not really matter to give a name to the disease – they have no resistance, there is nothing we can do.'

She looked at Belvedere for confirmation but he was concentrating on the tiny shrivelled form as if something about it had triggered a line of thought. Without responding, he leant forward and began to make his own examination, ignoring the stomach, delicately touching the sides of the skinny neck with the fingers of both hands. This seemed to confirm something. He reached down and delicately lifted away the tiny arms, leaning even closer to examine the undersides.

El-Assawy gave him a quizzical look so he held apart the stick limbs to offer her a better sight of the dark patches.

'There's a rash,' Martin interjected. 'We tried putting antiseptic cream on it but it doesn't seem to have done much good.'

El-Assawy stared at the dark blackberry efflorescence. 'You have seen this before?'

Belvedere nodded. 'Several times over the past year. It may explain where the child comes from. On the other hand it may just be another passing infection, like a new strain of malaria or the way everybody seems to get conjunctivitis all of a sudden, then just as quickly, whoosh, it passes.' He laughed slightly, as if bemused by God's little eccentricities in the matter of tropical health.

'But this isn't like that is it?' Martin interjected, trying to chivvy things along. 'You don't think it is just another stray bug, do you? And how come it tells you where this baby comes from?'

'Ah,' said Belvedere, with the relish of a suburban obsessive finally asked to explain his secret hobby. 'Now there you've put your finger on the really fascinating part of this whole thing.'

'And?' said Martin acidly.

'Well, it was only after I'd had a number of these babies with this new thing – the terrible diarrhoea, the glandular swelling, the skin rash as well – that I realised that all the children with this condition were not from local women.' He was getting a trifle excited now as if reliving the forensic thrill. 'Of course I couldn't always be sure because we often don't see the mothers. The babies are left outside or brought in by a third party. Of course that's what we're here for, we never . . .'

'Yes, yes,' Martin said, seething with frustration. 'And so . . .?'

'Well, when we did occasionally find out who the mothers were, I realised that they were all outsiders, from Zaire mainly, though sometimes Angola or even Chad. And you know the really fascinating thing was that they were always . . .' he dropped his voice to a whisper, '. . . prostitutes. A lot of Zairean women come to work in bars and nightclubs or they just attach themselves to long-distance truck drivers, they live with them for a time, until the man gets bored with them and drops them off somewhere. Then they try to get a job locally or hitch another ride. Anyway, their babies often had this wasting disease, wasting away to nothing. Feeding them was impossible. They always died.'

Martin's brow furrowed as he tried to extract some key fact, enmeshed inside the tale. 'What you seem to be saying is that this is some sort of sexual disease – like the clap?'

Belvedere sighed. 'I suppose that must be the logical conclusion.'

'So what's the rash – herpes?'

'Oh I think not – it's more like some sort of skin cancer.'

'Oh bloody hell.'

'MARTIN!' Alice was gripping the metal bedhead so tightly her knuckles were almost pointed. She rounded on the minister. 'Why just the babies? Why don't the mothers get it, whatever it is?'

'Oh they do. The city hospitals have had both men and women with the same symptoms – wasting away, the same rash. But the babies are weaker and die quicker and it's only them that we see here.'

This seemed to provoke something in El-Assawy. She had been following Belvedere's words as if they were a lecture, repeating his examination at each stage in his commentary – feeling the throat, looking again at the rash, but this reference to the city hospitals had clearly widened the issue.

'And the Ministry?'

He nodded. 'Dr Taboure informed the Ministry officially, they are supposed to inform the WHO but . . .'

El-Assawy grimaced. 'No bad reports wanted?'

Belvedere responded with a pained expression. 'Normally I wouldn't have been too bothered – these things so often flare up and die before anyone can do anything about them. But there is one truly worrying factor here – the women must be spreading it wherever they go. We have only a few cases but in Zaire or elsewhere, who knows? And if the governments hush it all up . . .'

Somewhere amongst the beds a baby snuffled. Alice clasped her hands behind her back, a teenager again – this was the end of all journeys, the terminus, the charnel house, this was where she was going to leave Simon.

Belvedere seemed to sense that his audience had had enough of his tale, especially as the end was a foregone conclusion. As a tragedy it lacked drama. He walked over to the door and held it ajar. Martin followed, leaving Alice and El-Assawy to resolve what they could.

The doctor bent to examine the little figure again, as if she found it hard to accept the old man's evidence. Alice kept a close watch on her, willing her to offer some sign of reprieve, some hint that it was not as absolute as Belvedere had made out. All she wanted was a suggestion that the diagnosis might be sketchy, that there was still a margin of hope, no matter how slight. That way she would be offering Simon treatment, not leaving him to die. But it was pointless to expect such grace. The doctor could guess her thoughts but had no ease to offer; that would have been a betrayal of the reality she herself had had to accept.

Alice felt the old wave of anger and self-pity wash over her. She was suddenly aware that she was still holding on to Baby. She lifted it up and looked at its pathetic triste face. Without quite knowing why, she leant over and placed it on the bed beside Simon. He lay on his back, arms and legs spread like a frog awaiting dissection. Baby was half-turned towards him, pale pink and naked. The recent bumping about had loosened the limp arms and flaxen curls and tampered with the eye weights so that one lid remained stubbornly locked open. It was, Alice realised, as if her unremitting wide-eyed melancholy had at last found its rightful place.

'I know he's a boy,' she said. 'But they sometimes like to play with dolls too, don't they?'

'I'm sure he will,' El-Assawy assured her, melting a little. 'It will be a comfort. But what about you – don't you need it any more?'

Alice shook her head.

A fly landed on Baby's face, nuzzled into the corner of the open eye, fell silent for a brief second, then moved off, zuzzing with frustration.

'You need money?' Alice said.

'The Baptists give us some, thanks to the Reverend Belvedere, though they are really a missionary organisation and sometimes we get boxes of Bibles instead of serum. I am Red Crescent, and I am only here because of the fighting in the north, not really the children.' She gave a weary shrug. 'No one is for the children.'

'I envy you,' Alice said.

This produced a dry laugh but she was not to be deflected. 'I think I knew it in Timbuktu, but I was still being torn apart. Things are clearer now. This is a mess but my having a screaming fit isn't going to help – not him, nor me neither. I just wish there was something I could do . . .'

' "Save the Children" is probably best – but it's whatever you choose really.'

The 'you' was delicately put, no emphasis.

Alice scanned the room, as if to fix it in her mind. It was her turn to feel that she had been given the answer to a question she had not yet formed.

'Are you happy?' she asked.

'Not especially. I'm usually too busy to think about it.'

'That's probably why I think I envy you.'

She could hear the swish of the fans as the women passed between the beds, the occasional sound of a child muttering through a dream. It was surprisingly soothing, even the night-club's distant electronic hum only added to the sense of calm. A cool saxophonist was improvising something jazzy yet infinitely slow, lingering over long breathy notes as if pondering what should come next.

The doctor had begun to move towards the door, explaining something that Alice had lost the thread of: '. . . money, yes – but getting the right sort of equipment. But information most of all. It is so easy to get cut off. It is as Belvedere said, we hear rumours but sometimes the government tries to hide the truth, because of pride or even because of the tourists.'

Alice was barely listening, her mind fixed on the two figures on the bed. She could think of no way of saying goodbye, yet without a gesture of some sort, it was impossible to avoid the conclusion that she was simply dumping her problem and sneaking away. She hesitated.

The doctor stopped her lecture. 'Come,' she said firmly. 'It's time to go.'

Martin too was held by the precipitous silences within the lilting music, caught as each plangent descent whispered into the night. It was nervy but soothing – he took deep gulps of night air, trying to clear his lungs of the hospital smells he had just escaped, trying to concentrate on Belvedere's preachy voice holding forth, explaining their surroundings.

'This was beautiful once,' he was saying. 'Plants in pretty pots, hanging baskets, a statue of the Virgin in blue and white – some French nuns were here for nearly fifty years. They kept it beautiful . . .' For a moment his voice trailed away then he rallied himself. 'They left.'

'Since when everything's gone to seed,' said Martin bitterly. 'Christ I used to believe all that shit about colonialism but now I know what it was like when the French were here, and what it's like now – and I'm not just talking about for whites, I mean for them, too. They must see it themselves, don't they?'

'I don't know – I don't know what *they* think, I've only been here twenty years.'

'Twenty! What for?'

'I sometimes wonder.' He laughed gently. 'No, my friend, the French did not solve the eternal problems of this or any other place. They made pretty courtyards and well-swept, wide boulevards and built a railway which burned up all the trees near Bamako and caused the soil to wash away.'

'Did you ever convert anyone?'

Belvedere shook his head.

'No one?'

'No. I was years in Timbuktu. Founded the mission there, but the Muslims don't convert or, if they appear to, it's because they're outcasts for some reason and they soon go back when their faith is tested.'

'Do you know Maktar Diop?'

'Knew him when he was a child – a lovely boy, perfect manners, the way they all have – until he went to America and got what is laughingly called an education. I knew his uncle, the one who's on trial right now. The most honest man I've ever met. The Diops are black aristocrats; the French brought a rag-bag of revolutionary ideas which even they have never fully digested. It's not so much that the Diops are in the wrong place at the wrong time, as in the wrong century at the wrong time.

'And Darwesh, Abdel Darwesh? He's no aristocrat?'

'He is the perfect example of a wheel turning on its own, quite independent of the rest of the machine. He manipulates a desert trading network as if it were the Middle Ages, only he's dealing in kalashnikovs and cocaine – he is quite without scruple, save the obligations of family.'

'Will you ever go home?'

'Home?' Belvedere tasted the word as if it were exotically spiced. 'I used to suppose so once. I imagined I would leave when there would be no one left to take care of me and it would be better to get back before anything happened – a fall, an infection. But that's over now. I'm needed here.'

'You mean the babies? The sickness?'

'Yes. There's no one else, just me and Dr El-Assawy. No one cares. I've tried to warn them, but they ordered me to keep silent. But they know. That's why they gave me this place as a hospice in which to hide it all away and why they were glad when Dr El-Assawy set up the camp in Timbuktu. Well, that's over. Young Diop closed it down and sent her and the babies here to rub their noses in it. I have to admire his audacity. It's such a pity he's burned out with anger.'

'I hate him,' Martin said.

'Yes,' said the old man. 'Yes, you would.'

The music from the club drifted back, a male falsetto voice sang 'yayayayayayaaaa' in a high unbroken line.

Alice came out and let El-Assawy lead her into the house.

'I guess we're off,' Martin said, following behind. 'Can't think what the hurry is.'

Alice's goodbyes were brisk, she thanked Belvedere and let the Egyptian embrace her, which surprised Martin, given the wall of ice she had thrown around herself over the past twenty-four hours. He wondered whether this promised a return to normality, but before he could work it out she was heading down the street, leaving him to mumble his own farewells and hurry after her.

The night-club had filled up. Through the railings Alice and Martin could see the dancing area crowded with couples, all of them wearing the same clusters of blue, white and red ribbons, jigging about, practising some jazzy footwork to tinny guitar licks. A dying voice descended a low, ragged diminuendo which suddenly bounced back into a high-pitched rebel yell, driving the dancers crazy, setting the ribbons jangling. Despite the press, the crowd left a space clear for the woman with the straight-out backside and straight-up breasts, now joined by a lithe young man in *tricolore* singlet and cut-away jeans, the man Alice had seen practising in the discotheque. Their movements were perfectly attuned, bumping hips to the beat, turning and wiggling back-to-back as if the man's spine could massage away the flesh between them. The other dancers were little more than an admiring amphitheatre for this erotic explosion. Alice paused; he was beautiful but it meant nothing.

'There's that Swede, Thorsten,' Martin said. 'Over there at the bar with the girl in the tight green dress – very tight. He's got some nerve, he's the only white face in the place. You'd think he'd feel out of it, yet there he is, at home by the look of him. Odd how people seem to get stuck here, Belvedere, Delmonico, funny really – they could be living in Manchester but they prefer here, who could credit it?'

He stopped, unable to tell if she was listening to him and feeling accused by her silence. 'You're not the only one who's upset,' he protested. 'I was going to be his father, remember?'

'You're disgusting,' she said, with a vehemence that rocked him. 'How can you say that when you never gave a damn? Margot was right – you always had a plan of your own. I was to be humoured, indulged if need be, pacified and manipulated whenever possible. And look where all this twisting and turning has landed us – you loathe Africa, a place you've been dreaming about for years – and I've ended up with nothing. And don't even think about telling me we can get back to normal. NORMAL! Don't make me laugh. There was no normal before and whatever there was, I certainly don't want it back again.'

They had come out at the storm drain. Alice took it at a run, jumping well clear of the treacherous bank and the filthy ooze below. Her face was set in stone. To their right the town was a black void, no challenge to the solitary power of the hotel, shining like the next century, every floor ablaze, the entire tower iced and pure.

Martin hurried up to the storm drain and took another run at the plank, but sweat was in his eyes and his foot slipped and he slithered down the bank, sinking into something soft. When he scrambled out he saw that his left shoe and trouser bottom were black with a sticky glutinous mess. He stood, exhausted and exposed, on the edge of the rocky field. His nose wrinkled – he smelt of the sweet sticky rot that rose from the depth of the ditch and he wanted to call out to Alice to tell her to wait for him – it was dark out there and he was suddenly afraid.

'Alice!'

'Be quiet,' she hissed, a hand motioning him to keep still.

He froze, he had seen what had caught her attention – a line of trucks, dozens of them, heading along the road that cut them off from the hotel. They must have come across the bridge and through the square, now they were heading into town – drab lorries with rows of men in makeshift uniforms holding rifles between their legs, a ghostly caravan, eerily picked out by the glow from the spotlit tower. White headlamps lit up the vehicle in front, red rear-lights the one behind, and leading the procession, Commandant Maktar Diop, standing in his jeep, a Roman general at the head of his little army, staring unflinchingly forward, enjoying his triumph.

'I'll be buggered,' Martin said. 'He's come to inherit his kingdom. He certainly looks the part.'

'Beautiful,' said Alice enraptured, as if the eerie spectacle had been laid on for her alone. Even when the last truck glided by and silence returned, she could not pull herself away. It was the dream she had never had. It was what she would have been had her street laid on a parade, her role, leading her troops into battle, ready to sacrifice herself for the cause, any cause.

But it was no use, Martin was already hurrying past, shattering the fragile vision.

'Come on,' he insisted. 'We'd better find Delmonico and tell him cement futures are up.'

They burst into the foyer at the stroke of midnight. The crowd of dancers in the dining room applauded wildly as the nets opened and hundreds of blue, white and red balloons floated down on to them. With a frenzied rush, amidst peals of hysterical laughter, everyone leapt to grab and burst them. Martin and Alice stood transfixed by this insane spectacle – *Le Quatorze Juillet*, dancing in the streets, accordions, love, laughter and a bottle of wine. The sound of exploding balloons was deafening – crack, crack, crack, crack. There seemed no end to it. Women shrieked – crack, crack, crack. It was a little eternity before Alice realised that the explosions seemed somehow sharper, more intense. Crack, crack, crack – not just in the dining room, but all around them, sharp explosions coming from outside. It was even longer before the first revellers heard the overlapping sounds. For a moment the two noises competed, con-fused by drum rolls from the orchestra, drowned by the shriek of paper rolls flicked out with feathers and the whine of plastic kazoos, all the ear-shattering cacophony of braying, drunken celebration.

For an instant, Martin's attention was caught by the sight of the little Japanese woman wearing a silver clown's hat, waving a French flag, while simultaneously trying to grab another of the unending stream of balloons. Another spate of bongs was followed by a loud, low rumbling boom. The vast chandelier swayed and tinkled merrily. It tinkled on through the dead silence which descended on the dining room as a solitary balloon struck a cigar and burst with an obscene and terrifying retort. Martin jumped at the sound. Everyone froze. The entrance doors slammed open. A posse of baton-wielding, helmeted soldiers in black Raybans clattered across the foyer and forced their way into the crowd. A woman screamed. The chandelier tinkled. The guards charged back, dragging Delmonico, blood streaming down his face. At the centre of the foyer, they paused for a second to get him upright. He stood, looking down at the red stain spreading across his beautiful shirt and blew on it, as if trying to clear away the little pool of blood. As they started hustling him out, his eyes caught Martin's and for the briefest second he seemed to shrug.

As quickly as they came, they were gone. Pandemonium broke out. Couples streamed out of the dining room, charging for the exits – Malians into the black night, tourists into the lifts, the waiters through service doors into secret oblivion. As the last body disappeared the chandelier flickered twice, then slowly faded to nothing. There was a moment's total darkness until somewhere high on the distant ceiling a solitary emergency bulb twinkled on, bravely casting an acrid lemon wash over the two figures standing dumbstruck in the abandoned space.

As the last of the limousines revved and screeched down the drive, the gunshots and artillery fire seemed to fade with them.

'Shit,' Martin said with feeling. 'Holy shit. I think we better get out of here.' But he did not move. His legs were clamped together and refused to budge.

'Go to the room,' Alice said curtly. 'I'm going for a walk.'

His lips mouthed the word 'walk' but no sound came out.

'Go on,' she said sharply. 'Move your ass.'

Martin made himself lurch towards the lift, stepping over a beaded evening bag which someone had dropped in the stampede for the door. Working on the emergency generator the lift doors opened with painful slowness. Martin got in and was borne aloft by slow degrees, almost unaware that he was moving.

Alice looked about and saw the sign to the swimming pool. She went down through the tunnel and resurfaced into air deliciously warm but refreshing after the day's heat. Lit only by moonlight, the village could have been a Polynesian dream. The soft moon glow made a spotless mirror of the water. The now unlit tower loomed, slab-like behind her, but Alice felt oddly detached from any sense of danger, immune in the shadows. Without street lights the stars had reclaimed the sky above the city. She pulled off her blouse, kicked off her shoes, let her clothes fall to the ground and walked to the edge of the pool. It was years since she had been swimming, which was strange when she remembered how much she'd loved it as a child. She had taught herself. There had been no one to help her. Her mother never swam, it was impossible to imagine her father taking her to the baths, appearing out of the men's changing rooms in a swimming costume, getting into the water with her. She had always gone alone, choosing a quiet corner, away from the rough and tumble, launching herself from the side, forcing herself to stay afloat longer and longer, until the miraculous day when there was no thought or effort, only the unstoppable progress to the far side in the knowledge that she could now swim and would always know how.

Naked, she perched, bird-like on the edge, her toes curled over the tiles. A proper dive was beyond her, so she simply let herself fall forward until there was no more ground and she was entering the water amazingly smoothly and skimming the bottom, her eyes open to a world of shifting squares and strange aqueous effusions projected by the moonshine above. Bubbles of silent laughter rippled from her mouth. She did a complete roll and as she turned upwards an explosion of white rain devastated her vision. It was beautiful. She continued round until she was touching the bottom and again there was that burst of white light, like a flash photograph that leaves everything momentarily hazy.

Her breath gave out and she rose to the top, breaking the surface with a last kick and turning to float on her back. The temperature was perfect, bodywarm yet still cooling. A third burst of white filled the sky, illuminating the huts and the tower with brief electric brilliance. Fireworks, she thought, Bastille Day fireworks – then she remembered what had happened and realised it was death that was

making such beauty. Out of the water she could hear the cause —
the dull thwump of shells, the sharp crack of anti-aircraft fire, their
beautiful work briefly lighting up the heavens, making the returned
darkness darker than before.

She climbed out and wondered what to do next. A shell-burst
showed her Mansa's hut with its stacks of fluffy towels. She went
over and gave herself a furious rub down, taking towel after towel,
scrubbing herself until every inch of flesh was alive with the
friction. More starbursts lit up the sky. She was not afraid, it was
all part of the great display Africa was laying on to welcome her
back to sanity. Meteors might ignite and cascade above her, yet
nothing could touch her, she was outside time and place, a naked
child in a make-believe village by an empty pond that mirrored the
whoosh and sparkle of a war that was not hers. And it was strange
how this aura of invincibility seemed to echo the things that El-
Assawy had been trying to say to her in the orphanage — she had
barely listened but somehow they had lodged in her brain — no one,
she had said, is for the children.

A long line of flak sprayed across the heavens but she had no
further need of illumination, the point was clear, she knew what she
should do and holding a last towel before her she walked back to the
hotel, abandoning her filthy clothes as if sloughing off old skin.

A single bulkhead lamp glimmered in the tunnel. The glass door
to the gym was dark. Alice thought of Margot and the African
trainer and wondered what the Pope thought of such things — was
using the mouth less of a sin than using a condom? Martin had
used rubbers before she went on to the pill. Usually such thoughts
were bitter, loaded with heavy irony, ending with the unpleasant
conclusion that she was really no more than a walking contraceptive,
a human rubber, prophylactic, final. This time it failed to bother
her.

She stepped into the foyer and stood at the centre of the polished
expanse of marble clutching the towel to her front, utterly unconcerned at her extraordinary nakedness. From the dining room came
a tinkling piano tune. She was not alone. In the darkened space a
curious shadow-play unfolded. Freddy was seated at the grand
piano, ineptly two-fingering a mawkish love dirge, while on the
dance floor, amidst a flotsam of perished balloons like an explosion
in a Durex factory, Margot was being slow waltzed in a tight clinch
by the ever elegant Dr Diop. Her head was laid on his shoulder, her

eyes were tightly closed, she moved with a fine delicacy, adrift on her dreams.

As Alice watched there was a sudden brief flickering from somewhere above her head, then a pause, then a brief spurt of light until, with a great effort, the chandelier rose from darkness to full force and was hugely and heroically ablaze. Its tiny sister lights twinkled on in the dining room and at the reception. The power-station was working again, there were lights on the drive outside but nothing was as flamboyantly alive as that preposterous sunburst above her. As its bulbs warmed to their task, the million facets of cut-glass began to tremble and tinkle like gentle rain. Alice laid back her head, let the towel fall to the ground, and stood, awash in its white cascade. She was Ayesha wrapped in cleansing, revivifying flame, purified and born again. The music tinkled on – she laughed at the thought – *She*, the tyrant-queen of her secret African realm. Her laughter said it all, she really was cured.

A stray balloon drifted up, glanced against a glowing bulb and exploded with a sharp crack like Diop's handgun. Alice bent to retrieve her towel and headed for the lifts.

Martin rose from the lavatory, accustomed now to the ghastly muesli spinning in the whirlpool flush. His mind was as confused as his lower bowel – a quick glance through the curtains *en route* to the bathroom had revealed a sunlit world emptied of all activity – no cars on the bridge, no boats on the river – though at least the bangs and flashes had stopped. He bemoaned his own stupidity – how could he have got himself into this mess? Of course it was all down to Delmonico, the devil figure who had seduced him into an act of incredible folly. At least he had succeeded in offloading the worst of their mistakes, now everything depended on things beyond his control, on who out there had won, and what, if anything, could be salvaged from the wreckage of his life with Alice?

She was still asleep. He had been surprised when he woke up and found her on the floor, her T-shirt crumpled over her like a loose tabard. He'd pulled it straight, gently, not wanting to wake her in case he provoked another burst of angry recrimination. He – they – needed time. Right now she was upset, it was only natural, but he felt confident enough that things would settle down. What worried him most was how peaceful she looked. He felt like shit and reckoned he must look like it – how then was she so calm?

He dressed in the same clothes as the day before and the day before that. They were filthy and smelled of farmyard slurry but there was nothing else; all his other clothes were covered in baby mess.

He eased open the door and slipped out. The corridor window offered another scene of utter emptiness save for a billowing mass of dense black smoke rising from somewhere in the centre of the town. It was the only sign that something terrible had happened, that and the empty streets and the total silence.

No one stirred in the dining room which was just as it had been at the moment of stampede – the floor scattered with curls of torn rubber and trampled plastic toys. No one had set up breakfast or seemed likely to do so.

Who could blame them, he thought, moving cautiously towards the door and risking a peep outside.

As he expected the guards were gone and there was something that looked like a bundle of old clothes dumped near the edge of the road. It all looked quiet enough but who could be sure? He wasn't sure which side he hoped had won – he loathed Mamadi for making him feel small but the thought of the oh-so-arrogant Maktar Diop in charge was terrifying. Better the old order – more chance they'd get the airport open and let them leave. But who *had* won?

He knew it was stupid, but everything seemed so peaceful he had to risk stepping out, just to see if there was any sign at all of what had happened. He wandered down the drive, curious about the bundle of rags up ahead. Of course it was dangerous, but he was unable to suppress his curiosity. Without the sprinklers the lawn was already hardening, another day and it would be singed and dead like everything else in Mali.

Halfway along, he realised that he was not approaching a pile of rags after all. His stomach lurched. A woman was spread-eagled, face-up, her dress above her knees, the blue, white and red ribbons dangling from her hair clamped to her face by a patch of congealed blood. Her shocked eyes seemed to accuse him of her violation. Her companion lay face-down, exposing the torn-away island of gore in his back where a high-powered slug had torn right through him, shredding the letters stitched onto his ill-fitting navy-blue canvas shift.

Martin gagged. It was Mansa, the left-hand side of his face just visible, a last defiant drool of saliva and blood running down his chin.

He turned at the sound of an approaching jeep. The driver was in uniform, but the passenger beside him was a rather battered Delmonico. When he climbed down, his movements were awkward. Both lapels of his once elegant jacket were half ripped off, the blood on his shirt-front had left a brownish stain, but it was his face which said it all – his left eye a puffy slit, the right a blood-engorged mound, darkish purple with a weeping sore at the outside corner. Someone must have tried to tidy him up, shaving a patch near the hairline where a cartoon bump had been crudely stitched leaving an outsize catgut bow, more like gift-wrapping than fine surgery.

He seemed unconcerned, staring at the corpses in the gutter.

'Poor bloody Mansa, eh? He was a fucking nuisance, but there was no need to waste him like that, no need at all. Ah well, he's not the only one, more's the pity.'

289

'Your tooth . . .' Martin said, shocked by the wide black gap which had appeared as soon as he had opened his mouth to speak.

'Only a crown. I swallowed it when they kicked me in the jaw. Get it back later I expect.'

'Why did they let you go?'

'Thank you for expressing it so delicately – what you mean is why didn't they put a bullet in me? Well, you're right to ask, 'cause it certainly wasn't a sudden realisation that they loved me – oh, no, no. It was touch and go – a night to remember, and may I never see another like it.'

He bent nearer, and winced with pain. 'It was brilliant really – two blackbirds killed with one very sharp stone.'

'So who won?'

'Won? My, my laddie, but aren't we the impatient one? This is far too good a tale to rush. First it all seemed to go young Diop's way. Having whipped the advance guard he decided not to wait for the famous twenty-ninth of July but to strike while they weren't expecting it. Ah, impetuous youth . . . What he couldn't know was that someone – I wonder who? – had tipped them off about his real strength and they had put two and two together.'

Martin fought to keep his face as blank as possible.

'Anyway,' Delmonico continued, 'yesterday afternoon the army pulled out of Bamako and headed south. The radio gave out that there had been an insurrection by troops in Kangaba – all rubbish of course. Then last night Maktar and his boys drove in – right in – can you imagine? No one stopped them, no one fired a shot in anger. You'd have thought he might have guessed something was wrong. Or maybe he did but decided to see it through – it is my experience that people get very funny about glory at such times, never understood it myself, but there you are. He got as far as the market – he even made a speech in front of the Post and Telecommunications building – all about a new dawn for Mali with liberty from tyranny and a return to idealism and hope. Actually, I made that last bit up, but I bet it's not far from the truth.'

Martin could just imagine it – the passion, the quotations from his grandfather's poetry. He had to admit it would have been a stirring sight to see.

'So then,' Martin said, 'the army sneaked back and blew him away.'

Delmonico laughed – an oddly innocent laugh.

290

'Not at all. You can't even guess the half of it. While all this liberating is going on down below, up on the hill in his crumbling palace His Excellency the President of the Republic is sitting surrounded by his bodyguards and a few up-country conscripts, all too well aware that young Maktar intends to sleep in his bed that night while someone who doesn't like him has sent his army on a jaunt downriver and that the only thing he can do is rally such miserable troops as are left to him and stand and fight.'

'What happened?'

'Fireworks. Didn't you see them? They were lovely – howitzers, mortars – French, Chinese, from all over the place, wham, bham, thank you ma'am. What a blood-bath. Even I didn't know Darwesh had those American missiles – that's Gaddafi, of course. The *Bibliothèque Nationale* is still burning. That's where the President took refuge. Such a blaze. Quite appropriate, really – he wrote a thesis on Molière at the Sorbonne.'

'So Diop won! And you're on top?'

'Whoa laddy, not so fast if you please. Yes, our Maktar almost died for the President, but then the trap was sprung. He'd almost wiped himself out with all this fight to the death stuff, so when the army crept back, he didn't stand a chance – beautiful really . . .'

For a moment he was lost in contemplation of the fine aesthetics of treachery.

'Then who won for God's sake?'

'Why, the MRN of course.'

'Mamadi's lot?'

'Yes, yes, he's one of them. They'd set the whole thing up. Let 'em knock each other out, then stepped in, neat as anything. Now a deal's been done, the President stays President, just for the look of the thing, so as not to upset the World Bank and all the other creditors, but the real power is the new Government of National Reconstruction led by General Abdillahi Diop with our mutual friend Mamadi as Minister of Defence.'

'Diop? I thought the Diops were the rebels here?'

'There are Diops and Diops,' Delmonico said, starting off towards the hotel. In the jeep, the soldier leapt to attention and saluted. Still confused, Martin hurried after the limping figure who was struggling to keep his right leg straight.

'I still don't see why they let you go. Why didn't they just blow your brains out? *You* betrayed them too.'

'Nonsense, without me there would never have been a show-down and they would never have come to power.'

He pushed open the doors and strained to peer at the great chandelier as if he had given up all hope of seeing it again.

'In any case,' he went on, 'they need me more than ever now that we have a policy of financial rectitude aimed at winning over the World Bank and securing a juicy loan. Goodbye Socialism, farewell propping up food prices, adieu buying off the discontented with social welfare schemes, hello the free-market economy.'

'But I . . .'

Delmonico wrinkled his nose and curled his mouth in distaste.

'Now that we are inside,' he said, 'I must point out that you stink like death.'

'I haven't any more clothes and we were so caught up with the baby I . . .'

'Got rid of it, did we? How was the sainted Belvedere? Living with El-Assawy, the Mother Theresa of Mali, I believe?'

'They seem like good people.'

Delmonico shrugged. 'As long as the Reverend keeps away from little boys – he nearly got lynched in Timbuktu for that. It was only young Maktar who got him out in time.'

'Is nobody good or decent in your world?'

'Are you proposing yourself for the post?'

Martin shook his head.

'Good, that's the first honest answer I've had for a long, long time.'

'So now you're riding high?'

'Sure am. Have you any idea what will happen when the free-market economy starts to bite? This place is a tinder-box, there'll be riots in the towns and secession in the provinces, general mayhem. Our new Minister of Defence is going to have to give his soldiers some new toys to hold all this in check. We are going to have a new army barracks near the Omnisports stadium – all made out of *loverly* cement. And they want one of those fancy French pill-box things, with a gunslit in front, outside every police post. But most of all they want arms, nice shiny new ones, with night sights and blast-your-brains-out bullets like they've seen in the movies.'

'And that's where you come in? Where do you get them?'

'Darwesh, maybe. He always has a line on that sort of thing. He's probably hiding out in the desert right now, but he'll be back soon enough. He and I are eternal. But you know the really funny thing about all this is that with little Master Mamadi in charge this will be the first arms deal I've ever done where I haven't had to bribe someone – doesn't seem right somehow . . .'

There was a sudden happy shriek as Freddy ran up and threw himself around Delmonico, who tried to hold him away, the better to protect his bruises.

'I do believe he's been crying. He must love me after all.'

'I think he does,' Martin said. 'Anyway you're both lucky to be alive.'

Delmonico looked suddenly deflated, as if the thought of his survival had punctured his usually impregnable carapace.

'They did for Thorsten,' he said bitterly.

'You mean they killed the Swede? Well, he was flying the enemy up and down, I mean he was a part of the operation wasn't he?'

Delmonico shook his head. 'That wasn't the reason. Oh sure, they picked him up at that bar where he always hung out, but that was just to make sure his plane was grounded for the duration. They'd have let him out when it was all over – they'll need ferrying over the desert now and in any case they don't usually kill white folk – it's too much trouble. No, that wasn't the reason.' Delmonico gave a dry laugh, more of a snort. 'He died a hero – oh yes, a hero. They'd picked up the tart he was with too, and when some of the squaddies decided they needed a spot of relief and got her stretched out over a table our Swede decided that they weren't behaving like gentlemen and tried to put a stop to it.' He shook his head, mystified by the unfailing perversity of his fellow men.

Martin was equally confused. 'But he told me that the first rule was always to act humble and never offer any excuse for trouble – just take whatever comes.'

'Very sound advice. Unfortunately he didn't take it – imagine – a hero for a cheap whore from the *bidonville*? She'd probably been fucked more times than we've both had hot dinners, and he'd probably only met her a couple of hours before, if that, yet he ups and starts telling these drunken thugs that they should desist, that she was his girl and that he wasn't going to stand by and let them abuse her.'

'And then?'

Delmonico shook his head again. 'Better not to know – not for the squeamish.'

'Why do you stay here? Why, when there's all this to put up with? What can it possibly be worth?'

But Delmonico was no longer listening. He and Freddy were staring at something across the room. Martin turned and saw a slow, solemn procession – six men in suits, bearing aloft a shiny black coffin with a rounded top and elaborate brass fittings. Behind it came Margot and her daughters with Alice to one side, all in black. It was this more than anything which puzzled Martin. Where had these deep mourning robes, these widow's weeds, come from? Margot even had a tiny pill-box hat, trimmed with a ripple of black veil which edged her forehead. Had she travelled with them or had they been quickly run up overnight? Behind the family came the rest of the holiday makers, as formally dressed as they could manage, all solemn-faced and sad-eyed – the English couple with their twins, the diminutive Japanese pair, he in a dark business suit, she in black skirt and blouse with a discreet pearl pin high on her left collar. Behind the cortège, two waiters dragged a trolley loaded with luggage. They were leaving. There would be no time for Martin to shower, in this neat subfusc crowd he could be garish and smelly.

'Goodbye,' Delmonico said. 'I hope all goes well for you.'

'And you. If you're ever in Manchester . . .' But the idea seemed so improbable he let it trail away. They shook hands and Martin made for the door.

'Oh, by the way,' Delmonico called after him. 'Get straight on the plane, as quick as you can.'

Martin wanted to ask why, but the bus was revving up and everyone was staring impatiently from the windows willing him to board. He turned to wave and caught a last glimpse of the strange Scotsman limping across the littered floor beneath the great chandelier, leaning heavily on Freddy's shoulder.

The coach had no sooner pulled away than there was a loud scream and a rush to the right-hand windows.

'I wouldn't,' Martin said, pulling Alice back. 'It's pretty foul – two bodies from last night.'

She hit the seat with a bump as the bus took the corner too fast for safety. The atmosphere was charged with nervous chatter and watchful glances to either side.

From the bridge, the river was empty of people, the abandoned pirogues rippling at their moorings in the gentle flow. Alice followed

294

the water's snaking progress to the misty horizon, wondering what had happened in Timbuktu.

'Farewell and adieu,' said Martin bitterly. 'I never knew a week could feel like a lifetime. It'll be good to . . .'

'I'm sorry,' Alice said sharply. 'But you'll have to slide that window open – it's impossible to breathe with you so near. If you could smell yourself, you'd die of shame.'

'Thanks a lot. I charge about sorting out all our problems while you use my shirts for nappies, I've no time to wash or change and you treat me like a leper.'

Despite the protests, he struggled with the catch until the glass slid back but only an inch or two. Alice shook her head. He was trying to get it to move a fraction more when he got his first sight of the truck they were overtaking. It was an open lorry, an old wreck of a thing, rattling along, belching filthy black fumes from a stovepipe exhaust.

'Martin!' Alice opened her mouth to scream but her cry was drowned by the horrified uproar of the other passengers as they saw the truck and its terrible cargo. The back was piled high with corpses, thrown in any-old-how, some in tattered uniforms, some virtually naked, bent, twisted, matted with blood, all with gaping spattered holes, wide-eyed and shocked at the unexpected ferocity of metallic death. High on the heap, passing the square windows like a film pulled through her fingers, Alice saw the unmistakable aquiline features, the high forehead and arrogant sensuous mouth of the one corpse she had hoped never to see or hear of again. This was why she had not asked what had happened. This was why she did not want to know who had won.

'Serves the bastard right,' Martin hissed in her ear, unable to keep the vengeful delight out of his voice. 'Levels the score for Simon.'

'It wasn't him,' Alice said. 'He wouldn't have done a thing like that – he was too honest, too . . .' She stopped at the point of saying 'beautiful' again. But he was – even splayed-out, in rictus, hideously vulnerable. Perhaps it was her money which had brought this carnage? His death, her gift to Mali.

As their driver accelerated to the limit of his engine, the death-car fell away.

'He's better off dead,' Martin said, persistently. 'There is no place for a romantic when it's all planning and co-operation. God knows what he would have done if he'd won.'

'It's funny,' Alice said. 'I used to think *I* was the conventional one, the one who would always go for the safe option – whereas you were the Bohemian, the give-it-a-try sort.' She blew through closed lips. 'Shows how wrong I was, even there. He really scared you, didn't he? In fact this whole thing has knocked the stuffing out of you. All you want to do now is scuttle back to Manchester, go home, shut the front door and breath a sigh of relief. And the really funny thing is, I don't feel that way at all. You can't begin to imagine how much better I am since we last drove up this road. I guess Africa was the big life test, the ultimate exam. And do you know what?'

'What?'

'You failed.'

'What are you driving at? Why did I fail? I did what you wanted, I found Delmonico, got us to Timbuktu, went out and brought back a child – it was hardly my fault it was duff. Whatever you wanted I did – so where's the beef?'

She fixed him with a straight look. 'Don't you see? You've said it all – it was whatever I wanted you to do. It was all about dealing with my obsession. No, no, let me finish – I realise I was unwell and that you had a hard time, but you weren't straight with me and you know it. We were on parallel tracks and now I've branched off, I'm not the same person I was a week ago, too many things have happened – things that can't just be brushed off. I know you in a way I never did before. I used to think you were a bit of a poet, not hidebound the way I saw myself. Now I know you're just adrift, there's no fixed point, you go where you're blown.'

He opened his mouth to protest but the bus lurched to a halt and people clammered to their feet, jostling down the aisle, keen to get away.

'That's ridiculous,' he began, but had to double up as someone brought a heavy bag tumbling out of the overhead rail.

Alice got to her feet and made for the door. As she stepped down, she caught the now expected tang of woodsmoke, the smell that would for ever mean Africa. She smiled, if there were fires then life must be returning to normal. Even the airport seemed to be managing a degree of bustle and confusion – their luggage being pulled from under the bus and thrown anywhere, the driver trying to sort out tickets amidst a barrage of noise and fuss, all of it suddenly drowned by police sirens howling up the road behind them, as a line of black Peugeots with motorcycle outriders came to a noisy halt at a gateway further along the terminal where a group of flustered attendants were hurrying to unroll a somewhat ragged red carpet.

Martin leant forward. A shiny Citroën, the flag of the republic slapping irritably on its bonnet, eased to the front of the line and out stepped a little figure in a military uniform at least two sizes too large for him, followed by a Junoesque lady in a billowing corn-flower-blue kaftan with op-art spiral embroidery in sharp orange and a matching headscarf, wrapped and piled like a huge scoop of ice-cream on her magnificent head.

Martin handed Alice the in-flight bag he had just wrestled over, and pushed his way free of the crowd to get a closer look at this apparition. These important arrivals were being greeted by a clutch of bowing and grinning airport officials. No one attempted to stop Martin. He stood for a moment on the fringe of the crowd until the great lady turned and caught his eye. The scars on her cheeks were almost U-shaped she was so radiant with pleasure.

'Why, Madame Josette,' Martin said. 'You look so . . . so . . . well just so happy.'

'Oh, I am, I am. We are the delegation. It is everything of my dreams.'

'Delegation?'

'Why yes, to the Wedding. The President and the General Diop are so occupied with *les événements* that they have asked *General* Mamadi and I to represent them. We shall sit in the Abbey and I shall no longer be *hors des choses*. You shall see me on the television, I shall wear pink now that I know that the step-grandmother will not be there. She, I have discovered, is a great authoress – I have been reading her *The Hell-Cat and the King*, a story of royal romance – Zenka is captured by wild tribal people, rescued, then falls in love with King Miklos. I recommend it most strongly. There are many, many more books by her so I shall have much reading to do. I shall go to Foyles. Ah well, *cher ami*, it is time for our ways to part.' She extended her hand; Martin caught it and raised it to his lips. She lowered her eyelashes in a delicate, unspoken *au revoir* before sweeping after her husband into the crowded concourse where a line had been cleared through the dense crowd of waiting Africans, squatting patiently beside their bundles, much as they had been when Martin arrived. He wondered if they could be the same people. There was no arrivals or departures boards, no announcements had been made since he got there, yet no one seemed in the least bit fussed. It was this, not the dirt or the poverty, or the crazy politics, which puzzled him most. Given the situation, the previous night's sudden explosion of violence seemed reasonable – what he couldn't understand was why they didn't do it more often. Why didn't they just rise up and tear this hopeless, ill-run useless airport to pieces with their bare hands, instead of merely sitting there, dead-eyed and docile, amongst their silent, obedient children, dozens of them, just sitting there, not even bothering to cry?

The Mamadis had been swept through the narrow building, out on to the tarmac, where a guard of honour stood at attention and a scratch military band oompah-pah'd its way through the *Chant du Départ*.

A pregnant 747 had hunkered down on the runway humming to itself, with the sort of high whine that drives dogs mad and which, if coming from a piece of ordinary household equipment, would prompt the owner to have it repaired. Men in orange overalls tickled its exposed underbelly. A chain of trolleys snaked towards an hydraulic platform which raised the bulky silver containers into the freight bay. Martin watched as an engineer lifted away a panel from the side of the nearest of the bulbous jets. The man looked quite puny against this expanse of metal, a tiny stick figure impertinently fiddling with an impossible spaghetti of red and green wiring. There was, Martin realised, more technology in that one machine than in the whole of Mali.

A solitary trolley drew Jack Zabriskie's coffin slowly across the tarmac, so close to the band he seemed to be having a military funeral. Martin felt suddenly lowered by the thought of the one character in their little drama whom everyone had ignored. He must sometimes have woken from his fever to find himself alone in a strange hotel room. No one had bothered with him, least of all his wife. Martin looked at Margot, but she was standing near the departure gates deep in the sort of intense conversation with Alice that Martin could only distrust. He turned away and saw that they were lifting the coffin into one of the neutral silver containers used to store in-flight meals. It was the final indignity, the ultimate humiliating loneliness, the final public proof that there was no one to care. Martin looked at Alice again but her eyes were fixed on Margot. What was the bitch telling her? He walked towards them but as soon as Margot realised he was coming she broke off and turned to the doctor waiting at her side.

'Dr Diop is leaving us,' Margot announced briskly as he approached. 'He has to take up his new duties – *Chef de Cabinet* to General Bamanda, the new Minister of Public Health.'

The Doctor smiled modestly, shook hands with Alice and Martin, kissed Margot on the cheek – right, left and right again – and muttered the usual things about having a safe journey and hoping to see them soon. Then he turned back to Alice and said, 'We shall be in touch as soon as I have the details.'

'I know the problem,' Alice said. 'It's really down to what they want. If the government goes on pretending it isn't happening, no one will get anywhere.'

Martin's brow furrowed – what on earth were they talking about?

'Do not anticipate failure,' Diop said, waggling a long finger in mock admonition.

'Excuse me,' Martin said. But he was too late, the doctor had turned and was immediately swallowed up by the advancing crowd.

Martin tried Alice: 'What was . . .?' But it was no use, they were now separated by a half dozen travellers, determined to get on the plane as quickly as possible. A soldier came across to try to restrain them – he was young, a muscle-bound squaddie in a sweaty singlet and baggy fatigue trousers – just the sort of character, Martin realised, who must have massacred Maktar and his boys or the Swedish pilot for that matter.

He held his rifle sideways to the crowd, a symbolic barrier. The atmosphere was tense, and Martin decided it would be better to keep out of Margot's way; he wasn't likely to come off best in any argument and there was no reason to invite trouble. As he turned to go he noticed that she was laughing and talking with the young soldier and whatever she was saying clearly amused him for he was grinning hugely and had completely forgotten his orders. By imperceptible degrees the passengers were edging forward until Margot and her squaddie were an island in their midst.

Martin strolled as nonchalantly as possible back into the bleak breeze-block hall. Through the glass panels he could see Mamadi inspecting the troops, walking beside a tall, bemedalled officer with a drawn sword, occasionally raising a sleeve to make a fingerless salute. Billowing and stately his wife sailed behind him, regally tipping her head in approval. Martin wondered if she would curtsy to the Queen. It would make a magnificent spectacle, like the last seconds of an exploded tower block when it seems to be held in a trembling dust storm before settling to the ground in a great soufflé of smoke.

He was passing a kiosk selling souvenirs and realised he had nothing to take back. Perhaps it was just as well, he had little need of the sort of memories a trinket might arouse. What he needed was amnesia. He glanced for a moment at the beadwork fly whisks, the elephant-hair bracelets, the zebra-skin footstools, at a brittle dried-out lizard, a stuffed desert fox, a bowl of semiprecious stones, carved and polished into shiny eggs, a cacophony of dead nature, true souvenirs of *La Sécheresse*.

The little Japanese woman was standing with her husband feeling the edges of a blanket made of animal pelts; soft, shiny and luxurious. Whatever the little creatures had been, dozens of them had died to make this sumptuous spread and Martin had a sudden, irrepressible image of her, naked on that sea of ticklish fur, squirming with pleasure. He fought it down. This desire for smooth, narrow flesh was destructive. There were more schoolgirls near one of the boarding gates, leggy in ankle socks, giggling and awkward. If he wasn't careful such lusts could lead into very dangerous areas – the image of the whirling dance passed before him, the girl/boy, all wide dark eyes and reddened lips and then the sudden, distorted face of the *doppelgänger* creature in the cistern, rubbing himself, masturbating wildly, fearfully strong. No, Martin told himself, he must keep with Alice. As long as he behaved she would get over this crazy mood she was in. It was the realisation that the baby thing was all over that was doing it. Once that had settled then he could start to piece together their lives. He would have to work on it, but her new thinness would help hold off dangerous temptations. He turned away from the Japanese and their erotic duvet – best not to expose himself to such dangerous thoughts.

At the top of the ladder a workman was taking down the photograph of the President in his library. Martin wondered how long this stitched-up arrangement would last, how long before another explosion changed everything round again. Perhaps their little civil war would get a short mention in *Time* or *Newsweek* in a few days, if he could be bothered to look. None of the waiting

Africans seemed concerned by their former leader's demotion or by the spectacle out on the tarmac – Mamadi was just another figure in a uniform doing what he had to do.

Martin gave up. In any case he needed a crap, the pain was back and would have to be dealt with pronto. He saw a crudely stencilled WC, and pushed through the door into a long corridor. There was another door at the end. He went in and gagged. The toilet had no seat, the bowl was filled to overflowing with paper and faeces, with more stained papers crumpled on the wet floor. The tiny slit window above the toilet was jammed closed and the hot dead air was soupy with sulphurous horrors, but at least the door locked, for he knew he had no choice but to try to relieve himself while making every effort to avoid the surrounding mess.

He lowered his pants just below his knees, desperately trying to prevent them from falling into the slurry on the floor, though this made it difficult for him to open his legs wide enough to straddle the bowl without touching it. The only solution was to bend backwards, holding the walls on either side with open palms. It was crazily precarious and no inducement to muscular release – it was hard to push open his sphincter while forcing out his arms. Furrowing his brow, he emitted a thin stream of mustard diarrhoea, coating the pile of paper beneath him.

It was over in one spurt but left the problem of how to clean himself. He gingerly lifted a piece of half-used paper from the floor and tore off the cleanest section which he scraped between his legs. Perhaps he would be able to towel himself off on the plane. He pulled up his pants, fastened them, did a little elementary primping then slid the bolt and flung open the door.

The shock hit him like a boot in the groin. Side by side, blocking his way, were Abdel-Kadar and the policeman with the knife. How he found the strength to slam the door and bolt it again Martin could not have said, but it was no sooner done than a mighty crash sent the wood smashing against its hinges. He tried to hold it with one leg but the rear wall was just too far away to brace himself against and when the second crash came the hinges barely survived.

The door held. Just. But he would have to get help. He carefully stood on the lavatory bowl, a foot on either side, and banged open the tiny window, but all he could see was a narrow strip of what he guessed must be a car park. If he forced his head to the left he could just glimpse a line of black Peugeots and behind them a row of camouflaged trucks. They had to be Mamadi's escort. When he twisted his head the other way, he saw a solitary jeep with two figures beside it, a man and a woman. Squeezing his head further into the space he got a clearer view. It was Margot of all people talking to the squaddie who had been sent to hold back the crowd, her livid red fingernails toying with the identity disc suspended at the point where his muscled cleavage disappeared into his olive vest. Christ, Martin thought, she's chatting him up.

'Margot!' he yelled. 'Help!'

Under any other circumstances her dismayed surprise would have been immensely gratifying.

'Help! Get me out of here! There's two men after me – one of them's got a knife, they're going to kill me – pleeeze!'

Her face registered disbelief, then the gradual suspicion that he was trying to make a fool of her. Then something suddenly twigged and a wide, malicious smile broke across her face.

'Alice said you didn't pay up for the kid – that's it, isn't it? They're after you for that.'

'Yes, yes. For God's sake, there's no time, they're trying to break the door in. You've gotta do something now – bring that squaddie, he'll be able to handle them.'

'No.'

'Eh – what do you mean "no"? They're going to kill me, kill me dead.'

'Good.'

The young soldier looked mightily confused, his puzzled glance moving between Margot and the desperate face at the window. There was no way of knowing what he made of the shouting match between these two crazy white people. Margot stroked his cheek reassuringly, smiled sweetly and tugged at his arm, leading him away. Just before they passed out of the frame, she turned to Martin and flashed him a little-girl look – raised eyebrows and fluttering lashes – which seemed to say, 'So sorry' – then they were gone.

'Pleeeze,' Martin yelled. 'Please don't leave me.'

He pressed his head into the narrow gap, squeezing as far as he could, trying to see where she was. It was no use. She really had left him to his fate.

'Pleeeeeeez,' he lifted his right leg to get further up.

'Pleeeeeeeeeeeeeeez'.

He stopped, there was no point. He put his right foot down,

missed the rim of the bowl and with an awkward twist stepped right into the gooey midden. Evil humours rose from the disturbed cesspit, a chemical cocktail of sulphur and fish. He tried to extricate his leg. It came up an inch with a wet noise like bestial lips smacking wetly over some disgusting pleasure. First it had been his left leg in the ditch; now at the last he had completed the circle of costive baptism. He rested his head against the tiled wall. It smelled of mould. He gave in, he was finished.

There was another crash. The door shuddered, bending the top hinge out at a crazy angle, the whole thing just held by a single mauled screw.

The military spectacle showed no sign of coming to an end. Mamadi had processed up and down the ranks several times and was now standing on a makeshift podium. His wife was seated a pace behind him, engrossed in a paperback as the troops executed a series of parade manoeuvres. The waiting passengers were beginning to fret but, after the violence of the night before, any complaints were muttered and subdued.

Alice was studying her reflection in a darkened window. It had been surprisingly quick and easy to pin up one of Margot's outfits – the shoes were wrong of course, but she had to admit there was something about dressing up which helped. Like the uniforms out there, it held you in and bucked you up, gave you a shield against the world where her jeans and T-shirt left her vulnerable. Armoured like Margot, she could cut a swathe through things.

The band was playing something jolly. She had no idea why the little man was holding this parade or why the tall woman behind him was nodding and smiling so regally. She saw Margot at last, talking to a soldier who saluted as she left him. At least she could guess what *that* was all about.

'Seen Martin?' she asked.

Margot looked blank. 'Nope. He's probably gone to the loo. He hasn't been looking too good these last couple of days – nor smelling good either. What a difference, eh? He's fallen apart while you've picked yourself up. You look great – though I'm less won over to the idea of your dedicating yourself to this do-gooding thing. Oh sure, go round with a box at Christmas if it makes you feel better but not for life, honey. You've been there with the school teaching, and anyway didn't you have enough self-sacrifice with that husband of yours?'

'I'm a joiner, what else can it be? Poor Martin, I'd feel a lot happier if I knew where he was.'

A discordant clash of cymbals announced the end of the march past. The Mamadis stepped down from the podium. There was another ripple of movement among the departing tourists who started to reach for their hand-luggage, expecting action at last.

'Where the hell is he?' Alice said, balancing on the balls of her feet to see over the heads of the Africans crowded about the concourse.

'I guess he isn't coming,' Margot said evenly.

'What makes you say that?'

'Oh, just the way he's been behaving. You must have seen him ogling young flesh. If that's what he wants, let him have it. Now's your chance to get out. Forget about him, he isn't worth it.'

The Mamadis were walking towards the front of the aircraft. Sensing the time had come, the other passengers began to straggle after them, afraid to get too close to the soldiers but determined not to be left behind.

'Come on,' Margot insisted. 'Time to get on board.'

'I can't,' Alice said flatly. 'I can't just leave him. Not like that. It's got to be done properly or it'll all be wrong – you must see that surely?'

'And what if he's left you? What then?'

'I don't believe it. There's something not right about all this. Martin hasn't got the guts to start a new life in a foreign country. It's not his way.'

They were alone on the tarmac. The others were now a distant bunch, held back from the Minister by a line of armed guards, walking crabwise after him to ensure that he was not trampled in the rush. Two air stewardesses hurried forward to direct the passengers to a rear entrance, leaving Mamadi and his wife to a reception committee of the pilot and his senior officers at the foot of the forward ramp.

'I'm not going without him,' Alice said.

'Oh, what the hell,' Margot said. 'He must be dead already. He's back there, in the toilet. There were two men trying to knife him for not paying them for the baby. He was locked in the john and they were trying to break the door down.'

Alice's first instinct was to run back into the terminal, but when she saw the dense crowd in the concourse something told her she would be useless on her own. She turned, looking wildly for help, until her eyes settled on the distant, imposing figure of Madame Josette, one foot on the stairs leading to the aircraft.

That was enough. Alice lowered her head and started running, feet thumping on the molten tarmac. She was amazed at her own speed. It must have been years since she did any real exercise, yet there she was, pounding along, driven by the terrible thought that all her new plans were about to end in disaster. Taken unawares, the guards were paralysed just long enough to let her within reach of her target.

'Please,' she yelled, still running. 'Please help me, someone's trying to kill my husband. Please help me . . .'

The nearest soldier made a grab for her but the large woman barked an order and he fell back.

Madame Josette returned her foot to the tarmac.

'What is this story?' she demanded.

Alice told her, garbling everything but somehow getting to the gist of the locked lavatory and the two killers.

His face a picture of confusion, Monsieur Mamadi stepped forward, clearly intending to interrogate this strange, demented white woman. His wife, however, had immediately realised the urgency of Alice's message and with an imperious 'Venez' stormed past him, quickly followed by the rest of their entourage. At her approach, the crowd in the concourse parted – even the most supine loungers scattering to right and left as she headed for the entrance to the narrow corridor. Alice had now drawn level with Monsieur Mamadi and could see that the lavatory door had caved in. Someone, presumably Martin, was trapped underneath it, using it as a last defence against the knife-wielding figure who was trying to pull it away, the better to get at him.

Abdel-Kadar was the first to realise that relief had arrived, pressing himself against the wall to avoid the onrush of Madame Josette. For her part, she seemed barely aware of this irrelevance, swinging her paperback and cuffing him away with a side swipe of the book, as she reached out with her free hand to grab the would-be killer by the scruff of the neck and pull him aside. Before the astonished man knew what was upon him, he had been wrestled into an arm-lock and yanked back so sharply he was starting to choke as the soldiers pushed through to get him into handcuffs and drag him away.

Another soldier lifted aside the broken door to reveal an utterly defeated Martin, prone amongst the filth and detritus on the lavatory floor.

Madame Josette raised the hem of her kaftan to protect it from the dirt.

'This,' she said, 'is what happens when you deal with dangerous men like Maktar Diop and Delmonico, but you would not listen to my good advice. Come. We are late.'

He struggled to his knees with painful slowness. There was a vicious red weal where his head had been forced against the tiles, a disgusting yellowish smear covered his right cheek and there was a damp patch over the front of his shirt.

'Come,' Madame Josette said, not unkindly. 'You cannot stay here.'

'Why not?' he said ruefully. 'I stink so bad I might as well.'

'Martin!' Alice said sharply. 'Stop it and get up.'

He obeyed. The curious procession filed back into the concourse. The prisoner was kneeling at the feet of the guards, his face already bleeding from several blows. Monsieur Mamadi was giving orders as more soldiers and dignitaries hurried up to see what had happened. Martin scanned the concourse, but there was no sign of Abdel-Kadar.

'Well,' said Madame Josette, looming over him. 'And what please was all that about? No, do not tell me – it was this baby. You have played with the fire and burned yourself.' She beetled her brows but somehow her expression was exasperated rather than angry. 'Still I shall not be hard with you, nothing shall spoil my wonderful journey. Come, it must begin.'

He followed meekly in her billowing train as she sailed across the tarmac once more. After a few more orders to the soldiers, Mamadi followed with Alice by his side.

'Thank you,' she said. 'We must be a terrible nuisance to you.'

He sighed. 'There are many things to clear up just now, that was the least of them. I am glad neither of you were hurt. What did you do with the baby in the end?'

'My husband found someone called Belvedere, the Reverend Belvedere – he's running a sort of hospice for sick children, they need help. You don't think that . . .'

Mamadi stopped her.

'Madame Beresford,' he said with a pained weariness, 'if there is one thing I dislike more than white people making a nuisance, as you and your husband have done, it is white people trying to be helpful, as you are now. Belvedere is one of those people who come to Africa to find a place where they have some meaning. If it was not sick babies it would be something else – sick cows maybe. Now please, my wife has her Wedding to go to, it is the highest moment of her life and I must not delay her. I go up these stairs here, which are reserved for VIPs, you go up the far stairs, there, to the rear of the plane. It's a system your people made up, not mine – strange, do you not think? Goodbye, Madame.'

He turned and began to climb the high steps, his head barely visible above the handrail.

Madame Josette moved forward to say farewell to Alice. 'He is sometimes a little sharp,' she said kindly. 'What did you want to say to him?'

Martin tried to edge closer. He had been unable to catch anything that Alice had said to Mamadi but was determined to know what would pass between her and Madame Josette – she, unfortunately, was blocking his way, shutting him out behind the broad expanse of her copious blue robe, leaving him dazzled by the throbbing orange swirls. Only stray, disjointed phrases drifted his way. He strained hard and made out the word 'Belvedere' and 'orphanage' but the rest was a garble. Worse, Martin could hear nothing of Madame Josette's response, but when Alice took up her case again, he knew from the odd disjointed words – 'prostitutes', 'Zaire', 'cancer' – that she was retelling the story as laid out by Belvedere and El-Assawy. Why Alice felt she had to offer this to Madame Josette was unclear until he heard her mumble something about how nothing was being done and how it really ought to be. Martin's frustration was acute. Why, with all their other problems, had she become so fixated on this unpleasant tropical malady? True, it had put an end to one of the craziest things they had ever got themselves involved in but, other than that, it was none of their business – surely? But no – he heard her say the fateful words 'I want to help' and realised that it was now something far beyond a mere passing interest, a topic of conversation, a moment's concern. He knew the danger in those words, especially to himself – but what exactly was she planning?

He tried to edge as far round the living impediment as he could without actually nudging her. With considerable effort he got himself to one side and found himself with a profile of that kindly black face.

'What,' Madame Josette asked Alice, 'do you intend to do?'

This was it. Martin leant forward, his neck stretched to the limit, but just as Alice opened her mouth to reply he felt someone tweaking at his shirt and heard a vaguely familiar voice, trying to catch his attention.

'I say, you wouldn't come over here for a group photo, would you?'

Seething with rage, Martin swung round to find Safari-suit, still bedecked with cameras and lenses, pointing across the tarmac to a sheepish group of their fellow holiday-makers, formed up in two lines near the far stairway.

'No, I bloody wouldn't,' Martin spat out, desperately trying to pick up something, anything, of Alice's reply.

'It's a question of communication,' he heard her say. 'Dr El-Assawy says that each country has someone who knows . . .'

'Please,' Safari-suit insisted. 'It'll only take a . . .'

Martin grabbed his collar and pushed hard. 'Go away or I'll murder you.'

'I only thought . . .'

'Don't ever think again, at least not anywhere near me. Now fuck off!'

'Just a happy memory of Africa.'

'Happy memory – happy memory – I have no happy memory – none of us has, you blithering moron, surely even you must have noticed something of what has been going on?'

The man pulled away, shaking his head at this gross injustice. Martin turned back but it was too late, Madame Josette was drawing herself up to her full height, shaking out the folds in her robe.

'Very well,' she said. 'I will talk to the General. We will see.'

Her head inclined to be kissed – right, left, right. She turned towards Martin, thought better of it and set off up the stairs, effortlessly rising in a cloud of blue and orange as if she had no need of a mere machine to bear her aloft.

Martin's shoulders drooped – his life was going into a tail-spin while everything conspired to exclude him from any knowledge of where the wreckage was falling. He had caught just enough to connect what he had overheard to Dr Diop's earlier remarks, but the little this added up to offered nothing but gloom for him. It was time to have it out, but when he looked for Alice she was already halfway up the far stairs and when he followed her on board, he found his way blocked by an Air France steward, who bluntly informed him that he was to stay at the back of the plane.

'It is the smell,' he said, indicating a seat by the rear toilet door. 'The other passengers would complain. You will sleep or perhaps you will wash? It is twenty minutes to take off.'

That said, he headed into the body of the plane, drawing a curtain across the corridor, leaving Martin in a private world of his own stench. He tried to pull himself together. If only he could slow down and think clearly – there had to be something he could do, something he could say to Alice that would get them back on track. But what?

He glanced at the tiny cubicle and shuddered – did he dare go in there after what he had just been through? He ordered himself to calm down, to get a grip. The steward was right, he ought to try and clean himself up – if he got some of the shit off, they might let him go through and sit with her, then he could try and persuade her out of whatever crazy scheme she was incubating. He lifted off his shirt and kicked away his shoes – the smell was far worse than he'd credited. No wonder they had blocked him off back there. He bent – not too close – and slipped off his socks, then dropped his trousers and left them in a puddle on the floor as he edged towards the toilet. He eased it open and saw himself in the mirror on the back of the door – a weird sight, he had to admit, naked except for his sordid underpants. It was an image that had the sloppy look of amateur theatricals – the brown smears on the face and arms could have been badly applied stage make-up. It reminded him of something specific – the brown stains, the dirty off-white nappy – all he needed was a spear.

He lifted his leg and did a little jig from one to the other.

'Uggabugga,' he said. 'Uggabugga – Uggabugga – Uggabugga.'

He was quite pleased with the effect.

'Uggabugga – Uggabugga – Uggabugga.'

He was a child again.

'Uggabugga – Uggabugga – Uggabugga.'

'Excuse me.' It was Madame Josette. 'Ahaa,' she said merrily. 'It is good that you have got over your bad time. So what is this –

309

traditional dancing? English folklore? In Brighton we had the Eightsome Reel and the Gay Gordons.'

He considered trying to explain the Coronation, the fancy-dress parade, the Zulu war-dance, but thought better of it.

'I was worried,' she said. 'I did not see you with Alice when I went to speak with her and wondered if you were in trouble again. Then they told me you had been made to stay here. You are punished – like a naughty boy. Which you are. Oh yes – I should be angry because you told lies, but I know you were trying to help your wife so I can forgive you. Now I think it is she who punishes you.'

She looked him up and down.

'I have come to help,' she said. 'And first you must get clean. Come. Sit there.'

She pointed to the toilet seat. He hesitated but her hand in the small of his back propelled him into the tiny space.

'Sit,' she commanded, producing a gauzy length of silk scarf which she dunked under the taps and wiped across the worst of the faecal smears.

'Good,' she said. 'Soon you will be clean, then you can try to talk with your Alice – I cannot tell you what to say, you must find the words yourself.'

He shuddered, the water was cold – but it was wonderfully soothing after the terrible turbulence of the past hours. He tried to clear his mind, to concentrate on this brilliant performance he was now required to make, the plan of a lifetime, but it was hard to think of anything while she continued to smooth away the filth and grime so gently.

'There,' she said, leaning back to appraise her handiwork. 'The front is good, well, good enough. Now lean forward and I will wipe the rear.'

He did as he was bidden and caught the scent of lavender – she was wearing something light and old-fashioned, so different from the brisk acidy perfumes most women wore. He let his head loll forward, settling his brow against her capacious bosom, purring softly to himself. He ought to think about Alice, about what he could say to save their relationship, but the water trickled down his chest and curved sensuously over his nipples and he purred deeper and trembled as she gently slid the scarf along the nape of his neck and down his spine. It was all too much after what he had been through. It was hard to tell whether it was washing water or a tear that was rolling down his cheek and on to his tongue. It was salty. It was a tear.

'Such a big baby,' she said.

'Alice is going to leave me,' he said. 'What am I going to do?'

She eased back his head and dabbed at his brimming eyes with the scarf. 'Come, come. Stand on the seat and let me do your legs.'

'But Alice . . .' he protested.

'On the seat, come.'

He obeyed.

'Turn.'

He turned. Water sluiced down his back and lapped around his feet.

'Alice is looking for some good work,' Madame Josette conceded. 'She wants – no – she *needs* to help.'

'And me?'

'Why do you ask? Even if I knew I could not help you. No one understands someone else's marriage – the people themselves do not understand. Come. Sit over here by the window and I will get her for you. And be careful – this may be your last chance.'

He did as he was bidden, feeling the nylon fabric scratchy against his bare flesh but unwilling to get back into his filthy clothes.

It seemed an age before Alice slipped into the seat next to him, but it was surely hopeful that she clicked on her safety belt and sat back for take off.

'I hear you're not feeling good?' she said, her voice less than concerned.

'You're going to leave me?'

'Yes.'

'I'll be on my own.'

'We've both been on our own for years, we just happened to do it under the same roof. I thought you were the gregarious one, with your big, crowded family. I put myself down as the solitary loner when all the time it was you who liked having space around you. You didn't really want someone else muscling in on your world did you? Mind you, I was wrong about myself too. You, me and baby? Hardly. We're too close to our own childhood to have a child – you're still imagining a life, not living it. I'm still looking for a gang to join.

'We still had something . . . still could have . . .'

311

'What? Sex died with the programme and whatever else there was died in that orphanage. The rest is shopping, cooking and laundry. No thanks.'

The plane was beginning to move away from the terminal building. Martin looked out and saw someone standing in the long grass at the edge of the runway, someone familiar, waving goodbye. As the plane gathered speed the boy waved wildly with both arms. Martin did a double-take, he looked amazingly like Abdel-Kadar. Was it possible? He narrowed his eyes and tried hard to focus on the distant figure but couldn't be sure. He raised his own arm to wave back but remembered the disapproving figure at his side and tried to pretend he was wiping the glass with his palm.

The plane roared on, the figure slipped away, Martin turned back to Alice.

'What's this new job you've got?'

'I haven't got a job – I'm trying to put something together, that's all. Monsieur Mamadi's just agreed to help, so it's possible.'

'Here in Africa?'

'Uh-huh.'

'But that was my dream. You've stolen it. You know I can never come back, they're waiting for me out there, they'll kill me if I ever set foot in Bamako again. Why? Why do you want to? You never did before. It was my idea.' The words caught in his throat but it made little difference, the plane was lurching into its stomach-heaving lift from the ground and all Martin could do was slump, defeated in his seat.

'*Uggabugga*,' he said.

'What?'

'Nothing, just being silly.'

They were airborne now and Alice got up to go.

'Bet it's raining at home,' he said morosely.

'I expect you're right.'

'You're not leaving straight away, are you?'

'Not unless you want it that way. I'll go back with you and get everything sorted out.'

He nodded. 'Yes, that would be sensible.'

She paused at the partition.

'You'll get by, Martin. Nothing touches you.'

The curtain fell behind her. He thought about following but was hardly dressed for a public appearance.

312

The plane was still quite low, its predatory shadow passing over limpet-shell villages, darkening those fading scratches in the hard red earth that marked the last frail signs of human labour, now cracked and silting under the encroaching drifts. Hell, Martin thought, real hell. How had he ever imagined he might live there?'

He could see the in-flight magazine sticking out of the seat-pocket in front, its cover offering yet another portrait of the Prince and his fiancée and no doubt another article on the marriage made in heaven. He took his biro and gave them frizzy beards and moustaches, making him cross-eyed and her a gap-toothed harridan. That was better. They could have a long and happy life together for all he cared, though he rather doubted their chances. He thought of Jack Zabriskie, somewhere underneath his feet, laid out in the silver catering container while his wife chatted up the cabin crew. She was a vicious bitch but he had to admire her instinct for survival. Perhaps she was right, sex was the answer – the reflections in the pool, the taut body enmeshed in cords of watery sunlight. Maybe it was the line he should follow after all? Stop fighting it. Dive in.

They were lost in swirling cloud. He could picture Timbuktu far below, sleeping through the thudding afternoon heat when even the mad boy would be hiding in the crumbling depths of the spiral cistern. Things had got too murky down there, staggering around the impossible labyrinth, confused by the dusty haziness deceptively masking the sun. He sat up as the plane emerged above pure white cloud under a brilliant blue sky. That was better – closer to heaven things were clearer, the distances infinite, the light like burning ice.